WRITERS REPUBLIC

MY DREAM ONE AND THE
LOST SOULS
KINGDOM

CHASMINE ARMSTRONG

WRITERS REPUBLIC L.L.C.
515 Summit Ave. Unit R1
Union City, NJ 07087, USA

Website: *www.writersrepublic.com*
Hotline: *1-877-656-6838*
Email: *info@writersrepublic.com*

Ordering Information:
Quantity sales. Special discounts are available on quantity purchases by corporations, associations, and others. For details, contact the publisher at the address above.

Library of Congress Control Number: 2023949003
ISBN-13: 979-8-89100-408-5 [Paperback Edition]
979-8-89100-409-2 [Hardback Edition]
979-8-89100-410-8 [Digital Edition]

Rev. date: 10/20/2023

I thank my parents, my friends, and family for never giving up on me. I appreciate, all the support you have given me over the years. But mostly I thank myself for never giving up on myself. I am very proud of myself, I made it this far. I would like to also thank the people I have mentioned above, for giving me strength to keep going forward. Then most thankful I am very grateful for is my passed away grandmother. Love you forever in my books and out of my books. You were and will always be my rock. Through keyboard and marker.

CHAPTER 1

THE BEGINNING OF A DREAM

Once upon a time there was a character named Hazel, Luna, and she had a sister named Luna. Also, there little brother Lee. That day Luna, Hazel, Lee, Luna, and Robert watched. Had to say goodbye to their mother leave, since she is moving to the rain forest for school for an entire year, of there lives. Robert was sad to watch his wife leave them for an entire year, but he was happy that Rose was doing something that she loved doing. Which was learning about nature. Rose waved good-bye got into her taxi and left to the airport.

"Hey, do you think she is going to be okay?" Says Luna. "Yeah, I think she will be fine. Mom loves nature, being in the rain forest will make her happier." says Hazel. Dad walks in the room where Hazel, and Luna. Dad looked sad still when Rose left them all to move to the rain forest. Hazel and Luna had no idea what the year was going to be like, without Rose in the picture. "Hey, Dad are you going to be alright?" Says Luna. "I am fine, it's just I will miss Rose your mother a lot. Anyway, I am heading to work. See you later." Says Dad. "Alright see you soon. I will start dinner later." Says Luna. Dad walked toward the door, grabbing his keys and heading out toward the car. Luna and Hazel heard the car start and pull away from the house. Luna and Hazel looked at each other. "You want to go out?" Says Luna. Hazel looked up at the stairs, thinking that she had homework to do, but hanging out with Luna was more fun. "Yeah, let's do that." Says Hazel. Luna and Hazel grab their coats and walk out the door. As they walk down the street, they see Britt and Mackenzie walking together down toward where Britt lives. Hazel and Luna walked toward them seeing what they were doing for the day. "What you guys doing?" Says Hazel. "Were just about to walk back to my house to sit on the couch to chill." Says Britt. "Sounds good can we join?" Says Luna. "Sure, there is no problems with that. My parents are both working." Says Britt. Britt, Mackenzie, Hazel, and Luna walk with Britt and Mackenzie toward Britt's house. Once they get there. No one was home. Immediately Britt laid down on the couch and turned on some TV. Everyone just sat there talking not really paying attention to the TV show that was on. Luna's phone went off. It was a message from Lee. "Hey, I don't know where you are right now, but I am going to my friends place, to play some games, then coming home later for dinner." Says Lee. Luna messages back. "Hey, we are just at Britt's house. That is fine, we will see you later for dinner as well." Says Luna. Luna puts her phone away, to see a commercial about a store, with there candies, movies, and slushies. Luna got reminded of her biological parents. All Luna could hear right now is the screams the gun shots in the store, that killed her parents and left her to be alone for the rest of her life. She was sent into foster care, and then she got adopted by Robert White and Rose White. But that day still haunts her. She missed her parents a lot. "Hey, Luna you, okay? You been staring at the screen for awhile now." says Hazel. Luna looked over at Hazel, Mackenzie, and Britt. They were all looking at her." Yeah, I am fine. Just thinking sorry." Says Luna. "Do you want something to drink?" says Britt. "No, I am fine. I just gonna go get some air." Says Luna. Luna gets up from the couch and walks out of the house to sit down on the chair on the Porch. Since Luna was alone outside on the Porch, she could not stop thinking about her parents, or that day. Then Luna's nose started to bleed and had a headache all the sudden. Suddenly Luna was back in that day for some reason. She was in the car where she was waiting for her parents to get back to her, so they could go to the movies with there snacks that they were buying. Then Luna heard gun shots from inside the store, Luna screamed trying to move to run toward inside the store, but she could not move. Once it went quiet cops drove toward the store, they went inside finding five people killed in the store. She just sat there experiencing her parents' death again. Suddenly Luna was back on the Porch where Britt lived. Luna got confused of why someone or something put her in that position again. Luna sat there crying on the chair. Luna heard someone say something. Luna looked up and saw a woman standing there on the driveway. "Luna, is it? Are you alright?" says the woman. "Yeah, I am fine. Just dealing with demons of my past." Says Luna. "Oh well. I do that to. "Trust me, it will get better." Says the woman. "What happened to you? How did you get through it?" Says Luna. "Time, was my key." Says the woman. Luna heard the door open behind Luna. Luna looked at Hazel opening the door. "Luna are you alright. I can hear you talking out here?" Says Hazel. "Yeah, I am just talking to this woman. Come out and meet her." Says Luna. When Hazel got out, she looked around and saw no one was there. "Who? Luna" says Hazel. Luna looked around and saw that the woman was gone from the driveway. "What she was just there, talking to me." Says Luna. "I think we should head home, and let you take a nap. It looks like you are not sleeping again…" says Hazel. "Hazel I am fine. I was just talking to someone I swear I was." Says Luna. Hazel stud there not saying a word. Then Hazel walked back inside to tell Mackenzie and Britt that they were leaving, and Hazel got their things. When Hazel got back out to the Porch. Luna was gone to. Hazel amused that Luna started walking toward their house, so Hazel took Luna's things and headed back home.

Finally, Hazel got home dads car was in the driveway again. "Hey dad. Is Luna home? I just got back from Britt's house." Says Hazel. "No, I have not seen Luna yet. Did you guys walk home together?" Says Dad. "No, I was getting Luna's things out of Britt's house and when I got back onto the porch. She was gone and I thought she would have walked back here." Says Hazel. "Well, I will text her while I am making dinner. Alright, we will find her." Says Dad. "Okay, I am just worried about her. She was not really talking the entire time that we were at Britt's place with Mackenzie." Says Hazel. "Hmm, okay. I will call you down for dinner in a few. It's almost ready." Says Dad.

Hazel heard dad calling Lee and Hazel's name for dinner. Hazel walked out of her room walking down the stairs to dad in the kitchen. Once Hazel got there. She found that dad was on his phone texting Luna. "Still no answer?" Says Hazel. "Yeah, I am starting to get worried about

her Hazel. I might want to go out going for her, while you guys eat."
Says Dad. "I don't feel hungry you should eat. I will go looking for
Luna." Says Hazel. "Alright, there is no use in arguing with you so, I
will just let you go I guess." Says Dad. "Thanks. I will be bringing Luna
back with me for dinner. See you in bit." Says Hazel. Hazel walked up
the stairs getting her backpack and her earbuds. Hazel then walked
toward the front door and left immediately to find Luna. As Hazel was
walking down the street, she continued texting Luna where she was.
But there no answer. Hazel continued walking down the quiet street. As
the sun went down. The streetlights turned on. Hazel just kept walking
around town, looking to find Luna.

CHAPTER 2

BACKSTORY OF LUNA

Luna is just walking around at a park to find that herself having no idea what park she was at. She also did not know where this park was where she was exactly. Luna pulls out her phone to find just about 10 messages, and two missed calls from Hazel. As Luna was going to see what was going on her phone died, and now Luna has no idea where she is anymore. So, she decides to sit on a bench for a bit. Then Luna sees a sign, realize what park she was lost in. Luna was at the park called Metallic Park. Which was just about an hour away from her house. But Luna just feels like sitting on the bench and looking up at the sky. As it starts to get dark a little. Luna goes to a dark place again in her mind.

"Luna is just a girl who I am trying to help find a home for her." Says Sam. After a couple minutes later, Sam hangs up the phone, Sam sits down on her bed looking sad, and concerned for Luna. Then Sam gets up from her bed and opens the door to out of her room. She walks toward Luna to see that Luna has just been staring at the news channel about her parents, and the other people that have passed on to. But for some reason the news channel was only focused on why or how Luna's parents died. Because apparently Luna's parents were rich, but very wealthy. Luna does not understand why her parent's kept things secret that Luna's parents were rich. "Hey Luna. You alight?" Says Sam. "Why is the news focused about my parents dying and saying things that are lies?" Says Luna. Sam just stud there looking at Luna. "You did not know that your parents were rich?" Says Sam. "No, I did not know that they were rich. They don't deserve to be dead." Says Luna. "To be honest no one deserves to die. I know that that is hard to hear, but that's how life works. It will be hard right now, but you have me to help you through it. I went through the same thing, as you. That is why I do what I do." Says Sam. Luna sat there crying a little, she did not want to hear what Sam had to say, but she was right. "Okay…" says Luna. "I know, that "okay". But you are allowed to do that." Says Sam. Luna sighs "What should I do now?" Says Luna. "Well first get some sleep. Here is the remote for the TV, and I should probably get you some blankets because it does get cold in here at night." Says Sam. Sam walks to her closet where there is, four cozy blankets, but Sam grabs the one comforter. Here is the best comforter that I sleep with when I sleep on the couch." Says Sam. "Thank you Sam. I thank you for what you have done for me." Says Luna. "Well, we have a long day tomorrow, Luna. So, try to get some sleep. I will wake you and make you some breakfast in the morning. Then we will go somewhere, where you will be safer." Says Sam. "Okay. Where are we going tomorrow anyway?" Says Luna. "You will see Luna you will see." Says Sam. "Alright night…" Says Luna. As Sam walks to the kitchen to turn the lights off and walks to the living room lamp turns that off to. Then walks to her bedroom and shuts the door to her bedroom. Now all Luna can see is the TV on still on the news channel. Luna does not even try to pick up the remote to change the channel, but all Luna does was just look up at the celling to see. That this world is hard to live in, but Luna closes her eyes, and thinks about tomorrow. Cause tomorrow is a better day. Finally, Luna falls asleep dreaming about her parents, and her at the theatres. Watching her favorite movie, but this time Luna's parents are talking to her after the movies. Saying that they are proud of Luna for being a beautiful, smart, funny, and they were happy to be Luna's parents while it lasted. Luna's parents gave Luna a big hug and kissed her on the cheek one last time. Luna's dad and mom then disappeared out of thin air. While hugging their daughter. Luna then felt pain, and angry in her dream, that her parents are gone from existence. Luna in the dream then punched the wall and screamed bloody marry. Then the dream turned dark, Luna then falls to the ground to cry loudly, and screaming "mom dad. Where are you. I LOVE YOU, please come back." Says Luna in the dream. Luna gets no reply of her parents coming back. She continues to cry on the ground in a ball. Still screaming Mom and dad where are you repeatedly. Until her strength is down, and she can't scream for her parents anymore. Luna now is just laying there in pain, her lungs hurting, and feeling weak in the heart. Then one more time Luna has the strength to say it quietly this time. "Where are you mom and dad. I love you, please come back." Says Luna in the dream.

"Luna are you okay?" Says Sam. "I heard screaming." Luna then wakes up crying to see that the living room light was on, and Sam just sitting on the ground. Luna then continues to cry in Sam's arms. "It's okay Luna, it's okay." Says Sam. Sam hugs Luna to try to cheer her up, but it was sort of hard cause Luna could not stop crying about the dream that she just had. Sam gets up and gets some water from the kitchen and walks back to Luna. "Luna, I got you some water to drink. It usually helps me when I cry this much." Says Sam. "Thanks Sam." says Luna. Luna just jugs the water down so fast that her head feels a little better. Luna then finally stops crying and has the voice to tell Sam what was going on. "Luna is everything okay? Did you have a dream about something?" Says Sam. "Yeah, I am fine, thank you sorry. I just had a bad dream about my parents." Says Luna. "Oh. What happened in the dream?" Says Sam. Luna goes now of what happened in her dream. Explains of what it was like seeing Luna's parents one last time in her dreams. "What were you guys doing in the dream?" Says Sam. "We were watching the movie we were going to watch the one that was in the movies yesterday. Then they hugged me and disappeared out of thin air." Says Luna. "I think that dream was closure for you, and your parents." Says Sam. "Really, you really think that?" Says Luna. "Yes, I think they came back in your dreams to say we are fine, and we are proud of you for being you." Says Sam. "Yeah, I just wish they actually came back for me." Says Luna. "I know." Says Sam, Sam looks at the time it says six am in the morning. "We mind as well get ready to go. What do you want for breakfast?" Says Sam. "Whatever you can make easy, or I can help you make breakfast." Says Luna. "Really you would help. Make breakfast." Says Sam. "Of course, I would. You gave me a place to stay for the night, and you are helping me, I am grateful for that Sam, and my parents always taught me to be nice." Says Luna. "Well, they were good parents then Luna." Says Sam. "Yes, they were."

Says Luna. Luna gets up to help Sam make some breakfast, Luna puts the toast in the toaster. Then Sam flips some eggs. Luna gets the toast out of the toaster and puts it on plates. Butters the toast. Sam gets the omelettes off the stove. Slides the omelettes on there plates. Luna and Sam eat their breakfast in silence. "Luna, are you finished eating?" Says Sam. "Yeah, it was great Sam. Very good." Says Luna. "What's wrong?" Says Sam. "I am just tired." Says Luna. "Yeah, I get it, but we must get ready to go now Luna." Says Sam. "Okay. I still don't understand why you won't tell me where we are going?" Says Luna. "Luna everything will be fine. This person I am taking you to is going to help. Now go get your things, and we will be on our way." Says Sam. Luna goes to the couch to pack her stuff. Luna walks to the door. Sam and Luna both walk out of Sam's apartment. Sam then locks the apartment door behind them, and they head to the car. Sam opens the door for Luna. Luna then crawls into the car. Sam shuts the door and walks to the driver's seat. Starts the car and Sam and Luna are on the way to where Sam has been talking about yesterday.

Hazel texts Dad. "Hey dad I have no idea where Luna is, she still has not answered my messages or my calls." Says Hazel. Dad texts back. It's okay Hazel, just come home. I don't want to of my kids missing right now." Says Dad. "But I don't like leaving my sister in the cold like this." Says Hazel. "This is me telling you to come home right now. Luna can handle herself Hazel. Come home right now." Says dad. "No, I want to find my sister. End of story." Says Hazel. "Well too bad. Come HOME right now." Says Dad. Hazel sighs, rolling her eyes. "Fine I will come home." Says Hazel. "Thank you see you soon." Says Dad. As Hazel began. Hazel begins to walk home in the dark. Hazel just thought about Luna and how worried Hazel is about her sister.

Once Hazel arrived at home in just about 30 minutes. Hazel opens the door to the smell of Dads cooking. Hazel then puts off her shoes and walks to the kitchen to find that Dad had a face of fear, and concern. "Oh, thank you. For coming home." Says Dad."Dad is everything okay?" Says Hazel. Dad walks over to Hazel to hug her tight. Hazel was mad at her father for making her come home, but Hazel still hugged her dad.

"I can feel that you are mad, but I am better with you at least home and not out there looking for Luna. She is family, but it's important that you are home. I don't need you and her missing." Says Dad. "I guess. I just hope that Luna is okay." Says Hazel. "Me to Hazel.". Says Dad. Hazel then grabs her supper and sits in the dinning room. Eats her food by herself in the silence, which she is not use to. Hazel is used to sitting in the dinning room with her sister, Lee, and her dad. But it's just her this time.

Hazel then finishes supper. Gets up from the table in the dinning room. Once she gets herself in the kitchen, she rinses her dish and puts it in the dishwasher. Hazel then walks out of the kitchen to the upstairs to her bedroom and changes into pj's. Turns on some music and charges her phone on her nightstand. Hazel then turns off the music as soon as Hazel hears her name being called by dad. Hazel then walks down the stairs to find Dad sitting on the couch. A little more worry on his face more now. Hazel then sits down next to Dad. Hazel hugs Dad tight and speaks. "Dad everything is going to be alright." Says Hazel. "Thank you, Hazel.". Says Dad. Hazel turns on the TV to watch a show with her dad, then Hazel's dad fell asleep on the couch. Dad was hugging Hazel tight, Hazel could barley move, but finally dad let go and Hazel got up and walked over to get a blanket to put on her dad. To let him get some sleep. Then Hazel walked up to the door thinking about going to find her sister, but then looking at dad sleeping. Hazel turned toward the steps and went up to her room, to get some sleep. Hazel just hoped that she made the right choice. A couple minutes later Hazel and Dad Fall asleep on the couch together. Hazel a little tearing up, and Dad hugging Hazel so tight.

"Hey. I have been at the park for awhile, and I just noticed that you have been sitting on that bench for about three hours. Are you okay?" Says the man. "Yeah, just got lots on my mind." Says Luna. "You are lost?" Says the man. "Yeah, I got sad, and I zoned out, and my body was doing the walking. Then we are here now. Sitting on the bench alone." Says Luna. "Do you live around here? I am just wondering because I could give you a ride home. If you want to get home before it's midnight. Cause its almost 8." Says the man. "Wait what I did not know it was that late." Says Luna. "Well, I can give you a ride home if you know your street." Says the man. "Thanks, sir I think my street is called square street?" Says Luna. "Alright hop right in the front if you want." Says the man. As Luna hops right in the front seat. She feels like she should not trust this person, but he seems nice, so Luna just sits there in silence. "So why were you on that bench for awhile?" Says the man. "I have no idea why. I just felt like sitting down, and it felt right for awhile." Says Luna. "Well, I hope you are okay. I do worry about kids your age sometimes." Says the man. "You should not worry about me. I am fine I just need some time to think about things." Says Luna. "Well, I do believe that you will be fine. I just like to make sure." Says the man. "I don't mean to be nosey, but what's your name?" Says Luna. "Right, I am so sorry. I forgot to introduce myself. My name is Rick. What's yours?" Says Rick. "My name is Luna." Says Luna. "That is a beautiful name Luna." Says Rick. "I am sorry if you think that I am kidnapping you, because I did not introduce myself, but anyway we arrived at your street already. I am so glad that I got to meet you, Luna. See you around." Says Rick. As Rick arrives at Luna's driveway at her house. Luna gets her stuff and gets out of the car. Before walking to the front door. Luna turns around to say something to Rick before she goes to bed. "Hey Rick." Says Luna. "Yeah, what's up did I drop you at the wrong house?" Says Rick. "No, you are fine. I just wanted to say thank you for driving me home." Says Luna. "Well Luna I got to head home and thank you for not assuming the worst out of me." Says Rick. "Okay I will see you around then, Rick. Also, Rick. Have a great night." Says Luna. "Thank you, Luna. I will see you around. I hope, see you." Says Rick. As Luna closes the car door. Rick starts to drive away and head home. As Luna still is waving away. Waits till Rick is out of eyeshot to let him keep seeing Luna keep waving bye. Finally, Luna heads to her front door, but when Luna opens the door Luna finds that her dad was laying down on the couch sleeping with the TV on. Hazel hugging him, and tears running down her face. As soon as Luna closes the door. Hazel and Dad wakes up. Dad basically and Hazel are jumping off the couch running toward Luna, giving her a big tight hug. "Dad Hazel. You are hugging so hard. I can't breathe." Says Luna. "Luna where were you. Hazel went out looking for you, then I tried calling you?" Says dad. "Hazel. My phone died, and I was at Metallic Park." Hazel. That Park is just about an hour away from here. Says Luna. "How did you get home?" Says Dad. "I got a ride from a nice man named Rick." Says Luna. "A man from a guy named Rick. Is that all you know about this man. Are you nuts, he could have killed you!" Says Dad. "I know that dad, but I had this feeling that I could trust him." Says Luna. "Well, you are here. That is all that matters. But still don't ever do that again Luna. I worry about you, Hazel and Lee." Says dad. "I know that is what you must do and that is your choice as a father." Says Luna. "Well, I have work in the morning. Good night, love you." Says Dad. "Love you to dad." Says Luna. As Hazel. As everyone walks up the stairs besides Luna. Luna walked into the kitchen Luna made herself some dinner for her because she has not eaten since breakfast. As Luna puts her food in the microwave. Luna keeps thinking about her parents, and how they died ten years ago. Luna has been a little depressed because Luna wants Hazel to know that Luna is adopted, and that Luna has already felt happy for Hazel to be graduating soon. As Luna pulls out her dinner out of the microwave. Luna walks toward the table in the dinning room. Sits down on the first sit that she sees. Luna hears dad's door open. Luna what you doing in here? Says Dad. "I am eating dinner. Why are you up. I thought you went to bed?" Says Luna. Just getting a water, and I see that you found the meal in the fridge I saved you, from dinner. Says Dad. "Yeah, it's good. I am going to bed after this." says Luna. "Alright. But are you alright. Why did you wander of." Says dad. "I wandered off to get some air, and I am fine." Says Luna. "You look sad though, have you been sleeping?" Says Dad. Luna sat there for a moment staring at dad. "Dad I just feel alone in this house. I want to tell Lee and Hazel that I am adopted, I am not Hazel and Lee's sister, real sister." Says Luna. Dad looked at Luna then said. "I can talk to Rose about it, and you are not alone in this house Luna, you are our family." says Dad. "because Hazel and Lee don't know that I am adopted, and you said not to say anything to them when they were born. Says Luna. I get it, it's just your adopted mom did not want her kids to know that you are adopted. I can say something to Mom if you want so you don't feel alone. Says Dad. Really?! You would say something to Mom." Says

Luna. "Yeah, I would, and if your mom does not like it, I will let you tell Hazel and Lee and Hazel anyway, but honestly, I don't think she will mind. I think she will be alright with it. Because we want you to be able to be yourself." Says Dad. "Thanks." Says Luna. Luna gets up from the dinning chair and hugs her adoptive dad. Luna had the biggest smile on her face. Even bigger than when Hazel was born. Luna felt less alone before Hazel came along in Luna's Life. Luna felt like she had a real sister. But always Luna knew that Hazel was not really her real sister, then Lee came along. Luna was excited to have a brother, but it's the same with Hazel. Because they weren't really Luna's siblings. Hazel and Lee were though. "Luna is there something else brothering you?" Says Dad. "I just miss my real parents. But I am so happy to have you all in my life." Says Luna. "I know. I am sorry to say this, but what happened to your parents?" Says Dad. "My parents died in a Maxx store. Shot in the head, along with three other people in the head as well." Says Luna. "Oh, my sorry. I was excepting them abandoning you when you were little." Says Dad. "They would never do that, dad. We were going out for the movies that night. We stopped by to get some candy to sneak in with the candy, but my parents were taking forever then I heard screaming and gunshots from inside the store. That was the last time I saw my parents. You know what they said to me. I will see you soon. Sit tight." Says Luna. Luna looks down at the table in sadness. "Luna it will be okay, they are in a better place now, and you have a new family. We love you with all our hearts. I know you miss your parents, but we love you so much, that is why me and Rose choose you to be our first child." Says Dad. "Thank you, dad. I love you to. I am going to head to bed now. I am sorry if I was a bother to you guys ever in your lives." Says Luna. "Luna you are never a bother you were a gift and a great reminder that we wanted to have kids like Hazel and Lee. Of course, we will be happy to see you happy. We care about you. Just tell me when you feel down." Says Dad. "Thank you, Dad, I love you, night." says Luna. Love you to Luna. Says Dad. Luna walks up the stairs to her bedroom.

Hazel walks out of the shadows and walks up the stairs, but Dad caught Hazel walking toward his room. "Hey Hazel. What are you doing up so late?" Says Dad. "Dad did I hear your conversation with Luna right? Is she adopted?" Says Hazel. "Yes, Luna is adopted Hazel. Please know that it was me and your mom's choice to keep that from you and Lee. To make Luna feel normal in this family. It was hard for Luna losing her parents at a young age. Me and your mom wanted to make sure that Luna had a great childhood." Says Dad. "Why would you and mom think that was a great choice?" Says Hazel. "I just thought that Luna would want to feel like. Her parents were us, and you and Lee to be her siblings. But I realize it would be lying to you and Lee, but also making Luna feel alone even more. It was wrong. I am sorry to have been lying to you and Lee about this. Which has been for eighteen years." Says Dad. "WAIT Luna has been here way before me? How long has she been around with you and Mom?" Says Hazel. "Hazel Luna was eight when we meant her. She was in foster care; she was looking for a new start Hazel. Me and your mom weren't sure about having our own kids like you and Lee. When we saw that there was a flyer about an adoption center around. Me and your mom went to the building to see what adoption would be like. We talked to woman. I am pretty sure their names were Sam and Polly I think, but anyway it was so worth it. Adopting Luna. Luna was mad that she was living with me and your mom, but I felt that day Luna grateful to have a family again. Me and your mom took awhile getting use to having to look after an eight-year-old. Then me and your mom were pregnant with you. We told Luna, and she had the maddest face, but when you were born. She loved you so much. Like an actual sister, and that is what I wanted for her. To have a friend and family. Luna looked after you. When she was ten years old, and we were so happy that Luna had a sister to play with. Then when Lee came into Luna's life, she was so happy. She was the happiest big sister I have ever meant. She was grateful to have family again like you and Lee. She loves both of you." Says Dad. "But why—Did she not tell me." Says Hazel. "I asked her to not tell you guys. I did not mention the reason why? But I told her that me and your mom wanted her to have a normal family. And now I realize that was a selfish thing to do. For you, Lee, and Luna." Says Dad. Hazel slides down slowly against the wall. To meet her hands on the floor in fear and confusion. "Hazel, I know this is a lot to take in, but everything is going to be okay. All that matters is that all my children are safe, and happy. But I must get some sleep. You should to. We will talk about this when you are fine with-it okay Hazel. I am sorry, I love you." Says Dad. Dad walks away from Hazel, but Hazel just sits there alone in the dark on the cold floor. Hazel finally has the guts to get up and walk to her room. Hazel, but only just does that. Hazel walks through the hallway where only Luna's and Hazel's rooms are across from each other. Hazel stops in the hallway to be staring at Luna's door to her bedroom. Hazel hears nothing in the room, but very loud music from headphones. Hazel looks down to see that Luna has a candle on in her room again. As the candle flickers in and out, Hazel turns around to see her door to her bedroom. Hazel walks in her bedroom to find all her lights on, and Hazel turns all of them off. thenHazel walks toward her bed and turns on some quiet music. Hazel Then closes her eyes thinking about what she is going to say tomorrow to Luna or to not say anything tomorrow. All Hazel wanted was a family that never told lies, but that has all changed today in minutes.

Luna looks up at her skylight. Sees nothing, but darkness, clouds, stars, and the moon. Luna just keeps looking up at the sky hoping to see something as a sign for that Luna's parents are safe, and okay. Luna then suddenly sees a shooting star. Shooting across the sky, it was bright and beautiful. Luna then knows that her parents are okay and safe. Wherever they might be. Before Luna goes to sleep. She opens her journal and writes what happened today. Couple minutes Luna was done writing in her journal. Luna gets out of bed and puts it on her desk in a safe place. Luna turns off her desk lamp. Then walks back to her bed. Now Luna is just laying down on her bed in the dark with a candle on. Luna then turns around to her nightstand where the candle was, and there was a picture of Luna real parents in a picture frame. Luna then looks at the picture in sadness. Luna blows out the candle. Turns around looks up at the skylight. Luna then makes a long sigh out of her mouth again in sadness. Luna's eyes started to then form some tears crying out of her face. Luna closes her eyes and goes to her happy place in her dreams. Luna falls asleep with her headphones on loud blasting music in her ears.

"Luna we are here." Says Sam. "Where are we?" Says Luna. "We are at an adoption center. I know what you are going to say. I don't want to be here. Is that right." Says Sam. "Yeah you are right I don't want to be here. I never imagined being forced into an adoption center." Says Luna. "I know, but this place will help us find you a new home. Luna. I know you might hate this idea, but everything will be okay. Polly is the nicest person I know that will help you get out of this place as soon as possible." Says Sam. "Okay I will give this place a try, and who is Polly?" Says Luna. "She is my best friend. We meant at college, and she loves what I do for kids like you. She basically helps me get the kids that I bring here new homes. To live in for a better life then living on the streets." Says Sam. "How many kids do you get to bring to this place?" Says Luna. "Let's just say a lot of kids, there is another after I drop you off to. I must pick them up soon as well." Says Sam. "Already Jez. You are a busy woman Sam." Says Luna. "Yeah, I am. Speaking of busy we should get you in the building and meet Polly already. You will love Polly she is super nice." Says Sam. As Luna and Sam get out of the car and approach the building. Sam knocks on the door. Suddenly the door opens. On the other side of the door finds a woman with long beautiful brown hair, eyes that are green as the wicked witch of the west, and a casual outfit with jeans, and a sweater. "Polly hey, how are you." Says Sam. "I am great. Who is this? Another kid in your hands waiting to find a new family or home." Says Polly. "This is Luna. Her parents passed away yesterday." Says Sam. "That is horrible I so sorry Luna." Says Polly. "It's okay. It was not your fault." Says Luna. "Come in, come into my amazing business that I love with my heart, and of course you to Sam." Says Polly. "I will come in, but I do have to pick up another kid that there parents abandoned them on a bus." Says Sam. "No Sam it's okay if you must go now. I think that kid needs you right now. I can make sure that Luna is safe." Says Polly. "Are you sure Polly?" Says Sam. "Yeah, I will be fine. I love kids." Says Polly. "Okay, Luna I will be back in an hour or so. I promise. Polly means it when she welcomes you with open arms. Just try not to break any rules. Okay. I will see you soon." Says Sam. "Okay, see you later then Sam." Says Luna. "Okay I will see you guys later then. I will be back Luna. I promise." Says Sam. As Sam walks away from Luna and Polly. Sam walks out the front door. "Wow

I have never seen Sam promise anyone like that besides me ever before. Sam must really like you then Luna." Says Polly. "Well, I like her a lot she helped me for a night, and she supported me." Says Luna. "Yeah, she is pretty good at that stuff. So anyway, let me show you to your room that you will be staying in for a little bit. Until people come to here and adopt." Says Polly. "Okay." Says Luna. "Why you look sad Luna?" Says Polly. "Yesterday is still affecting me." Says Luna. "It's okay. I just want to make sure that you are okay that's all. Yeah, I am fine. Thanks Polly." Says Luna. Polly walks Luna to her room for a stay over if she wants or needs to stay over in the care center. "Okay got everything to just sit down and relax for awhile?" Says Polly. "Yeah, I will be fine for awhile, thanks Polly, and nice rooms. I have one to myself. Wow." Says Luna. "Yep!! You sure do." Says Polly. "The phone rings from downstairs. I will be right back Luna. I just must answer this phone call." Says Polly. Polly walks down the steps to the front desk. Luna is alone in this room. The walls are the color white. There are bookshelves in one side of the room, then a desk in the same area, then just a single window that has the most view of the city. The window can still open, and there is no screen on it. There is also a window ledge outside on the side of the building. Suddenly Luna hears her name being called downstairs. "Luna!! Are you hungry for lunch?" Says Polly. "No, I am fine thanks though Polly." Says Luna. Luna then walks toward the bed that was in the room that was assigned to Luna. Luna lays down on the bed hoping that Sam will be back sooner. Then Sam had said to Polly and Luna.

Luna then wakes up from a nap that she did not even know that was happening in the first place. "Hey Polly. Where is Luna?" Says Sam. "Well, she is upstairs. I have not really seen her for at least hour. I think she fell asleep." Says Polly. "Oh okay. I am going to go check on Luna then." Says Sam. "Okay. And where is the kid you were going to bring or help?" Says Polly. "That kid just needed to be dropped off at his grandparents' place. I got there, and it was a little boy. His lawyer says that he was already claimed for if anything ever happened to his parents or decided to have abandoned him or abuse. So, he had God Grandparents. Is literally all I had to do was drop that boy off at his grandparent's place across town." Says Sam. "Well, that is good that he has his grandparents to have as a family, and it was good that his parents put the little boy's grandparents as God parents." Says Polly. "Yeah, I thought so to. But I still felt bad leaving him there alone without saying much because his grandparents were so happy to see him, but he was so sad. That his parents left him all alone. I think I saw a tear go down his face. He also barely said anything in the car ride." Says Sam. "Yeah, I still think it was sad that. That little boy had to handle in just minutes or seconds. Then realizing that his parents have choose not to come back for him. Which is sad for me to see or hear about. I mean what happened to Luna is bad as well I just can't believe most of these kids get abandoned or there parents passing away. I always feel bad for these kids. Cause they all know what it feels like to lose someone special in their lives." Says Polly. "I totally understand. Therefore, we are friends Polly. Because you get me a lot." Says Sam. "Well, I try to get you, and it always seems to work out for me all the time." Says Polly. "Well, I promised someone that I would be back, and I am back. I should probably go see Luna for a little bit." Says Sam. "Okay. Her room is 03." Says Polly. "Thank you, Polly. I really appreciate what you do for me and these kids. Thank you so much Polly." Says Sam. "No problem. After all it's my job and my hobby." Says Polly. Sam walks up the stairs to room 03. Sam sees that Luna is just laying down on the bed in the room. "Hey Luna. I am back like I promised. I brought you a donut." Says Sam. "Oh you did not have to do that Sam." Says Luna. "I felt like giving you a treat for being patient with this entire thing. It's a lot to take in all at once." Says Sam. Sam gives Luna the donut. Sam Sits down on the bed. Luna and Sam just sit there just chatting away for such a long time. That Sam started to think about wanting to stay in contact with Luna if she ever needed help. But then Polly yelled up at Sam and Luna. To come downstairs. "Hey Polly, what's up?" Says Sam. "I just meant these two people they have never adopted before. They just want to see what it is like to be a parent." Says Polly. "Alright what are your names?" Says Sam. "I am Robert and this is my wife, Rose." Says Robert. "Nice to meet you guys. How did you find my building?" Says Polly. "I found this flyer pretty much everywhere I looked. Then I searched this building up on the network, and found this place was close to where me and Rose are staying. So, we wanted to come to the building to see what you guys to offer for adoption? Or who is up for looking for a new home?" Says Robert. "Well, there are lots of kids here looking for new homes everyday. We can talk in my office if you like, and I can show you some pictures of the kids and files of them to." Says Polly. "Sounds good we will see you in the office then." Says Rose. "Okay I will be right with you I just need to grab one more file from my friend here Sam. Sam can you give me Luna's file. Please." Says Polly. "Sure, here you are Polly." Says Sam. Sam gives Luna's file to Polly. Polly walks with Rose and Robert to Polly's office to talk business. "What was that about?" Says Luna. "That was Polly getting new customers for her business as an adoption counselor." Says Sam. "Should I be worried that Polly has a file on me?" Says Luna. "No, you should not. That file helps you be an option for being in a new home." Says Sam. "What does it say about me?" Says Luna. "It just has your birth, personal story by the police and how you got into the adoption center. Also, when you arrived here in this building. It also has your parents' names on the files and their phone numbers, but that might be cut off because they have passed on." Says Sam. "Wow that is a lot of info about me." Says Luna. "Yeah, but Luna just think that file will help you get a home faster because that file is strictly not allowed to lie about where you are from or what happened to you or who you are. That file is everything to know about you and that is a great thing." Says Sam. "Yeah. It's just government stuff makes me nervous." Says Luna. "Oh, did not know that about you, but Luna you are fine. That file just makes sure that you are cable of having a family." Says Sam. "Okay that makes me feel a little better now that you have said all those things.: Says Luna.

As Polly finishes up talking to Rose and Robert. Polly points toward Luna just sitting on the steps toward the upstairs quarters. Polly opens the office door, and Robert and Rose look toward Luna. Rose and Robert talk toward Luna sitting alone on the steps and speak. "Hey are you, Luna?" Says Rose. "Yeah? Why are you wondering?" Says Luna. "Luna, they want to adopt you today. They are going home today so. What do you say do you want to go home today with them, and have a family again?" Says Polly. Luna Sits there for a second looking at Sam for an answer and Sam just nods her head. Like Sam is saying to Luna.

Go for it. They seem like nice and decent people. Luna then looks back at them. Then stands up and speaks. "Yeah, let's give this a try." Says Luna. In a concerned voice. When Luna is not looking Sam walks to the room that Luna's stuff was in and walks down the stairs toward Luna and gives her. Her backpack. "Luna here have your backpack, and I am so happy you found a family already. That was fast." Says Sam. Luna Says nothing, but all Luna does is hug Sam tight. Sam swears she feels that Luna is crying a little in Sam's arms. Luna then lifts her head and speaks. "Thank you, Sam for everything. I am going to miss you." Says Luna. "Me to kid, me to. Be good to these people okay." Says Sam. "Okay I will see you around then. I think?" Says Luna. "Do you want my number if you ever want to call or visit me?" Says Sam. "Yeah, I would love your number Sam." Says Luna. Sam writes down her number on a piece of paper that has been in her pocket for some time. "Luna. I am serious be good with these people you are so lucky to have these people in your timeline. Specially when they have come on the first hour of you being in this building that is super lucky in my opinion." Says Sam. "Yeah, I would say so to. Because I was not really excepting to get adopted so quick." Says Luna. "Yeah, me to, but I am so happy for you Luna. I hope to see you around." Says Sam. Luna goes into Roses and Robert's car. Sam closes the door for Luna one last time. Of a car door. As Robert drives away out of the town. Sam waves bye until Luna can't see Sam anymore. Luna all thinks about just Sam, and how Sam helped Luna be here today. Luna is super grateful for Sam's help, but she is also nervous about being a daughter two new people in Luna's life. Luna was tired though. So, Luna faded into a nap and a deep sleep. Rose and Robert were as nervous as Luna was about being apart of someone else's life. As Rose looks in the back seat to see that Luna was sleeping. Rose just keeps looking at this beautiful girl that has lost her parents, and she has no idea who she is about to let in her house. The car ride goes on for another hour or so. Still with Luna sleeping in the back seat of the car.

Finally, they arrive at Robert's and Rose's house. "Hey Luna. Sorry to wake you, but we are home." Says Rose. Luna opens her eyes to find Rose opened the car door to let Luna out of the car. Luna gets up, and looks at the house that Luna will be staying in. "Luna this is your new place." Says Rose. Luna just stares at the new house. Luna is nervous to say anything to Rose or Robert. "Luna, do you want me to take your stuff to your room?" Says Rose. "Sure." Says Luna. "You don't have to be afraid to say anything you know that right?" Says Rose. "Okay. I am just sort of still getting use to being adopted or living in a new house." Says Luna. "I understand Luna. I have never gone through what you are going through, but I am sure that everything will be okay. Me and Robert never thought of adoption first either. We expected to have a child first and then adoption. Not sure though." Says Rose. "Rose, can you come help me with the groceries." Says Robert. "Okay honey I am coming. And Luna your room is on the left upstairs." Says Rose. Luna walks up the stairs to a bedroom that use to be a guest room, but now it's Luna room. Luna still felt weird about living in a new room. Luna was only thinking about how awkward it is for Luna, Robert, and Rose. At the same time though.

Couple hours later dinner was ready. "Luna come down the stairs. We made something for dinner." Says Rose. Luna walks down the stairs to see what they made for dinner. "Come in Luna, I have made us all food." Says Robert. Luna walks in the dinning room to sit down and eat dinner with Robert and Rose. "Here Luna some chicken." Says Robert. "Thanks." Says Luna. "No problem. Do you want anything to drink? We have juice, pop, and some water or chocolate milk." Says Robert. "I will just take water please." Says Luna. "No problem I will get that for you." Says Robert. "Robert come over here for a second." Says Rose. "Yeah, what's up honey." Says Robert. "Are you sure it was a great idea adopting a kid today?" Says Rose. "Rose, are you kidding I love Luna. I mean she is quiet, but she is a shy girl. Shy girls usually get along with people like me. So yeah, I think it was a perfect idea to get a kid today." Says Robert. "Okay. I just feel that Luna is different then other kids or people." Says Rose. "Why would you say something like that Rose?" Says Robert. "Luna just has a different aura then everyone else I know. I just have a bad feeling about her." Says Rose. "Why would you have a bad feeling about her?" Says Robert. "I feel like she is the kid that rich parents died. Also, that Luna's parents before us were not her parents." Says Rose. "How would you know this, Rose? We don't even know Luna. We just meant her today, and you are making sure that Luna is not safe to be around, or Luna is an experiment. Is that what you are basically describing Luna to be like?" Says Robert. "Yeah, she looks similar in news paper from almost three years ago." Says Rose. "Rose we will talk about this later. I have been meaning to give our daughter some water for just about to minutes now." Says Robert. Robert grabs a cup and pours water into the cup. Robert walks into the dinning room with the water in his hand gives it to Luna. "Thank you, Robert." Says Luna. "No problem, Luna. You know you can call me by dad if you feel comfortable, but unless you feel not comfortable with that you don't have to call me that." Says Robert. I will just call you Robert for a little bit. Until I get comfy, I am still getting use to having a new family that's all." Says Luna. "It's okay take your time." Says Robert. Rose walks in the dinning room with two glasses of wine. The glasses of wine are for Rose and Robert. "So, Luna. Where are you from?" Says Rose. "I am from the city of Patine." Says Luna. "Wow I never really thought you were from there. That is sort of far from where we found you." Says Rose. "Rose what are you doing?!" Says Robert. "Are you nervous around me?" Says Luna. "No, I just want to know why and how you got here from all the way from there." Says Rose. 'Simply my parents moved closer to a job that they wanted, and here I am here with you now. I wish my parents never took their jobs around here. They would probably still be alive." Says Luna. "Okay Luna. I am sorry about Rose she just has some trouble trusting new people in her life." Says Robert. "It's okay." Luna says. Luna, Rose and Robert just ate in silence for the rest of dinner. Luna gets up first and walk toward the kitchen to rinse her plate. Puts the plate in the dishwasher. Luna then walks up the stairs in a quiet matter. "Rose what was that!?" Says Robert. "I am sorry that I am trying to find out who Luna is. I just don't like having someone in my house that I don't know Robert. It's going to take me awhile to get use to it." Says Rose. Rose then gets up walks to the kitchen with her wine glass in her hand. Rose then goes in the fridge gets more wine. Then walks to the living room with the wine glass in hand and sits down on the couch. Robert then gets up rolling his eyes and taking Roses dish though the sink and puts his dish though the sink to. And puts both dishes in the dishwasher. Robert then just stands in the kitchen. Then Robert decides to walk up the stairs to Luna's room to check on her. Robert opens the door to see that Luna was just laying on the bed listening to her music. "Hey Luna. Sorry to bother you, but I am just coming up here to apologize for Rose." Says Robert. "It's fine Robert I am fine with it. I have been talked like that before I am used to it already." Says Luna. "I am still sorry about her. But anyway, did you like what I made tonight for dinner." Says Robert. "Yeah, it was pretty good thanks for supper." Says Luna. "No problem. Well, I will leave you. So, you can get comfy for the night." Says Robert. Before Robert was about to walk out of Luna's new room. Robert turns around to speak one more. "Hey Luna, this room gets sort of cold at night. There is a closet right across from this room just outside of this room. There should be blankets in there. If you are cold, you are welcome to grab as many as you like." Says Robert. Robert turns back around to face the door that goes out to the hallway. Closes the door behind him to. Robert goes back downstairs to talk to Rose. A couple hours later everyone goes to sleep.

Luna's dream. "What is this place?" Says Luna. "Welcome to your destiny. My future Time Witch." Says the woman. "Who are you?" Says Luna. "I am the Time Witch right now, but you are going to replace me, Luna." Says The Time Witch. "Look Time Witch I am not going to replace you ever. Because I have no freaking clue because you would choose me to take your place. My parents just died recently." Says Luna. "I know your parents died recently, we watched them die." Says The Time Witch. Luna stands there looking at the Time Witch as if Luna has seen a ghost. "What do you mean you watched my parents die?" Says Luna. "We simply helped the murderer." Says The Time Witch. "Why would you help the murder kill my parents!!" Says Luna. "We had no choice. They were meant to die in that Maxx store Luna. We are sorry to have let that happen to you. It needed to happen." Says The Time Witch. "NO, you can't just come in my dreams to just tell me that my parents deserved to die. YOU CAN'T do that!" Says Luna. "I know you are still hurting that your parents have passed on, but we need you to be with us Luna. We need your guidance to save the world in three or two

22

years from now. I don't me to spoil your life with these people that are now your adoptive parents. But they have two kids, and you are friends with one of those kids. It is the most powerful person that is being born. The last time someone was born in this world was a thousand years ago that was the most problem that we see in our time schedule. They almost destroyed this world. Cause they kept getting powerful every time they read a spell in a book. Then they decided to want to use that power to almost destroy the world. Then we as Timekeepers had to use the most powerful spell to banish them. We have no idea where that person went to, but it worked. But Luna we won't have to do that again to your sister Hazel. Unless you jump in to become friends, supportive, mainly just be there for her don't leave her alone. She will figure out her powers when she is eighteen, and I don't really want to see another child become evil again. Because of there powers. You also seem to be close friends with this girl when she is born." Says The Time Witch. "Wow you are just wow. You spoiled my life. And why is this Hazel so important to be friends with? And you say that I will be friends with this kid Hazel. Who do you think you are, and why is this Hazel so important to be friends with?" Says Luna. "You will be fine. It's important because the world depends on it. It's your destiny. I am sorry that we killed your parents, but it was time for them. Before I go, I will be watching you. Until we meet you again." Says The Time Witch. Then The Time Witch was gone out of existence as if she was never there. Luna then wakes up, sweating in the guest bedroom. Also feels this pain on Luna's. Luna turns on the lamp to find that there is a new marking on Luna's arm. The marking on Luna's arm has the symbol of beautiful markings. Luna is not sure what it is really, and she does not know how it got there. But the marking looks like it has a star in the center and three pentagrams with tiny stars in the roped circle. Luna just keeps staring at it. Finally, Luna falls back asleep with the mysterious markings on her arm.

CHAPTER 3

THE POWER!?

Dad wakes up to make everyone breakfast. Hazel then comes down the stairs tired more than usual, but Hazel says good morning to dad. Hazel then comes down the stairs tired more than usual. Hazel says good morning to dad. "Morning sweetie. How was your sleep?" Says Dad. "It was not good at all." says Hazel in a tired voice. "Why was it so bad? Says Dad. "I just could not even sleep. I was trying to sleep, but I just couldn't." Says Hazel. "Well, I am making everyone breakfast. Also going to drive you and Lee to school." Says Dad. "Why do I have to go Dad?!" Says Hazel. "You must go because this is your last year, and I want you to graduate." Says Dad. "Fine I will go to school." Says Hazel in a sigh voice. "Thank you. You will be fine." Says Dad. Lee and Luna walk down the stairs as if they were only coming down the stairs to have some breakfast. "Dad what's for breakfast?" Says Lee. "You will find out right now son." Says Dad. Dad puts some eggs and bacon on Lee's plate, also Hazel and Luna's plate. Lee, Luna, and Hazel eat their breakfast. "Hey Luna, what are you doing today?" Says Dad. "Can I just stay home today? I am tired." Says Luna. "I think you should be getting a job Luna. I think this because you have been doing nothing at home really the past few years. I also thought that you wanted to move out one day." Says Dad. "Yeah, I do one day, but why do I have to work for it now?" Says Luna. "Because Luna houses are expensive, and I won't be paying rent. Also, that I want you to get out of the house doing something." Says Dad. "Fine. Where are jobs right now?" Says Luna. "I will drive you if you want." Says Dad. "I need to look what is applying first." Says Luna. "Okay I will come and pick you up later when I have break today. I will be back here for you at noon. So be ready." Says Dad. "Okay I will see you then." Says Luna. Luna walks over to the sink in the kitchen rises her plate off. Puts the plate in the dishwasher. Then walks out of the kitchen, walking up the stairs to her room. "Hazel Lee. You ready to go yet?" Says Dad. "Yeah, I just need to wash my plate." Says Hazel. "Okay. I will meet you guys out in the car." Says Dad. Dad walks toward the front door out to the car. "Hazel. How bad is high school?" Says Lee. "I will tell you one thing it is boring." Says Hazel. "That works for me." Says Lee. Hazel and Lee walk to the car outside. Hazel sits in the back with Lee. Mostly they sit in the back of the car because it is only fair if the youngest kids sit in the back of the car. That is what Dad thinks anyway. So, Hazel and Lee sit in the back seat of the car. Dad starts the car and drives backward onto the road. Then drove toward school.

A few moments later. Hazel and Lee were dropped off at school at the front door, Hazel walked toward her locker to put her stuff in her assigned locker. Hazel had to head to the restroom first before she went to her first class that was emailed to her in the morning. Hazel walks in the bathroom that she first sees. Hazel washes her face as she looks in the mirror. She notices a star mark on her wrist. She never seen this mark on her before. All Hazel could think of was that this mark was never here before on her wrist. Hazel tried washing it off, but it just stayed on her wrist. Hazel reached for her bag. Pulled out a sweater then put that on and hid the tattoo that she never got. Hazel then walked toward her class then ran into some friends of hers Brittany and Mackenzie. "Hey Hazel, what's up?" Says Brittany. "Oh, nothing I am just heading to class before late." Says Hazel. "Well, that is a good thing, but me and Britt just wanted to say hi." Says Mackenzie. "Hey guys." Says Hazel. "Hazel why are you rushing like this. You usually are excited to see us?" Says Brittany. "I am. I just want to make it to class on time... I usually don't really care about going into class, but this year I care." Says Hazel. "Okay see you later then Hazel." Says Mackenzie. As Hazel continues running in the hallway to the closest closet that she could find. Hazel then feels as though her arm is in even more pain than two minutes ago. Hazel then slides down on the floor to her knees. Hazel holding screams so no one knows about her pain, but then Hazel then realizes she must get to class in two minutes.

Hazel fights through the pain and walks to her classroom holding her arm tight in her sweater. As Hazel walks in the classroom. She sees that Mackenzie was just sitting there in one spot next to the spot that Hazel usual sits in this classroom. Hazel walks over to the seat and sit downright next to Mackenzie. "Hey again Hazel. I did not know you were taking this class with me." Says Mackenzie. "I did not know you were interested in taking Art as well." Says Hazel. "Well, I am into painting, and I also mostly love the idea of having something important in the world because there is a lot of stuff going on in the world with art and technology. So, it's mostly just thinking about what is a great and a job that will get us somewhere, I guess." Says Mackenzie. "Good point. I am taking art because I enjoy it a lot" Says Hazel in pain in her arm. "Hey are you alright. You have been holding your arm this entire conversation." Says Mackenzie. "No, I am fine it's just I slept on my arm weird last night." Says Hazel. "Well, it also looks like you have not even slept either. Is everything okay?" Says Mackenzie. "Yeah, everything is fine I just had a bad dream last night." Says Hazel. "Okay. Just know that you can talk to me. I am here for you." Says Mackenzie. "Thanks Mackenzie I just need to figure out some things that's all." Says Hazel. Alright just let me know, if you need to talk." Says Mackenzie. As soon as the conversation was over the teacher walks in the room. Then the bell rings to queuing the classes to start.

After when Hazel's first class was over. Hazel still felt the pain on her arm. Hazel wanted to see why it hurt so much. Hazel moved the sleeve out of the way so Hazel could see the marking. When Hazel lifted the sleeve off her arm, to see that the mark was growing on her arm. Hazel looked shocked and scared of what this mark was doing to her. "Hey Hazel. What's up." Says Brittany. Hazel pulls up the sleeve so fast that Brittany could not even see the mark on her arm. "Is everything okay?" Says Brittany. "Ah yeah everything is fine Brittany." Says Hazel. "Yeah, Mackenzie is right. You seem tired and are you doing, okay?" Says Brittany. "I just had a nightmare and I slept funny on my arm." Says Hazel. "Okay, but Hazel if you are in that much pain you should probably go to the nurse's office." Says Brittany. "Okay. Don't worry about me. I will be fine." Says Hazel. "I will always worry about you

Hazel because you are my friend, and I care about you!" Says Brittany. The bell rings again. Everyone walks toward their next class, but Hazel just stands there in a frozen shock. Hazel then feels a hand on her shoulder. Hazel turns around and sees a boy asking what is wrong. Hazel says nothing, but Hazel then realizes that Hazel was not in the hallway at school anymore. Hazel was surround by clouds, dark clouds. Then Hazel turns around to find a throne of some kind. The boy says to Hazel that, that throne could be hers if she let's this pain go through her veins. Hazel screams out why me. The boy then says because you are the chosen one to guide us to be better people than ever, our chosen protector. You would be the protector of our dimension. But before the boy could finish what he was about to say to Hazel wakes up in a hospital bed. Dad looking down at his daughter. The most caring and worried eyes Hazel has ever known or seen. The doctor comes in. "Hello Mr. White, your daughter has been dealing with lots of pain all day. I don't know what from, but something is growing in your daughter's arm." Says Dr. Whales. "What kind of thing is growing in my daughter's arm?" Says Dad. "We are not sure, but can we do an X-ray on your daughter or anything that we think that will help her." Says Dr. Whales. "Yeah, do anything that will help. Shot I just remembered I must pick up Luna to drive her to a job placement that she picked out." Says Dad. "Okay we will call you Mr. White about the news." Says Dr. Whales. "Dad wait please don't go." Says Hazel in a weak voice. "Yeah Buber?" Says Dad. "I don't want you to leave me here." Says Hazel. "Honey you will be fine. They are doctors. They are here to help you." Says Dad. "Yeah, we are here to make sure that everything is fine with your arm and yourself Hazel." Says Dr. Whale. "Okay just be back soon please." Says Hazel in a weak voice. "I will honey just relax." Says Dad in a comforting smile. Dad leaves the room walks down the hallway. "So, Hazel we will be right back to take you to the X-Ray room." Says Dr. Whales. "Okay…" Says Hazel.

Lee goes to his next class science. "Hey, are you Lee White?" Says Mr. Brown. "Yeah, what's up?" Says Lee. "Well don't be worried, but I just thought it would be good if you knew that your sister Hazel is in the hospital, and your dad is coming to get you early." Says Mr. Brown.

"Wait what happened to Hazel?" Says Lee. "Well, they found Hazel on the ground unconscious, and she was burning up." Says Mr. Brown. "Well okay thanks for telling me that. I am also new here. Where is this classroom." Says Lee. "It is just down that hall the first right." Says Mr. Brown. "Thanks so much." Says Lee. "Well, you should just come with me. Cause I think your dad is coming now?" Says Mr. Brown. "Oh okay. I don't know the teacher that is teaching me science. Would it be possibly if you told them that I will not be coming?" Says Lee. "Yeah, sure I will tell Mr. Bobby that you won't be making it to his today." Says Mr. Brown. Lee and Mr. Brown walk to the parking lot to find that Lee's dad was waiting there for awhile. "Hey Lee get in the car." Says dad. "Okay, okay. Why are we going so fast?" Says Lee. "We are going fast because your sister Hazel is in the hospital. Did Mr. Brown tell you?" Says dad. "Yeah, he did, but he did not tell me why?" Says Lee. "Yeah, because we don't know what is wrong with Hazel." Says dad in concern. "Dad, is Hazel going to be fine." Says Lee. "I have no idea, but she is strong." Says dad. Yeah, she is strong. I remember the time she broke her arm. She healed so fast that she started swimming again in the pool, that we used to have." Says Lee. "Yeah, I remember those days. I used to call Hazel the fish in the family." Says dad in a sad voice. "Dad Hazel will be fine." Says Lee with a smile on his face. "Thanks son. I love you, Luna and Hazel. You guys are special to me. I don't think I could live with you guys being in pain, or not around anymore." Says dad. "When I say everything will be fine. I mean it will be fine. I love you to dad." Says Lee. "You are one of the most positive kid I will probably have." Says dad. Dad looks at his son for a few moments and realizes that he is so proud at his son. Then continues driving to the house to drop off Lee there.

"Well Lee I am just going to go get Luna at her new job that she just applied today. I don't think she starts till Monday." Says Dad. "Alright. Hey is Hazel going to come home tonight?" Says Lee. "I have no idea, but in the pain, she was in... I don't think so." Says Dad. "Okay." Says Lee in a voice that Lee is clearly trying to hide from dad. "Okay I will see you soon Lee." Says Dad. "Yep, I will be here." Says Lee. Dad drives toward Luna's new workplace.

"Hey Luna, I am here to pick you up." Says Dad. "Okay. I just need to sign out." Says Luna. "Wait what are you working right now?" Says Dad. "Yeah, I am." Says Luna. "You can't leave for me Luna so just text me when you are done your shift." Says Dad. "Oh okay. I did not know that." Says Luna. "Okay see you as soon as you text me. I am going to see Hazel in the hospital." Says Dad. "What did you just say!! Did you just say that Hazel is in the hospital?" Says Luna. "Yeah, she is in the hospital for an arm problem. There is something seriously wrong with Hazel." Says Dad. "Okay I am coming with you." Says Luna. "No Luna you can't, you are working right now." Says Dad. "But it's Hazel... dad please." Says Luna. "Luna you can come after when you are done working." Says Dad. Dad walks away from Luna. Dad walks out of the store where Luna got her new job at. Dad gets in the car and drives to the hospital.

"Where is my dad." Says Hazel in a pain voice. "Save your strength Hazel. I am sure your dad will be here soon." Says Dr. Whales. Dad walks in the hospital room where Hazel is staying in. "Honey, I am here." Says Dad. "Dad make the pain stop." Says Hazel in a screaming voice. "What is wrong. The pain was not that bad an hour ago?" Says Dad. "We are not sure what is happening right now, but we are just letting it course through her veins." Says Dr. Whales. "WHY. Are you doing that?! She is in pain. Have you examined her arm?" Says Dad. "Yes, we have but there is nothing that we can do. She has something that we have never heard of or seen." Says Dr. Whales. "Well figure it out Doctor!" Says Dad. Dad walks toward Hazel. Sits right next to Hazel holding her hand. "Hazel it's going to be okay." Says Dad in a concerned voice, and more worried than ever. "How do you know." Says Hazel in a weak voice. Hazel's eyes close as if she has died. Hazel's breath suddenly slowed down a lot. "Hazel. Hazel. HAZEL. Doctor. DOCTOR" Says Dad in a yelling voice. Dr. Whales walks in the room to see that Hazel has passed out again. "Mr. White." Says Dr. Whales. "Your daughter has fallen into a coma." Says Dr. Whales. "What. Hazel fallen into a coma." Says Dad. "Yes. I am sorry." Says Dr. Whales. "You should have been doing something than letting her get in that position. You guys should have not been writing notes down in your books." Says

Dad in an angry voice. Dad then storms out of the hospital to pick up Luna from her new job.

Dad arrives at Luna's new workplace. "Luna, are you done working?" Says Dad. "Yeah, I just signed out they let me go for the day. My shift ends at 5 everyday of the week." Says Luna. "Well, I am glad that you like working here Luna." Says Dad in a sad but happy voice. "Dad what's wrong I know that voice. You are trying to hide something from me. Aren't you?" Says Luna. "You see right through me." Says Dad. "So, what's wrong!?" Says Luna. "Hazel has fallen into a coma." Says Dad. "What. How did this happen." Says Luna in a worried voice. "I am not sure right now. Is all I know is that the doctors barely did anything to stop it from happening. Or I am just angry right now." Says Dad. "Dad I am sure that Hazel will be fine." Says Luna. "You should have seen the way the doctors were doing nothing to stop it from happening. Is all I could hear was that Hazel was in so much pain. She was begging it to stop." Says Dad. "I could not watch anymore. So, I stormed out with a fight with the doctor." Says Dad. "It would hurt me to see Hazel I hurt either. I would have done the same as you did, but then I would regret yelling at the doctor. The doctor was doing the best they could for Hazel." Says Luna. "You are right Luna. Let's just go home to your brother and make some food. This has been a long day." Says Dad. Dad and Luna walk to dad's car. Starts the car and drives back home to make some dinner. The drive was quiet. Luna did not know what to say. So, she just looked out the window of the car. Just watching the trees roll by as dad was driving pass them all. Finally, Dad and Luna arrive at home. "Lee we are home." Says Dad. "Hey Dad and Luna. Where is Hazel?" Says "Lee. She is still at the hospital. Hazel is in a coma. Right now..." Says Dad. "Oh... I didn't know that." Says Lee. "It's okay. Let's just get some food into us." Says Dad. Dad walks toward the kitchen to start making food. "Hey Dad, do you want my help?" Says Luna. No, I should be fine. Besides I was hoping to escape by making food all by myself. If that is okay with you Luna." Says Dad. "No, it's fine whatever makes you okay. I just thought that you would want to have some company." Says Luna. "Thank you, Luna. You are always going to be an amazing supportive girl." Says Dad as chopping up some vegetables. Luna walks out of the kitchen more worried about Dad even more now. "Luna what's wrong?" Says Lee. "Have you noticed that dad just wants to cook all by himself? He usually likes it when I cook with him." Says Luna. "Yeah, I know, but maybe it's best if we just give dad some space. He just found out that Hazel is in a coma, and he did not take that well." Says Lee. "Yeah. You are right." Says Luna. "Okay I am going to set the table for supper." Says Lee. Lee walks into the kitchen to grab some plates, forks and knives. To set the table up for supper. Luna walks toward the living room to sit on the couch. Luna then spaces out for awhile. Then Luna sees that Hazel is just sitting there in her very spot that she sits in the living room. Then Hazel walks toward Luna in her spot to hug Luna. When Luna was crying about her first boyfriend breaking up with her. Hazel says. "Everything is going to get better. If he is the one that broke up with you. He does not deserve you. You deserve love and truth, not someone that wants to leave you for anyone else. But I will always be here with you Luna. You are my big sister. You will never lose my love." Says Hazel. "Luna dinner's ready." Says Dad. Luna gets up and walks toward the dinning room. "That was fast cooking." Says "Luna. I was in the kitchen for awhile. Then I was yelling for you for 10 minutes. Are you okay?" Says Dad. "No, I am fine dad. I am fine. I just lost time, I guess." Says Luna. "Alright let's eat then if everything is okay." Says Dad. As Luna, Lee, and dad eat supper without Hazel. Luna, dad and Lee have all looked and tried to make this bad news about Hazel being in the hospital not a thing. They just want Hazel back making everyone laugh once again, but all they see is an empty spot at the table. There hearts gravel down to the bottom of there chests. Finally Lee talks first. "How was your first day working." Says Lee. "It was fine. I think that I will really like it at the flower shop." Says Luna. "Well, I am glad that you are fine with the job." Says Dad. Dad looks down at his plate in a sad moping face. "Dad Hazel will make it out of this. She is the strong sister and daughter that I think that we will ever have." Says Luna. "Yeah, I agree with Luna. Hazel will get through this, and we will be able to be a full family again." Says Lee. "Well, I am done eating. I have work tomorrow should probably going to bed. Oh, before I go. Luna be ready early. I will get you to work as well, and I am leaving early tomorrow. Lee, are you going to be fine in the morning by yourself? Getting up and walking to the bus stop." Says Dad. "Yeah, I will be fine. I am excited have the house to myself in the morning." Lee says in a happy voice. "Yeah, I will be up early tomorrow dad. I love you." Says Luna. "I love you to. Good night kids." Says Dad. As Dad walks to the kitchen with his empty plate. Puts it in the dishwasher and walks out of the kitchen walking toward his bedroom. All Luna and Lee could hear was a door then shutting behind dad quietly. "Well Lee I am going to bed to. I have work in the morning" Says Luna. "Night Luna. Have a great day at work." Says Lee. "You excited to have the house to yourself for an hour?" Says Luna. "Yeah, I get to have a shower, then deal with school, and I hate school. Do you think that you are going to hate tomorrow?" Says Lee. "We will see, Alright. Night Lee." Says Luna. Luna gets up. Walks to the kitchen and puts her dishes in the dishwasher. Luna walks up the stairs past Lee's closed door. Luna now crawls into bed with her journal in her hand. Writing about what happened today. Just about five minutes later. Luna puts her journal under her pillow. Begins to fall asleep with her music on. With one candle on.

"Hello sir, how are you doing?" Says Dr. Whales. "Where is the girl that you are talking about?! With the coma." Says a man. "Wow you are right to the point sir, aren't you?" Says Dr. Whales. "Just show me where the girl is." Says a man. "Okay. Okay. She is just upstairs." Says Dr. Whales. As the man and Dr. Whales walks up the hospital stairs to Hazel's room. The man looks down at Hazel evilly. The man then walks closer to Hazel's bed. "So, this is what is on her arm? Then huh." Says the man. "Yeah, she was in lots of pain. When her dad arrived in the room she screamed and begging her dad to make the pain stop. Then she fell into the coma." Say Dr. Whales. "That is very unfortunate. I really wanted to get to know the guardian." Says the man. "What is the guardian?" Says Dr. Whales. "See that on her arm. That is the star symbols of the guardian's queen. Right now, this young girl is being transformed into a canon that will surround her with hate or darkness. She is dreaming of her worst dreams right now. It's like torture to her." Says the man. "Is there anyway we can stop it?" Says Dr. Whales. "No because it's this girl's destiny now, but here is the thing. I want to take her for myself."

Says the man. "What are you talking about? You can't take this girl. She will be noticed missing." Says Dr. Whales. "Yeah, and I don't care. She is my project now. Pick her up boys." Says the man. "Well, I am afraid that I am going to have to stop you from doing that." Says Dr. Whales. "So be it." Says the man. The man grabs a gun out of his pocket. Pulls the trigger on Dr. Whales. Dr. Whales falls to the ground trying to hold all his blood in his body. But the bullet went right through Dr. Whales. Dr. Whales' hand grown weaker to the ground and his hand was in the blood. "I did not want to do that Dr. Whales, but I need this girl." Says the man. The man walks out of the room with his soldiers carrying Hazel out of the room. Walking down the stairs. Opening the hospital entrance door. They walk toward a truck. They put Hazel in the back of the truck covered in chain to make sure the body won't make banging noises. The man and his soldiers go to the front seat of the truck. "Hey, can you guys be in the back with the guardian. Just stand there watching her." Says the man. "Yes sir." Says the soldier. The soldiers walk to the back of the truck to get in where Hazel was just laying there. A soldier gets in the back with the guardian. Then one of them just outside of the truck so someone can lock the truck from the outside. The other soldier walks to the front of the truck to drive the truck back to base. "Alright let's head back to base." Says the man. The soldier starts the truck and drives away from the hospital in the darkness.

Luna walks down the stairs to grab a glass of water. But before Luna continues to the kitchen. Luna can hear something downstairs. Like crying. Luna walks down the stairs slowly and the living room light is on. Luna could see that dad was sitting on the couch crying. As Luna got closer to the living room. she could hear dad's cries louder. Luna had no idea what to do at that moment. She has never seen dad cry before. Dad just continues to lay on the couch crying and crying. Luna finally makes a move toward the kitchen to get a glass of water. But Luna noticed the crying stopped as soon as the step made a noise. "Who is there?" Says dad. "It's me Luna. I just came down to get a glass of water." Says Luna. "Oh okay. Did you hear anything?" Says dad. "Yeah dad. I heard you crying. Are you going to be, okay?" Says Luna. "No, I am really worried about Hazel. I called Dr. Whales just a couple minutes ago to try to check up on Hazel, but there was no answer." Says dad. "I mean it is late. The hospital would be closed right now, and Hazel would probably be sleeping… in the coma." Says Luna. "Yeah, you are probably right." Says dad. Luna and dad just stare at each other for a little bit, but then Luna walks toward dad in the living room to sit right next to dad on the couch. Luna then hugs dad so tight. Dad hugs back. Luna swore that she felt a tear on her shoulder. "Well, I am going back to my room to try to get some sleep Luna. Remember be ready in the morning. I love you." Says dad. "I love you to dad. I am here if you want to talk. I love you so much." Says Luna. Dad gets up off the couch. Walking toward his bedroom. Luna continues to get that glass of water. Then Luna walks to her bedroom to go to bed.

Luna's alarm goes off at six in the morning. Luna gets out of bed to get dressed for work. Luna walks out of her bedroom all dressed and ready for the day of working. Luna walks down the stairs to make some breakfast. "Morning Luna." Says dad. "Morning dad I am just making some breakfast right now." Says Luna. "Alright while you are doing that, I am going to turn on the news." Says dad. Dad walks out of the kitchen toward the living room he went with his cup of tea. Dad turns the news on.

Hello morning everyone. Watching the news, I am afraid that we have such disturbing news today. The hospital around our area has found a dead body by security this morning. The body was Dr. Whales, one of the best doctors around, I am also afraid to say one of his patients was kidnapped last night as well, known as Hazel White. Anyway let's move on to the weather for today.

Luna hears the TV from the kitchen as she was making breakfast. Luna then runs toward the living room to make sure Luna was not just hearing them saying that Hazel was kidnapped, But Luna heard right. Hazel has been kidnapped. Dad walks out of the living room not saying a word to Luna. At all. All Luna saw was that dad had a face of angry and sadness. All mixed together he was scared even more now. Luna tries to see where dad went. Luna finds that dad's door was shut. Luna knocks on the door. There was no voice saying come in, but Luna goes in anyway. Luna finds dad just staring in space looking horrible than usual. "Dad are you alright?" Says Luna and biting her lip. "What do you think?!" Says dad. "I know dad. I know. Hazel was kidnapped, but they will find her I believe it." Says Luna. "No Luna they won't. The news just wants stories to make people talk about things. No one takes my daughter." Says dad. "Dad, I know this is hard for you to move on and keep going, but everything will get better. This was just like my situation. I found you and mom to love and be part of a family again. That was the best thing that I could ever have, and you were always there for me. Now it's my turn." Says Luna. "Luna I just need to be alone today. I will drive you to work later." Says dad. "Don't you have to work today to?" Says Luna. "Yea I do, but my boss will understand." Says dad. "So, you are like not going to work today." Says Luna. "I don't feel like it. Luna can you just leave my bedroom please." Says dad. "I will leave your room, but all I ask for you is to not let this Hazel being kidnapped take over your life dad. You can make it through this. I know it." Says Luna. Dad just continues to just sit on his bed saying nothing. It's like he was trying to keep himself from saying something that was going to hurt Luna a lot, but he just kept it in. Luna walks back toward the kitchen to continue making her breakfast. Luna walks toward the dining room to eat her breakfast. Dad then walks in the room sitting in his spot. "Luna I am sorry. This is just hard for me to process. I never thought that my daughter or my children would ever get kidnapped... You ready to go?" Says dad. "No, but I will be after when I am done eating breakfast." Says Luna. "Okay. I am going to go start the car to warm it a bit." Says dad. But before dad walks out of the house. Lee walks down the stairs. "Hey Dad, where are you going?" Says Lee. "I am just going to go start the car." Says dad. "Oh okay." Says Lee. Dad walks out of the door and shuts it loudly. "What's wrong with dad?" Says Lee. "Dad just heard some awful news about Hazel." Says Luna. "What's wrong that could make dad so mad." Says Lee. "Hazel was kidnapped last night." Says Luna. "Oh yeah that would do it." Says Lee in a voice that he was trying to make Luna smile, but of course it did nothing. "Lee, I think you should just get ready for school." Says Luna. "Yeah, I am going to go have a shower." Says Lee. "Alright. I will see you later." Says Luna. Lee walks toward the bathroom. Dad walks back in the house. "Hey Luna, are you ready now?" Says dad. "Yeah, I am. Can I just put my dish in the dishwasher?" Says Luna. "Yeah sure. I will meet you out in the car." Says Dad. Dad walks out of the house. Luna could hear the door slam and hear dad's footsteps. Luna puts her dish away in the dishwasher. Walks toward the door to outside. To see that dad was already in the car just waiting for Luna to get in. "Are you ready? You got everything?" Says Dad. "Yeah, I got everything thanks dad." Says Luna. As Dad drives toward Luna's new workplace. Luna tries and wants to talk, but she says nothing in the car. Cause she does not want to make things worse for dad. Luna could see the angry in dad's eyes, but so scared at the same time. Luna hates seeing dad like this. All Luna can do is hug dad and say that everything will be fine. But Luna even knows that is bullshit, to say to someone that is going through kidnappers that have Hazel. Luna has no idea why the kidnappers would want Hazel so bad to kill a doctor for her sleeping body. "I will text you when my shift is over." Says Luna. "Alright I am going home for awhile, but I might do what you said earlier. Go to work… maybe." Says Dad. "Okay just shot me a message if you need me okay. I love you dad." Says Luna. "I love you to. Honey and will do." Says Dad. Luna gets out of the car and waves to her dad in the car, but Dad just kept driving. Luna is not going to be sad about dad just driving away immediately. Luna knows that dad is going through the worst situation right now that a dad can go through in their life. Missing one of his children, and not having contact with them is the worst feeling in any parents' life. Luna walks in the store to sign in the back room of the shop and meets up with her boss.

"Well, I guess we are just going to have to find another way to getting inside of this witch's head somehow." Says the man. "Sir there is no way in her head. She is in a coma. Not a human one… anymore." Says a solider. "What are you talking about?!" Says the Man. "She is gaining power in her coma. Or that she knows that she has been kidnapped and she is trying to keep answers from coming out." Says the solider. "Well, isn't she just amazing. She learned that fast. Right?!" Says the Man. "We will find away to make her give signs or talk." Says the solider. "Well, find it!" Says the Man. "Yes, sir we are working on it right now." Says the solider. The solider just walks away from the man in sort of fear in his eyes. The solider then looks at the man. His dark black hair really represents his soul. His gray eyes they are so hard to read they are far to mysterious to explore. He would be a scary sea to explore. The solider goes back to his station after he was done trying to read the man. "Guardian, why must you fight. I am your follower. We are just here to help you. Put down your powers and listen to me. I will make sure you are safe." Says the Man. The man looks down at Hazel. "I will do anything for you. My niece." Says the man. "Sir we might have found something." Says a solider. "What is it?" Says the man. The man and the solider walk toward a computer screen and see that there was a file on the PC screen. It was Hazel's Sister, but everything about her. Even more than Luna knows about herself. "Who is this?" Says the man. "This time Witch is Hazel's Sister, but here is the thing she has no idea who she is. I think we can use her." Says the solider. "Alright go get that Witch than. Bring her to me. Make sure she does not use her magic or know anything about directions to coming here." Says the man. "Cause if this girl knows where she needs to go to get help. She can summon help. These Witches are powerful than you think. Make sure she is unconscious when bringing her here." Says the man. "Yes sir. I will make sure the new prisoner will not know." Says the solider. The solider already knows where to go get Luna. Luna is just a few couple hours away from here to. The man walks back to Hazel. The man puts his mouth in Hazel's ear and whispers in her ear. "I am getting your sister. Change your actions. I am not afraid of killing someone for answers." Says the man. The man feels a fight through Hazel. "So, you can hear me? Then. I won't hurt your sister. Unless you wake up and answer my questions." Says the man. The man feels nothing, but pain, fear, and concern. "Hazel, I don't want to hurt you or anyone that you love, but I want answers I have been waiting for you to arrive in this world for 100's of years. I have watched people I love die, and I want to know why I can't die. I have watched my parents call me a monster. My own parents hate me because of who I am today, and somehow in my research that I have been doing my entire life leads to you. You are the only one that can stop this. I just want to know what I am. I can read people's thoughts. I can make things live or die. I am like the grim reaper." Says the man.

The man still gets no answer from Hazel. "Fine I guess you can listen to your sisters screams in a few hours. Time Witches hate handling with there future. Cause they are not allowed to see or feel or cheat it. I am going to enjoy having a grip on your sister. You see Hazel, A time Witch got involved in my life and ruined everything. With my family, my girlfriend and my best friend. They ruined everything for me, so I won't go easy on your sister as I am with you. Make your choice now." Says the Man. The man then walks away from Hazel in frustration, but as the man walks away Hazel starts giving intense rays off the charts on the machines that she was connected to. Like as if Hazel was screaming in her head for help.

Hazel's realm inside her head. Hazel panics as the scary man walks away from her. Hazel just thinks of an idea that she would have never known that she could do it or she would have never thought of it. Hazel is going to send a warning message to Luna. Hazel knew everything about Luna now because. Even though her eyes are suck in a coma and she can not open her eyes. The stars for some reason are giving Hazel, knowledge of the world and the universe. She does the warning message making Luna have a vision. Hazel waves her hands around making a vision that will only get to Luna on time. Hazel hopes that the man won't find out what Hazel has done to keep the answers for what the man wants. Hazel is not sure why she is so valuable to him so much. Hazel only thought that she was a teenage girl going through drama at school, but now Hazel must deal with this entire thing that she never wanted. The message was sent to Luna. Hazel then sits down on a chair to wait for what happens next. She hopes that it will be great news that Luna won't get kidnapped.

It's almost the end of the day already. Lee thinks of that in his head he is so excited for the day to be over. As Lee was done thinking about that the announcements come on. "Hello everyone, good afternoon. I want to do something before classes are over for the day. These years getting involved in any sport or club. If you are interested in getting involved in stuff like that. The gym is the place that you are welcome to come to, or you can stay in class and learn. We would love it if you all got involved in something for this year. But we will always be here to help you anyway. Okay have great rest of your day." Says Mr. Bones. As soon as the announcement was done. Kids just booked it out of there seats. Lee was just sitting there thinking. Lee gets up and walks to the gym. Lee enters the gym looking around at the clubs and sports. Lee walks around for awhile until he saw something interesting that he might want to try. He has been playing basketball by himself for awhile. That is pretty much the only thing that he enjoys doing. For his spare time. Lee walks up to the table and asks. "Hey, can I sign up for basketball." Says Lee. "Sure, you are welcome. What is your name?" Says the girl. "My name is Lee White." Says Lee. "Wait, are you that girl Hazel's little brother that literally fainted in the hallway, then sent to the hospital and then kidnapped?" Say the girl. "Yeah, that's my sister." Says Lee in a sad voice. "Hey, I am sorry for your sister. I hope she will come home safe for your shake." Says the girl. "Thanks umm." Says Lee. "Oh right." Says the girl in a laugh. "My name is Sam." Says Sam. "That is a nice name." Says Lee. "Thanks. I think that Lee is a cool name as well." Says Sam. "Thanks my dad suggested it to my mom." Says Lee. "Hey, you seem like a nice guy and fun because you are signing up for a sport that I play to." Says Sam. "Oh you play basketball to? I thought they just put people in these booths or areas." Says Lee. "No, they choose people that are involved in these sports or clubs." Says Sam. "Oh I see. Well, it's a cool thing what this school puts together, then." Says Lee. "Yeah, it's alright. I am so excited to start playing basketball though." Says Sam. "Why so excited?" Says Lee in a happy confused way. 'I am just so excited because I love playing basketball so much. I just have the biggest confidence with playing this sport. It just brings me closer to my heart, for some odd reason." Says Sam. "That is great to hear, that someone like you has a big connection. That is soooo much fun." Says Lee. "Yeah, I love basketball. My dad taught me how to play when I was grieving over my moms passing." Says Sam in a sad voice. "Oh… I am so sorry about your mom." Says Lee in a sad voice. "Oh, it's fine. She passed when I was eight. I do still miss her though." Says Sam. "Yeah, I bet. My mom is all the way across the world researching the environment in the jungle." Says Lee. "Is she an environmentalist?" Says Sam. "Yeah, she loves plants and the worlds natures. So, she decided to make a living out of it." Says Lee. "That is cool. My mom was a painter. I am also pretty sure she would have wanted me to be a painter." Says Sam in a laughing voice. "Why's that?" Says Lee. "Let's just say that I am great or good at drawing and picking out colors." Says Sam. As Sam puts her sketch book in front of Lee. "Wow this is good drawings. How long have you been drawing?" Says Lee. "I have been drawing since I was six. I enjoy drawing a lot to as much as basketball, but basketball keeps me moving forward. Drawing keeps my fingers moving and my imagination." Says Sam. "You have quite the talent and the activity Sam. I have never meant a-." Says Lee. "A girl like me." Says Sam in a laughing way. "Yeah, I have never meant girl so active, but so into the arts." Says Lee. "Well, you have meant me. Well, sign your name. I got to close the booth soon." Says Sam. "Right. Let's sign up me!" Says Lee in a laugh and a sigh. Lee picks up the pencil and writes his name on the boy's basketball side of the school team. "Alright you are all set up." Says Sam. "Hey Sam?" Says Lee. "Yeah, what's up." Says Sam. "This might be weird to ask, but can I have your number I don't have many friends and my family is a little sad right now. Also, this is my second day here at this high school." Says Lee. "Sure, you can have my number." Says Sam. Sam gets a piece of paper. Writes down her number on it. Then gives the piece of paper to Lee. "Thanks Sam have a great rest of your day. I will talk to you later." Says Lee. "Yeah, see you, Lee." Says Sam. Lee walks away from Sam his heart beating fast a lot more usually. Lee walks out of the gym walking toward his locker. Lee grabs all his stuff out of his locker. Lee walks out of the school toward the bus station to head home. Lee gets in his bus that he is assigned to get a ride from everyday to go home. As the bus drives away, Lee can't stop thinking about Sam.

"Hey dad I am home." Says Lee. There was no answer. Lee walks around to see if Luna or dad was around, but Lee did not find anyone. Lee grabs his phone out of his pocket and messages dad. "Hey, where are you and Luna at?" Says Lee. Dad texts back." I am just out getting some food right now, and your sister Luna is still at work." Says Dad. "Oh, okay I just wanted to know that's all." Says Lee. "Okay. I will see you soon Lee." Says Dad. "Okay. See you later." Says Lee. Lee walks up the stairs holding his schoolbooks and taking his backpack up the stairs. Lee closes his bedroom door behind him. Lee opens his laptop to do some homework from school of the second day. Lee thinks that homework is not meant to be on the second day of classes. But he does it anyway.

"Hey Luna." Says the manager. "Yeah, what's up?" Says Luna. "I am sorry to do this, but can you stay a little longer it's a bit busy today, and we got to do this decorating for our sale this weekend." Says the manager. "Sure, I will stay a little longer. I have one question though? How late will I be so I can text my dad to come and pick me up?" Says Luna. "I think you might be a little longer. Maybe like 9:30." Says the manager. "What!!??" Says Luna. "What, what is wrong?" Says the manager. "No everything's fine. I am just usually in bed by 10." Says Luna. "Oh, I see. Do you want me to ask someone else?" Says the manager. "No, it's fine I will stay. That was just a little surprise for me that is all." Says Luna. "Okay perfect just let me know if you have any question, Luna." Says the manager. "Well, I have one question. You have not told me your name yet? What is your name?" Says Luna. "Oh, I did not tell you, my name. I don that sometimes. Sorry, my name is Eva." Says Eva. Eva walks away from Luna and goes to the back room where the other flowers are. Luna grabs her phone out of her pocket to message dad. "Hey dad. I might be a little late for dinner tonight, so I am just saying I will walk home later. I will see you tomorrow morning or tonight. I am coming home around 9:30. I love you." Says Luna. "Oh, that is fine. Thanks for messaging me for what's going on. So, I don't have to drive to your workplace later?" Says Dad. "Nope I will be fine walking home." Says Luna. "Okay, I am probably going to be sleeping when you get home though, but I hope you are enjoying your new job." Says Dad. "Oh, trust me I am enjoying working with this company." Says Luna. "Well, I am happy that you are." Says dad with a smile emoji on messages. "Okay I should get back to work." Says Luna. "Okay I will talk to you later." Says Dad. Luna puts her phone back in her pocket and continues to work for her job for the rest of the day. But as Luna continues. Her mind flashes an image of Hazel. Luna this is a warning message. "Be careful tonight they are coming for you now to. Be careful." Says Hazel in the vision. Hazel then disappears out of thin air, before Luna could say anything. Luna has a concerned and confusing facial expression, but Luna just must get back to work. Luna still has no idea what that was. All Luna knows is that Hazel is alive, thank God. Luna then just works for the rest of the day to be thinking about what just happened.

Dad puts all the groceries in the car out of the shopping cart. Dad walks to the shopping cart drop off area to. Drop off the shopping cart. Dad walks back to the car. Dad starts the car driving toward home.

"Lee I am home." Says Dad. "Hey dad." Says Lee. "I am going to be making two just for two tonight." Says dad. "Why where is Luna?" Says Lee. "She is still working, and her boss needed her to stay longer." Says Dad. "Well, I guess it's just the two of us then." Says Lee in a sigh. "What's wrong son?" Says dad. "I just miss us being together. That's all." Says Lee. "I know I miss it to. But we need to just hope that Hazel will be safe coming home in the future and hopefully Luna can come home as early as she can." Says dad. "Yeah, I agree, but I guess life had other plans for our family." Says Lee. "Well, I am going to get some supper made." Says dad. "Hey dad you little better?" Says Lee. "Yeah, I just needed some space for a bit." Says Dad. "Its okay dad. Take your time. Healing is a process that requires patience." Says Lee. "How did you become so wise? Lee." Says Dad. "I don't know I got it from you. Because you always seem to see the good in things and I seemed to have learned positivity from your actions." Says Lee. "Well, I am glad that one of my kids is grateful for what is in front of them in life." Says Dad. "Yeah, I am grateful besides my sister Hazel getting kidnapped by an unknown person." Says Lee. "Alright Lee I should make some dinner for us." Says Dad. "Okay I will be in the living room watching my show." Says Lee. Lee walks toward the living room. Dad stares in the distance as Lee walks away from him, but then dad snaps out of his spacing phrase. Dad turns around from the living room and walks toward the kitchen. Dad gets out the chicken out of the fridge, puts it on the counter, chops it up, puts it on a pan, and finally the final touch is salt and pepper. For chicken anyway to him. Turns on the stove and grabs some vegetables out of the freezer, gets a pot out of the cabinet, fills it up with some cold water to boil on the stove. Dad grabs some cold vegetables out of the bag full of greens. Fills the water pot full of vegetables. He sets the stove at five for heat, he grabs a spoon and stirs the food inside the water pot for a minute. Dad grabs the sauce out of the fridge to put on the chicken. Dad sits and waits for the chicken to be fully cooked and checks on the vegetables.

"Lee dinner's ready." Says dad. "Okay I am coming." Says Lee. Lee walks into the kitchen grabs a plate of food, walks toward the dinning room. Lee sits down in his spot; Lee then looks around the dinner table sees that it is just dad and him sitting at the dinner table. Lee then looks down at his food. "What's wrong son?" Says dad. "Oh nothing... it is just weird not having Hazel or Luna at the dinner table. With us." Says Lee. "I will tell you what son. It is weird not having them here, but they will be back soon." Says dad. "Yeah, you are right." Says Lee. As Lee and dad continue eating dinner in silence. Dad grabs his phone out of his pocket and messages Luna. "Hey, it's just dad messaging. We have way more food at home if you are going to be hungry when you get home. You are more then Welcome to get some out of the fridge. Love you have a great shift." Says dad. Dad sends the messages. Dad puts his phone in his pocket. After half hour. Lee and Dad get up from the table in the dinning room. From after a nice dinner chat just dad and Lee. They still feel weird not having everyone around the table, but like dad said everything will be fine. Lee and Dad go to the kitchen to clean up. The dishes. Dad starts the dishwasher; Lee cleans up the pots and pans that dad has used for the past two days. Dad and Lee turn on some music as they clean the kitchen. "Lee thanks for being here for me." Says Dad. "Dad I will always be here for you. I love you." Says Lee. "I love you to son." Says Dad. Lee and Dad stare at each other for a moment, then they open their arms to hug it out. "Well, we should finish up the kitchen then I might go to bed and see you guys in the morning." Says Dad. "Sounds like a plan." Says Lee. As Dad and Lee finish up cleaning the kitchen for the night. Dad walks out of the kitchen with a glass of water. Walks toward his bedroom and says goodnight to Lee. "Night Dad." Says Lee. Lee walks out of the kitchen, up the stairs toward his bedroom. Lee opens his bedroom and walks into the room. Lee turns on his lights in his bedroom sop he could see what PJ's he was putting on. As soon as he had his PJ's on, he walks toward the light to turn off the lights. Lee crawls into bed putting his phone on charge, Lee grabs the closet blanket next to his hand. Lee hears his phone buzz. Lee grabs his phone to see who was messaging him currently. It was Sam. Lee messages back. "Hey, what's up." Says Lee. Sam messages back. "Nothing much you? I am just laying in bed right now." Says Sam. "Yeah, I just got in bed. Me and dad were cleaning the kitchen, so we don't have to do it tomorrow. Lol." Says Lee. "Well at least you guys are still getting things done around the house. Lol." Says Sam. "So true. Otherwise, our house would be a mess. Lol." Says Lee. "Yeah, especially when you are not going to have a sister around for awhile until they find Hazel." Says Sam. "Oh you, don't know do you?" Says Lee. "Know what?" Says Sam. "I have two sisters. My oldest sister's name is Luna, she is just working late tonight." Says Lee. "Oh, sorry I did not know that. LOL." Says Sam. "No, it's fine. You don't know everything about me. Lol." Says Lee. "I thought I did. Lol." Says Sam. "Well, you have so much to learn." Says Lee. "I guess I do. But Lee I must go get some sleep. I will see you tomorrow at school. See you later." Says Sam. "Night Sam." Says Lee. Turns off his phone, puts it back on charge, struggles up to his blanket, and falls asleep.

"Luna." Says Eva. "Yeah, What's up?" Says Luna. "I think you are good to go for tonight. It's getting late. I must get home and go to bed. I will see you tomorrow." Says Eva. "Alright I will see you then, bye Eva." Says Luna. "See you tomorrow. We have another big day." Says Eva. "I will be there." Says Luna. Luna signs out. Luna then grabs all her stuff from the back room. Luna grabs her phone then messages dad. "I am heading home see you soon. Love you". Says Luna. Luna continues walking down the street, but then Luna hears some footsteps following her or running toward her. Luna then remembers Hazel's message, and Luna totally forgot. Because of all the tasks she had to do for the day. Then Luna notices that there is a car slowly following her beside her on the other side of the road. Then someone runs at her from the dark alleyway to grab her. Luna then screams out. "What do you want?!!"

Says Luna. "You are coming with us. Back to your sister." Says the solider. "You have Hazel. Where is-"Before Luna could finish. They have tranquilized Luna to sleep. The Soldier's grab Luna's sleeping body and put it in the back seat of the car. The soldiers get in the car with Luna's sleeping body. The soldiers drive away the opposite direction from her house with dad and Lee there alone for sure now. The soldiers call the man. "What??!!" Says the Man. "We have Luna. We are on the way back Sir." Says the soldier. "Okay. That is the best news I got all day, thank you." Says the man. The man hangs up on the soldiers. The soldiers continue to drive back to base.

CHAPTER 4

WHERE ARE THE SISTERS?

After the ride to the base. The soldiers bring Luna inside the building tied up. The soldiers walk in the base to the commander's quarters. "Sir Luna is here. Where should we put her?" Says the soldier. "Put her where Hazel is. I set up a perfect place for Luna to do her best work to wake up Hazel." Says the man. The soldiers walk Luna to where Hazel is being kept. Luna wakes up in a cage a few hours later. Luna opens her eyes to notice that Hazel was laying down on a platform of some kind she was restrained. Luna notices that she had a chain on her ankle, and a man walks toward Luna. "Hey, Luna. Your awake." Says the man. "Where am I?" Says Luna. "You are at my base very far from home, but at least you are close to your sister. Are you the big sister?" Says the man. "What have you done to her?!" Says Luna. "I have done necessary things for her." Says the man. "She is not your experiment." Says Luna. "I know. She is destined to be our guardian though when you wake her up." Says the man. 'What are you talking about?!" Says Luna. "I am talking about a new future for Hazel and all of humankind. She will rule us forever, she will guide us, she will be our guardian." Says the man. Luna looks at the man and realizes how creepy this man is being about Luna's sister making this world different or something big. "Luna, you look scared. I will tell you what, you don't need to be scared. Because your sister would never hurt you. She loves you with all her heart." Says the Man. "What is the point?!" Says Luna. "The point is that she will listen to you, and maybe we can get some answers together." Says the man. 'I will never help you. Whoever you are. Hazel would never help evil like you, and since I did not listen to my sister's vision of warning me to be careful. Of course, cluelessly forgot about it." Says Luna. "Hazel sent you a message to be careful. Wow she has been growing while I have not been looking." Says the man. The man walks toward Hazel. The man whispers something in Hazel's ear. Luna was trying to listen to what he said, but Luna was to far away from Hazel's sleeping body. "Hazel don't do that with your other family members. We know where they live. We also have your sister here now. We can hurt her now. If she ends up dying." Says the man. He could feel Hazel crying inside in her realm. The man was trying to listen to Hazel's voice, but it was in a language that no human has never heard of. The man once again feels that Hazel is crying inside. The man pets Hazel on the head. "I don't want to be your enemy Guardian. I just want you to be free." Says the man. Luna tries and tries to struggle out of the chain on her ankle. "Don't try it, you are just wasting energy for yourself Luna. Those chains held me over 100 hundred years by my parents. They tried and tried to kill me repeatedly, but they failed. The point is that I was a powerful being, and it will carry a Time Witch for me." Says the man. "What is a time witch?" Says Luna. "You are a time witch, that is why you got a clear message from your sister. I will tell everything to Hazel, that is you are adopted." Says the man. "You can't because she is sleeping, and she can't hear." Says Luna. "Oh, she can hear. She heard me sending soldiers to get you, and here you are, but she tried to warn you. But she failed of course." Says the man. "She did not fail-"Says Luna. "Then why are you here." Says the man. "I did not know what it meant." Says Luna. "A Time Witch takes those kinds of messages serious because it tells them futures for them." Says the man. "I didn't know that I was a Time Witch." Says Luna. "Yeah, you did not know, because your real parents knew, and never told you." Says the man. "How do you know my parents?" Says Luna. "I know your parents because they were traitors when they found out about you. That when your mother was pregnant with you. They left this place and never came back. They tried to hide, but we found them lots of times. You see they use to be one of these soldiers that kidnapped you. Then they died in a robbery." Says the man in air quotes in an evil laugh. "YOU KILLED MY PARENTS." Says Luna. "NO, no, no... my soldiers did." Says the man. "YOU MONSTER, they were good people." Says Luna in a cry of hatred. "No, they weren't because they worked for me Luna. They went with my command over 20 years. I am pretty sure they enjoyed it until you came. I had to kill them because they knew about me." Says the man. "But you let a kid blame herself for 10 years." Says Luna. "I don't care. My parents were meaner than I am. I take lives and I can make people suffer for eternity. That is why they hated me. Because I accidentally killed our dog." Says the man. "I don't care about your dog." Says Luna. "Ouch… that hurt, you have your mom's sass. I like it, but that is not going to get you through this Luna. What will get you through this is that you, do as I say. Maybe you and sister will make it out of this alive." Says the man. "HAHAHA, I will make sure that we make it out of this alive." Says Luna. "You are lucky I need you alive for the Guardian to awaken, girl." Says the man. Luna sits there looking at her sister still sleeping. Luna then makes her eye contact at the man. "Well, I am going to leave you and your sister. Don't do anything stupid Luna Roswell." Says the man. Luna just sat there stunned, by that name. She has not heard that name in years. He walks away and the door closes behind him. Luna then makes her eye contact at the chain on her ankle, then at Hazel. "Hazel if you can hear me. I am sorry, I did not want you to find out that I was adopted this way, and now I know who killed my parents. I will get us out of here." Says Luna. Luna sits down on the floor in sadness.

Dad gets out of bed. At 5 am in the morning. Dad picks up his phone to look at his messages, and there was a message from Luna from last night. Dad goes to the kitchen to make his coffee. Do his daily morning stuff. Dad puts the dishes away from the dishwasher. Dad turns on his book plugs his ear buds in and continues putting the dishes away.

Dad looks at the time after he is done putting the dishes and the pots away. He notices that Luna was supposed to wake up a few minutes ago. Dad messages Luna to get up, then he realizes that might not work so he goes up the stairs to Luna's room. Dad opens Luna's door. Luna was not there. Dad messages Luna one more time. "Where are you?" Says Dad. Dad messages again "LUNA this is not funny answer your phone." Says dad. Dad stares and tries to see if Luna is going to text back, but there was no answer. Now dad was worried for sure now. He was blaming himself that he should have not listened to Luna. He should have gone to pick Luna at 9:30. Now dad gets out of Luna's room and drives to the police station.

Dad enters the police station. "Hello, how can we help you today." Says a police officer. "I want to file a missing person. My daughter Luna." Says dad. "Oh, you are Mr. White aren't you." Says the police. "Yeah, I am Robert White." Says dad. "I am so sorry about your daughter Hazel and now you are saying that your other daughter is missing. Is her name Luna." Says the police officer. "Yes, I know it. I feel that it might be the same person that kidnapped my daughter Hazel." Says Dad. "Okay, begin filing a missing persons report. My name is Officer Roswell." Says the officer. Officer Roswell and Dad walk to his office to talk about where Luna was before she went missing. "So, where was Luna before she went missing?" Says Officer Roswell. "She was working late, at her new workplace." Says dad. "Where does she work?" Says Officer Roswell. "She works at Flower life shop." Says Dad. "Okay thank you. We will go question them for where she possibly went or tried to go. We will find your daughters." Says Officer Roswell. "Thank you so much. Please tell me about any updates for where Luna went or is." Says dad. "I will try, but you go on with your day Robert. I will call you." Says Officer Roswell. "Okay, thank you so much Officer Roswell." Dad walks out of the office. Dad gets in his car to drive back home.

Lee wakes up at seven in the morning. Lee gets his phone off charge. Lee puts a sweater on and walks down the stairs. Lee hears the front door open. "Dad where did you go?" Says "Lee. I went to the police station." Says dad. "Why? What happened?!" Says Lee. "I don't know if I am right, but I think Luna has been kidnapped." Says dad. Lee looks at dad like he has seen a ghost. "Lee are you okay?" Says Dad. "No, my other sister has been kidnapped." Says Lee. "I know, but the police are now looking for Hazel and Luna." Says dad. "Why don't you just look where Luna's phone is. You basically put trackers in our phone." Says Lee. "I totally forgot about that. Thanks for being a smart-ass. It finally is useful." Says Dad. Dad looks in the app to track Luna. Lee's phone is right on top of dad's icon. Hazel's says its across town or across the country in a forest. Dad shows Lee where Hazel and Luna are.

They almost lost it. They just thought about showing this info to the police, but then Dad thinks about wanting revenge for kidnapping his daughters. So, he decides he wants to go find Hazel and Luna all by himself. "Dad, I know that face, don't do it whatever you are thinking." Says Lee. "Lee, I want to know if Hazel and Luna are okay." Says Dad. "Whoever kidnapped Hazel and Luna they must have a reason for it." Says Lee. "They better have an amazing reason because they are going to get a knuckle sandwich." Says Dad. Lee stares at dad for a bit, then Lee realizes that dad just misses his daughters. Lee does not say anything because he does not know how that feels to be missing his daughters or just kids in general. "Lee you should get ready for school." Says Dad. "Oh, shot I should I have basketball practice today." Says Lee. "Oh, you signed up for a sport at school. That is fantastic for you Lee." Says dad. "Yeah, I also meant this nice person as well while signing up." Says Lee. "What's his name?" Says Dad. "Her name is Sam, she loves basketball." Says Lee. "Oh, it's a girl." Says dad in a goofy look. "Yeah, it's a girl. I really think that we could be great friends." Says Lee. "Well, I am glad that you are meeting new people Lee. I am happy for you." Says Dad. "Thanks dad. I should get in the shower wash myself up and eat. Then get to the bus on time." Says Lee. "Yeah, I got to go pack up for the journey to find your sisters." Says Dad. "Are you serious?! You are going after that tracking. What if it's a trap." Says Lee. "I will be fine Lee. But if I don't make it home tomorrow or tonight you have the house to yourself. Keep it clean please." Says Dad. "Fine, but please text me. I can't lose you to." Says Lee. "You won't I promise. I will be home with your sisters." Says Dad. "Okay just be careful." Says Lee. "I will, now go get ready for school." Says dad. "Okay, I love you dad." Says Lee. "I love you to." Says Dad. Lee walks toward the bathroom to have a shower. Dad walks toward his bedroom to pack up for the journey to finding Hazel and Luna. Dad packs a few extra clothes, shower products. He walks toward the kitchen to grab a few snacks and a few drinks. Dad walks back to his room. He bends down to reach something under his bed. Dad grabs out a case of some kind. There was a gun in it, with 50 bullets and extra packages full more of bullets. Dad grabs all the bullets and the gun. Puts it in the bag in a safe area where no one will look. "Alright I am ready to go." Says Dad. Lee gets out of the shower with a towel on his hips. Lee looks over at dad. "You are going." Says Lee. "Yeah, Lee I am brining them home. I will try to come back in three days." Says Dad. "Okay, but I am holding that against you if you don't come back in time." Says Lee. "Deal. I will be back I promise, I must do this. I will text you tonight." Says dad. "Okay that sounds like a deal. I will get going myself I am little behind on my morning schedule." Says Lee. Lee walks toward the kitchen, then he realizes what time it is he starts running up the stairs. Gets dressed so fast and makes an easy quick break then runs out the door. Running toward his bus stop. Dad locks the door but leaves the extra key so that Lee can go into the house while dad is looking for Hazel and Luna. Dad walks toward his car holding his bag. Dad puts his bag in the back seat of his car, and dad shuts the car side door of the back seat. Dad walks toward the front seat of the car. Dad opens the car door looking at his house. Dad pauses for a second then he continues starting the car up. Dad backs out of the driveway and puts his phone on the GPS stand. Dad begins to follow where Luna's location is.

"Hey Sir." Says a soldier. "Yes, what is it." Says the man. "I think someone is tracking Luna's phone." Says the soldier. The man realizes that Robert was tracking them. "Let him come." Says the man in an evil laugh. "Alright sir, whatever you want." Says the soldier. The soldier puts the phone next to the man and the soldier walks out of the room confused of why the man would not want to destroy the phone instead of literally making it so that someone can find them so easily. But then he thought of that the man was smarter than anyone. So, he might have a plan up his sleeve. "Come after me brother." As the man looking at the phone. Says in an evil laugh. With an evil grin.

"Hazel, can you hear me." Says Luna. Hazel does not respond. "Of course, you can not respond though. Cause you are in a coma. Hazel just give me a sign that you can hear me." Says Luna. As Luna says that a few seconds later a light flickers a little. "Do the light flicker again if that is a yes." The light flickers again. "Okay, Hazel I am sorry for lying to you about me being your sister, I did not want you to find out that way." Says Luna. The light flickers double the time it did before. "What does that mean Hazel?" Says Luna. Then Luna falls to the ground in a deep trance like as if Luna was in a coma to. Luna wakes up in a different area, but this area Luna is not chained in a cage. "Where am I?" Says Luna. "You are in my head." Says Hazel. "Hazel. How am I in your head." Says Luna. "I transferred your conscious in my conscious." Says Hazel. "Are you okay?" Says Luna. "Yes, I am fine actually, I feel normal. For some reason I think this is who I am really. I always felt something missing in my life." Says Hazel. "I am sorry for lying to you this entire time though about me being adopted." Says Luna. "Luna, I knew for three days now. I was just shocked." Says Hazel. "Wait how did you find out." Says Luna. "I found out when the night that you went missing for awhile and the person dropped you off at home." Says Hazel. "Oh, that night. When me and dad were talking." Says Luna. "I don't know why you guys would keep a secret like that from me and Lee. I would have been fine with it." Says Hazel. "I thought that to, but Mom and dad wanted to keep it a secret." Says Luna. "Whatever the reason was, I think it was a stupid reason. They were probably just thinking about it to much than they feared the truth, so I guess they just kept it to themselves." Says Hazel. "Yeah, that could be it to, but I don't know why?" Says Luna. "Well anyway is everyone fine at home?" Says Hazel. "I don't think so. I mean dad is the worst right now, and now he is probably really worried about me." Says Luna. "Yeah, he would be." Hazel and Luna stare at each other for a few moments. Luna runs toward Hazel to hug her. Hazel hugs Luna back. "I am so glad you are okay Hazel." Says Luna. "I am glad I have someone to talk to." Says Hazel. "This might be a bad time, but why does this man want to wake you up so bad, and why does he need me to do it." Says Luna. "He wants me to give him answers of who he is really, and I don't know who he is. But you can wake me up by using your powers that he says that you have." Says Hazel. "I don't know what I am anymore. Hazel, and how do you know what you are?" Says Luna. "I just have this feeling. I have never thought so full of who I am. I also keep seeing this woman, she is on fire. There is also a bird." Says Hazel. "A woman with a bird?" Says Luna. "I also keep seeing a queen with black feathers, and she can heal and kill with her fire that she uses to do her poison. Then the woman covered in fire can bring balance, death and life." Says Hazel.

"Hmmm, we will find out who these people are, but right now, we got to find away out." Says Luna. "I don't think there is away out of here. I feel something surrounding me, right now." Says Hazel. "I will find out what it is surrounding you." Says Luna. "I feel someone coming." Says Hazel. Hazel touches Luna. Then Luna wakes up in the room once again in her chair with her chain on her ankle. Luna saw that the man was in the room with them, once again. "Well morning. You are a light sleeper just like your mother." Says the man. "What do you want?" Says Luna. "Relax Luna. I am just here to give you food. Also, to tell you both that your dad is tracking this place. On your phone Luna." Says the man. "How do you know that?" Says Luna. "I have your phone right here." Says the man. The man shows dad's icon getting closer toward where they are, but then the man laughs. "Why are you laughing?" Says Luna. Because your dad is a fool he is coming into a trap. Your dad has always been a fool." Says the man. "You know our dad?" Says Luna. "I have a file of everyone in the world, and you will soon find out the truth about everything girls." Says the man. "What do you mean the truth?" Says Luna. "You will find out. Very soon" Says the man. "What do you mean?" Says Luna. "You will find out soon, Luna." Says the man. The man places down Luna's food in the room on the floor. The man then turns around to look toward Hazel. The man then walks toward Hazel. The man looks down at Hazel. Then the man pets Hazel's hair. The man looks at the machine that Hazel is connected to. To see if she has done anything. The man writes down some notes. Then walks away bringing the checkboard with him and walks out of the room. "Hazel, can you let me back in your dream land. I need to check on you." Says Luna. "There was no respond until there was a light flicking once, very lightly. Hazel is that a, no?" Says Luna. The light flickers bright. So, Luna just takes that as a yes. Hazel does not want to talk right now. Luna eats her food on her own.

"Lee there you are." Says Sam. "Hey Sam, What's up?" Says Lee. "I am fine, just going to go practice before the actual practice for basketball. Do you want to come and join me?" Says Sam. "Sure I just want to put some of my stuff away in my locker." Says Lee. "Okay I will come with you then." Says Sam. Sam and Lee walk down the hall. "Hey, Lee I am curious have you ever hanged out with a girl before besides your sisters?" Says Sam. "No not really." Says Lee as Lee puts his schoolbooks away. "Well, just know that you are really a kind guy. I really like you." Says Sam. Lee blushes a little bit looking inside his locker for a long while. "Is everything okay?" Says Sam. "Yeah everything is fine. I am just happy that you and I are friends." Says Lee. "Yeah, I really like having another person that understands me. A lot. Thank you for being yourself. Because every time I meet someone new, they all act not themselves, and I find out the hard way that they don't like having me around as a friend. As soon as someone starts hanging out with me, they find someone else to hang out with and I find out they were just using me to look like an interesting person for other people." Says Sam. "I don't do that I stick with the right people Sam. I really think me, and you are going to be amazing friends." Says Lee. "Yeah, I am pretty sure that is the case as well." Says Sam. Lee closes his locker. "Oh, you are done in there, sweet. Let's hit the gym to practice for a bit." Says Sam. Lee and Sam walk toward the gym together. As they walk down the hall, they notice that everyone is staring at Lee and Sam. "They must think that we are dating." Says Sam in a laugh. Sam and Lee just keep walking down the hallway toward the gym ignoring everyone staring. As they arrive the gym. Lee and Sam walk in the gym together with a basketball ball. Then Sam turns on some music in the gym. Then Sam bounces the ball toward Lee to play.

"Hello there miss." Says Officer Roswell. "Hey? What's up." says Eva. "Does a Luna White work here?" Says Officer Roswell. "Yeah, she has not been in all day. I am sort of busy doing her job right now, and sort of not in the mood to talk about it. I am sort of mad at Luna right now for not showing up for work." Says Eva. "Well Mrs....." Says Officer Roswell. "Mrs. Stone." Says Eva. "Well Luna went missing last night." Says Officer Roswell. "Oh, yeah, I did not know that. I did not picture Luna skipping jobs. She seems like a nice girl." Says Eva. "Well Mrs. Stone has she been dealing with anything that could help me with her absentness." Says Officer Roswell. "No, she looked normal. Working like everyone else." Says Eva. "Okay thank you. Also, what way did she go home, or did she take a bus?" Says Officer Roswell. "I have no idea.

All I saw that she walked in the back room to sign out then we said bye. Then she said that she would be here today to help. Then walked out that door. That was the last time I saw of Luna." Says Eva. "Okay thank you for your help." Says Officer Roswell. Officer Roswell walks out of the shop, and as walking to his car. He notices that there was a wallet on the ground, and intense tire tracks that go backwards. Then he notices that the tire tracks go to the other side of the street. Then it ends. Officer Roswell has nothing, but a wallet that belongs to Luna. Officer Roswell takes the wallet with him in his car. Drives back to the police station. Officer Roswell arrives at the police station to talk to the chief. Officer Roswell opens the front door to the police station, walking toward the chief's office. "Hey Chief." Says Officer Roswell. "Yes." Says the chief. Officer Roswell gives him Luna White's wallet to the chief. "I found a clue, that Robert White was right about his other daughter missing." Says Officer Roswell. "Alright I get the point put her up for a missing person, and we will put her on news tonight." Says Chief. "Okay I will find the sisters for you chief." Says Officer Roswell. "I will call the dad." Says Chief. The chief calls Robert White. "Hey Robert, you were right about Luna being missing. We found her wallet outside of her workplace." Says the chief. "Who is this?" Says Dad. "This is the chief. Officer Roswell said that you would want me to call." Says the Chief. "Thanks, but I am a little busy right now. Sorry." Dad hangs up the phone. Dad gets out of the car to put the gas in his car. Dad then notices that it is close to the end of the day. Dad looks on the phone map to see how far he is. He is still far from where Hazel and Luna are. Dad thinks he should stop for awhile message Lee and get some sleep and then leave in the morning. Dad pulls up maps to see the closet place to stay the night. He sees that there is a motel just 10 minutes away from where he is. Dad gets the gas out of the side of the car. Then starts the car driving toward the motel that is near where dad is. Dad parks his car in front of the building. Then dad gets out of the car. Dad walks toward the front door of the motel and sees that there is a woman behind the front desk. "Hey excuse. Mrs." Says Dad. "Yeah, what's up, would you like a room?" Says the front desk lady. "Yeah, can I just have a one bedroom for one night. I am leaving early in the morning." Says Dad. "Okay here is your key. The number is your room." Says the front desk lady. Dad takes the key from the lady at the front desk. Dad walks to the room that was given to him. Dad sees the room number off the key and walks up to it. Dad opens the door, walks in the room. Dad places his key on the nightstand. Dad grabs his phone out of his pocket to text Lee where Dad is right now. "Hey Lee. I know you are probably on the bus or doing something, but I am staying in a hotel. I left the extra keys under the carpet for the front door so you can get in and out of the house. I want you to lock up for the time being. I might be getting Hazel and Luna out of where they are in two days, I will see you later. Love you Son." Says Dad. "Oh, and eat something real, I still care about you." Says Dad. "I will eat good tonight. Is it okay if I have someone over for a night?" Says Lee. "Sure, just be responsible." Says Dad. "Thank you, dad. I love you." Says Lee. Dad sees that Lee just goes off online and assumes that Lee will be fine on his own.

Lee messages Sam. "Hey. You can come over for the night." Says Lee. "Oh sweet. Do you have a basketball court?" Says Sam. "Yeah, I do." Says Lee. "Nice, we can practice for the game." Says Sam. "Yeah that works out perfect." Says Lee. "I will be there soon." Says Sam.

Sam arrives at Lee's house parking her car in the driveway. "Hey Sam. Welcome to my house." Says Lee. "Yeah, pretty nice place." Says Sam. Lee lets Sam in his house to get some dinner ready. "So, what do you want to eat for dinner?" Says Lee. "I know a place that has the best food and best of all it will give us a good deal on decent food." Says Sam. "Oh where?" Says Lee. "Alright come with me, fine sir." Lee and Sam. Get in Sam's car. Sam drives away from the house and toward to unknown neighborhood that Lee has never seen before. And they finally arrive at the destination of where Sam was talking about. "We are here Lee. Welcome to my brothers, but he is not really my brother he just feels like a brother to me." Says Sam. "Oh sweet place. Yeah, and the best part is that we can drink beer because the owner barely cares." Says Sam in a smile. "Wow this place is something, and you drink alcohol?" Says Lee. "Yeah, who doesn't." Says Sam. "Wow I have never seen this side in any girl before. You are cool." Says Lee. "Yeah, I think so to." Says Sam. Sam and Lee walk toward a table to sit down. A boy comes walking over to Sam and Lee's table. "Hey Sam, what's up?" Says the boy. "Hey, Dale what up man." Says Sam. "Sam have you been drinking again, or something?" Says Dale. "I am fine I just got a great new friend that I am showing him this place, and I am going to want some beers. Lee will to, right Lee?!" Says Sam. Lee thinks about this deeply, and Lee nods his head for yeah. Dale walks away from Sam and Lee's table to grab their drinks. "So how is the visit to my favorite spot?!" Says Sam. "It is neat." Says Lee. Lee thinks in his head, still thinking of this girl that I never knew under the pencil or the ball. "It is neat! That is all you can say. Wow you need to come out of that house of yours more. I think this place is an amazing. Look around, it is literally a style that I dig." Says Sam. "Yeah it is a sweet place I will give it that." Says Lee. "Thank you." Says Sam in a laugh and a smile. Sam and Lee just sit there drinking their beers and chatting away about somethings that made Lee really open his eyes. Dale walks over. "Hey, guys do you want anything to eat." Says Dale. "Sure, I will have the cheeseburger, with no tomatoes, and pickles. With fries." Says Sam. "For you Lee?" Says Dale. "I will have the bacon back burger with no tomatoes, no onions, no pickles, no mustard and is that it on the burger." Says Lee. "Yeah, now there would be lettuce, ketchup, and the back bacon with some normal bacon." Says Dale. "Yep, perfect thank you, Dale." Says Lee. "No problem it will be 10-20 minutes." Says Dale. "Thank you, Dale, I so much appreciate you." Says Sam. More chatting with beers. Sam asks for more beers. Lee is still figuring out who Sam is a little bit more. Sam starts to look tired. Maybe there is something going on at home she is not telling Lee about, Lee wonders what it could be? The food comes to the table, and Sam picks up her burger and eats as though she has not seen food in a week. But Lee sips on his beer and eats his burger normally. Sam and Lee continue to chat away. Sam gets more beers to drink. "Okay Sam that is enough beers, for you sorry." Says Lee. "Why Lee don't you like drinking beer." Says Sam. "It tastes good, but you are drinking a little too much. Is there something wrong at home or at school?" Says Lee. "No. Just let me have the beer." Says Sam. Waves at Dale to come over to there table. "Yes?!" Says Dale. "Sorry if that was rude of me to wave you here, but I just want to pay for the bill, and I am taking Sam home." Says Lee. "Wait I want to stay with you for a sleep over." Says

Sam. "Sam are you sure you just don't want to go home?" Says Lee. "No, I am fine, I really like you, Lee we have so much in common that is why I wanted to hang out tonight with you." Says Sam. Lee thinks about letting Sam stay over the night at his house. Lee thinks it might be a little bit cheaper to get a taxi and to just get a ride to one house instead of two, and Lee thought that maybe Sam did not want to go home tonight for some reason. So, Lee decides to let Sam stay with Lee at his house for the night. "Okay Sam you can stay for the night. Let me just pay for the bill first before we leave here, then we can go home and get some rest." Says Lee. "Yaa I am staying with you tonight." Says Sam. Lee pays for the bill. Lee grabs his phone out of his pocket and calls for a taxi. The taxi arrives in about two minutes. Lee carries Sam to the taxi and puts her in the back seat of the car. Then Lee gets in the back as well. "Where to." Says the taxi driver. "Russell St 189". Says Lee. The taxi driver drives to Lee's house. The taxi driver arrives at Lee's place just about in 20 minutes. Lee picks up Sam, and pays the taxi driver the cash, and the taxi driver drives away in the dark. Lee carries Sam to the door. Lee opens the door with one hand. Then Lee places Sam on the couch, just letting her lay down for a bit. Then Lee walks back to the front door and locks it. Lee goes to find a blanket for Sam, places it on her sleeping body. Lee just sits on his chair that he likes to sit on, and just stares at Sam sleeping. Then Lee looks at his phone for some messages, and there was one from dad. Saying that he is staying at a motel, and that he might be available to get Hazel and Luna back in about three to two days maybe. So, Lee has the house to himself for a little longer. Lee starts to fall asleep looking at Sam. Lee thinks that Sam is peaceful when she is sleeping.

CHAPTER 5

WHO IS GRIM AND THE WINGS

Lee wakes up before Sam does. He realizes that he slept in the living room light on. Lee gets up off his favorite chair. Lee walks to the kitchen to get some water. "Lee where are you?" Says Sam. "I am just in the kitchen." Lee gets some water for Sam as well since Sam drank many more beer than Lee did. Lee walks with the water in his hand toward the living room. Lee gives the water to Sam. "Thank you. You did not have to get me a water though. But I will take it." Says Sam. Sam sips on the water, and Lee sits down on his chair. "Lee why don't you come sit next to me?" Says Sam. "Okay, I guess. If that is what you want." Says Lee. Lee gets up from his favorite chair and walks over to sit right next to Sam. Sam leads on Lee. "Did I do anything last night bad?" Says Sam. "No, you didn't do anything. We went to your favorite spot your restaurant and met Dale." Says Lee. "I don't remember that." Says Sam, she has a face as if she is hiding something. "Hey, Sam are you okay?" Says Lee. "I don't know. I don't think I am ready to tell you to." Says Sam. "What's going on? I won't get mad; Sam I am worried about you." Says Lee. "Thanks, but I think I will tell you when I am ready to." Says Sam in a face that makes Lee worry even more. "Okay I will wait, but please don't wait to long Sam." Says Lee. Lee and Sam just stare at each other for a few moments. "I think that we should get ready for school it's Thursday." Says Lee. "Yeah, do you want me to give you a ride?" Says Sam. "Sure. Oh, wait your car is at the restaurant. We will just walk to school today. I will just have a shower then we can go" Says Lee. Lee walks toward the bathroom to have a shower, listening to music. Sam just sits on the couch. Sam then picks up her phone and sees that there were messages angry messages from her dad. "WHERE

ARE YOU!" Says Sam's Dad. Sam messages back. "Hey dad, I am so sorry that I did not come home last night, but I wanted to just tell you that I am coming home tonight, and I will see you soon. I am going to school to. Oh, and I am at my new friend's house, right now." Says Sam. Dad messages back. "No, you don't get to just go to your new friend's house. When you come home tonight you are grounded. You need to tell me where you are all the time." Says Sam's Dad. "You can't talk to me like that Dad." Says Sam. Sam puts down her phone. Lee comes out of the bathroom seeing Sam looking like she is going to cry. "Sam what happened." Says Lee. "Nothing just… nothing." Says Sam. Sam looks down at the floor looking sad more than usual. "Sam are you sure you don't just want to tell me, what is going on. Maybe I can help?" Says Lee. "You can't Lee, it's something between me and my dad, that we are going to talk about it tonight. I also don't want you to worry about me I can handle what dad says to me." Says Sam. "Then why do you look so sad, Sam. I will also never stop worrying about you, you are now my friend, and I never leave my friends in the dark." Says Lee in a smile. "You are a good friend Lee, but me and my dad's issues should not be your problem." Says Sam. "Okay. Whatever makes you happy. I am going to go get some clothes. Then we can head to school." Says Lee. "Okay." Says Sam. Lee walks up the stairs to his bedroom to get some clothes for school on. Lee walks down the stairs in clothes. Sam is now dressed as well. Sam grabs all her stuff off the floor. Lee and Sam walk toward the front door of the house, and Lee grabs the house key. Lee locks the front door to the house then puts the keys in his pants. Lee and Sam begin to walk to school. Since Sam forgot her car at the restaurant last night.

Dad wakes up late. Dad looks at his alarm clock, dad basically gets up so fast. He grabs all his stuff so fast. Runs to the reception desk. Dad gives the reception desk back their keys for the room. "Thank you for letting me stay." Dad almost forgets to pay them; he gives them way more than he needed to. But before the reception could even say one word. Dad was gone running toward his car, he does not even have the time to have breakfast. Dad turns back on the tracking app to see where he must drive. Dad turns on some music and continues his journey toward Hazel and Luna.

"Good morning, Luna and Hazel. Looks like your dad started moving again toward you guys." Says the man. Luna looks at the man in angry. "What's wrong you don't want your daddy to save you or that you don't want to be here anymore. Well Luna if you wake Hazel up. I will let you and your dad go free, and you both won't lose anyone that you love. That is all up to you Luna. Do you want your dad to die?" Says the man. "No, don't hurt him please." Says Luna. "Good, good. Then wake up Hazel. Then your dad can have you back or you can go free." Says the man. "What about Hazel? Are you going to let her come home with us? If not, I will just keep her like this." Says Luna. "Well then, I will kill your dad." Says the man. "Then for sure I won't wake Hazel up ever if you kill dad." Says Luna. The man walks toward Luna. The man puts his hand on her neck just about to choke Luna and he does. The man starts choking Luna, then Luna has a vision of something.

"Grim come here son." Says Grim's father. Luna standing there in a sort of feeling like a dream like Hazel's world, but anyway Luna sees a little boy that looks like the man choking her in real life. "Grim we love you so much." The father hugs the little boy named Grim. Then a woman walks out of the house that the father and the little boy was sitting on a Porch. They were all hugging. Even the little boy. Then the vision ends.

Luna stops getting choked. When Luna comes back to reality Luna looks at the man as though she has known him for a long time. "What!? You want to do something useful for me now." Says the man. Luna looks at the man for a few more seconds, than finally says something. "Are you that little boy named Grim?" Says Luna. The man looks down at Luna as if she said something that the man has heard of. He looked scared out of his mind. "How did you do that? Shot your powers are getting powerful, now I need to get you waking your sister up before you see my future from that world." Says the man. "Who are you? You are that little boy aren't you." Says Luna. The man walks out of the room shutting the door behind him. "Hazel, we need to talk, bad. I am not kidding. I saw something about the man that we have no info on. Please let me in that weird place again. So, we can talk." Says Luna. Suddenly Luna wakes up in Hazel's world once again. "What is it that you wanted to talk about Luna?" Says Hazel. "I wanted to say that I had a vision of a boy that looks like the man that is basically keeping us here." Says Luna. "Really. What else did you see?" Says Hazel. "I saw his family in the middle of nowhere, but there was a house where they must have lived before." Says Luna. "Did you hear anything, or did they say anything?" Says Hazel. "They said my son Grim we love you." Says Luna. Hazel looks at Luna thinking so hard, then ever before Hazel has ever thought before. Hazel than looks like she has a great idea. "Luna let me touch you, and you try to image that memory that you had. Maybe I can see what you saw more." Says Hazel. "Okay, let's try it." Says Luna. Luna walks closer to Hazel touching her hand, than Luna and Hazel fall into a deep sleep in the dream land where Luna was before. Luna and Hazel watch what Luna saw earlier. A boy looks like the man in real life. Then the vision ends as soon as the family hugs each other. Hazel and Luna wake up in Hazel's dream land. "Well, that is the man." Says Hazel. "How do you know? Your eyes are closed." Says Luna. "Okay I know my eyes are closed, but I sense that, that little boy is the man that kidnapped me in the hospital." Says Hazel. "Okay, fine so the man does have a name. His name is Grim. Who names their child that?" Says Luna. "I don't know, but Luna he has said somethings way before he caught you, he has said to me that he can touch things and kill them, but when the things are dead already, he can bring them back. But now he has it under control he says, but he wants to know more about himself. He thinks I know things." Says Hazel. "So, are you saying he is the grim reaper? Cause that is basically the angel of death. The Grim reaper can bring things back, but only if he wants to." Says Luna. "Yeah, it makes some much sense now. The man is the grim reaper. The angel of death." Says Hazel. Luna and Hazel stare at each other for a moment realizing that they miss doing this kind of stuff together. Then suddenly Hazel starts screaming in pain. "Hazel what is wrong?" Says Luna. "I don't know." Says Hazel in a screaming voice. Then suddenly there was wings behind Hazel on her back. The wings were so black, as the man's hair. Then Hazel stops screaming in pain. "Hazel are you alright?" Says Luna.

"Ow that hurt." Says Hazel. "Hazel, you have wings now, like black wings. As dark as the night sky." Says Luna. "Well, I guess my powers are-"Says Hazel, before Hazel could even finish her sentence Hazel has a vision. "Hazel are you okay?" Says Luna. Luna touches Hazel's hand, and sees what Hazel sees. There was a crowned woman sitting on a throne with the same wings that Hazel just grew on her back, but then a bird flies right on the woman's arm. The woman starts petting the bird. As the bird gets petted on the head. The bird flies into the air then burst into flames then ashes fall to the ground, then suddenly the bird few seconds later the bird reforms into a baby bird. Then Luna looks that is the bird of rebirth. It was a phoenix. Then the woman picks up the bird petting it again. Then the woman says a word. "You are reborn again, my beautiful bird. You have lived for hundreds of years." says the woman. The bird flies into the air again and lights a flame on the woman. Then the woman gets up from her throne. The birds flame lights her up as if she is doing the same thing as what the bird did a couple of seconds ago. Then the woman lights up in flames to. The ashes form together, and the woman is now a little girl, but still very beautiful, also still has the black wings on her back. Then the vision ends there. Hazel is just sitting there trying to figure out what that meant to Hazel really. But of course, Luna knows what it means. Luna has done lots of research about myths and creatures that use to be real, but they all died because of the humans, but somehow the mythic creatures made it with Hazel somehow. "Hazel, I know what that vision means if you are trying to figure out what it is." Says Luna. Hazel then turns around to face Luna. Like she was waiting for Luna to tell her what it meant. "Well, what does it mean?" Says Hazel. "Well, it means that bird is the phoenix." Says Luna. "I know what bird it is, I did study with you, but I don't know what the message is saying." Hazel looks down on the ground still trying to figure out what the vision means. Then Luna looks at Hazel's wings. Luna realizes that woman must have been Hazel's past or that was her Anne sister, from the past. "Hazel, I know what it means. I think?" Says Luna. "Well, what does it mean." Says Hazel. "Okay. I think it means that was your Anne sister from the past or that could be you. Did you notice the wings are the same color?" Says Luna. Hazel looks behind her looking at the wings, then looks at Luna like she was a genius. "Now that is something that I would have never thought of. Thank you, Luna. That is helpful. But I have never had these wings before and now they are in my life. I have no idea what is going on with my life, now. I am sort of confused of who I am becoming Luna." Says Hazel. Luna stands there for a few seconds then finally says. "You are going to be fine. But I will give you one piece of advice. Pay attention to these visions that you are having because they could really help you find away to find out who you are becoming exactly." Says Luna. "Yeah, you are right. I am going to have to get you out of my head. I must think for awhile sorry." Says Hazel. "Okay, but just don't wait to long okay. I will talk to you later." Luna walks to Hazel and hugs her bye. Hazel then makes Luna get out of her head. Luna wakes up back in the room where they are being kept.

"Sir what's wrong." Says a soldier. "That Time Witch is learning fast about her powers to. To fast. My brother's kids are learning to fast about there power." Says the man. "What do they know? Now." Says the soldier. "I think Luna knows, my parents. When I was choking her, her eyes were in the back of her head, so I think she was having a vision of my past with my parents. She also said my name. I have not heard that name in years." Says the man, he looks scared out of his mind. "What was the name." Says the soldier. "I can't say the name, and if I could, I would never tell you." Says the man. "Oh. What is your name. We just call you sir all the time." Says the soldier. "Don't. Even try to get answers from me. Just let it go." Says the man. "Okay what is your story then? We are all so curious." Says the soldier. The man walks closer to the soldier whispering in the soldier's ear of the man's story. but before the man could finish his story. A sudden darkest comes out of nowhere, then there was a scream by the soldier. The soldier was screaming in death and the soldier dies at a dark figure's feet. "Hello again. Nephew. I told you not to say your name ever. Unless you want my help with figuring out who you are." Says the dark figure in an evil laugh and grin. "I don't want your help. Now go away." Says the man. "Remember you have to say my name, to dismiss me. But I must warn you, if you say your name again one more time. I am going to be staying. So don't say your name if you want me to stay away." Says the dark figure. The man then thinks for a few seconds. "You want my help don't you." Says the dark figure in an evil grin. "No, I don't." Says the man. "Then dismiss me Grim. I don't have time for your games." Says the dark figure in angry. "Why did you make me like this? I want you to make me normal again." Says the man. "I can't do that Grim, you are the decent of me. You are the next Grim reaper. That is why your parents named you that. You see Grim, your mom was my sister. So that makes me your uncle." Says the dark figure. "I don't want to be the next reaper, and you will never be my uncle." Says the man. "You see boy I am already your uncle. Now if you mind sending me that would be great. So, I can go do my job taking souls. Unless you need my help Grim. If not send me away!" Says the dark figure. "I have one more question?" Says the man. "Why do you kill when I say my name, then appear in front of me?" Says the Man. "It's about the that curse that your mom put on you and that witch use to be your friend but went to brother's side. Oh, how is Robert, by the way?" Says the dark figure. "I have not seen him, and I don't want to see him because he could have helped me fight you off." Says the man. "Oh, Grim you are just a joy aren't you." Says the dark figure. "What does that mean?" Says the man. "You don't want to talk to your own brother? Why, why are you letting him get closer to you then? Especially his children" Says the dark figure. "How do you know that I have them here?" Says the man. "If I stay long, I get info on what my clients are keeping from me. I know your secrets boy. If you want me not to know anything, SEND ME AWAY." Says the dark figure. "Fine!" Says the man. "Wait you want to know more, don't you?" Says the dark figure in an evil grin. "I have one more question to ask, why me uncle, why me. Why am I the next Reaper." Says The man. "You are the next Grim Reaper because..." the dark figure stands there for a few moments looking at his nephew. Finally, the dark figure says. "Because your mom asked me to curse you after you killed the werewolf. She wanted you to suffer like me." Says the dark figure. "Why does this werewolf keep coming back and kick my ass, the werewolf was going to hurt someone, and I killed it to defend us?" Says the man. The dark figure just floats there for a few seconds looking at his nephew. The dark figure walks over to his nephew. "Nephew Grim I want to show you something." The dark figure puts both of his hands on Grim to show why uncle skull cursed Grim like this. Grim goes into a trance.

Grim sees him when he was young. With the wolf attack. Little Grim grabs a silver knife because little Grim knew how to kill a werewolf, from studying of how to kill supernatural creatures. Little Grim defended himself with the sliver knife. But the Grim that was watching his past watched little Grim killing the wolf. Then Uncle Skull puts his hands off his nephew looking down at him. "Yeah, I know I killed a wolf, but what's the point?" Says the man. Uncle skull puts his hands back on to show Grim what it means. Grim sees mom and Grims's uncle talking to a witch that was once Grims's friend. The witch was Gretel, his mom said something. "So, are you the witch Gretel, that I have been hearing that can help me with something?" Says Grims mom. "Yes, you have heard right, but I only help once. So, this better be good or you are wasting my time." Says Gretel. Grims's mom then pulls out a knife with blood all over it. While Uncle Skull was standing there, carrying money to pay for the deal for Gretel helping with what Grims's mom was asking for help with. Gretel then looks at the knife. "So, you murdered someone?" says Gretel. "Yes, I murdered my daughter Amy, because she was using her powers to hurt people, and I think I went a little to far this time." Says Grims mom with a worried face. "So, what do you want me to do?" Says Gretel. "I want you to hide this knife I used, or can you destroy it?" Says Grims mom. "Well, I can destroy it, or I can take your memories of ever having a daughter and burn the body and no one will even know that you had a daughter." Says Gretel. "Yeah, that works. So, if they find anything I will not know her, and I won't be giving an honest answer. Thank you so much Gretel." Says Grims mom. "This is an expensive price, are you going to have enough. If you don't pay me for my work, there will be consequences to not paying me back." Says Gretel. Grims mom looks at Gretel for a few moments. "I will pay you everything you say for this job. Just please I don't want anyone else to know about this." Says Grims mom. "Okay, give me the knife." Says Gretel. Grims mom hands over the knife, but as soon as Grims mom hands over the knife it turns into ash. Grims mom just seemed to be nervous about why that knife just faded like that into thin air, but she got what she wanted. She wanted the knife is gone, that is all that matters. "Come here, let me take your memories of having your daughter Amy, I am going to take yours to Skull." Says Gretel. Grims mom walks toward Gretel. Gretel puts her hands on Grims mom's forehead, and suddenly Grims moms head starts to glow then there was a blue light coming out of Grims moms head into Gretel's head. Gretel was taking Grims mom's memories for safe keeping. Once Gretel was done taking Grims mom's memories. Gretel walked toward Uncle Skull. Gretel tried to take his memories, but it did not seem to work. Uncle Skull then said. "Gretel I am dead you can't take something that is dead." Says Uncle Skull. "Fine, but you must make a deal with me Skull." Says Gretel in an evil grin. Gretel was smiling at Uncle skull that entire time as Grims mom pays for most of her price. For the work that Gretel did for taking Grims mom's memories away and destroying the knife that killed her daughter. But then Grims mom says. "I will pay you the rest in two days, just please be patient." Says Grims mom. "I am holding that against you Cynthia, you better pay the rest in two days or someone you love will be cursed for the rest of there lives." Says Gretel. "Fine so be it, but just know this I will get the rest of my payment." Says Cynthia.

Uncle skull then gets grim out of his memories. "Uncle skull what was that?!" Says the man. "That was your mom making a deal that she made with your witch friend then Cynthia your mom failed to pay the price on time." Says Skull. "What happened? Then" Says the man. Uncle Skull puts his hands back on Grims face.

Grim then sees Cynthia, Emerald, and Gretel talking. "So where is the rest of your payment Cynthia?" Says Gretel. "Cynthia who is this?" Says Emerald. "She is Gretel the witch." Says Cynthia. "But why is she here?" Says Emerald. "Cynthia, have you got everything to complete your payment or are you going to let someone face your consequences? And have your memories back" Says Gretel. "Cynthia what did you do?" Says Emerald. Cynthia then tries to run, but then Gretel uses one of her spells to make Cynthia freeze in spot. "So, you did not get the rest then. I guess you are going to have to face my consequences." Gretel then touches Cynthia's forehead. Giving Cynthia her memories back, then the knife appeared at Cynthia's feet. Then Gretel's next thing she did. "Let's find out who Cynthia loves the most." Says Gretel. Gretel closes her eyes, then she turns to Emerald. "Pay the price Cynthia, but since I gave you the knife and your memories back to you, I will make Emerald pay for consequences of not paying me back." Says Gretel. Emerald looked scared of what Gretel was thinking, Emerald just stared at Gretel paralyzed. "No please. Curse me. She does not deserve that. I am sorry." Says Cynthia. "Too late. We had a deal Cynthia, and you accepted my terms. Now you and your sister shall pay the price, of breaking a deal with me." Says Gretel. Gretel begins to chant at Emerald. Cynthia tries to get out of Gretels grasp, but of course she could not get out of the spell. Emerald then started screaming and transforming. Into a hairy beast. "ONCE, THE FULL MOON RISES, YOU SHALL BECOME A BEAST AT NIGHT. RIP PEOPLE TO SHEREDS, COVERED IN THEIR BLOOD. YOU WILL BE STRONG AS THE WISE WOLF OF THE NIGHT, YOU WILL BE A WEREWOLF OF THE NIGHT. I CURSE THEE EMERALD. I CURSE THEE EMERALD. "Says Gretel. Gretel stops chanting. Then Emerald stopped screaming. Skull then arrives where he heard all the screams of Emerald being cursed to be a werewolf for the rest of her days. "What happened here! I heard screaming from the forest." Says Skull. When Skull made it toward them. He saw that his sister was on the ground and Cynthia frozen in spot and Gretel just standing there. Skull wanted to say something to Gretel, but then Gretel teleported away. As soon as Gretel was gone Cynthia ran to her sister and hugged her. "What happened?" Says Skull. "Leave me alone. You DID THIS TO ME. I WANT NOTHING TO DO WITH YOU." Says Emerald. Emerald gets up and runs away from Cynthia. Cynthia tries to run after her sister, but then Skull grabbed Cynthia's arm. "What are you doing?! Let go of me, I got to go after her." Says Cynthia. "No, you don't you give her space. She needs time." Says Skull. Cynthia then stopped trying to get out of Skulls grip and she stud there looking what way Emerald went. Cynthia shredded a tear down her face. Then Grim was standing back in the present where Skull was a shadow of darkness.

"Why have I never found out about this about my family." Says the man. "We never wanted to talk about this stuff ever again. We were all ashamed of what happened." Says Uncle Skull. "Wouldn't you care about what your sisters went through?" Says the man. "Yeah, I used to care, but not until they both betrayed me." Says skull. "What did they do to you?" Says the man. The dark figure floats there for a bit then tells Grim about what happened. "You see. We used to get along well. We used to love each other once as well. Us against the world. We hated our parents. Well, I did because they blamed me for there sisters' death, and it was an accident." Says Skull. "But what happened between you guys?" says Grim. "Once Emerald realized that she could make a deal with Gretel and get her to be normal again they both turned on me. They cursed me away and to be like this. When you came. Gretel made it so that if they have a boy, he will replace me to be the Grim reaper. Which is you." Says Skull. Grim stud there, looking at Skull, not saying a word." So yeah, your aunt Emerald deserved to die that day, when you killed her. I thank you for that." Says Skull. "You think I am like you. You are wrong. I had no pressure in killing my aunt Emerald, I thought she was a werewolf. End of story for that." Says Grim. "I still thank you for my revenge, my sisters were monsters. There is no such thing as normal Emerald. I am still pissed at her, for what they did to me." Says Skull. "Well there not even alive…" says Grim. "I know, but I have been dead my entire life, since I am the Grim reaper right now. I sense their souls in the lost soul's kingdom." Says Skull. "How did Emerald get to deal with Gretel, Gretel knew that Emerald was Cynthia's sister." Says Grim. "Gretel only accepted to make the deal with Emerald because, Emerald came with money, all the money that our parents had, and then she asked to be normal again. But for some reason the deal was broken because of Gretel. Gretel betrayed Emerald at the end, but the deal still went and sent me away here. In this form, but since Cynthia did not pay full last time. For there deal. Gretel decided to screw over Emerald and make Emerald normal for a couple days. Then when those days wore off. You were there and you killed her, and Gretel still had our parent's money. Emerald was dead to. Then my curse was just to get you to break my curse, but since the curse can never be truly broken. There always has to be a grim reaper in this world." Says Skull. "Wow, you guys screwed our family over." Says Grim. "No, Cynthia did. I and Emerald wanted nothing to do with magic, but Cynthia wanted to make sure that her murder was hidden from the world, but only to do that was to keep Amy alive. That was Cynthia's curse. Amy herself." Says Skull. "I will still never help you though. Even though it was never your fault. You, Cynthia, and Emerald screwed up this family." Says Grim. "Whatever you say Grim. You will always be my cure to my curse, for the rest of my life. No matter what you say or do." Says skull. "Yeah, I know, you will never help me, but you got something from Gretel. She made you this way like I am today, but you don't have it bad as me, and I think you would like to know that I can fix you. You just need to summon me one more time." Says skull. "What who messed up my life" Says the man. Skull's red eyes looks down at his nephew and sighs in fear. "I did, and once again Gretel cursed the one that I loved, and that was you. She cursed you. She banned also banned us from asking help from her ever again. Even though she only does one wish for each person in the world." Says Skull. "Well, why curse me?" Says the man. "Gretel was getting sick of us all from the same family making deals with her, and not paying her back. So, she banned everyone in our family from ever making deals with her ever again." Says the dark figure. "Uncle Skull, what if I was friends with that witch." Says the man. "Oh yeah, I knew you were friends with Gretel. She talked about you before she cursed you and my sister." Says Uncle Skull. "What did she say?" Says the man. "Well, let's just say that she was not happy with me, but she felt bad for cursing you. I think she had something like a crush on you or something." Says Uncle Skull. "Or she just trusted me. Because I was the only one who actually paid her back." Says the man. "What did you help her with or ask for?" Says uncle Skull. "Well, I asked for lots of easy shit. And you guys kept asking for hard things." Says The man. "What. You knew a little bit of her deals with us?" Says Uncle Skull. "Yeah, but not the stuff you have been telling me about." Says the man. "Well, I am glad you got along with that witch." Says uncle Skull, in an angry voice. "Well, I am sorry that she did not like you. You needed to gain her trust first and pick easy tasks for her to do." Says the man. "Whatever nephew. I must go now, but I still cared a lot about your mother. Cause she never betrayed me." Says uncle Skull. 'Well, if you are mad at me, you are the one who made me this way." Says the man. "No, I am not mad at you. I am mad at the witch who agreed to make me this way." Says the dark figure. "Why are you mad at the witch that made you this way? If you think about it. It's more likely your fault and my mom's fault?" Says the man. "First, of all you are right about that, but I can still be mad at my decisions." Says the dark figure. "I have one more question." Says the man. "What is it?" Says the dark figure. "Why did mom seem to always hate me?" Says the man. "Are you serious?! you killed her sister, and mine." Says the dark figure. "Yeah, but she never told me that I had an aunt that was cursed as a werewolf." Says the man. "Yeah, because your mother never really liked telling or remembering her mistakes, in the past." Says the dark figure. "Well, I was around when she was making deals with my friend Gretel the witch. Now I know why Gretel hated you all." Says the man. The dark figure just floats there looking down at his nephew. The dark figure looks sort angry than usual; the man's uncle was trapped in a curse that he could not hurt anyone or anything. So, the Man should be lucky that his uncle is not in his real form yet. "So, are you just going to ask more questions or are you going to send me away so I can go do my job?" Says the dark figure. The man then continues his last question. "Again, why did mom hate me so much?" Says the man. "She told me why she never loved you, but it never felt like the real answer. She made me confused. And I also wanted you to never find out why she hated you. But since she is not around anymore. Your mother was not really the nicest person to other people. I don't know why she hated you so much, but she did love you somewhere in that heart of hers. somewhere." Says uncle Skull. "Of course, but she loved Robert more the most. Robert was always the loved son." Says the man in an eye roll. "Yeah, your mother loved Robert so much for some reason, and I never knew why your mother loved Robert more than you. I wanted to find out why, but she never told me." Says uncle Skull. "Aren't moms supposed to always love their children no matter what." Says the man. "Yeah, but your mom has a gut, and she tends to follow her gut." Says Uncle Skull. Uncle Skull looks down at the floor and then looks back at his nephew, as through he knew something, but he had a right not to tell. Someone walks into the room. "Sir, we need you right now. Robert is getting close." Says a soldier. "I need to go uncle Skull." Says the man. "Okay, but before you go and dismiss me, I have to say one more thing-" Says Uncle Skull. "I dismiss you the Grim reaper from where you stand." Says the man. Then Uncle Skull disappears out of thin air. But the man, then realizes that the man dismissed his uncle fast before he could say what he was going to say. The man walks out of the room toward the camera room. As the man walks, he was thinking about why the man was so interested in what his uncle was going to say. On the other hand, he can never call his uncle ever again. He was cursed for a reason.

The man walks into the camera room. "So, what is your plan now sir?" Says a solider. "He is not showing up here. When he was sleeping, I put Luna's phone so where else I am going to talk to my little brother." Says the man. "Smooth boss smooth." Says the solider in a big sigh. The man then turns around to the solider who sighed. "Is there something wrong?" Says the man. "No there is not, I think it was a great idea." Says the solider. "Good, because I did not want to kill you, right here and now. Because I am going to need all here people." Says the man. The man then just sits there watching his brother drive closer to the location where the man wants Robert to be. To meet him later.

Lee texts Sam. "Hey, are we going to hang out for lunch." Says Lee. Sam texts back. "Sorry, but my dad picked me up early and I can't talk right. Sorry, I will talk later." Says Sam. Lee puts his phone away, more worried about Sam, and why did her dad pick her up so early to just talk to her? Lee walks down the hallway alone to his locker. Suddenly Lee feels that someone is watching him. But Lee just continues to get his lunch and go to the café to eat. Lee shuts his locker and continues to walk toward the café for lunch. There were basically no seats left for Lee to sit at, so he sits down near the stage and eat his food, then Mackenzie and Brittany walk over to where Lee was. "Lee, do you want to come sits with us over there?" Says Mackenzie. "No, I am fine, you go enjoy your lunch." Says Lee. "It's the least we can do for our friend's little brother, come sit with us. It's better than sitting on the floor near where students throw out their lunch." Says Mackenzie. "Okay fine I will come sit with you two, but I would have been fine sitting here on my own." Says Lee.

"Really the floor, you are something just like your sister Hazel." Says Mackenzie in a laugh. "What's that supposed to mean?" Says Lee. "She is always wanting to be alone or something. But she is a great friend, and whoever is related to her I am their friend or whoever is her friend I am their friend. That is pretty much how I like to be. I just like to help people find there way around." Says Mackenzie. "Okay I am hungry let's just go sit." Says Lee. Lee Mackenzie and Brittany walk to a table and sit down. Lee finally grabs his sandwich finally eating in peace.

A moments later the bell rings for lunch to be over. Lee just sits there finishing his lunch. Lee gets up to eat one more bit of his sandwich, then gets up and basically starts running toward his locker to put away his lunchbox, and grabs the next class books, and basically slams the locker door then runs to class as fast as he could. Lee arrives in class right as the bell goes. Lee grabs a sit and sits down at a desk.

An hour later the class ends and the day for classes as well. Lee walks out of the class starting to walk toward his locker, to grab all his stuff out of his locker. His home stuff to take home. Lee opens his locker, grabs his coat, homework books, and his backpack along with his laptop. Lee walks toward his bus to catch a ride to his house. Lee opens his music app, turns on some music. Then he texts Sam to make sure that she was okay, but there was no response. Lee was getting worried about Sam super bad. Lee then sits down in his seat on the bus and sits there listening to music and waiting till his stop.

Lee then gets a message from Sam. "Hey Lee, I am sorry, but I can't come to school tomorrow. I am sorry. You go to basketball practice tomorrow. The couch texted me if I was coming, but I said no of course." Says Sam. "Sam is everything okay at home, you have not texted me back in three hours." Says Lee. "Yeah, everything is fine, I am just going to stay home tomorrow that's all." Says Sam. "Sam if there is something wrong, please don't be afraid of telling me, okay. I am your friend. Friends don't leave each other in the dark." Says Lee. "Lee everything is fine. I just can't come to school tomorrow." Says Sam. "Okay. I am trusting you on that." Says Lee. Lee then puts his phone in his pocket.

As he put his phone away. The bus stops for his stop. Lee gets up from his seat and walks toward the door out of the bus. Lee walks toward home. As he walks toward his house, he thinks about what he is going to have for dinner.

"SAM get down here right now." Says Sam's dad. Sam puts her phone away in a hiding place so she can text Lee or the cops later. Sam walks out of her bedroom down the main floor. "Yeah dad, what do you want?" Says Sam. "I want you to cook dinner, clean the kitchen, and the living room." Says Sam's dad. "Okay I will get on with it then." Says Sam in a sad voice. Sam starts to make dinner in the dirty kitchen. While Sam's meat is cooking Sam cleans the kitchen, rinses out the sink, washes the spare dishes on the counter that they used yesterday, Sam grabs the broom and sweeps the floor. Then the final chore for the kitchen was throwing out the garbage for the past few nights. Sam grabs the garbage out of the bin and tosses it out in the laundry room near the back door of the house. Sam's dad walks in the kitchen. "Oh yeah can you also do the laundry tonight. We also have a guest tomorrow as well, and I am picking her up tomorrow for supper. So be on your best behaver Sam, or you will be forced off the basketball team for the year." Says Sam's dad. "Okay I will." Says Sam in a sad voice. Sam walks back into the kitchen to check on the food for dinner tonight. "Dad supper is almost ready." Says Sam. Good. "Well while you are waiting for the meat you should go throw out the garbage now, so you don't have to do it later." Says Sam's dad. "Yeah, okay." Says Sam. Sam hurries to the laundry room to get the trash into the bin outside. Sam walks out the back door to the backyard to throw out the trash in the bin. Sam walks back to the back door of the house and checks on the meat in the oven. "Dad the meat is ready pretty much." Says Sam. "Good." Says Sam's Dad. Sam's Dad gets up from his chair in the living room to the kitchen to grab some food and eat in the kitchen for supper. Sam's dad sits down in his chair to eat some food. He bites into the meat, and immediately yells at Sam. "Sam why does it taste spicy?!" Says Sam's "I put in some spice a little on top of the meat. I thought it would taste good." Says Sam. "Well clearly it does not please me at all. So, get me some meat that does not have spice on it." Says Sam's dad. Sam's dad gets up from his chair and walks back into the living room to sit on his comfy chair. Sam removes the spice from all the meat that she just cooked. "Dad I removed the spice from the meat." Says Sam. "Alright bring it here." Says Sam's dad. Sam walks in the living room with the plate in her hand toward her dad. Sam gives her dad the plate. Sam's dad takes the plate right out of her hands desperately and angrily out of Sam's hands. Sam's dad bites into the meat. "Alright go along eat some meat with the spice on it, and get your chores done tonight, and have a shower you smell." Says Sam's Dad. Sam walks toward the kitchen to eat some of the meat that Sam's dad does not like. Sam tastes the spice, and she thinks that it is good. But she thinks that it is spicy a little too much. Sam eats the meat and rises her dish. "Sam come get my dish out of the way and start the dishwasher. Also, can you mop and grab me a water and a beer." Says Sam's Dad. "Yes dad." Says Sam. Sam goes back to the kitchen to grab Sam's dad some beer and water. Sam walks back with the water and beer in her hand to give to Sam's dad. "Thank you, now go do your chores." Says Sam's dad. Sam walks back to the kitchen with her dad's plate in her hand to put in the dishwasher. Sam puts all the dishes away that can fit in the dishwasher to clean. Sam starts the dishwashers. Sam cleans the counters and the cupboards. Sam cleans the windows. Sam cleans off the table in the kitchen, and Sam mops the kitchen floor. As Sam finishes cleaning the kitchen she walks toward her dad. "Hey, can I clean the living room. Now?" Says Sam. Sam's dad looks up at her then says. "Fine. Oh, and clean your room and do the laundry. Then you are done for the day." Says Sam's dad. Sam's dad turns off the tv and walks to his room to clean up there for tomorrow. Sam cleans up the couches she puts back all the pillows back on the couches that were on the ground, and she puts the blankets that were also on the floor. Sam then picks up all the beer bottles that dad was just drinking right now. Make sure that they are empty. Cause Sam's dad does not like wasting a good beer. Sam puts all the bottles that were empty which was pretty much all of them. In the recycling bin in the backyard. Sam walks back to the living room to grab the vacuum so she could make the carpet a little nicer. Sam then cleans the windows for the living room as well. Sam walks over to her dad's chair with the vacuum and vacuum's the chair with all the crumbs on it. Turns off the vacuum and puts it back in the closet. Sam looks around to see if there was anything that she missed. There was nothing to do besides get the laundry out of the living and put it in the washing machine. Sam looks at the pile of laundry. Sam then thinks and looks down. She says in her head. This is going to take me all night. Sam picks up the pile of clothes and walks with it to the laundry room. Some of the clothes flew while she was walking toward the laundry room. So, she had to go back and get them off the floor in the living room. Before her dad saw them on the ground. Sam just picks up all the clothes in time to get to the laundry room. Her Dad yells for Sam. "Hey. Sam. I now just feel like sitting down. So can you grab all my beer bottles in my bedroom and get my laundry as well. Oh, and vacuum as well. Then you are done." Says Sam's dad. Sam walks toward her dad's bedroom, she is usual not allowed in his room, but only for chores. Sam picks up 20 more beer bottles and kicks out all the laundry on the floor from her dad's room. Sam walks back toward the kitchen to throw out all the beer bottles in the bin in the kitchen. Sam walks back to her dad's room and picks up all the clothes that were on the floor to the laundry room. Sam walks back toward the laundry room to put it in the pile of needing to be cleaned. Then starts the first batch of clothes. Then Sam sneaks up in her bedroom to get her phone out of her hiding place. Sam looks down the stairs to see her dad on his chair watching tv with another beer bottle in his hand. Sam runs back to the laundry room to continue the final chore. Laundry. Sam turns on her phone to find some music or listen to a podcast that she listens to. Sam stuffs her earbuds in her ears so loud, so she did not have to have the background noise in her podcast time. A couple minutes later she did not know that her dad was yelling for her, so her dad came in behind her to smack her in the face. "DID I SAY THAT YOU CAN HAVE YOUR PHONE OUT?" Says Sam's dad. "No, you did not. You said nothing about me being allowed to have my phone out with me while cleaning the entire house." Says Sam sarcastically. "Don't get like that or I am going to break that phone." Says Sam's Dad. "Dad please I just want to listen to my podcast while I clean. Why is it so bad if I have it with me? I am almost done all my chores." Says Sam. Sam's dad looks at her with angry. Then he smacks her again and grabs her phone and smashes it on the ground. "NO." Sam says. Sam kneels to her knees trying to put her phone back together. "Clean this up and finish the laundry and go to your room." Sam's dad walks out of the laundry room and sits back down on his chair. Sam cries kneeling at her broken phone. Then she gets up and throws it away in the garbage. Sam then finally finishes the laundry three hours later just staring at the washing machine and the dryer. She was also folding the laundry. "Sam one more thing throw out the recycling, then go to your room." Says Sam's dad. Sam walks over to the bin and walks out of the house with the bin in her arms to the backyard. Sam dumps all the beer bottles in the bin in the backyard. Sam walks back with the bin in her arms walking back inside. Since it was sort of cold outside at this hour. Sam then goes into the shower quick. When done Sam goes up to her room, but before she could even walk one step up the stairs. "Sam, can you turn off all the lights. I am going to bed." Says Sam's dad. Sam walks toward all the rooms that have the lights on and turns them all off in sadness of losing her phone from her dad. "Oh, good you turned off all the lights." Says Sam's dad. "Yeah." Says Sam in sadness. "You showered I am amusing." Says Sam's dad. "Yeah, I had a shower." Says Sam. "Good. Now GO UP TO YOUR room. Remember you are still grounded for a week." Says Sam's dad. "Wait I thought I was grounded for tomorrow and today." Says Sam. "No, you are now grounded for another week now because I caught you on your phone, while cleaning." Says Sam's dad. "That's not fair. That is going to affect me. Can I still go to basketball practice at all?" Says Sam. "NO you are grounded. You are also making your sentence longer being down here, do you want it to be three weeks. I am going to enjoy making you work around this house. I will do that. Whatever it takes for you to learn your lesson to not having your phone down here while cleaning or talking back to me." Says Sam's dad. 'Okay. I am going upstairs, but it's still not my fault that you get me to do everything around here all by myself. It sort of get's boring not listening to my podcasts and you just sitting on that damn chair all the time." Says Sam. "Okay kiddo. You just earned yourself another week of being grounded. GO TO YOUR ROOM." Says Sam's dad. "Fine. But just know I hate you." Says Sam. Sam runs up the stairs to her bedroom and slams the door behind her. Sam then crawls into bed crying so much that the entire world for her is blurry with tears in her eyes. Sam gets up from her bed and locks the door to make sure that her dad won't come in the middle of the night to hit her on purpose while sleeping. Sam then grabs her secret laptop to message Lee good night, turns on her podcast to listen to, and falls asleep underneath her blanket with her laptop on all night long.

CHAPTER 6

SAVING THE PRINCESS

Sam wakes up with her podcast on standby. Sam is terrified to go downstairs to face her dad in the eyes, but she must make breakfast, and she wants to grab a glass of water for her morning start. Sam gets out of underneath her blanket head downstairs to grab that glass of water. Sam looks down the stairs to check if her dad was at the bottom, but as she walks slowly down the stairs, to the left is her dad's bedroom. The door is shut and usually she sees her dad on the chair to the right, so Sam walks to the kitchen without encountering her dad yet. Sam gets a glass out of the dishwasher to pour some water in it. Sam hears her dad's door opening. Sam panics, so Sam just freezes in spot standing there staring where her dad is going to walk toward in her eyeshot. Her dad looks like a wreck walking toward the coffee machine. He does not say a word. Sam starts to walk away then she feels a hand on her shoulder. "Sam, where are you going." Says Sam's dad in a voice sounding as though he is going to puke. "I am going up to my room to get changed." Says Sam. "Okay." Says Sam's Dad. As Sam's dad continues to make his coffee. Sam walks up the stairs to text Lee, to tell all her teachers that she won't be coming today. Since it's Friday they won't really care, but Monday and for the rest of the week next week and for the next two weeks ahead she won't be allowed to go to school because she is grounded for three weeks. Sam closes her door to her bedroom. There is a message on her shared phone app from Lee saying. "Hey, good night. Sam I am sort of worried about you please answer me." Says Lee. There was another message. "Sam are you there? I am only worried because you said you are not allowed to text or something, and now you are not answering, and you usually do. Sam please don't do this game, ghosting." Say Lee. There was one more text from Lee. "Sam. I can't really sleep right now, it's only because I can't stop thinking about you, I just want to know if you are okay that's all. But I am going to try to get some rest for school tomorrow, but I will see you tomorrow." Says Lee with a smile emoji. Sam then looks at the message in sadness because she knows what she is going to have to say the bad news. So, Sam messages Lee back. "Hey, Lee. I am sorry for not answering you last night. Me and my dad had an argument. He got mad and threw my phone across the room, so know I am texting on my last piece of tech my laptop that I used literally all night long to listen to my podcast. But then I fell asleep underneath my blanket. I also did not know that you would be texting me at that hour. I thought you would have gone to bed by then." Says Sam. Sam was not going to be excepting a reply, but she got one from Lee. "Yeah, it's okay. I just was worried about you, and why did he throw your phone across the room? Does your dad have problems?" Says Lee. "I can't say Lee. Also did you get sleep." Says Sam. "Yeah. I pretty much fell asleep as soon as I turned on my music for the night and texted you that last message." Says Lee. "Oh good. I am glad that you got that much, but Lee please don't be worried about me please. I just want me and my dad's nonsense to be between us to." Says Sam. "Okay, but if something happens, I will be coming to you. Still your own dad throwing your phone across the room is a little worrying me. For you." Says Lee. "Lee I am fine I can handle myself. But can you do me a favor. Tell my teachers that I will not be making it today for classes again." Says Sam. "Yeah, I will. Wait why are you not coming today." Says Lee. "Lee, I can't really tell you. Sorry, but I must go now. Enjoy your day. I wish I was coming to be honest." Says Sam. "Okay, but text me if you can. Sam why don't you ask your dad if you can come to school then?" Says Lee. "Lee, I can't ask him, he is the one who said that I am not allowed to come to school today and for the next three weeks." Sam sends a sad face emoji. "Wait what!! You can't come to school for three weeks; you are going to lose the basketball team." Says Lee. "I probably will." Sam sends another sad face emoji. "Sam, do you want to keep the basketball team. You should sneak out of your house then come stay with me for awhile. I still don't know when my dad is coming back." Says Lee. "Lee, I have to go now. we will talk later. Bye." Says Sam.

"Okay, see you later…" Says Lee. Sam closes her laptop and hides it underneath her blanket. "Sam, can you come down here please." Says Sam's dad. "Coming." Says Sam. Sam walks out of her room into new clothes. Sam then walks down the stairs to see that her dad was excepting her to come down. "Sam, can you go to the store for me to pick up some beers or wine." Says Sam's dad. "Dad, I can't buy beer or wine." Says Sam. "I DON'T Care I want more. Now go and get me some and take this money." Says Sam's dad. Sam's Dad gives Sam hundred dollars in cash. Sam takes the money out of his hands. Sam walks up the stairs to get her coat and boots on. Sam walks back down the stairs out of the front door and starts walking to the closest beer store. As Sam walks to the store, she thinks about what people would be thinking that if they saw a kid go into a beer store, and watch Sam walk out of the store with the beers. I think they would be asking questions; Let's just say Sam is sort of terrified to go in. Sam arrives at the beer store. Before she goes in, she looks down at the ground then she turns around to make sure no one was following her. Sam finally goes into the store, walking in scared. Someone comes up to Sam. "Hey, how are you doing today. I am also here to help if you need it." Says the salesman. "Thanks, but I got this from here." Says Sam. "Wait are you a kid, how old are you?" Says the salesman. "I am 18, I am just here to pick up some beers for my dad." Says Sam. "Why doesn't your dad just come here himself? Cause you are not old enough to buy here. You look like you are 15." Says the salesman. "I know I am young, but I have money and I will never come back. I just need this stuff for my dad, or he is going to ground me again for another week of being forced to stay home, and I can't miss any school days anymore. So please just let me buy the beer and we can never see me here again please." Says Sam. "Okay I will tell you what. I will let you buy, but only just once. I am also going to hold that against you. I want to never see you here again unless you are a good enough age to buy on your own. Okay. Go on buy your beers and don't touch anything else." Says the salesman. "Thank you, and I won't touch anything. I know where my dad get's his beers in this store." Says Sam. Sam walks to the aisle that she walks with her dad in, and she sees the beers that he buys all the time. She grabs them and walks to the cash register. "Okay you find what you were looking for." Says the salesman. "Yeah, it was where I thought it was, thank you so much again. I am so sorry for causing you trouble." Says Sam. "It's fine, just don't let your dad push you around anymore. Cause he should know that you are not allowed here." Says the salesman. "Yeah, I would rather be at school right now…" Says Sam looking down at the floor. The man just now notices the bruise on Sam's face. "Hey what's your name?" Says the Salesman. "My name is Sam." Says Sam. "Who smacked you?" Says the salesman. Sam then notices that her scarf was falling and showing her dad's abuse to everyone. Sam then adjusts her scarf. "Sam why are you to hide the bruise?" Says the salesman. Sam then starts to grow a tear on her face. The salesman has a concerned face looking down at the troubled teenage girl that is just trying to be liked by her own father. "Sam, I know you are scared, but please if you know anyone that can help you get out of this situation with your dad I would it. Because it's bad for you to be involved in a toxic relationship with your father or anyone that is abusing, getting you to buy their beers for them, and forcing you to not be allowed to go to school that just makes anyone sick. I am sorry, but your dad does not deserve you or these beers. Beers can make anyone stupid; I just hope your dad can open his eyes in time to see that you are a great daughter. I care about my customer. Your dad is a horrible man. A father never should hit his own children." Says the salesman. Sam just stands there looking at the man. In sadness that Sam's situation is scary. The man was right Sam does not deserve to be treated like this. Sam then starts to cry a little, but she hides her tears so well that the salesman couldn't see her crying at all. "Sam if you ever need me. I am here for you." Says the salesman. Then the salesman bends down under the counter digs through his backpack and grabs some piece of paper grabs a pen off his counter. The salesman writes numbers on it and gives it to Sam. "Call me if you are in trouble." Says the salesman. But Sam just gives him the money and does not say a word or takes the phone number. Sam just continues to walk home and pretend like nothing happened. Sam could not believe that the salesman gave her beers and almost gave her his number because he saw a bruise on Sam's face.

Lee keeps looking or excepting a text message from Sam, but there was still nothing to be seen or heard from. Lee still grows worried about Sam, or how Sam's dad threw her phone across the room. He can't study or think straight right now. He only can think about Sam right now. He sends her another text. Once again Mackenzie and Lee bump into each other. "Hey again Lee." Says Mackenzie. Lee does not answer Mackenzie. Then Mackenzie notices that Lee looks full on worried than she has ever seen him before. "Lee are you okay?" Says Mackenzie. Lee just notices that Mackenzie was talking to him this entire time. "Lee are you alright?" Says Mackenzie. The speakers of the high school call down Lee to the office. Lee then stops spacing out and starts walking toward the office to see why he was called. "Hello Lee White." Says Mr. Brown. "Hey? Why was I called, did I do something wrong?" Says Lee. "No of course not. You did nothing wrong we just need info on why Sam Bows has not come to school today, and the couch is asking where Sam is. She was supposed to help with something today and her dad is not calling back. We are sort of worried about her as well, the couch was excited to do practice with her today as well." Says Mr. Brown. "Yeah, she was the one that got me wanting to join the team for the year." Says Lee. "That is nice to hear that you joined because of Sam. But anyway, do you know anything about why Sam is not at school today. She is not really the kind of girl that misses school on purpose." Says Mr. Brown. "I think she said that her dad is not-" Says Lee. Lee has huge headache as he was going to say something. As he kept trying his headache gotten worse every time. As he stopped talking the headache stopped. "Is everything okay Lee." Says Mr. Brown. "Yeah, everything is fine I was just going to say that she was not feeling good or something like that, and her dad does not feel great either that is why he is not calling back." Says Lee. "Oh, okay that changes a few things. If you do end up finding something or tell me the truth that would be great to know. You may go now." Says Mr. Brown in a concerned, but he knows that Lee is lying to the principal. But Mr. Brown felt like he was being forced to lie. Lee gets up and leaves the office and heads to his locker. He messages his dad. "Hey, dad I know you are still probably driving right now, but I am just saying. I tried to tell the truth to the principal about where Sam is and that her dad is a threat to Sam. But I had this huge headache it was like it was telling me not to tell Mr. Brown the truth. I tried to fight it, but it kept getting big of a headache and then it stopped when I stopped." Says Lee. There was a late reply from Dad. "Sorry boy I was out of Wi-Fi for a second. I am getting close to the girls, and what is going on over at the house and who is Sam?" Says Dad. "Sam is the girl that you said that I might have a crush on. Which I don't, but anyway her dad I think is abusing her." Says Lee. "Oh, that is bad. Why was there a big headache stopping you from telling the truth?" Says Dad. "I don't know dad it just happened today. I have never had this issue before." Says Lee. "Lee I am so sorry, but I am about to run into no Wi-Fi zone. I will text you later, I love you Son." Says Dad. "Okay bye, I guess." Says Lee. Lee puts his phone away in his pocket then looks through his locker fishing out his lunch bag for lunch time. Thank God Lee thinks. He is so happy that lunch has finally came. Lee walks toward the Café to sit alone again. Except there was barely in the café today. Because since it's Friday half of the school does not even bother coming in school today. So, Lee sits anywhere. He finds a sit that he likes to sit. Lee gets out his laptop puts his buds in his ears and listens to a video from village videos where he watches random videos. Lee then has an unexcepted person. "Hey. Can I sit with you?" Says a guy. "Sure?" Says Lee. "So why are sitting all the way back here. You know this is where the popular kids sit. So, on Monday I am pretty sure you will not be allowed to sit here because these popular kids are mean here." Says the guy. Lee pulls out his ear buds to talk to this boy and closes his laptop. Lee looks at the boy and sees that the boy has beautiful brown hair. He wears a leather jacket. He has one piercing in his left ear. Lee looks deep into his dark green eyes. "Yeah, I know the popular kids sit here, but are they here?" Says Lee. "Smooth, what's your name. My name is Lance." Says Lance. "My name is Lee." Says Lee. "Oh, you are the kid who is basically living by himself right now, and both sisters missing." Says Lance. "Why does everyone keep talking about my sisters?" Says Lee. "Because it's interesting nothing like that has ever happened in this city, that's all." Says Lance. "What has happened in this city? That is boring, and everyone has to talk about my sisters." Says Lee. "Nothing just fun and not even one murder, but maybe one or a few murders on the other side of the city. I lived on the other side of the city once. I did not like it over there, and then my parents got a job over on this side." Says Lance. "I am very happy that you have everything great for you." Says Lee. "Thanks, but last year my parents passed on so now I live with my grandparents. But I do still have my friends. It's just they all are now hanging out with the cool kids. The cool kids are basically stealing my friends." Says Lance. "That's not nice. You seem like a good guy to hang out with." Says Lee. "Yeah, I thought so to, but every time I talk to my friends, they don't believe me anymore so now I am here trying to make new friends that won't go into the cool kids group." Says Lance. "That makes sense. You can join my group with Sam and me if you want." Says Lee. Thanks, that means lots to me. So where is Sam Bows?" Says Lance. "Wait you know Sam?" Says Lee. "Yeah, she is my ex-girlfriend. We used to date, but her dad was a little much for me, so I broke it off. Besides Sam did not look happy with me, and I have seen you and her together. I think she likes you more than she ever liked me. But I think she still sees me as just a friend." Says Lance. "Wait you guys dated!" Says Lee. 'Yeah, for three months at least, I am pretty sure her dad did not like me either." Says Lance. "Lance why do you think Sam likes me? And why are you being nice to me?" Says Lee. "I am being nice to you because you seem like a decent guy, and I want Sam to be happy. I still care about her, but not in that way anymore. I just still care lots about her because I want to be friends again with her." Says Lance. "Thanks? I think?" Says Lee. "We are cool Lee. I just wanted to see who you are, and I think that Sam likes you because. You are nice, smart, funny, and handsome." Says Lance. "You think I am handsome? You barely know me." Says Lee. "Yeah, I do because. Look at yourself you have brown hair, blue eyes as the ocean, and you just wear casual clothes everyday. You don't wear things like I do. I am also pretty sure she does not like what I wear sometimes. I think she likes your style way more." Says Lance in a laugh, but also looks down at himself. "I think you look cool. I would not want to change myself if I looked like you, but all I can say is that I think I see Sam as a friend to me anyway." Says Lee. "Oh Lee. You don't know how I see how you look at Sam do you. You look like you are crushing hard on Sam. I get it you don't want to come out and tell anyone that you like Sam. But Lee, I think she feels something for you to. So, one of you should ask the question before its to late. Before you get in the friend zone." Says Lance. "Lance, I don't think you are right." Says Lee. "What I am always right with love. Except the time when I asked her out. I liked her, but she did not feel the same for me. But when I see you and her together, I see so much more possibly you guys surviving together longer than me. Also, Lee, what do you feel in your heart when you are around her." Says Lance. Lee pauses for a second looking at Lance as though he was right. Lee does feel something in his heart that he has never felt before in his life. "Well, what do you feel Lee?" Says Lance. "I feel butterflies." Says Lee. "Lee that is love what you are feeling. When you have the touch of the of butterflies. You feel that worry about if she is going to say no or yes. That is how you know when you have a huge crush on any girl." Says Lance. "Again, why are we talking about this, to me?" Says Lee. "I am looking out for you Lee. That is what is going on. Lee when you see Sam, I want you to try to ask her out." Says Lance. "Why?" Says Lee. "Because it's an experiment for how you struggle or that you chicken out and just move on with your life. By I mean that, you change the subject, or you walk away." Says Lance. "Lance I am not trying that." Says Lee. Before Lance could say something. The bell rings. Lee packs up his stuff and grabs his lunch bag. "Wait Lee." Says Lance. "Just think about it okay." Says Lance. Lee walks away, but as he walks away, he can't stop thinking about what Lance has said to him. Lee arrives at his locker, then starts walking toward class. "Hello everyone, If you signed up for the basketball team. Head to the gym and couch herrings will do the rest, thank you for listening and have a great rest of your day thank you." Says the speakers in classrooms and the hallways. Lee walks to the gym.

Dad keeps looking at his app to see where Luna's phone is, then dad realizes that it is just around the corner he is a little nervous, but happy that he is getting close to where Luna has been kept and possibly where Hazel is being kept as well. Dad turns the corner. He sees an abandoned building in front of him. It looks burnt, down and the perfect spot to be keeping his kids. Dad then gets out of the car. Dad then gets his weapon out of the trunk. Dad closes the trunk as he walks away from his car. He pushes the button to lock his car. Dad starts walking toward the abandoned building, he walks cautiously toward the building making sure that there were not people on top of the building, but there was no one around to watch for anyone. For warning anyone for intruders. But Dad kept going. Finally, dad arrives at the front door of the building. Dad opens the door there was just one squeak, cause the door was rusted a little bit. But dad keeps going. Dad walks into the building excepting people to be inside, but there was still no one to be seen. Robert is starting to think that someone just placed Luna's phone here to give her dad hope to finding his kids again, but before dad decided to walk out in disappointment going back home without the girls. He hears something in the back room. Dad walks toward the sound that he heard, Dad then notices that Luna's phone was making that noise. Dad walks over to pick up Luna's phone to take it with him, but then when picks it up he hears someone calling his name or yelling. "Are you here brother?" Says a voice. Then the voice gets closer and closer to dad, then the light turns on, and he sees his brother Grim. "GRIM!?" Says Dad. "Hello Brother." Says Grim. "You found your daughters phone nice work. I needed to see you." Says Grim. "What did you do to them, and where are they!" Says Robert. "Relax brother they are just another hour east from here." Says Grim. "Why do you want my children?" Says Robert. "You don't know do you?" Says Grim. Grim starts laughing at how his brother does not know. "Luna is a time witch, and your daughter Hazel is the next guardian." Says Grim. "What do you want with my kids that's so important to you?!" Says Robert. "I want your kids. To give me answers of why I am the next reaper, but I already sort know somethings, so they are basically useless to me." Says Grim. "Grim don't do anything to them please they are just kids." Says Robert. "So, Robert did you know that we have a sister, but Mom killed her cold blooded because she was powerful or something and we never meant her." Says Grim. Robert stares at his lost Brother. Robert thought that Grim was dead or banish to where Uncle skull was. But guess not. "You see brother mom is always seems to be the bad guy at the end. She is the one who made her own sister into a werewolf. To try to cover herself up with the murder of our sister, and all the blame crawled to our aunt Emerald. I hated her, she hated me to, so it was fine, but I was always jealous that she loved you more. SHE IS THE ONE THAT MADE

ME HATE MYSELF. Uncle skull cursed me this way. I can't even say my own name because it will kill a person, or it will summon Uncle skull and I am sick of him telling me that he can fix me and YOU. You walk around having a family. I tried to have a normal life, but all I got was my mom hating me, and my uncle saying that I can never say my own name." Says Grim in angry. "I am sorry Grim, But the reason why our mom does not love you anymore like she did before. It's because you killed Aunt Emerald." Says Robert. I know that. YOU THINK I DON'T know that. Uncle Skull showed me everything. He showed me that we had a sister, and my best friend was the one who cursed me." Says Grim. Grim looks at his brother Robert and walks over to him. "You know what Robert; you want to know why I am mad at you for having all the good stuff coming toward you. Because you wanted nothing to do with me and my group. I wanted you to join my group, but all you did was run away with my love. YOU stole Rose from me. I also just realized you took in Luna and Luna's parents were apart of my group as well, but then they just magically left my group because they had Luna and wanted nothing to do with the group anymore. I warned them that there was going to be consequences to their actions. Of course, they finally hit the consequences. When they went into the Maxx's store. They were fools to walk into that store excepting to buy candy for Luna and keep going to see the movie. They were full of it." Says Grim. "Wait you are the one who killed Luna's parents?!" Says Robert. "Yeah, Robert they knew things inside this circle, and I could not have the risk of two petty parents wanting to protect their child. And accidentally saying something to anyone." Says Grim. YOU Are the monster in this situation. You ruined Luna's life. Why, would you do that. Luna's parents wanted to forget everything that happened in your group, and you come back looking for them to just kill them. Grim that is not you." Says Robert. "I DON'T CARE ABOUT ANYONE ANYMORE. You took everything away from me, you had mom loving you all the time, you were the golden child. I hated you more than mom. Then started to hate you all, but then I meet Rose she was beautiful and so kind. THEN YOU CAME IN. Stole her from me." Says Grim. "Remember you wanted me to be in that group of yours. It was not my fault that Rose was there and choose me instead of you. I know I was the golden child, but I had problems to. You were the smart one." Says Robert. Grim stands there looking right at Robert in even more angry than ever before. "Robert the world does not need smart people to be happy. The world is always full of love, and mom clearly did not or ever love me. That is why I am mad at everything because everything should be love, but of course mom always showed me nothing, but unhappiness." Says Grim. Robert stands there looking at Grim for a few moments than realizes that Grim was right once again. The world is made from love. "Grim the thing that you need to learn more about the world is that you need to be accepting of yourself. If you are not accepting of yourself then people won't love you." Says Robert. "Stop it." Says Grim. Robert stands there in spot not saying anything. Grim, turns around to walk away from Robert a little bit. They both don't know what to do anymore. But stare at each other. "Grim I know you hate me, but can you tell me why you kidnapped my children." Says Robert. "I already told you. I needed answers, but of course I did not get those answers. I got them from our uncle. That is possibly the worst place to get my answers or anyone that knows uncle skull." Says Grim. You're right again about that. Grim I know that you are having issues with life right now, but I just want to take my daughter's home. I love them lots. I have left my son home alone for three days I am probably going to have to head home soon." Says Robert. "Robert. I DON'T CARE ABOUT YOUR SON. I care about what I am getting in return from getting your daughters back." Says Grim. "FINE, WHAT DO YOU WANT." Says Robert. "I WANT TO BE NORMAL; I WANT TO BE ABLE TO MY NAME AGAIN, WITHOUT SUMMONING MY UNCLE SKULL." Says Grim. "Okay, how can I help with that." Says Robert. "YOU CAN'T! Uncle is the only one who can, he said so himself." Says Grim. "Then summon him, Grim. Say your name. To summon him." Says Robert. "Robert, you are dumb. The reason why I cannot say my name is that he will be able to do anything he wanted for many years. Which was to take anyone's soul for no reason. Gretel told why she cursed him." Says Grim. "What is the reason Grim?" Says Robert. "Don't you see our uncle wants every soul to himself. He also wants me to become like him." Says Grim. "Grim. If I try to summon him would bad things happen to you or me?" Says Robert. "Sir, we need you for Hazel and Luna." Says a solider though the speakers in the building. "Who was that?" Says Robert. "A solider of mine. What do you want?!" Says Grim. "We need you to see this, what Hazel is doing right now, she is talking to Luna, I think. Because Luna is sleeping. And we think that Hazel can transfer people in her head to chat with them." Says the solider. Grim was a little pissed that this entire time he could have just went into Hazel's head. "Well brother I will see you later, oh and no I am the only one who can summon Uncle Skull." Says Grim. Grim teleports away, but before he disappeared there was a chain on Robert's ankle. "GRIM COME BACK RIGHT NOW." Says Robert. But there was nothing. Grim chained Robert for a reason. But Robert did not want to find out that reason, so he starts looking around to find something to get him out of this chain.

Grim arrives back to his base. "Well, take me to Hazel." Says Grim. "Yes sir." Says a solider. Grim and the solider walk to Luna and Hazel's area where they are being kept. The solider opens the door to where Hazel and Luna are staying.

"Hazel someone walked in the room." Says Luna. "Yeah, and I think I know who. Uncle Grim. I still can't believe dad hid that from us. That he had sibling's." Says Hazel. "Yeah, how do you think I feel. Your uncle killed my parent's." Says Luna. "Yeah, you win, that is worse than lying to me for my entire life." Says Hazel. Hazel hears a voice from the outside. "Hazel, I know you and Luna are in there talking about me. This machine that Hazel is connected to is now telling me what you guys are thinking. But of course, you can't talk to me, because you are in coma, but you can meet me if you so desire. I want to give you answers, and I am pretty sure that Luna knows her answers already so, let her out of your brain and let me in Niece." Says Grim. "Luna. Do you trust me..." Says Hazel. "Hazel don't let him in, I can touch you, that means he can touch you as well." Says Luna. "I know he can, but I have magic now. Luna I will be okay. I want to know what is going on with my family." Says Hazel. Luna stands there looking at how brave Hazel has become. "Okay I trust you Hazel, just don't be stupid." Says Luna "I won't. Now let me let you go for a few. I will bring you back I promise." Says Hazel. "Okay." Says Luna, Luna walks toward Hazel. To let herself get out of Hazel's head. Luna wakes up in the room with Grim standing above Hazel. "Alright now let me in Hazel." Says Grim. "Don't you hurt her; I will find away out of these chains. I will hunt you down, like you did to my parents." Says Luna. Grim turns around to look at Luna, then turns back toward the solider whispering in his ear. Then the solider grabs a walkie talkie out of his pocket, and Luna hears her name in that sentence. Then Luna sees that at least ten soldiers walking toward Luna. One of the soldiers, walk over to Luna and unchain her from the ground and handcuffs her wrists. The ten soldiers drag Luna out of the room in a mask as well. "Hazel let me in, or your adoptive sister dies. I know how to kill a time witch." Says Grim. The lights start to Flicker then Grim falls on the ground. Grim is now in Hazel's head. "Good Choice, niece." Says Grim. "Don't call me that." Says Hazel. "I know you are mad at lots of things right now, but I am here to tell you the truth unlike your father." Says Grim. "What do you want me to know, so you can get me to hate my own father." Says Hazel. Grim looks around in Hazel's brain, but it's like a huge library there is some many books on the ground, the ground is like clouds and when you look up it's dark and full of stars everywhere. Grim looks amazed then he looks back at his niece. He realizes how beautiful she is, then he looks at the wings like he has seen them before. "When did you get those wings?" Says Grim. Hazel takes a second to answer because she is still mad at this man, for except Hazel to answer all his questions, but if she doesn't Luna dies. "I got these wings yesterday when me and Luna were talking." Says Hazel. Grim walks closer to Hazel to see if he has seen these wings before, and he now recognises them from a book that is full of his mom's books that he took when he killed them. "Do you know something about these wings?" Says Hazel. "I think I do?" Says Grim. "I will tell you about what I know about the wings if you work with me. I can help you get out of this coma as well." Says Grim. Hazel looks at her uncle for second she is tempted to accept, but she fears the price or what he wants from Hazel. "What do you want from me?" Says Hazel. "I just want help becoming normal again, and I am sure that you can make that job easier than me summon my uncle Skull for help. I ran out of safe summoning for him. I don't want to make it possible for him to hurt anyone." Says Grim. "How do I know that you are not going to double cross me?" Says Hazel. "I will let your father and Luna go free. Without consequences, they will be allowed to go home in peace, and they will be not bothered by me." Says Grim. Hazel hesitates for a second but accepts Grim's deal. "Deal, I will help you if you do the end of your bargain." Says Hazel. "Good I will. I always do. I have something for you then." Says Grim. Grim walks up to Hazel holding out his hands toward her face. "What are you doing?" Says Hazel. "I am showing you where I have seen your wings. I don't know who had them, but I saw them in my mom's book somewhere. I ignored it because I thought those wings didn't exist until I saw them on you." Says Grim. "I want you to let my family go first." Says Hazel. Grim stands there for a few seconds looking at his niece. "Alright I will let your family go, then we shall begin." Says Grim. Hazel then let's Grim out of her head. Grim wakes up on the floor and gets up. Whispers to the solider that was still there next to his sleeping body. Then he walks out of the room with Grim.

"Hello Luna, you are free to go home with your father." Says Grim. "What did you do to Hazel. Where is she?" Says Luna. As Luna asked that question a solider opened the cell door then escorted Luna to a better teleporting spot so. Grim can get Luna back to Robert. "Where are you taking me?!" Says Luna. "I am taking you back to your father. He was close finding you guys." Says Grim. "What do you mean? He was close to finding us?" Says Luna. "Luna stops with the questions!" says Grim. Grim and Luna arrive to where Grim usually teleports around the world. Grim puts his hands on Luna shoulders. Grim's hands were so cold as if he was dead, but then Luna notices that they were somewhere else, and Luna turned around to see her adoptive father on the ground chained. Luna runs toward her dad hugging him. "Dad, you are okay." Says Luna in a grateful voice. Dad hugs back, Robert basically starts to cry. "Oh my god it's really you." Says Dad. Grim just stands there rolling his eyes, then the chain on his brother's ankle was gone. Before Grim could teleport away Robert yelled at him. "WHERE IS HAZEL!?" Says Robert. "I made a deal with her. I would let you guys go free and she would help me find another way of becoming normal again. I will see you another time Brother." Says Grim. Grim then teleports away before Robert could stop him. Robert looks down at the floor, then he just sighs and turns around to see Luna just standing there looking at dad. "Dad it's going to be okay." Says Luna. "How do you know? You don't know my brother." Says Robert. "I think we can just head home. I am tired I was sleeping on the floor for three days." Says Luna. "Okay I will drop you off, then I am coming back for Hazel. Cause Grim says that you guys were an hour east from here." Says Dad. "Fine, but just don't be stupid dad. I think it's sort of a great idea to just let this happen and then we can get Hazel. Because she is still in that coma, and I don't know what kind of deal that your brother made with Hazel, but it probably was a good deal, to let us go. So maybe we should trust Hazel that she will defend herself and be home soon." Says Luna. "But Luna you don't know who my brother is. He killed our parents, our aunt Emerald, and your parents." Says Robert. "Dad, when I was with Hazel, she gotten braver, she has wings and magical powers now. She can defend herself. She's got this and I trust her." Says Luna. Dad looks at Luna for a few moments then thinks about what Luna is saying. Luna was right. "You must trust that Hazel will be alright and come home soon. Okay Dad, I am getting hungry so. Let's head home." Says Luna. Luna grabs her adoptive dad's hand and hugs him. To make sure that everything is going to be fine. As Luna and Dad. Get in the car to start driving toward Lee's tracker. Dad gives Luna's phone back to her. "Thanks dad, for holing my phone." Says Luna in a laugh. Dad starts the car and drives toward home. "Text your brother that we are heading home now, and it will take us a couple days. Maybe just two-three days." Says Dad. Luna messages that to Lee, those exact words. Lee responds. "Wait. Luna is that you?" Says Lee. "Yeah, it's me, Dad found me." Says Luna. "Is Hazel coming home to?" Says Lee. Luna pauses for a second, before Luna could say anything. Lee texts back before Luna could ever try to text back. "She is not there is she." Says Lee, he sends a sad face emoji. "Yeah, she was basically the one that got us out of a bad situation. She made a deal with your uncle." Says Luna. "Wait I have an uncle. What did I miss?!" Says Lee. "Yeah, it's a long story." Says Luna. "Well, I am just playing basketball right now. I will see you later, I guess. Or like you said in three days. You guys better call me tonight." Says Lee. "Okay we will. I will chat with you later." Says Luna. Luna then exits where she was messaging Lee. Then all these notifications come out of nowhere. There were so many messages for her from her manager. Luna was scared to open them, but she had to see what they said. The messages were like where are you or you are so fired. For promising a lie, then Eva texted back. "Hey, you are not fired I don't know why I am texting a kidnapped girl. I am sorry, I just hope you are safe, and I will get to see you soon." Says Eva. Luna texts back. "Hey, Eva I am so sorry for not showing up, and how did you know I was kidnapped?" Says Luna. "Oh my god Luna you are okay. Thank God. We are going to need your help tomorrow is that okay? Oh, and the cops came by to see what happened to you. You were filed a missing person by your dad." Says Eva. "Oh okay. Well Eva I am so sorry, but I am days away right now. The kidnapper took me out to the other side of the country like three days away from where we live. Dad came to get me and Hazel, but I was the only that made it." Says Luna. "Oh, so your sister is passed on." Says Eva. "No, she is with the kidnapper still." Says Luna sending a sigh emoji. "Oh okay, well Luna, I just hope you will get back home safely. I must go. But have a safe trip with your dad home. I will see soon like in three days." Says Eva. "Yep, see you later." Says Luna. As she sent that message Luna saw that Eva's profile page become offline. Then Luna looks out the car window while music was turned on, while dad was driving toward home.

Sam was on her bed looking up at the celling then Sam hears a yell by her dad. "SAM GET DOWN HERE. We have guest." Says Sam's Dad. Sam gets up off from her bed, and closes her bedroom door behind her, then walks down the stairs. "This is my girlfriend Patricia, behave or your grounded for an extra month." Says Sam's dad. "Nice to meet you, Patricia." Says Sam. Patricia just looks up and down at Sam as if she was just an opinion and she was not liking the opinion. But Sam does not say anything. "Sam me and Patricia are going to sit on my favorite chair, and I want all the beers in there in two minutes. Also, can you please just start making dinner anything, but your spicy meat." Says Sam's Dad. "Okay Dad." Says Sam. Sam walks into the kitchen looking for the beers that she brought earlier. Of course, of she found them in the laundry room, she grabs the entire case and puts it right next to her dad's chair, but Dad and his girlfriend were not there, but his door was closed, and Sam swore she could something in his room. Sam walks away toward the kitchen and continues to make dinner and pretend that she did not just hear something in there. Sam looks through the fridge. Sam finds vegetables to make, then she thought of what her dad likes. Stir fry with meat, rice and vegetables. So, Sam goes through the freezer to find good meat. Sam finds chicken, so she pulls that out and puts it in the sink. Sam closes the fridge door. Sam looks for some rice, Sam grabs rice out of the cupboard. Sam puts all the ingredients on the counter. Sam turns the oven on to the right temp, fills a pot with water and boils it.

Lee calls for take out, since it was take out Friday and Lee was so excited to try take out Friday by himself. Lee is, but still thinking about what Lance said to him about how Sam has a crush on Lee and Lee has a crush on her to. But Lee calls his favorite Pizza place and orders his favorite pizza. "Hello Pizza Pizza Plaza here, what can we help you with today." Says the pizza person. "Hey, I am wanting to order a pizza for tonight." Says Lee. "Alright what kind of pizza would you like to have tonight?" Says the pizza person. "I would like to have a pepperoni cheese and bacon pizza oh and can I get cheese bread with that as well, and Pop with that as well." Says Lee. "Sure thing, do you want it delivered or is this for pick up." Says the pizza person. "Its for delivery." Says Lee. "Alright, where is your address young man." Says the pizza person. Lee continues to say his address, but as he tells where his address is he has one of those big headaches again, but the pizza man got the address. "Alright we will be there in an hour. Since your food gets 20 minutes and then we take 40 minutes to drive to your house. We will see you soon." Says the pizza person. Lee hangs up on the phone. Lee goes to get some money out of the jar for take out Friday. There is just enough for Pizza and what he ordered. Lee takes out all the money, puts it in his pocket and goes on his favorite chair. Lee sits down on his chair; Lee gets out his phone sees that there is still no message from Sam. He is still super worried about her. Then messages again. "Hey Sam, can you please get to me, so I know that you are okay. I am just worried about you." Says Lee. Lee sends the message. But no reply.

"Dad Patricia supper ready." Says Sam. Dad and Patricia walk out of her dad's room messy. Patricia's blonde hair was messy and her buttons on her shirt were undone. Sam's dad's fly was open in his jeans and her dad was not wearing his belt, like he usually was. Sam grabs plates and fills three plates for Patricia, Sam, and dad. Sam picks up all three of them and puts them down on the table where everyone is sitting, of course Patricia and Dad were sitting next to each other, and Sam's dad always got to sit across the table from them. She was not comfy with sitting next to them anyway. "Sam, can you get me and my girl here some wine that you brought us." Says Sam's dad. Sam gets up from her sit, and Sam remembers that she did not buy any wine she looks through her dad's secret wine batch, and there was just exactly one left. She was so thankful. It was also the best wine her dad loves this wine. Sam brings two whine glasses with her to the dining room. Sam places the whine glasses and the wine in front of her dad. But before she could walk away Sam's dad grabbed her hand. "Can you pour the wine for us please?" Says Sam's Dad. Sam opens the wine and grabs one glass for dad and pours it for him and places it down in front of him and picks up Patricia's wine glass pours it in the glass. Before Sam places the glass down her hand slips and the wine that she just poured in the glass went all over Patricia's skirt and shirt. "HEY! This is new!" Says Patricia. "I am so sorry." Says Sam. "Okay Sam. Me and you in the kitchen right now." Says Sam's Dad. Sam and Sam's dad walks toward the kitchen. "Sam what was that." Says Sam's Dad. "It was an accident I did not mean to do that to Patricia." Says Sam. Sam's dad smacks her on the face harder than last time. Hard enough to make her bleed and stumble to the ground. Sam starts to cry a little.

Lee feels lots of pain and sadness in his chest. Then he sees Sam on the ground crying, bleeding and her dad above her hitting her more. Then first thing Lee gets off his chair writes a note for the pizza guy and leaves the money on the note. Lee starts running like the wind toward Sam's house, but here is the thing Lee does not know where Sam lived, but something was telling him where to go.

Few moments later Lee was at Sam's house. Lee busted into her house. Lee saw Sam on the ground bruised as if she was a grape. "HEY!! STOP IT." Says Lee. Sam turns toward Lee. Sam never told where she lived. "STOP it." Says Lee. "Who are you boy?!" Says Sam's Dad. "None of your business." Says Lee. "Oh boy you came at a bad time. You should go before I change my mind to do what I had done to Sam." Says Sam's Dad. Lee walks over closer to Sam's dad. "Well, I am fully in your house, so what are you going to do about it." Says Lee. Sam's dad tries to hit Lee in the face, but Lee dodged faster than Sam's dad's fist went for his face. Lee then smacks him faster though and does not miss Sam's dad's face. Sam gets up from the floor. "Lee stop please." Says Sam. Lee turns toward Sam looking at a scared girl bleeding and crying on over. "Lee please, I am fine." Says Sam. "GET OUT OF MY HOUSE. YOU TO GIRL. I NEVER WANT TO SEE YOU AGAIN. JUST GO, GO." Says Sam's Dad. Sam and Lee walk out of the house walking toward Lee's house he knows where that is. As they walk to Lee's house Sam is just walking spaced out at this point, she is scared. "Sam are you okay." Says Lee. Sam does not answer, but she just kept walking in Lee's arms toward his house. A few streets ahead Lee and Sam arrive at Lee's house with the pizza on the porch and the money gone. Lee opens the front door of his house, picks up the pizza puts it in the kitchen. Sam is just standing out on the porch looking in at the dark night, as Lee walks out on the porch it starts to pour like cats and dogs. "Sam, do you want to come in?" Says Lee. "I guess…" Says Sam. Lee guides Sam to the chair in the living room. Lee goes to the kitchen to get some ice for Sam for her face. It's very purple. When Lee comes back in the living room to see that Sam was crying again. Lee sits next to Sam, puts the ice on her face. Sam puts her face in Lee's chest. Then Sam's arms are now around Lee's sides. Is all Lee could feel right now was Sam's pain, but Lee just hugs and keeps the ice on Sam's face. Then Lee notices that Sam fell asleep in Lee's arms. Lee gently places Sam on the pillow. Lee finds a blanket on the couch. putting the blanket on Sam to keep her warm for the night. Then Lee watches over

Sam while she sleeps. Lee does not feel like eating so, Lee climbs on the couch to lay down watching Sam peacefully safe and sleep. Sam sleeps with her bruised-up face and a little bit blood dripping on the pillow. Lee starts to fall asleep on the couch. With no blanket on.

CHAPTER 7

THE QUEEN OF PHOENIXES

Sam was in her bed at her dad's house, suddenly she hears her yelling her name. Sam walks down the stairs. Once Sam got downstairs, her dad got up from her chair and started to yell at her. Then Sam saw a woman standing behind him. She walks over to her father staring at him. For some reason when her mother standing there looking down at a crazy man yelling at her daughter, he could not see him. "Girl, I am talking to you. Did you hear me?!" says Sam's dad. "Yeah, sorry I was listening, my mind just took me." Says Sam. ***"Don't let him treat you like that. Sam"*** says Sam's mom. Sam just looked at her, not knowing what to say. "Get me a beer Sam." Says Sam's dad. Sam walks into the kitchen getting a beer for her dad. Sam did not realize that her mother was following her. ***"Sam, darling, why do you let your dad talk to you like that."*** Says Sam's mom. "He will hurt me, if I don't get him a beer." Says Sam. ***"Don't get him a beer. Don't let him treat you like that. You were always a sweet girl. You don't deserve what he does to you."*** Says Sam's mom. Sam stud there looking at. "You were not there, for me in my life." Says Sam. ***"I would have been there for you, I just died... that's all."*** Says Sam's mom. "Why did you die, you should have been there, for dad and me. Dad hurt me more than you, dying." Says Sam. Sam's mom just floated there. Sam was waiting for her to say something. But there was nothing. Sam walked into the living room, with the beer in her hand to give to her dad. Her dad was sitting down on his chair just watching TV. Sam's mom was in the room again, but this time she did not say anything. Then she suddenly was in a different time. Sam saw her as a little girl just running toward her mother. The young Sam hugged her dad and her mother. They went into the car together. They dropped her off at school, then they left. Sam, the older Sam saw what her parents did together all day. Sam then realized that this was her last day being alive. In a couple hours, Sam's mom was going to die of a car crash. After awhile her parents were shopping, getting groceries for dinner. They went back into there car, starting to drive away. As they started to drive onto the highway. Sam then saw a car that was going to hit them. "WATCH OUT! MOM WATCH OUT." Says Sam. Then bam the car slammed into Sam's mom's car. Sam ran toward the car, seeing if they were still alive. Of course, her father was still alive, Sam went to the driver's seat. Sam saw blood all over her mother's neck. "Mom, please don't leave us. Please don't leave us." Says Sam. Sam stud there by her body for a long time. Her moms body then faded, like everything else around her. Then she saw herself as the little girl again. Her dad sat down on the chair that he always sits on. He drank a beer for the first time, knowing that his wife was never going to come back. "Daddy? When is mom coming home?'" says little Sam. Sam's dad looked at her, he lifted his hand almost smacking her in the face. But Sam's dad just drank the entire beer can. As the time that Sam's dream or past kept going further through, of her dad drinking and her getting abused by her own father. Little Sam grew up as an abused kid, without her mother to save her from the abuse. Even the harsh words got to the little Sam and broke her heart. The words became into abuse, Sam would be covered up with bruises on her face and tears stained on her skin from crying herself to sleep. Every morning that went by Sam's dad would be drinking a beer in the morning. When her dad saw her, he would look at her angry and say to her. "I hate you; you made my wife die. You are not my daughter." Says Sam's dad. Sam's dad continued to drink on his chair while Sam would be trying to make her dad proud of her, but he never looked once at her ever again. Only harsh words and abuse was given to Sam for years to go by. Sam wakes up sweating and crying. Lee was up on the couch on his phone. Lee saw that Sam was up and crying. Lee put his phone down and walked to the chair, to hug Sam. "It's oaky, you are safe now." Says Lee. Sam just sits on the chair crying in Lee's arms. "Why did you never tell me that your dad hit you?" Says Lee. "I was never allowed to, and I thought it would get better and I would be able to forget about it." Says Sam. "Well, now you can forget that ever happened to you, and stay here with me." Says Lee. Sam hugs Lee, in tears. "Your face looks swollen. Do you want some ice, for your face." Says Lee. "Yeah, that would be nice, can I also get a water please." Says Sam. "You sure can. I am here for you." Says Lee. "Thanks Lee." Says Sam in a weak voice. Lee walks toward the kitchen getting water and some ice for Sam's face. Once Lee got back into the living room, with the water and the ice. Lee sat next to Sam, giving her the ice and the water. "That feel better?" Says Lee. "Yeah, thanks." Says Sam. Sam and Lee just sit there in silence looking at each other. Lee could feel, how much pain Sam was in, but she felt better for some reason. Lee suddenly then gets a message from Luna. When Lee looked back at Sam, she was sleeping, with the ice pack on her face. Lee pulled back the chair, so the ice did not fall off her face. Lee then grabbed a blanket for Sam. Lee walked out of the living room, letting Sam get more sleep. Lee grabbed his phone out of his pocket again to see what Luna was saying to him.

"Dad Lee just messaged me." Says Luna. "Okay what did he say?" Says Dad. "He said Sam is staying at the house, her dad kicked her out and was beating her anyway." Says Luna. "Well text him okay, she can stay." Says Dad. Luna messages back. "Who is Sam?" Says Luna. "I think it's Lee's new girlfriend." Says dad in a smirk. "Oh really." Says Luna in a laugh and has the same face as dad. As she says that. Luna then looks down at the car floor. "Hey, what's wrong?" Says Dad. "I just wish I could have helped Hazel get out of there." Says Luna in a sigh. Dad then looks right at Luna then looks back at the road. "Luna, I am worried to, but my brother has a good heart. He would never hurt anyone. Unless he had to. Which I don't see a reason why. Grim would hurt Hazel." Says Dad. "Yesterday you said, he said that he killed my parents and your aunt." Says Luna. "Yeah, he did. But Grim is a good brother. Not the part where he killed your parents and other stuff, but he was a good brother to me. I was not to him; I deserve what he said to me. About how he hates me, and other stuff." Says Dad in a sad voice. "If you believe that your brother won't do anything to Hazel, then I believe that nothing bad will happen then, but I still don't trust him… though" Says Luna. "I know, you don't have to trust him." Says Dad. "Now let's just listen to music for awhile." Says Dad. Dad turns up the music in the car, but Luna turns toward the car window and just stares at the trees going by.

Grim walks into Hazel's room where she is staying, but it's a different room. Hazel is attached to more machinery to watch what is going on in Hazel's head. Where Grim can talk to Hazel. They had to change Hazel out of her clothes into shorts and a crop top shirt. But she was still restrained to a flat table that just laid her straight down. Her beautiful long brown hair was underneath her back, and there were tubes scanning information out of her head into a machine that is uploading to their data base for information of that Hazel knows. That also means that she can't hide a secret from them anymore. "Hello Hazel. I am back, but this I want to chat." Says Grim. Hazel does not respond nothing happens. "Hazel, I did not just let your family go for nothing. I will go get them." Says Grim. Before anything happens Grim sits down in the chair that he likes to use when he goes into her head to talk to her. The lights start to flicker a little bit brighter than usual. Then Grim falls asleep and wakes up in Hazel's head. "Good choice." Says Grim. "You did not say you would connect me to more machinery." Says Hazel. "Well, I want to know everything about you. Those wings you have on you is the exact same as my big sister Amy. Which is your aunt." Says Grim. "Wait my dreams of that woman of phoenix's, is your sister. The queen of phoenixes." Says Hazel. "What is the queen of phoenixes?" Says Grim. "The queen of phoenixes is the protector of phoenixes themselves, and your sister has been in my head for awhile now. I have been getting visions of her, with a bird that helps her stay young." Says Hazel. "When were you getting these visions? And how" Says Grim. "I don't know. I just started getting them, when I got into this place in my head." Says Hazel. Grim stud there thinking and looking at Hazel. Hazel did not know what Grim wanted her to tell him. She knew nothing really, but all she knew was the phoenix queen was her aunt and Grims's sister, long lost sister. "What do you know of your sister?" Says Hazel. "All I know is, my mom wrote a journal about her, how she has the wings her abilities. I did not know she was a queen." Says Grim. "Well, I did not know I was visioning my aunt." Says Hazel. Hazel wanted to ask questions, but she thought too much about Grim killing his own parents and Luna's parents as well. Hazel just did not want anyone else to get hurt. "So, Hazel. If you help me find out what happened to my sister. I will think about letting you go. Sound like a deal." Says Grim. "How do I know I can trust you." Says Hazel. "Well, get started to trust me. Cause if you don't help me. I will make sure that you are here for awhile." Says Grim. "Fine, but you must answer these questions. To get me to trust you." Says Hazel. Grim rolled his eyes. "Fine I will answer your questions." Says Grim. "Good. Then we have a deal. Why did you kill Luna's parents?" says Hazel. Grim stud there looking at Hazel. "Why do you want to know that?" Says Grim. "Because Luna is my sister." Says Hazel. Grim once again rolled his eyes. "Fine, I killed her parents because her parents knew too much about my group and I could not have that. So, I had to do the hard thing, to kill them." Says Grim. "I am sure that they could have lived in this world with Luna, and they would probably not have told anyone about your group." Says Hazel. "Not safe to take a chance. So, I took the safe choice." Says Grim. "It sounds like the selfish choice. You made Luna, no, a little girl an orphan." Says Hazel. "You think I care?" says Grim. Hazel looked at him. "There is just something about you. You could make better decisions; I know that you are not as bad as a person that everyone thinks you are. You just need to open your eyes to the right path." Says Hazel. "Well, I made that decision to protect my group and my secrets. That is who I am, you are wrong about me. I am not a good person." Says Grim. "I slightly disagree with that." Says Hazel. "Well, start agreeing with that." Says Grim. Hazel sighs. "Alright next question. What happened between you and my dad?" Says Hazel. "Hazel. I did not let your family go, so you can ask a million questions. I want to start with knowing where my sister is, what the queen of phoenixes is. I don't want to find out, what I already know." Says Grim. "Well, to bad. I want to know things." Says Hazel. Grim walked up to Hazel, grabbed her neck and squeezed Hazel's neck. "I am not playing your game anymore." Says Grim. As his eyes glowed red and horns grew out of his head. Suddenly Grim let go. He started to hear his uncle laughing at him. Grim did not want to be like his uncle. Grim let go of Hazel, his eyes stopped glowing red, and his horns disappeared. Grim stud there looking at Hazel, then he walked away from her. "What are you?" says Hazel. "I don't know, that is why I want your help. Not to play games with me!" says Grim. Hazel walked over to him and touched his hand. Grim pulled away. "What are you doing now." Says Grim. "Trust me. Please." Says Hazel. Grim had no idea why he trusted Hazel, he gave her his hand, and Hazel's eyes rolled in the back of her head. Grim was confused what was happening. "I see." Says Hazel. As Hazel's eyes went back into spot. "What do you see?!" says Grim. "I see you, Grim. Pain, betrayal, jealousy, and hatred. You hated my dad and my grandmother Cynthia." Says Hazel. Grim pulled his hand away from her and looked at her deathly. "Grim. It's okay, I don't blame you. You look like you have been through a lot. Your entire life. Your right about your mother being cruel to you, but my father. I mean I never knew that I had an uncle and an aunt. But whatever you and my dad went through I am sure that you can work it out." Says Hazel. Grim wanted ignore Hazel. Once Grim looked into his eyes, he saw something that he has not seen before. He saw hope and love. Grim suddenly felt relaxed. Being around Hazel, for some reason. He felt drawn to Hazel, when Hazel looked at Grim, Grim just for some reason was relaxed. He did not know what else to say. He just looked into Hazel's eyes, like he was drawn to a comforting hug. Suddenly Grim hears his name echoing in his head. Hazel could hear it as well. "Hazel, can you let me out." Says Grim. Grim woke up in the chair in the room, with his soldiers running around in spot. "What the hell is going on?" Says Grim. "Sir, someone is breaking in." says a soldier. "Well do you know what they look like?" Says Grim. "No." says the soldier. "WHAT DO you mean NO!" Says Grim. "We can't find what entrance they are trying to get in." Says the soldier. Grim walks over to the cameras frustrated at his soldiers. Finally, he finds where the person is breaking in. Grim recognizes the person. Grim then runs to the west wing to greet his best friend at the door. "Let him in. He is a friend." Says Grim. They looked at each other, then opened the door.

Lee walks into the living room checking on Sam, making sure she was awake or sleeping. When Lee walked into the living room. Sam was awake. "You doing okay?" says Lee. Sam groans on the chair, in pain. "I am doing better than yesterday. It just hurts that's all." Says

Sam. "Let me check the bruise." Says Lee. Sam moves the ice off her face. The bruise on her face looked better, but when Lee touched her head. Sam was hot to the touch. Lee got worried right away. "What's wrong?" says Sam in a weak voice. "You have a fever." Says Lee. "I don't feel hot." Says Sam. "I am going to get a thermometer out of the kitchen." Says Lee. Lee walks out of the living going to the kitchen. Once Lee got back, he put the thermometer inside her mouth. Once it started beeping in her mouth Lee took it out and it said 150 degrees. "What does it say." Says Sam. "It says 150 degrees. This is not natural. I might have to take you to the hospital." Says Lee. "I am fine. I just want to lay down on this chair, for a while." Says Sam. Sam passed out on the chair again. Lee felt her pulse. It was slow and she was boiling. Lee picks up Sam and decides to ignore Sam and go to the hospital. As Lee walked down many streets to get to the hospital. He finally made it, in about 30 minutes. carrying Sam around town. "I need a doctor, please." Says Lee. A doctor walks up to Lee. "What is the meaning of this?" says Doctor Collins. "My friend Sam feels hot, and she has been sleeping all day." Says Lee. "Why is she bruised all over her face." Says Doctor Collins. "I did not do that. Her dad did. I got her out of that house last night." Says Lee. "Alright. I believe you kid, but I need to get her a room. Right now." Says Doctor Collins. "Yeah, for sure." Says Lee. Doctors walk over to Lee, to take Sam into a hospital room. As the doctors took Sam into a room. Lee went to go sit down in the waiting room. To his surprise. Lance was there. Lance then noticed that Lee was sitting in the waiting room. "Hey, what are you doing here?" Says Lance. "Sam has been sleeping all day and she has a fever. I started to get worried about her." Says Lee. "I see. So, you do care about her in the way I thought you guys did for each other." Says Lance. "Lance, I am just making sure that she is alright. I might have feelings for her, but her health comes first." Says Lee. "Yeah, that is what a true boyfriend would say." Says Lance. "What are you doing here?" says Lee. Lance stud there looking at the floor, then back at Lee making eye contact. "I am volunteering and visiting my brother in the hospital. He is not doing well." Says Lance. "Oh. I am sorry." Says Lee. "Thanks, but we are getting through it. It was hard when my sister died, and our parents left us, and I had to raise my siblings by myself." Says Lance. "Wow, I did not know that about you. I am sorry." Says Lee. "I don't really like talking about it a lot. My brother and sister used to ask me what our parents were doing all the time. I would lie to them. Cause they wanted to know when they were coming back." Says Lance. "Yeah. I don't know what I would do in that situation either." Says Lee. "Can we talk about something else. I don't really want to remember who my parents were." Says Lance. "Okay. Sorry." Says Lee. Lee and Lance just stare at each other. Not knowing what to say. A few minutes later. "I should probably get back to volunteering. I will talk to you and Sam later. Nice seeing you." Says Lance. "Yeah, nice seeing you to Lance." Says Lee.

Sam opens her eyes to see that she was somewhere else. The doctor sees that she was up. "Oh, good you are up. I will go get Lee then. I will be right back." Says Doctor Collins. "Wait, when did I get here." Says Sam. "You got here three hours ago." Says Doctor Collins. Sam did not say a word. Doctor Collins comes back with Lee behind her. "Oh, thank god you are alright." Says Lee. "Why did you bring me to the hospital?" says Sam. "You passed out again, your pulse was slow, and you had a fever. I thought you had a concussion or got sick or something." Says Lee. "Lee, I just don't like hospitals. It reminds me of dark times." Says Sam. "Well, I was worried about you. I hope you can forgive me, for bringing you here. I just wanted to make sure you were fine." Says Lee. "He made the right choice bringing you here. From you being beaten by your father, you got a concussion, and it somehow caused you to get a fever." Says Doctor Collins. Sam just sat there not saying a word. Sam looked at Lee. "You told them, that my dad was beating me." Says Sam. "Yeah, I did because it is the truth." Says Lee. "Can me and Lee have a moment." Says Sam. Doctor Collins looked at both them and then walked out of the room. "Why did you tell them that." Says Sam. "Sam, why are you mad at me for worrying about you. I just wanted to make sure that you were okay, is that so bad." Says Lee. Sam sighed and looked at Lee in the eye. "No, its not. I guess I am just tired and frustrated. I don't know why I am getting mad at you." Says Sam. Lee grabs a chair to place it next to Sam's hospital bed, and Lee grabs her hand and holds it tight. "I will always be here for you." Says Lee. Sam grabs hold of Lee's hand, and they just stare at each other. Lance walks past Sam's room. Lance looks inside the room from the window of the door. Then Sam noticed that Lance was looking right at them from outside of the room. Lance tried to hide from Sam's vision. But it was too late. "Lee why is Lance here?" says Sam. "He volunteers here, at the hospital." Says Lee. "You know what he did to me to break up, our relationship." Says Sam. Lee was making a curious face. "He cheated on me, with one of my best friends, and she ended up using me to get close to Lance, to steal him from me." Says Sam. Lee looked at the window, Lee got up from his chair to open the door and say to Lance to leave Sam alone. "Sam, I want to say sorry. For what I did to you." Says Lance. "There is nothing you can do about it. You and her betrayed me, as people leave my eyesight at once." Says Sam. Lance looked down, then he left the room to Sam and Lee. "Lee, if you ever see Lance again. Don't ever talk to him again. I don't want anything to do with him. At all." Says Sam. "What if he is trying to change." Says Lee. "Are you trying to get me to hate you to. HE has never tried to change once, in his life. I heard rumors that Lance has done this to other girls. He gets in a relationship with someone, then he cheats on his girlfriend with her best friend and then the best friend suddenly wants nothing to do with there friend ever again." Says Sam. "Wow. That does sound bad…" Says Lee. "Yeah, it does, doesn't it…" Says Sam. "I don't really know what else to say about that. Cause he said something to me, that made me. Like you, more than just as a friend…" Says Lee. Sam looked at Lee funny. "What do you mean?" says Sam. Lee breathes in and out heavily. "Here goes nothing…" says Lee. "What are you talking about. Lee, you are scaring me?" says Sam. Lee sits down back on his chair and holds Sam's cold hands. "Sam, I have a crush on you." Says Lee. Sam just sat there not saying a word. "You… you have a crush on me?" says Sam. "Yeah." Says Lee. Playing with his hair and all red on his cheeks. Sam looked away for a second, then back at Lee. "Hmmm…" says Sam. "Are you mad at me. I am sorry." Says Lee. "No, I am not mad at you. I just… I just don't know how to feel about that right now…" Says Sam. "I understand. Do you want me to leave?" Says Lee. Sam just stared at Lee, with no words to say to him. "Alright I will leave. I will come back in the morning." Says Lee. Lee puts the chair back and walks out of the room. Suddenly Lee felt his phone buzzing in his pocket. It was Luna calling Lee. Lee answered Luna's call. "What's up Luna." Says Lee. "Just calling to make sure that you are alive and okay." Says Luna. "Oh. Well, I am alive and stable I guess." Says Lee. "what's wrong?" Says Luna. "You just called me at a bad time. I am just tired." Says Lee. "Oh, I see. Well, we are almost close to town. We will probably be home tomorrow." Says Luna. "Okay. Good to know. Thanks, I will talk to you later then." Says Lee. "Are you going to hang up on me?" says Luna. "I mean you were just checking on me, it's not like you were checking on me for something else right?" Says Lee. "Yeah, I just wanted to make sure you were doing okay, by yourself at home." Says Luna. "Well, like I said. I am fine. I am just tired." Says Lee. "Well. Okay. I guess we will talk to you later, if we have nothing to say to each other." Says Luna. "Yeah, I will talk to you later." Says Lee. They stay on the phone for a minute then Lee, finally hangs up on the phone with Luna and continues to walk home in the dark. Being sad over Sam.

As Sam sits in the hospital bed alone. Sam feels a pain in her side, she looks down at her. There was blood coming out of her body. Sam then pushes the red button for a nurse. Then Sam passes out again. Before she completely passed out. She heard a nurse, or someone walk into the room, and yelling for help. Then Sam went down sleeping, because of blood loss.

"I thought you were dead." Says Grim. "Well, I am alive." Says Grim's demon friend. "Jack it is great to see you." Says Grim. "Well, I am glad that someone missed me." Says Jack in an eye roll. "Why what's wrong?" Says Grim. "My girlfriend was mad at me." Says Jack. "Why was Polly not happy to see you?" Says Grim. "I don't know. But I sort of don't want to talk about it." Says Jack. "Well, okay. I got to ask you a question anyway. How did you find this place and why are you here?" Says Grim. Jack looks at Grim for a few moments and finally says. "I need your help. I was lying about seeing Polly. Someone after me and my friends." Says Jack. "Really? Who." Says Grim. "I have no idea, but I think you and Gretel can help me." Says Jack. Grim pauses for a second then answers. "Jack. I have no idea where Gretel is. I have not seen her in six years." Says Grim. "Wow it's been a while then. Well since you are the only one, I can find right now. Can you please help me? Is all I know about these things. Is that they have dark wings as dark as the night sky, and no face." Says Jack. Grim gets up from the chair and searches what his friend Jack was talking about and Jack got up from the chair and walked over to Grim, looking into a book about creatures. "That is the creature that has been chasing me." Says Grim. "Well Jack you are being hunted by weeping shadow angels." Says Grim. "What are they?" Says Jack. "They are former angels from heaven, but the ones that are chasing you right now are banished. So, they are basically dead angels, and they weep for pain. Have they ever got close to you?" Says Grim. "I don't think so?" Says Jack. But Grim knew that Jack was lying too Grim. "What was the dream about? You need to tell me. Someone that you know might be in danger. You might be in danger!" Says Grim. "Why did they choose me?" Says Jack. "They choose you because you are a demon. It makes them strong and there master strong as well. With a demon's souls in their grasp, they can feed on your soul and somehow travel to this world in their full form." Says Grim. "How do you know all this Grim?" Says Jack. "Because my uncle might be the master, of these creatures that are going after you." Says Grim. "Can you tell your uncle to get his minions to stop hunting me?" Says Jack. Grim stares at Jack for a few moments. "I can't. and I won't." Says Grim. "Why not? I really need you to tell him to get his damn weeping shadow angels off my back." Says Jack. "I CAN'T summon him anymore Jack. I used my last card to say my name, and if I say it, he will be free from his curse then he will literally want to take your soul." Says Grim. "I can summon him since I am a demon." Says Jack. "You are going to summon my uncle?" Says Grim. "Yeah, I am going to do this Grim. I need place right now, cause other demon people are after me, and I have not gotten any sleep for weeks." Says Jack. "You have not changed one bit. Have you?" Says Grim. "Nope, I have not changed one bit." Says Jack. "Fine, do what you must do, but I am staying out of the room where you are summoning my uncle. Because he is going to trick me into saying my name, and I can not afford that right now." Says Grim. "Okay, Grim. Whatever you say." Says Jack. Grim leads Jack to the room that he will allow him to summon his uncle into his base. They arrive at the room. "Here is the room that you can summon my uncle, just remember. Don't be stupid.

My Uncle Skull does not like being disturbed at times like theses. I feel that he will be in the best mood tomorrow to talk to you about making a deal with you by stopping his weeping shadow angels from coming after you." Says Grim. "Thanks. I am sort of glad that you don't want to join me with talking to your uncle. Because I need the full concentration with this spell." Says Jack. "I guess we are good then. Do you need a place to sleep for the night?" Says Grim. "Yeah, that would be nice." Says Jack. "Well, follow me. Old friend." Says Grim. "Grim you are a total lifesaver." Says Jack. "No problem I will show you to your room that you can stay in for the night." Says Grim. Grim and Jack walk out of the room that Jack will use tomorrow for a summoning spell. Grim and Jack talk for awhile, while walking down the hall to Jack's room.

"Do you think she is okay?" says Lance. Sam opens her eyes, she wakes up in the same room as before, Sam feels pain in her side, but there was no more blood. "What are you doing in here?" Says Sam. "Sam it's okay. You just lived your life. If you did not push that button, you would have probably died." Says Lance. "GET OUT. I don't want to see you." Says Sam. "Sam, I am sorry what I did to you, but please I am just trying to help. Please." Says Lance. "No, you hurt me. You cheated on me. With that traitor as a friend. She used me to get close to you, and you continued dating her. GET OUT." Says Sam. Lance just stud there not knowing what to say. "Sam, I know I hurt you, and I am sorry. I should have known how to treat you better. You did not deserve that." Says Lance. Sam just sat there in tears. Sam tried to hit Lance in the face, but Lance just kept letting Sam hit him in the face. "Sam, calm down, your stitches are still healing. You need to stay still, for a couple days. Just relax." Says Lance. Sam listened to Lance only because he was right about her stitches healing. "Your lucky Lance. But I still don't want you here. Get out of my room." Says Sam. "Fine, I will. Just don't move. Lee would be sad to see you in pain tomorrow." Says Lance. Then Lance walked out of the room, leaving Sam alone in the room.

"Luna we are just stopping here for the night at a motel to have somewhere to sleep." Says Dad. "Okay sounds good. I do want to sleep in a bed for the night." Says Luna. "Yeah, me to. I had some bad sleeps lately, but anyway I will go get our room for the night, and you get our stuff and meet me in the front area where I will be getting our key." Says Dad. Dad walks toward the reception area as Luna opens the trunk of the car. Luna grabs important stuff to bring in the inside of the room that they will be staying in for the night. Luna has all dad's stuff and then she picks up her stuff that she would possibly use for the night. Before Luna closed the trunk door, she remembers that she wanted or promised Lee that we would call him tonight, so Luna grabs a tablet out of her bag in the trunk. Luna closes the trunk door and heads to the front reception area. Luna arrives to the reception centre to find that her dad was just waiting for her on a chair a comfy chair. "Dad I got everything for the night." Says Luna. "Good, I got the keys." Says Dad. Luna and Dad walk toward the room key number. Dad opens the room door for Luna so she can place down the bags. "So, dad. Do you think you are going to have enough energy to call Lee tonight?" Says Luna. "Yeah, we can call him in a few moments. I just want to get changed into PJ's first." Says Dad. "While you do that, I am going to have a shower, then we can call Lee." Says Luna. Luna walks toward the bathroom turning on the shower. Dad gets changed into his PJ's and crawls into his bed that he is sleeping for the night. "Okay dad. You ready to call Lee?" Says Luna. "Yeah. Let's call." Says Dad. Luna walks over to her bag that she put the tablet in. She goes into message life and call Lee from there. Lee answers the phone. "Hey, why are you calling me?" Says Lee. "We said we were going to call you tonight remember." Says Luna. Oh, right sorry. I forgot that you wanted to call me later..." Says Lee. "Wow Lee. You must be tired." Says Luna. "Yeah, it's been a long day..." says Lee. "What's wrong boy?" Says Dad. "Nothing dad. I am just in a situation..." says Lee. "What kind of situation?" says dad. Lee just looks at Luna and dad. "Son we are almost home. If you don't want to chat right now that is fine." Says dad. "I am sorry. I think, I will just talk to you later." Says Lee. "That's okay son. Have a good night. We will see you soon." Says Dad. Lee hangs up the phone. Dad sighs. "What's wrong dad?" says Luna. "I wish your mom was there with him, so he was not alone at my house, dealing with whatever he is going through." Says Dad. "Well, we will be there soon." Says Luna. "Yeah, we will... Let's head to bed." Says Dad. "Night Dad." Says Luna. Dad turns off the lights in the room. But Luna struggles to fall asleep. When dad was out like a light. Luna tries to close her eyes, and finally falls asleep. "Luna. We need to talk." Says The time witch. "Wait it's you again." Says Luna. "Yep, it's me. We need to chat about the future again, but this time you can not tell anyone about this at all." Says the time witch. "What is it? That I must keep a secret from everyone. What else am I supposed to do. I let Hazel get captured. You did not warn me of that happening." Says Luna. "I could not warn you because that would be ruining the future for you and me. And yes, you must keep this to yourself, or you will be ruining everyone even worse than everyone is right now." says the time witch. "Okay what is it!" Says Luna. "Your father has a sister, she is dangerous, but she does not come till a long time. But the real threat right now is Skull the most powerful grim reaper of all." Says the time witch. "Who is skull?" Says Luna. "He is Grim and your father's uncle. He was banished to a realm that he can not leave unless Grim says his name one more time. Grim is being smart right now, but he can't hold it any longer." Says the time witch. "What can he not hold any longer, saying Grim?" Says Luna. "Yeah, Grim was cursed to never say his name ever. If Grim says his name one more time. This world that you are living on will be hell for everyone. Skull has done some awful things, to get what he deserved in the end." Says the time witch. "So, what do you want me to do about that?" Says Luna. "Just make sure that Grim does not say that name or just try to contact Hazel to warn her about it, but don't tell her anything about me, or the future." Says the time witch. "I can't contact Hazel she is all the way where Grim is." Says Luna. "Luna you are a time witch, you can contact anyone around the world. just need do what I am doing right now." Says the time witch. "Wait you are contacting me in my dream right now. are you even real?" Says Luna. "Yeah, I very much real Luna. I am just in a different dimension right now." Says the time witch. "What is your name or is your name just the time witch that comes in my dreams?" Says Luna. "My name is Ruby, but Luna, I need you to do this task please. All the time witches are grateful that you are helping all of us." Says Ruby. "There is more of you?" Says Luna. "Yeah, the time witches spend out in the entire universe to watch over everyone. Luna, I need you to do this for all of us. Including you. You are a time witch now to.

We protect the past, present, and the future. We make sure everything is the way it must be, but also the way it should be it has to be this way for everyone. We don't like working this way, but it protects time and our loved ones. I believe that you can be one of the best time witches out there." Says Ruby. "Thanks Ruby, but I don't know if I could ever be a time witch because I tell the truth all the time and that I don't like lying to my family about stuff like this." Says Luna. "I know you hate it, but Luna it is so worth it. You will be saving others from danger." Says Ruby. "Okay. I will try to finish this task easy and gently." Says Luna. "Okay. I have much faith in you Luna. I think you are going to be the best time witch that most of us will probably live, but Luna I must go now. I have other time witches to contact." Says Ruby. "Okay see you around. Wait- never mind" says Luna. Ruby disappears out of nowhere, and Luna is now in her own dream land dreaming about what Rubies task is for Luna. Luna feels so much pressure on her for doing a big part for the world. But Luna also feels confident in herself. If this mysterious lady that calls herself the time witch known as Ruby. Believes in Luna then Luna will try to believe in herself as well for this task.

CHAPTER **8**

THE PAST OF REBIRTH

A seventeen-year-old girl was on a hospital bed. A nurse came in with a doctor to help the seventeen-year-old-girl give birth to her child. "Okay, Mrs. Thorn you are going to need to push out that child right now, I am here to help you just do that okay." Says the doctor. "Okay." Says the seventeen-year-old-girl. "Okay we are ready for you to push." Says the doctor. The seventeen-year-old-girl listened to the doctor and started pushing out the baby. "Okay one more push." Says the doctor. The seventeen-year-old-girl screamed out the baby into the doctor's arms. "It's a girl Mrs. Thorn." Says the doctor. The seventeen-year-old-girl looks over at her child. As they are cleaning her off and making sure the baby is healthy. As they were getting a towel for the seventeen-year-olds child. They saw that there was an interesting birthmark on the child's arm. It almost looked like a bird mark, rising their wings in the air, but they just gave the child to the seventeen-year-old-girl wrapped in a towel. The seventeen-year-old-girl held her child and looked at her, as if they were the only people in the world. The doctor walks over to Mrs. Thorn. "Hey, I am sorry to interrupt, but do you know what your child's name is?" Says the doctor. "Her name is Amy Amber Thorn." Says the seven-year-old-girl. "That is a beautiful name." Says the doctor in a happy smile. As the doctor walked away, the seventeen-year-old-girl looks back down at her baby child Amy. All her troubles were gone for a couple hours, until the hospital called her parents. The seventeen-year-old-girls parents walk into the room. "Who is the father, Cynthia!? And why did you not come home at all to get help." Says Cynthia's "mom. Because you both would have judged me, and I am not telling you who the father is." Says Cynthia. "YOU BETTER TELL US WHO THE

FATHER IS!! NOW." Says Cynthia's Father. "I am the father." As a young boy walks into the room and the same age as Cynthia. "Who are you?" Says Cynthia's mom. "I am Troy." Says Troy. Cynthia just looks at Troy, his looks really made Cynthia feel special. Because Cynthia always thought she was just a bookworm and not beautiful, but Troy made her feel special and beautiful. As Cynthia looks at Troy's beautiful black dark hair, then Troy walks over to Cynthia. "Hey Cynthia, can I hold our child?" Says Troy. Cynthia gives Troy Amy Amber Thorn to her father. Amy grabs hold of Troy's finger and opens her eyes to see her father looking down at her. "She is beautiful just like her mother, what's her name? Cynthia." Says Troy. "Her name is Amy Amber Thorn." Says Cynthia. "Wait, you put my mom's name in there?!" Says Troy. "Yeah, I did. I thought it would be a beautiful middle name with Amy." Says Cynthia. Troy grabs a chair, while holding the baby in one hand, Cynthia was worried that Troy would drop her, but he never did. Troy sits down on the chair he picked up. "Well Cynthia, we are here to tell you that. Me and your father are moving away far away." Says Cynthia's mom. "Wait why are you moving away?" Says Cynthia. "Don't you see Cynthia. We did not want you to have a child when you were seventeen years old, so we are moving away from you, and we never want to see you again." Says Cynthia's mom. Cynthia's parents then walk out of the room, as they did Troy gave Amy to Cynthia and ran after her parents. But before Troy could even say one word Cynthia stopped him from getting up. "Don't it's not worth it. They were bad parents anyway, but I am going to make sure I am the best. I am going to show my parents that I am not a mistake, or it was a bad idea having a child at seventeen. Even though I did not want children till I was thirty, but when I looked in Amy's eyes. I could never let her go. She is just so beautiful." Says Cynthia. "I agree, Amy is a beautiful child, but you got one thing wrong in the that sentence." Says Troy. "What?" Says Cynthia. "You are not a mistake you are the best thing that happened to me, and you are beautiful just like Amy." Says Troy. Cynthia hugs Troy for that. Troy and Cynthia then hold their child in their arms. Cherishing these moments with Amy. Amy touched Troy and Cynthia's heart at the same time. There bound was never to be broken, they were the cutest family that anyone has seen in a very long time. The next day,

Cynthia and Troy go to there houses. When Cynthia goes to her house. No one was there, her parents left her stuff in her room, and they left a letter saying "We put the house up for sale. So, if you want to move in with Troy, that is fine, but we still don't want to see the child again or you or Troy. Bye forever Cynthia". Cynthia looks down at the letter it was her mom's writing she could recognize her writing. Then Cynthia picked up the letter, then threw it in the fire out of angry while she was holding Amy in her arms. Cynthia then walks to her room, places Amy in a safe spot where Cynthia could still see Amy. As Cynthia started packing her most prized possessions and her clothes. As Cynthia was done pretty much packing up her clothes and her stuff. She saw something she could not believe. Amy was holding fire in her hand, and she was playing with it to, and the birthmark that Amy had on her arm was glowing. Cynthia grabbed all her stuff, put it outside so fast. She then called Troy to come to her house to help get her stuff in the car. Then Cynthia runs back in the house still seeing fire on Amy's hands. She was laughing, but then she dropped some fire on the wooden floor. Before the fire could start completely burning the house down. Cynthia grabs Amy off the chair and runs out of the house. Cynthia and Amy got out of the house just right on time. Then Troy's car comes in from the left side. Troy runs out of the car asking what happened. "Why is your house on fire?" Says Troy. "Let's just go I will talk to you later about why. We must go fast. Maybe this is a sign that we can move on with Amy, our child together." Troy looks at Cynthia for a moment. "Okay, let's get your boxes in the car." Says Troy. As Troy and Cynthia put all her belongings in Troy's car. Cynthia and Troy get in the car and start driving away so fast as the house stopped burning down. Cynthia turns around to see her house one last time, it was black as ash. Cynthia had closure in her heart that the house she was raised in. Was burned down she was happy a little that she was moving in a place with Troy and her child was just on her lap just sleeping like as if nothing happened. Troy turns on some quiet music. The quiet music was then helping Cynthia get some sleep as well. Troy then looks over at his new family, and he smiles at how both were sleeping.

A couple hours later Troy found a rest stop and stopped for the night in a motel. Troy wakes up Cynthia gently because Amy was still sleeping on Cynthia. "Hey Cynthia." Says Troy in a quiet voice. Cynthia then wakes up to see that it was dark out and Amy still sleeping on her lap. Then Cynthia sees that Troy found a place to stay the night. "Good idea, you need rest to." Says Cynthia in a quiet a voice. Troy get's out of the car, to walk to the front door to the reception to get a room for the night. Amy was still sleeping like an angel. Cynthia opens the car door quietly to keep Amy from waking up, but it was hard to not wake her up. She was a heavy sleeper apparently. Cynthia carries around Amy to the door where Troy went toward, and Cynthia walked in the building. As Cynthia walked up to see if Troy got a room for the night, he was having trouble with his money. Cynthia then walks up to the front desk to give the key holder extra money. Then the key holder gives them a key to there room. Cynthia and Troy walk to the room that was given to them for the night. Cynthia places Amy down in a basket that Cynthia brought in so Amy can sleep in her own space. Troy then goes into the bathroom to wash his face. Cynthia is basically just crawling into bed at this point to. Troy crawls into the same bed as Cynthia. Before Troy could even say good night to Cynthia she was sleeping like a dead person. Then Troy closes his eyes and get some shut eye to.

"Cynthia." Says the Time Witch. "Who are you?" Says Cynthia in a soft tired voice. "I am Ruby the Time Witch. I am in your dream tonight to warn you to be carefully of your Amy, yes, your little girl. Be careful." Says the Time Witch. "Why are you telling me to be careful about a little harmless girl? She was just born yesterday." Says Cynthia. "Cynthia your little girl burned your childhood house down." Says the Time Witch. "Well, I can handle her, she is my daughter. Don't ever come back here to just tell me that my little girl will do harm." Says Cynthia. "Alright, but you are right she won't do harm in these ages, but she will learn more about herself as she grows up to know who she is." Says the Time Witch. The Time Witch then vanishes out of nowhere, then there was nothing, but darkness in Cynthia's head.

"Hey Cynthia wake up. I think we should get back on the road again." Says Troy. Cynthia flips over to see Troy holding his daughter in his hands. Cynthia was very happy to be waking up like this, this was going to be every morning and she is loving it so far. Cynthia gets out of bed getting dressed. Troy was already dressed and packed for the rest of the journey to finding a place to call home for now on. Troy and Cynthia always wanted to run away together and now they are. They are getting the first part of there running away together starting today. Troy and Cynthia always dreamed of living away from people in the middle of the forest so, Cynthia and Troy went toward the nicest forest in their favorite country all the way back in BC. It was perfect for a new start, and that area barely had anyone around, is all they could see was mountains and trees everywhere they looked. So, Troy started driving toward BC, Troy and Cynthia knew it would at least take a week to get there or more, but they were willing to make a new start. So, they went for BC.

CHAPTER **9**

NEW BEGINNING

"Cynthia look. We are finally here in BC. It took us awhile, but we are finally here. Let's drive in the forest a little deeper more into there. I want to make sure that we will be far from everyone like we always talked about I will make this happen for us Cynthia." Says Troy with the biggest smile on his face. Troy continues driving down the path till the end of it, it took at least an hour before we finally hit the edge of the perfect spot in the forest. Troy wanted to have the most beautiful view in the forest, finally he found that. What exactly he found was a waterfall in the distance flowing off a mountain, and underneath the edge where he stopped, when he got out of the car to see what he was working with, at the edge of the mountain that they were on there was hundreds of trees in the distance. Looking down that is all he could see was trees and that beautiful waterfall. Then Troy runs to the back of the car and brings out some stuff out of the trunk. Troy gets out of the bag that he grabbed was the tent he, Cynthia and Amy would use for awhile for there house or shelter for a couple days or possibly longer. Or if the rain was bad, they would sleep in the car for a night, it depends. But everyday for such a long time for months. Troy would go to the closest town to buy wood and supplies for a couple nights. Then finally the cabin that they always wanted was done, they were done staying in their tent or their car for nights and days. It was a real challenge to build a nice simple cabin that was right off the edge of the mountain, and he finally finished it. But now since they spent lots of money building their cabin, they needed more money to feed them and Amy. So, Cynthia went to go find a job in the town were. Troy always went to go get their wood and food supply. Luckily there was one job that really caught Cynthia's attention. She worked at a restaurant called Snowy cabin. She wanted to work there because it remined her that Troy built a cabin in the snowy weather and the rainy weather. So, she wants to always remember that her boyfriend never stopped working in the cold weathers or bad weathers. Cynthia never knew that Troy was that much of a hard worker, but now that Troy knows that he can build that kind of stuff he went for a job that he can build for other people. He did earn more than Cynthia, but Cynthia just wanted an easy job. Cynthia took time before working lots like Troy. Troy worked way more than she did with building stuff. He was getting paid 20$ an hour, Cynthia would just get calls in if it was busy, but Cynthia would still bring Amy with her to work because she did not have a babysitter, but then one day someone went up to Cynthia and asked if she wanted a babysitter so that Cynthia could work more and not have to bring her daughter Amy to work every time. Cynthia showed the girl where Cynthia lived. The babysitter was surprised to hear Cynthia's story. They lived right off the edge of the cliff. Cynthia opened their house door; it was very beautiful. As the babysitter walked into Cynthia's and Troy's house you could see a nice area that you put up your coat and shoes in a closet area. Then the first thing you see as you walk forward, an open kitchen connected in the living room with a fireplace, and nicely done stairs to the second floor and finally the biggest pain for Troy when building this house, it was the most open window of all you could see the water in the distance and the trees that Troy saw the first day that he ever built this place. "This place is beautiful who built this place?" Says the babysitter in an excited and surprised voice. "My boyfriend built this place. His name is Troy Thorn. I so agree with you on how this place is beautiful I swear Troy built this place out of love, patience, family, and beauty. I have no idea though what or how he was building this place out of? I have no idea. You could probably ask him he is coming home soon, anyway." Says Cynthia. Cynthia and the babysitter walk toward Amy's bedroom, Cynthia places Amy down in her crib. "So, this is her room as you can see. It is messy in here. I just want to put Amy down for her sleep time and I will show you the rest of our home, so you know where everything is, so you don't have to look around for where everything is." Says Cynthia. "Okay I will just be in the living room then." Says the babysitter.

The babysitter walks out of Amy's room into the living room, as Cynthia puts Amy to bed, Amy starts talking. "Mama." Says Amy. Cynthia could not believe it. Amy is talking and saying Mama. Cynthia kissed Amy on the forehead. Sang her lullaby to get Amy to close her eyes. Finally, Amy was sleeping in her crib that her dad made as well. Troy pretty much made everything in this house. As Cynthia walks back Troy was walking in the house. "Hey Cynthia." Says Troy. "Hey Honey." Says Cynthia in a smile. Cynthia walks over to her boyfriend and kisses him on the lips and gives him a warm hug. "What's with all the love honey?" Says Troy. "Oh, nothing you are just going to be happy even more." Says Cynthia. What, is it Cynthia, is it Chinese food?" Says Troy. "No, I was thinking about getting that tomorrow though. But there is someone in the living room that is happy to be wanting to babysit Amy to help us both." Says Cynthia. "Cynthia, you know that we are going to have to pay for there services, right?" Says Troy. "I know I got enough money to pay her for a bit." Says Cynthia. "Okay. I will help pay to, but I will probably forget so if I must pay in a little bit just remind me. Where did you find this babysitter?" Says Troy. "At work. I am mostly excited for this babysitter because I don't really feel comfy with bringing Amy everywhere I go. I don't mind bringing her with me to the store, but my job. I don't think my boss likes it when I bring my kid to work everyday. I am pretty sure he has been talking about me. About bringing my Amy everywhere in town. I feel like there is eyes all over me in town." Says Cynthia. "Well, you are not wrong. I have been hearing about this woman bringing her baby to work every time she is working, but I did not know it was you and Amy they were talking about. I also always stud up for them." Says Troy. As they froze in spot staring at each other as if their love has grown into this house already. There love has grown stronger and more precious to both forever, they know that they are going to want to grow old in this house together for the rest of there lives. "Let's go get to know this new babysitter that you found." Says Troy. Troy and Cynthia walk the babysitter around there home to show her the rest of the house, so the babysitter knows where everything is. They learn the babysitter's name at the end of the tour around the house, her name is Flare Mc'blair. "Thank you so much for showing your beautiful home to me. If you need me to start a day, just call my number and I will be back here any day you want, just not the days I am off, because there is always a reason why I am off, and my email is also on that card." Says Flare as she gives Cynthia her card for babysitting. "No thank you for asking if you could babysit my Amy, I really appreciate it thank you so much Flare." Says Cynthia. "No problem I am always here for the kids, I want children day for myself, but right now I am trying to get in college and get enough money to move away from here." Says Flare. "That sounds like a great plan Flare." Says Troy. "Thanks. I think so to. Flare looks down at her phone and checks to see what time it is. I should get going it's getting late, and I have a baby to sit tomorrow, so I will see you around, and remember everything you need to know about my days off are and will be sent to you once week because I put down the schedule that I do for everyone that needs me to look after their little ones. I need your email too." Says Flare. Cynthia writes down her email, and Flare takes it right out of her hand, and puts it right in her pocket. "Alright I should start walking back home." Says Flare. "Do you want a ride home?" Says Troy. "I am sure that you and Cynthia just walked up here to the cabin. I won't mind giving you a ride, because that driveway is more of a pathway, it's about three to two hours away from town." Says Troy. "Oh okay, if you don't mind. I mean I was just going to walk to town, but that works to." Says Flare. "Okay I will give you a quick drive home." Says Troy. "Okay Troy I will have some dinner ready when you come home." Says Cynthia. "Okay, honey. See you soon." Says Troy, Troy gives a big kiss on the lips to Cynthia. Then Troy and Flare get in Troy's car. They start the car and start driving toward wherever Flare lives. Cynthia walks back toward the kitchen to start making some supper for her and Troy.

Four hours later. "I am home Cynthia." Says Troy. Cynthia had some supper already made up for Troy when he got home from dropping off Flare to her house. Troy looks in the fridge to see what Cynthia made Troy's favorite, well second favorite. Spaghetti and meatballs, Troy grabs a plate out of the cabinet above the oven. Troy puts the Spaghetti and meatballs in the microwave to warm it up.

As Troy finishes eating dinner. He gets up and rises off his plate and putting his dish away in cabinet. Cynthia walks in behind Troy surprising him wearing a sexy bodysuit. "Hey Troy. Look behind you." Says Cynthia in a flirty voice. Troy turns around to see that Cynthia had her hair down straighten out, her beautiful dirty blonde hair really brought out her brown eyes. The suit was revealing her breasts, her breasts were together very tight in that suit that she was wearing. Is all that Troy could see was her breast were in between a V-neck? The suit was red. Cynthia came a little closer to Troy, so Cynthia could whisper in Troy's ear. He pinned her down to the table and kissed her on the neck. Then Troy whispers in Cynthia's ear. "Do you want to head to the bedroom?" Says Troy in a whisper voice. Cynthia replied "sure." In a flirty voice. Troy Picks up Cynthia walking up the stairs to the bedroom. As they walked in their bedroom, all you could see is candles all over the place except for the bathroom and the bed of course, Troy pinned Cynthia to the bed. As Cynthia was looking up at Troy, she could see through the skylight, that they had in their bedroom. Cynthia then thinks there is so many stars out there tonight it was possibly the most beautiful sight she has ever saw in her life. Troy then walks toward the open window that also gave him a hard time to put together, he closed the blinds. Then there was only the light coming from the skylight from the stars and the candles that Cynthia lit up for this moment. Troy then goes back toward Cynthia on the bed. Cynthia was already under the blankets; Troy then joins underneath the sheets. Troy does the first move; Troy takes off his shirt and throws it across the room away from the candles, then Troy takes Cynthia's bodysuit slowly unzipping the front of it down to the end of the zipper. Then when the bodysuit is undone Cynthia, unzips Troy's jean pants and takes them off and throws them where Troy threw his shirt. Troy takes off Cynthia's body suit puts it where Troy's clothes are. Now Troy and Cynthia were in their underwear and Cynthia was in her bra now. Troy made the second move kissing her all over her body and her neck most importantly, as he was doing that, he was unstrapping her bra. He threw it across the room with the pile of her clothes. Cynthia pulls off Troy's underwear and throws it across the room where the other clothes were. Troy rubs Cynthia on the hips, pulls off her underwear then and throws it across the room aiming for the pile of clothes again. Troy and Cynthia get underneath the covers once again, but naked this time. Troy then gets on top of Cynthia, Troy kisses Cynthia all over her body. Cynthia kisses Troy on the lips, Cynthia was purposely making it easy for Troy to kiss her neck, Troy just noticed that Cynthia was pointing her neck to Troy's lips. Cynthia then flips over for top of the advantage. Cynthia then makes the third move by getting Troy inside.

An hour later Troy and Cynthia were worn out. As Troy blew out the candle. He started walking back to the bed where Cynthia was. As soon as he crawled in bed, he could feel Cynthia laying on top of Troy as he laid down. Troy and Cynthia, they both look up at the stars. "Wow, my wish did come true." Says Cynthia. "What was your wish?" Says Troy. "My wish was to sleep next to you every night like this and look up at the stars and make more wishes." Says Cynthia. "Your wish is my pressure, I helped you make that wish come true, you are my beautiful star, Cynthia." Says Troy. Cynthia Hugs Troy tight. Troy could feel her falling asleep, her hug grew lose. Troy looked over on his chest and saw that Cynthia's eyes were closed. Troy kissed her on the head, Troy closes his eyes falling asleep watching the stars grow bright in his vision.

The next morning of course Cynthia was still sleeping as Troy woke up to her sleeping in the same spot on his chest. Troy lifted her off his chest gently. So, Troy did not wake her up. Troy knows that Cynthia does not like waking up this early, but Troy always woke up at this time to have some morning time and some chores. Especially when they live in their own house now. Troy is still working on a garden outside, so he goes out there to work on it. As Troy gently puts Cynthia on the other side of the bed, there was barely a blanket on her and it was sort of cold in the mornings around here, so he put the blanket on Cynthia to keep her warm. Troy picks up all the candles that were on the floor from last night and he puts them where they belong. Troy picks up the clothes where they threw their clothes last night and puts them in the laundry hamper. Troy grabs some new clothes out of the dresser and puts the clothes on. That were morning clothes, that he liked to wear in the morning. Troy then shuts the door quietly to the bedroom and walks downstairs to the main floor bathroom to wash his face, have a shower. After he was done in the shower, he went to Amy's room to check in on her and she was wide awake standing up in the crib. "Dada." Says Amy. Troy walks into her room and picks up Amy and congrats her on saying dada for the first time. Troy picks up Amy to take her to the kitchen to get her something to eat for the morning. Troy puts Amy in the highchair warms up some milk and feeds Amy the milk. Troy then grabs something out of the fridge which was baby food and places it in front of Amy. Amy eats the food that was given to her, Troy makes some breakfast for himself and sits down in his spot that he sits in every morning drinking coffee, eating some waffles with butter and maple syrup. Like always Troy turns on the TV to the news for the mornings, but now Amy was done eating her breakfast. Troy gets up from his seat picks up Amy's dish rises it off in the sink then puts the dish away in the cabinet where it was before. Troy washes off Amy's highchair. Troy eats his breakfast quick, drinks his coffee to wash the food down, then Troy grabs some water from the tap sink, and drinks out of the glass cup. Troy rises his dishes and puts them back in the cabinets. The kitchen was and always will be cleaned for the rest of the mornings, Troy always keeps his house clean. Troy picks up Amy from out of the highchair then moves the highchair back to its spot. Troy walks toward Amy's bedroom to get Amy into different clothes for outside near where Troy is going to plant some plants in his garden. Amy slips right into her clothes quick like always. Troy picks up Amy and walks right toward the outside in the warm sun. All Troy knows that it was way warmer outside then in his house. He did not know why though, but he likes it the way everything is. As Troy gets out of the house he puts Amy in his trousers, big pocket. As Troy walks down to his garden that he has been working on he places Amy down in a safe place where Troy could see her crawling or walking around. "Dada." Says Amy. "Yeah, what is it?" Says Troy in a silly voice. "What is this?" Says Amy. "Well, my little princess that is a flower that your mother loves so much." Says Troy. Amy stands up and picks up dirt. "Hey, what are you doing with that dirt princess?" Says Troy. "I don't know, can I eat it?" Says Amy. "No, don't eat dirt. That is what grows and keeps our plants alive, and it does not taste good." Says Troy. Amy throws the dirt back on the ground where she pulled it from. "What are you doing, dada?" Says Amy. "I am gardening. Do you want to try Amy?" Says Troy. "What is gardening?" Says Amy. "Well, it can do a lot of things. It could make you more organized. The point of gardening in life is just making your garden beautiful for someone that you love truly. You know who I love?" Says Troy. "Who, do you love Dada?" Says Amy. "I love you and your mother." Says Troy. "Are you making this garden for mom?" Says Amy. "Yeah, I am. Making this garden for your mom, but I am making it for you to, my little princess." Says Troy. "Can I help make this Garden for mom?" Says Amy. "Sure, you can sweetie, come here. I will show you the simple start of making a garden." Says Troy. As Troy shows Amy how to dig holes in the flowerbed Amy falls backwards into her dad's arms. Troy hugs Amy so tight that it was making him feel more blessed to have a kid that wants to learn how to garden. He loved Amy so much.

Three years later. It was Amy's third birthday. Amy was turning three years old today. Amy then blew out her candles. As Amy did that her blow was heavy for the cake. The candles blew right off the cake. Troy and Cynthia looked at each other as they were pinning down the cake. "Amy your powers are growing every year." Says Cynthia. "Aren't they ever!" Says Troy in a sigh. "Honey we will be right back don't blow on anything or touch water or try to control the earth or try not to conjure fire. Just stay put, me and your dad. Are just going to go chat for a second." Says Cynthia. Troy grabs Cynthia by the arm and takes her into the living room. "What is wrong? Is everything okay?" Says Cynthia. "I am just worried about Amy's powers. She does not know how to control it and she is just a little girl. She just turned three today. Don't get me wrong I love Amy so much, but I don't want anyone to know what Amy can do with just a blow or her thinking about something and it just poufs right into her hand. I am just scared that she is going to hurt another kid on accident." Says Troy. "You don't think I fear that happening. I am terrified, but you and I need to stay calm and steady, and everything will be fine. I will teach her to control the air when she blows, but it will be hard like you said." Says Cynthia. "How do you know it's going to be okay?" Says Troy. "I know it because I have it to Troy. She got my gifts of having powers just like me when I was a kid, just like her age and that was the time that my mom still loved me. She taught me to be calm and no panic or my powers will go off again." Says Cynthia. "Wait she got these gifts from you? Why did you not say anything that you had these powers?" Says Troy. "I was afraid that you would not love me anymore. So, I never told you anything about my powers." Says Cynthia. "Well. Cynthia, you don't have to worry about that. I loved you no matter what. I sacrificed lots for you. I really do love you. Just please don't be afraid of ever telling me about these things, okay." Says Troy. "Okay. I won't keep anymore secrets from you anymore." Says Cynthia in a smile. Troy and Cynthia walk back into the kitchen where Amy was sitting in her chair waiting for someone to cut her a piece of her cake. Troy cuts a piece of her cake and places the piece of cake on a plate. Amy picks up the fork in front of her and starts to eat the cake that Troy gave to her. Then Cynthia and Troy get a piece of cake to make there lives a little sweeter, but then Amy looks at them. "MY Cake." Says Amy. "There is no way you are eating this cake by yourself Amy Amber Thorn." Says Cynthia. Then Amy looks up at her mom. "Fine eat my cake." Says Amy. Troy starts to laugh a little. Then Cynthia laughs as well.

CHAPTER **10**

FIRST DAY OF SCHOOL

Nine years later. "You ready to go to school like you always wanted." Says Cynthia. "Yeah, I am so excited to go to school for the first time in my life. I loved being home schooled, but I am wanting to experience being in person for learning." Says Amy. "Amy, I love you, but you must be careful with your powers okay. I mean it." Says Cynthia. "I will be mom, I know both you and dad are scared that I am going to lose control, but I won't I promise." Says Amy. "Okay. I trust you. I will drive you to school." Says Cynthia. As Cynthia and Amy get into Cynthia's car, Cynthia starts the car and drives toward school.

"Okay we are here. Are you sure you just don't want me to keep you home schooled?" Says Cynthia. "No, I am fine, I am ready for this mom." Says Amy. "Okay, I will see you later then, I love sweetie." Says Cynthia. Amy gets out of the car and walks toward the school building. Cynthia drives away back home. Amy looks outside to see where her mom was, but of course she was gone. Amy walks to the principal's office, to find out what to do or where her class is. "Hey, where is the principal?" Says Amy. "Who's asking?" Says The woman at the front office desk. "My name is Amy Thorn. I was asked to come to this office before I am go to classes." Says Amy. A man walks out of the office seeing what the commotion was about. The principal looks at Amy and invites her in his office to chat. "Okay, so you are Amy Thorn, right?" Says the principal. "Yeah, I am Amy Thorn, my mom is Cynthia Thorn, and my dad is Troy Thorn." Says Amy. "So, it says on your file that you have been home schooled till now, right?" Says The principal. "Yeah, I have been home schooled by my mom she was just worried about me going to school, but then I finally convinced her to let me try to go to school in person." Says Amy. "Okay, is there a reason why your mom was nervous to let you go to school in person?" Says the principal. "Yeah, she was worried that I would get bullied at school." Says Amy. Don't worry everyone here at this school is nice and forced with there studies. I am verry happy that you wanted to try school." Says the principal. "Yeah, I am excited about going to school and making new friends. I would like something normal in my life." Says Amy. "Well anyway I will lead you to your new class, your classroom will be with Mrs. Gates. She is an English teacher, and she also teaches art, but she loves teaching kids in general. So, she basically is free to teach you what you want." Says the principal. "That's good, I am excited to meet her." Says Amy. "Okay, let's get you to class, Shall we." Says the principal. "Yes, we shall." Says Amy. Amy and the principal walk to Amy's new class. "Mrs. Gates, I have a new student here for you." Says the principal. "Oh, hello how are you?" Says Mrs. Gates. "I am good, how are you?" Says Amy. "I am fantastic, my name is Mrs. Gates and what's yours little one." Says Mrs. Gates. "I am Amy Thorn." Says Amy. "What a beautiful name." Says Mrs. Gates. "Alright I must go now Amy, I will see you around the school. If you need anything from me just comes to the office and I will be there." Says the Principal. The principal leaves the classroom walking back to his office. "Alright Amy, take a seat and we will begin my lesson for the day." Says Mrs. Gates. Amy goes and picks a seat at the back of the classroom. Every student in that room was looking right at Amy as she was walking down the row of desks. She sat down in the right corner of the room at a desk, and the lesson began as Amy sat down.

An hour later for lunch time. Amy looks through her backpack and finds one bag that had her lunch in it that mom made for her. Amy looks around to find a seat, but there were no more tables left, but just the floor. Amy sits down on the floor near a nice plant. Amy eats her sandwich in peace until someone walks up to her. "Hey, why are you sitting on the floor?" Says a girl. "There are no more seats, the tables are all being used, and I don't mind sitting on the floor." Says Amy. "You can come sit with me and my friends if you want." Says the girl. "Sure, if you don't mind." Says Amy. "I don't mind, you look new around here and I like making lots of new friends." Says the girl. "Yeah, this is my first day of classes or school in general in my life. I have been home schooled." Says Amy. "Oh, you have been home schooled? I think that is cool. Why would you want to come here, and ruin that fun? I hate it here. I would rather have been home schooled, but my parents don't have time for me." Says the girl. "Really you would rather be home schooled than not making friends." Says Amy. "Yeah, the only reason why I am still here because I have friends here that I enjoy hanging out with. That is the only reason why I like school." Says the girl. "By the way my name is Amy." Says Amy. "That is a cool name, and what's that on your arm?" Says the girl. "It's my birthmark." Says Amy. "That is a cool. I thought it was a tattoo for a second then I realized that we are young to have tattoos. Oh, and my name is Jade." Says Jade. "I love your name, and no its not a tattoo." Says Amy. "Thanks. Let's go meet my friend group." Says Jade. Jade and Amy walk to Jade's usual table and there were four girls sitting there waiting for Jade. "Hey guys this is Amy, she is new at this school. Amy these are my friends Nina, Emma, Olivia, and Eva." Says Jade. "Nice to meet you, Amy." Says Nina. Nina looks so beautiful she had long strawberry orange hair, and hazel eyes. She was eating a salad with a sandwich. She was wearing a short skirt, the skirt was colored red and white, it looked plaid, and she was wearing a black tank top shirt with a white coat on. "I really love your hair." Says Amy. "Thank you." Says Nina. "My name is Eva it's nice meeting you." Says Eva. Amy see's that Eva has her hair up and again Eva is beautiful to she has brown dark hair and it's long, but it's up in a ponytail. She was wearing ripped jeans, and she was wearing a black shirt that showed her belly. And her eyes were ocean blue. "I am Emma." Says Emma. Emma had her hair curled down; her hair was long like everyone else in the group. Her hair color was blonde, she wore glasses, and she had a book in her hand. Emma was wearing a hoodie that was black. But she was wearing ripped jeans as well as Eva. "Hey, my name is Olivia." Says Olivia. Olivia was cool looking, she was wearing a leather jacket, the leather jacket was black as her hair and Olivia's eyes were bright as the sun, her eyes were topaz color, and her bottoms black ripped jeans, and she had a chain hanging off it. Then Amy looks back at Jade realizing that this group was good to be true, but Amy did not want to sit on the floor, so she sat down with them. As the group kept talking about gossip around the school and Emma was not paying attention because apparently, she is the smart one in the group. She does not like gossip or failing testes or exams and everyone else did not care at all. "So, Amy Jade tells me that you were home schooled before you came here. Why did you decide to come here?" Says Nina. "I wanted to come to school to see what school was like in person." Says Amy. "Hmm. Interesting. If my parents home schooled me. I would love it; I would never come here to see what it is about. Amy if you think that they are going to teach you anything. You are probably wrong. School literally teaches you nothing." Says Nina. "Well, that is what you think, but I must say it is a little more exhausting at home." Says Amy. "If you say so. But I would totally stay home all the time because this place is hell." Says Nina. "I so agree with you on that, Nina." Says Eva. Olivia was looking at Nina smiling and thumbing up to that, she had her earbuds in, but Olivia knows mouth language. That means that Olivia can hear mouths. "See even Olivia agrees to that." Says Nina. Someone walks up to there table. "Hey, girls. Can I have a seat." Says another girl. "Sure." Says Jade. "Who is this new girl?" Says the girl. "Oh, right that is Amy." Says Jade. "Oh, you're the new girl in Mrs. Gates class. My name is June." Says June. "That's a pretty name." Says Amy. As Amy was looking right at June. She was wearing tights that were black with white cats all over them, and she was wearing a crop top that was white. She was wearing a skirt above the tights as well. Then Amy looks at her light blue hair with her headphones on. The girls continue talking about hot guys at the school and how they would rather be home schooled like Amy was once. Before she came here to see what school was like.

Two hours later. Amy messages mom to come to pick her up from school. A few moments later her mom was right in front of her while Amy was not paying attention. Amy gets up from the bench she was sitting on and walks toward the car. "How was your first day?" Says Cynthia. "It was cool. I met some people." Says Amy. "Oh, that is great honey." Says Cynthia in a smile. "Where is dad?" Says Amy. "He is still at work." Says Cynthia. "Oh, what time will he be home?" Says Amy. "I am pretty sure that your dad will be home at five for dinner tonight."

Says Cynthia. "I am going to tell him all about my day at school." Says Amy in an excited voice. "I am glad you are liking school in person so far." Says Cynthia. Cynthia looks toward where she was driving, but she looked nervous about something.

An hour later Cynthia and Amy arrive at home. Amy gets out of the car and shuts the door. Cynthia gets her bag out from the back seat of the car, then locks her car and walks toward the house. "Amy, what do you want for dinner?" Says Cynthia as Cynthia shuts the front door behind her. "I have no idea surprise us. I have homework to do." Says Amy. "Okay, I will look around the kitchen then." Says Cynthia. Amy runs to her room to start doing her homework, then she feels something from her phone. She picks up her phone to see a message from book life, there was a friend request from Nina, Jade, Eva, Emma, and Olivia. Then there was another one from June. Amy accepts their friend requests on book life. Then as soon as she accepted their friend request's there was a group made with Amy in it. Amy messages Hi. Then there was a hi emoji from everyone in the group. Then Nina messages, "Does anyone want to be a group for the book report assignment from Mrs. Gates." Then Jade messages "Sure!! I would love to." Says Jade. Emma messages "Sure what the heck, let's do it!" Says Emma. "Then I will call in this group chat, I want this done now, my dad wants to go shopping in three hours and I said I want to go, but he found out that I have an assignment. He said if I get it done on time then I can go." Says Nina. "Okay make the call." Says Jade. Then suddenly there was a call request on Amy's phone screen, Amy taps the accept button. "Hello Amy, welcome to the call!" Says Olivia. Eva, Jade, Emma, Olivia, and Nina were in the call. "Okay so what is this book about, Emma." Says Nina. Emma looks at the screen as if she did not even know her own name. "Yes, Emma I am talking to you." Says Nina. "Of course, you talk to me because I am the smart one in the group. I am starting to think that I am in this group because you guys are just using me for my brain." Says Emma. "We are not using you for your brain you just, don't talk a lot in the group." Says Nina. "Oh really. That is cool of you, Nina. I just thought you Nina of all people was just looking for me or the kind of person to be in the group because I am smart or whatever you think about me." Says Emma.

Someone walks into Nina's room. "Nina what are you doing on the phone?!" Says Nina's stepmom. "Mom, I am just working with my friends on a book report that Mrs. Gates gave to us as homework." Says Nina. "Okay fine, but if you want to go shopping you better have something in an hour then I know for sure that you are committed in doing schoolwork." Says Nina's stepmom. "What does that mean?" Says Nina. "I am talking about if you don't get your work done in an hour you are not allowed to go shopping for a year." Says Nina's stepmom. "WHAT." Says Nina. "Yeah, I am watching your grades and I keep watching your clothes, your clothes are growing, but your grades are not." Says Nina's stepmom. "So." Says Nina. "Clothes won't get you through years of your life, so please if you want to prove me wrong change your grades, please." Says Nina's stepmom. Before Nina could say something, Nina's stepmom walks out of the door. Everyone on the call even Olivia did not say anything, until Nina broke the silence in the call. "Okay, Emma give me a topic to talk about." Says Nina. Emma takes a second to say something, until Emma says something that Nina does not except. Emma even puts her book down for this. "Nina are you okay at your house. That sounded serious. I know how much shopping means to you." Says Emma. "I am fine Emma, just give me something interesting to say something in the book report." Says Nina. Emma takes a second to change the subject, then Emma gets up from her chair and grabs the book that the report is on. Emma flips through the pages then she stops on a page. "Okay I got something easy and interesting for you, Nina." Says Emma. "Okay, that sounds good, hmm what page is it. I can read it." Says Nina. "The page is 45. It is the first thing you see." Says Emma. "Yeah, this is perfect, thank you Emma. Mrs. Gates will totally like this. But this is something that you would do." Says Nina. "Yeah, it is the one I was going to do, but you need it way more than me." Says Emma in a smile. Nina then looks at her camera looking right at Emma. I swear that Nina had a tear in her eye for Emma helping her. "I knew you were more than a smart brain, Emma. You won't regret this." Says Nina. "No problem, if you need my help, I can help you. I don't mind." Says Emma. "Thank you so much Emma, but I think I got the rest of this from here." Says Nina. "Okay. I am glad." Says Emma. "I am going to mute myself. I am about to turn on some music while I work." Says Nina. "Okay. Just unmute if you need my help." Says Emma. Nina mutes herself. Is all everyone can see now on Nina's cam is her headphones are on her head. And she's writing notes in a notebook. "Okay, so everyone I am going to start working on my backup report. That one that I gave to Nina was just to give me time, but I am feeling like I want to challenge myself today. So, I am doing a harder one." Says Emma. Emma then mutes herself without any warning. "So, what is everyone else doing." Says Jade. Amy looks in the book to find an interesting part of the book. "I found a part that looks interesting." Says Amy. "Okay, I think I found something to." Says Olivia. "What about you Jade?" Says Eva. "I think I found one on page 100. It sounds fun and dark, but also interesting." Says Jade. "Yeah, I found something on page 50. That is totally my kind of page. It is sporty, but also a vacation. It is about a girl on a vacation then finds a passion of sport along the way." Says Eva. "Yeah, that does sound like you Eva." Says Jade. "Yeah. I am pretty set on it, so I am going to mute as well. I will probably unmute and say bye because I do have practice in an hour, I just wanted to get this done before practice started." Says Eva. "Okay. I hope you get finished in time." Says Jade. Eva mutes and starts working on her part of the book report. "Okay, Amy I am going to mute to as well, because I must go to my dad's farm soon, so I must get this assignment done." Says Jade. "Okay, see you later then." Says Amy. On the call, it was just Amy and Olivia in the unmuted chat. "So, Amy what are you interested in doing or do you have an idea of what you are doing for the report assignment." Says Olivia. "I have no idea. I am more of an adventurous person. I live near the mountains and my dad built this house for my mom." Says Amy. "Well, I have a suggestion for you. Look on page 60. There is a girl or boy I can't remember. I was reading that part of the book and the person is adventurous. The person like's wandering around the forest at night or day. At any chance they can. Then one night they find something amazing. A cave they have never seen the cave before, but the point is that they went adventuring inside the cave and they found a stone that the person's town puts in the centre of the town, and it symbolizes the town to this day." Says Olivia. "That sounds interesting. Thank you, Olivia, what are you doing for your assignment?" Says Amy. "I am doing an assignment about a girl that puts on of her savings into music, the girl starts failing and then almost gives up. Then her music was noticed by her friends then her friends showed their friends and kept going viral then she was famous, and she continued making music for her career. That I am interested in writing about. Because myself I am into music a lot and I want to be a song writer one day, so this story would be good for me." Says Olivia. "That sounds cool." Says Amy. "Yeah, I think so to." Says Olivia. "Well, I should probably get to work. I am studying for music after this so, yeah." Says Olivia. "Okay, I will talk to you later. Oh, and thank you again Olivia for helping me find something to write about." Says Amy. "No problem, I am always happy to help." Says Olivia. Then Amy was the only one on the unmuted chat. Olivia muted herself and left her camera on like everyone else did. Amy saw everyone just writing in their notebooks. Emma was writing so fast that Amy could barely keep track of her hand. Amy then mutes herself as well. Amy gets up from her chair and grabs the book and finds the page that Olivia was talking about, and Olivia was right it was interesting to be writing about. Amy gets her headphones then a pencil. Amy opens her notebook that Mrs. Gates gave to Amy today. Amy writes down the date of today. Amy reads the report story then starts writing about the girl. An hour went by, Amy was done about the girl finding the stone. Amy gets up from her chair and puts the notebook and the assignment book, that Mrs. Gates gave to Amy, so that could do her work and have something to hand in to Mrs. Gates. Amy puts the two books in her backpack. "Amy dinner is ready." Says Cynthia. Amy walks over to the phone to see if anyone was on, and everyone was still on. Amy unmutes and sees that everyone has their headphones off there heads. "Hey, everyone. My dinner is ready, so I got to go. I will see you all later." Says Amy. "I should go to. I am done with my assignment and my practice is starting soon so I should leave to." Says Eva. "Yeah, me to my dinner is ready as well, my mom is yelling at me, I also want to work on my music later." Says Olivia. "I should go to my dinner is ready, then me and dad are going to the farm to help grandpa." Says Jade. "I am DONE." Says Nina in an excited voice. "I am so happy; I can go shopping and send this to Mrs. Gates tomorrow." Says Nina. Emma looks like she is still working on the assignment. "Are you still working on yours Emma?" Says Jade.

Emma realizes that everyone was looking at her and asking her a question. "Oh no I am just working on something else." Says Emma. Then everyone hears someone yelling up to Emma's room. Something about dinner. "I should probably go to. My supper is ready, and my mom does not like to wait." Says Emma. Then Emma left the call. "I should go to, I am going to go eat, then I am going shopping." Says Nina in a happy scream. Nina left the call as well. "I got to go now, my mom and dad are yelling at me." Says Eva. Eva leaves the call as well. "I should go to; I will see you guys tomorrow." Says Olivia. Olivia leaves the call. Now it was just Amy and Jade in the call. "Well, I hope you are enjoying being in the group Amy, but I must go to. I should go eat then I am going to the farm with dad to my grandparents, but I will you tomorrow." Says Jade. "Okay. I will see you later. I should go to because my mom said dinner's ready." Says Amy. "Okay I will see you tomorrow then." Says Jade. Amy and Jade end the call together. Amy puts her phone on charge and walks to the kitchen to eat some food. As Amy walks into the kitchen. Dad and mom were setting the table and getting the food out of the oven. "You made us lasagna!" Says Amy. "Yeah, I sure did. I know that you love lasagna and you seemed happy about school today, so I wanted to celebrate for you." Says Cynthia. "Thank you, mom. You did not have to go through the trouble." Says Amy. "No, it's fine I felt like a pasta anyway." Says Cynthia. Amy walks over to grab some food and some bread. Amy sits down eating her supper. While Dad sits down to eat as well. Amy talks about school the entire time that everyone was eating supper. "I am so glad that you enjoyed school, then Amy. Also, Jade seems very nice." Says Troy. "Yeah, she let me in their group, and we finished our assignment from Mrs. Gates, our English teacher today." Says Amy. "Well, I am excited to meet these friends of yours." Says Troy. "Well Amy, do you have anymore homework to do?" Says Cynthia. "No, I think I have finished it all with everyone on the call today." Says Amy. "Okay. Do you want to watch a movie with us?" Says Cynthia. "Yeah sure. I would love to." Says Amy. "I will make some hot chocolate then." Says Troy. "Make popcorn to honey." Says Cynthia. "Yes ma'am." Says Troy in a silly voice, but then Troy walks over to Cynthia and kisses her on the head. Cynthia and Amy walk into the living room. Amy sits down where she sits all the time, then Cynthia sits where she sits with Troy on the couch. Troy then walks into the living room and sits right next to Cynthia. Amy knew that was going to happen because they loved to cuddle on the couch all the time. "What movie are we watching?" Says Amy. "I don't know, you pick." Says Cynthia. "Are you sure?" Says Amy. "Yeah, I am sure that what movie you choose we will enjoy." Says Cynthia in a laugh. "Okay, I will choose then." Says Amy in a sad voice. Cynthia looks at Amy, as if Amy had something to say. "Honey what is wrong?" Says Cynthia. "You guys just always fall asleep when I choose a movie." Says Amy. "Oh. Honey it's not your fault it is just that we are tired. All the time." Says Cynthia. "Oh, right you guys do work everyday." Says Amy. "Yeah, that is why we are tired all the time. Work is very tiring sometimes, right honey." Says Cynthia. "Yeah, that is the truth sister." Says Troy. Amy chooses a movie; they sit on the couch eating popcorn, then an hour later Cynthia and Troy fall asleep in each others' arms. Amy just keeps watching the movie a little longer, then she starts to feel a little bored of the movie. Before Amy could turn it off, she saw that the movie was going to end anyway. "Mom and Dad, I am going to bed." As Amy said that they both woke up and realized that they fell asleep again. "Good night honey." Says Troy. Amy shuts her door behind her. Amy turns on some music in her ear, then started listening to full blast music in her ears. Amy turns off her light next to her and begins to fall asleep as soon as she turned off her light. "Hello, little one." Says the Time Witch. "Who are you?" Says Amy. "I am your guardian. I am here to help you use your abilities right. I want you to make sure that the world does not fall apart." Says the Time Witch. "How did you know that I have abilities?" Says Amy. "Like I said I am your guardian I know everything about you and my children." Says the Time Witch. "What do you want from me?" Says Amy. "I just want to help you know how to use your powers. I don't want you to lose control." Says the Time Witch. "Well, you don't have to worry about me losing control. I know what I am doing." Says Amy. "I am sure that you know what or how to use your power, because your mother Cynthia taught you how to use them or to control them and contain your angry or stress and fears, but that is and was just the beginning of your training. You need to know what you are using your power for. Are you defending people you love or are you destroying people you love?" Says the Time Witch. "How do you know my mom's name?" Says Amy. "I know her because I talked to her a long time ago, and I was waiting for a good moment to come to you and chat with you." Says the Time Witch. "Just stay away from me and my mom." Says Amy. "Amy don't be afraid of me. Your power will get out of control if you try to leave my dream realm." Says the Time Witch. "What do you want, from me though? For real?" Says Amy. "I want to help you." Says the Time Witch. "I am okay on my own, thanks." Says Amy. "I know you would be fine, but your kind grows quick." Says the Time Witch. "What do you mean my kind grows quick?" Says Amy. The Time Witch looks right at Amy in the eyes. "Amy, you are one of the most powerful witches out there." Says the Time Witch. Amy looks at the floating woman telling her that she is a witch more powerful than she thinks. "Amy. I know I should not be coming in your dreams like this, but you need to know that you are capable of things that you don't know about yourself yet. You can lose lots of control over yourself, emotionally and mentally. Your power is based on feelings and emotion. If you lose your emotion, you will either lose much control over yourself. Your parents don't even know how to get you out of that trance that you can get stuck in. That is why I am here, to teach you to not lose that control. You are doing fine right now, but when you keep aging Amy. Your power grows stronger than one day you won't be available to control it anymore." Says the Time Witch. "How do you even know what kind of power I have? I am starting to think you are not just, my guardian." Says Amy. "Fine my name is Ruby, I am a Time Witch." Says the Time Witch. "So, you can see my future?" Says Amy. "Yes, in fact I can see everyone's future, I am only focusing on you though, right now." Says the Time Witch. "I will listen to you if you tell me what happens. There must be a reason why you are worried about me and my power." Says Amy. "I am afraid that I can't tell you that. Because it's against my rules and my oath of being a Time Witch." Says the Time Witch. "Fine, what are you here for or what do you want to help me with?" Says Amy. "I am here to warn you to watch who your friends are." Says the Time Witch. "What does that mean?! I just meant new people and you are saying they are going to betray me?!" Says Amy. "No, just watch them and you will see what I mean." Says the Time Witch.

Amy stands there looking at the floating woman in front of her, then suddenly Amy sees her looking around like someone was calling her name. "I must go. I will see you soon. Amy. If you need me or want to chat. Think about me or say my name." says the Time Witch. Then suddenly the Time Witch was gone, and Amy wakes up in bed confused of what just happened. Then she looks down and notices that her birthmark was glowing. Amy looks out her window and sees that it is still dark out. She sees that her alarm clock says it is three in the morning. Amy lays back down on her back to go back to sleep.

CHAPTER **11**

THE SLEEPOVER

"Hey, Amy wake up honey. You can't sleep in anymore. I am your ride to school, and I have to work soon." Says Troy. "Okay, dad I am waking up." Says Amy. "Damn Amy you alright?" Says Troy. "I am just tired I had a weird dream last night. With woman came in my dream last night saying I must be careful about my powers and watch over my new friends." Says Amy. Troy then turns back to Amy as if he knew something about this woman that comes into people's dreams. "Honey, what was this woman's name?!" Says Troy. "Her name was Ruby, she says she is a Time Witch. Why do you know her?" Says Amy. Troy freezes for a second then gets off Amy's bed. "Honey, be ready to go to school in three minutes I will buy you breakfast at a breakfast drive thru. Just be ready in that time spam." Says Troy. "Okay?" Says Amy. Troy get's out of Amy's room, so Amy could get into her clothes for school. Amy is all dressed and ready to go, but Amy just needs to grab her schoolbook and her phone then she is ready to go. Amy walks out of her room, to see suspicious looks from her mom and dad toward Amy. "Okay, you ready honey." Says Troy. "Yeah, I am ready. I got everything." Says Amy. "Okay, good. Let's head out then and get you to school." Says Troy. Troy and Amy walk out of the house toward Troy's car. Amy opens the passenger seat door. Puts her backpack on her lap. Troy starts the car and drives toward Amy's school. The car ride was quiet. Until Amy talks. "Why were you and mom looking at me like you know something about that woman I talked about this morning to you?" Says Amy. "Amy. That woman is real. That woman went into your mom's dreams way before you were even one years old. That woman is not to be trusted. She was right about you having abilities, but she told us something that scared us both." Says Troy. "What did she tell mom?" Says Amy. "She said that you were going to lose control at some point in your life, but you are doing great. I am sure that you won't lose control and do anything stupid. I think that you can handle your powers." Says Troy. "Thanks dad." Says Amy in a lost voice. "Are you alright though?" Says Troy. "Yeah, I am fine." Says Amy. "Okay, but if you have something on your mind. I want you to tell me about it." Says Troy in a concerned voice. "Okay, I will." Says Amy. Troy then just continues looking at the road for lots of safety reasons. Then he finally arrives at Amy's school. Amy starts to get out of the car, but before she could even touch the sidewalk her dad grabs her and hugs her tight. "Amy, just know I care about you so much, and I love you." Says Troy. Amy hugs back tight. "I love you to dad. Are you okay?" Says Amy. "Yes, I am fine. Is it bad that I wanted to hug my daughter without question?!" Says Troy in a laugh. "No, I was just wondering why you are hugging me like this. Like something bad is going to happen." Says Amy. "Amy, nothing bad will happen to you I will make sure of that. I love you very much. You are my princess I will always love you and care about you." Says Troy. Amy and Troy hug for another few seconds than Amy realizes that she should get to Mrs. Gates class before the bell rings. "Dad let go of me. I should go." Says Amy. Troy let's go of his daughter. Amy then get's out of the car and shuts the car door. As Amy walks away from the car. Troy pulls down his window to yell at Amy. "I love you Amy Amber Thorn." Says Troy. Amy yells back. "Bye dad." Says Amy in an embarrassed voice, but also happy voice. Amy walks up to the school front door and walks toward her locker then runs toward Mrs. Gates class for English. Amy walks into the classroom on time just before the bell rang. Amy walks toward her seat to sit in her spot from yesterday. As Amy sits down Mrs. Gates begins the lesson like always.

Troy text messages Cynthia. "Cynthia, what do you think Ruby said to Amy?" Says Troy. "How am I supposed to know?" Says Cynthia. "I was just giving it a shot, if you knew something, but I guess not." Says Troy. "Aren't you supposed to be at work?" Says Cynthia. "I am at work. I just can't get that conversation out my head that I had with Amy." Says Troy. "I know, I don't trust that Ruby Time Witch woman. She just keeps coming in our lives like this. I don't know what her deal is." Says Cynthia. "She can probably sense that we are talking about her." Says Troy. "Yeah, you are right. I should probably get back to work now honey. I will talk later." Says Cynthia. "Yeah, I should to. Love you." Says Troy with a heart emoji. Cynthia then sends a heart emoji with kissy face then goes offline. Then Troy puts his phone in his pocket and walks back to his workstation.

"Amy. Psst Amy." Says Jade. "Hey Jade, what's up." Says Amy. "Do you want to hang out with us at Nina's house tonight?" Says Jade. "Sure, I will have to ask my parents about it." Says Amy. "Yeah, do that first. I will send you her address and the time to come over. We are all going shopping since Nina wanted to go shopping, with us." Says Jade. " Oh nice, and thanks that would be very helpful." Says Amy. Jade gets her phone out of her pocket to message Amy the details. Suddenly Amy's phone makes beep sounds from out of her pocket. "Okay, everyone it is time to hand in your personality assignment that I gave to you all last night. I hope that some of you got it done. Because I got another assignment here that will be allowed to be due in three days which is Friday. I am giving you three days for this assignment because it's going to take longer than the personally report assignment." Says Mrs. Gates. Everyone gets up with a piece of paper and returns the book that came with the assignment. Amy gets up and walks to the front of the room toward Mrs. Gates. Amy drops her assignment in front of Mrs. Gates then walks back to where she was sitting. "Thank you everyone who has handed in your report assignment I glad that some people care to do my tasks." as Mrs. Gates looks at a boy that has not got up and handed it in let, Mrs. Gates knew that he was not done his yet. "I will get mine done right now. I just have to finish one more sentence." Says the boy. "Okay, that works. Thank you, Austin." Says Mrs. Gates. Then Mrs. Gates turns around and walks back toward her desk to take her seat. "Okay I will be giving you all break except for Austin until he is done doing the assignment that I wanted done last night or today in class. Then I will be talking about the new assignment that everyone will be starting tonight, thank you enjoy break." Says Mrs. Gates. Literally everyone except for Austin gets up from there seat to sit next to there friends to talk, and the girls get up and walk back where Amy was sitting, and they start talking with Jade about what's happening tonight. "So, Jade did you tell Amy that I am having a sleepover tonight." Says Nina. "Yeah, she said that she would come over tonight." Says Jade. "Cool, I am excited for you all to see what I have done to my room last night before I went to bed." Says Nina. "What did you do to your bedroom last night?" Says Olivia in a sarcastic voice. Everyone starts to laugh a little to how Olivia said that. "I have done something that you guys would never except, but mostly my dad wanted to do it to my room, so yeah." Says Nina. "Okay, now I am curious. Can you give us a hint?" Says Olivia in a sarcastic voice again. "Olivia stop that." Says Nina in a laughing voice. "It clearly makes you all like me more, so I do it because I like to." Says Olivia. "So, are we going to be doing the assignment tonight?" Says Emma. "I just want to relax. I like Mrs. Gates, but why does she must give us an assignment when we are having a sleepover tonight." Says Nina. "It's her job to give us things to do, so we can graduate and get out of here." Says Eva. "Yeah, I know, but why tonight. I just finished last night. I would be fine doing one tomorrow, but of course the world must go against me." Says Nina. "It will be fine. Maybe we could finish it tonight before we go to sleep. I am coming tonight so many I can help us get it done then we can watch movies for the rest of the night." Says Emma. "That sounds very nice, Emma. I love your plan, but I am totally finally getting that make over to you, that I wanted to do for so long. Probably for a year now. But of course, you say no every time." Says Nina. "I know, I just don't think looking good, does anything for you. That's all." Says Emma. "I am sure it will do something for you Emma. I see a beautiful girl underneath those glasses and that causal sweater and jeans. I think boys will be talking to you. Also, you won't be just smart you will be beautiful even more than me probably." Says Nina. "Nina I am not beautiful; I don't wear make up for a reason or do what you do." Says Emma. "Emma, you helped me do an assignment last night and I want to return the favor. I promise I won't do anything extreme." Says Nina. Emma stares at Nina for a second this says. "Okay, you can give me a make over, but not to extreme like you said." Says Emma. "Okay, thank you so much Emma. I promise you will be thanking me." Says Nina in a happy voice and Nina gives Emma a big hug. Emma then looks at everyone confused, Emma did not except Nina to hug Emma for a make over. Nina then let's go of Emma. Nina has the biggest smile on her face, everyone has not seen Nina this happy before. Then Mrs. Gates yells out to the class. "Okay, everyone head back to your seat. I want to make this assignment example quick." Says Mrs. Gates. Everyone heads back to there seat as everyone is sitting back in their seats. Mrs. Gates talks about the new assignment that is due on Friday. As Mrs. Gates finishes up the assignment example the bell rings. Of course, Emma was the last one to get out of class because she was writing down notes for tonight to finish it in a day. It seemed that it was Emma's goal to finish tonight. Emma than gets up fast running after the group. The group then sits down at there lunch picnic table to eat their lunch in peace. Emma was reading over her notes that she took and ran off out of the room after she realized that everyone in the class was gone. Eva was eating salad and drinking a smoothie that her mom made for the morning. Jade was eating a sandwich and with the side there was chili it smelled so good. Olivia was eating a wrap with feta cheese, and she was grabbing something out of her bag possibly more dressing for the wrap. Then there was Nina she was looking at shopping apps and eating pasta that looked tasty as well. "Guys I love this store it is at the mall that we are going to as soon as everyone comes to my house for the night." Says Nina. "Where or who made that chili that you are having Jade?" Says Amy. "I made it last night with my grandpa and dad last night. I ended up sleeping at the farm last night it was late when we all went to sleep. But since I had to come here for school, I had to get up at four in the morning to pack up and be ready to get to school for today, so I have been up for awhile now." Says Jade. "Wow, do you have more?" Says Amy. "Yeah, but it's at home." Says Jade. "Okay, guys I think we can finish this assignment tonight. We just need to do separate tasks then be as detailed as we can be." Says Emma. Olivia puts off her headphones. "Emma, I think, that we need to do this on our own. Like separate assignments." Says Olivia. "What why. I have to do this assignment on my own." Says Nina in a concerned, but also winey. "Yeah, I think so." Says Olivia. "I could probably ask if we could do it as a team in the next period with Mrs. Gates." Says Emma. "Yeah, do that." Says Nina. "Okay, do whatever you want, but don't except good news. Make sure you also except news that you might not like." Says Olivia. Nina then looks down at her phone, sighing. "Everything will be fine Nina, just ask for help if you need it." Says Olivia. "I just think I am going to screw it up. I am not good at being organized and doing this kind of stuff. I am interested in fashion and how I look like Emma says." Says Nina. Emma does not notice that Nina was talking about her at all. "See Emma is so forced into her work then I am. I don't care about working hard like Emma does. Right now, she looks like me when I am shopping." Says Nina. "Wait what. Are you saying about me?" Says Emma. "Nina is saying that she thinks that she is bad at studying and she looks at you and basically saying that you are more forced than her." Says Jade. Emma then looks at Nina. "Nina, you are smart. You did not even ask me for help once in the personally report. I think you can do this with us or alone you just need to relax your mind and just look at the question. Realize what you see with what the question is asking you to do, and just do that. I was nervous saying what was on my mind in a lower age and look where I am today. I am sure that you can do it either way Nina, but if you do need my help I will help." Says Emma. "Thank you, Emma that made me, feel a little better?" Says Nina in a questioned voice. "What, I was like you once, but not really. I feared being me because I thought I would have looked like a nerd or a loser or just the person that does not have friends, but I look around and I see my friends and I am a nerd, but not the kind I thought I would turn out to be really." Says Emma. "Wow, I did not know that you had that much belief in me Emma?" Says Nina. "I believe in you Nina. You have been a great friend to me for a long time, and you deserve the best kind of friends, even though you are more in your looks and not to your studies, but I still think of you as a great friend." Says Emma. "Wow you are full of surprises today aren't you ever." Says Nina. "What does that mean?" Says Emma. "I did not know that you could interact with people this much. I was right you are more than a person that has their face in a book, you are also a person that cares about people." Says Nina. "Thanks??" Says Emma. The last few moments for the rest of lunch break Emma were just reading her notes over again and Nina was on her phone looking at clothes and her favorite stores that the girls will be going to later maybe. Suddenly the bell rang, the warning bell to head to class. The girls get up and pack their stuff and head to their lockers to grab the important stuff for Mrs. Gates class, then they all walk toward Mrs. Gates class.

Two hours later. Class was over, and all Amy had to do is text message her mom to come and pick her up from school. Amy is going to ask if she can have a sleepover at Nina's house tonight. As Amy was done messaging Cynthia to come get her because Amy was done school for the day. A few moments later Amy's mom was in front of her. Before Amy could walk toward Amy's mom's car Jade came yelling and running toward Amy, when she got closer to Amy Cynthia looked outside of the car wondering who that was running and screaming at Amy. "Jade what is it?" Says Amy. Jade stops running and screaming as soon as Jade is panting standing there in front of Amy. "I came here to tell you something." Says Jade out of breath. "To tell me what?" Says Amy. "My ride is canceled, and I was wondering if I could get a ride. then my mom will come get me and you to drop us off at Nina's house tonight? Is that fine." Says Jade. "Yeah, that sounds like a fine plan than I can work." Says Amy. Jade and Amy get in the backseat of the car, and before they could just go. Cynthia was wondering who this person was that was in the backseat of her car. "Who are you again?" Says Cynthia. "I am Jade, Amy's friend." Says Jade. "Oh, you are that girl that let Amy in your group, thank you for that." Says Cynthia. "No problem your daughter is a nice person, but anyway I got everything for the sleepover at Nina's house tonight. Did Amy tell you that me and her are going to a sleepover tonight?" Says Jade. "No, she did not tell me that." Says Cynthia. "I kept forgetting to tell you, but then I was thinking it was better to tell you in person. So, can I go with Jade to Nina's house for the night." Says Amy. Cynthia looks at the backseat of her car, and Cynthia looks deep into Amy's eyes. Cynthia starts to go back and see her beautiful daughter's eyes when she was a baby, Cynthia could not start a fight with those eyes. Cynthia sighs. "Yes, you can go, but you must tell me next time okay." Says Cynthia. "Thank you, mom. I love you." Says Amy. Cynthia turns back toward looking at the front of the car which is the road. Cynthia continues to drive, and Amy and Jade were talking about school, the group and the sleepover. Suddenly time threw. Amy and Jade suddenly looked out the car window. They were at Amy's house. Cynthia gets out of the car and gets the groceries out of the trunk. Amy and Jade get out of the car walking toward the house, Cynthia was behind them with bags. Amy left the door open for Cynthia, so she can close the door behind her. Amy shows Jade around the house saves her room last for the tour. Once the tour was done Amy and Jade walk toward Amy's room. Jade grabs out her phone, opens a message app. "I am going to message mom to come and get us." Says Jade. "Hey, mom can you come and pick me up at my friends house it might take awhile to get to it, the driveway is long. Like an hour long, but before you come and get me can you pack me my sleepover stuff and bring it with you because me and Amy are going to have sleepover at Nina's house." Says Jade. "Yeah okay, I will just look on the app that I can track you on. Or easier just send me the address of where you are right now." Says Jade's mom. "Okay, I will send it in a second." Says Jade. Jade gets out of the messaging app and goes into a tracking app and copy and pastes it to Jade's chat with her mom. "Okay I will see you two soon, be ready." Says Jade's mom. "Okay, love you see you soon." Says Jade. Jade puts her phone in her pocket. Amy and Jade sit around Amy's room talking about the girls. Finally, two hours later Jade's mom arrives at Amy's house. "Honey, Jade's mom is here to pick you guys up." Says Cynthia. "Okay, we are pretty much ready." Says Amy. "I will meet you out there Amy. I just need to chat with mom for a few." Says Jade. As Jade walks out of Amy's room out to where her mom is. Amy gets into different clothes and looks around her room to make sure she did not forget anything. Amy walks out of her room, walking toward the outside of the house. Amy sees that Jade and her mom were talking. Amy pretends that she didn't hear anything about what they were talking about. Jade walks away from her mom and her mom is walking into the car to start the car. Then Jade walks in the back seat of the car. "Okay, Jade. Where are we going?" Says Jade's mom. "We are going to Nina's house. Do you know where she lives." Says Jade. "Yes, I know where Nina lives, you made me drive you to her house loads of times." Says Jade's mom. "I know, you have." Says Jade. Jade's mom makes a sigh noise and starts her car driving toward Nina's house. As Jade and Amy talk in the back seat of the car, once again they were talking about the girls in the group. They talked about that for awhile then they started talking about Mrs. Gates.

Three hours later they arrived at Nina's house. It was huge. There was a pool, a gate that buzz you in and it opened as soon as it saw our car. Amy and Jade get out of the car. Jade gets her stuff out of the trunk and Amy puts all her stuff on her back. "Mom, I will see you tomorrow love you. Thank you for also dropping me and Amy off." Says Jade. "No problem honey I will see you tomorrow after school." Says Jade's mom. Then Jade closes the trunk as soon as Jade closed the trunk. Jade's mom drove away. Then Nina was walking out the front door to see who was here first. "Oh, hey guys." Says Nina. "Hey. Nina. Is anyone else here?" Says Jade. "No not yet. But I am glad you guys are here. I am starving." Says Nina. Nina, Amy and Jade walk into Nina's home. Nina gives Amy a tour around her house. It feels like it takes awhile, and it does take awhile. Amy, Nina and Jade go to Nina's bedroom to drop off their stuff. Amy looks around Nina's room it's beautiful it has four couches. "That is a lot of couches Nina." Says Amy. "I know right. Since I have sleepovers more, I told dad to get me four couches in my room, so lots of my friends don't have to sleep on the floor." Says Nina. Amy looks around more Nina's room. Amy thinks of Nina's room very luxurious and big. There was a balcony as well, but it was small, but still had enough room for one person to sit out there eating or just chilling out there. "So, what do you guys want to do while we wait for everyone else?" Says Nina. "I have no idea, but this place never fails to blow my mind." Says Jade. "I know right, I LIVE HERE." Says Nina in loud scream. But it was a happy scream. "Lady Nina. I think a friend of yours is here." Says a maid. "Is that a maid?" Says Amy. "Yeah, her name is Jasmine, she is the nicest and the only maid here." Says Nina. "Oh, stop it Lady Nina." Says Jasmine the maid. "Alright let's go see who else made it at a decent time." Says Nina. As Nina, Jade and Amy walk toward the front door to see who else is here. Nina opens the gate to let them in, and then walks out of the front door to see it was Emma. "Emma, you made it. I am glad." Says Nina. Nina opens her arms to hug Emma. Of course, Emma was not paying attention she was reading her notes that the assignment was about. Then Emma gets out of her trance as soon as Nina's arms touched her. "Oh, I am here." Says Emma in a laugh. "Yeah, you are." Says Nina. Then Emma's mom's car makes a honk noise, and everyone saw a wave out of the driver's seat window. Then the gate closed right behind the car. "Well, let's get that bag in my room Emma." Says Nina. Emma was totally not paying attention again; she was focused on reading the notes. As soon they go inside the gate buzzer makes a noise. It was Eva's mom's car. Nina pushes the button to let her mom in. Eva's mom pulls up to the front door. As Eva opens the car door, she gets all her baggage out of the car. "Eva why do you have so much stuff? It's not like you to bring you this much." Says Nina. "I am about to organize it, cause half with stuff is my sport stuff." Eva throws stuff that apparently, she does not want to bring with her in for the sleep over, then suddenly a ball falls out of the bag she picks it up and puts it back in the car. "Eva seriously you need to organize your bags more. I need to go." Says Eva's mom. "Sorry, but I just have so many sports to play." Says Eva. As Eva organizes her bags someone else buzzes in to let them in. Nina walks up to the button and pushes it. Finally, Olivia was here the last one. Her dad dropped her off, and then gets out of the car. Closes the car door and walks to the front of the house with her bag on her back. Olivia's dad waves at Olivia. "Bye Dad, love you." Says Olivia. "Oh, your dads back home?" Says Nina. "Yeah? He is. He just got back last night." Says Olivia. "What tour was he on now?" Says Nina. "He was on the most forgetful one. I don't really care about it that is why I forgot about it." Says Olivia. "Alright then, you are still having trouble with your dad." Says Nina. "Yeah, he is excepting me to want to leave to go on tour with him and leave my life behind for awhile. I am busy to; I have school and friends here." Says Olivia. "Yeah, that is a good point, but didn't you always want to go on tour with music you love music. Music is your life." Says Jade. "Yeah, you are right, but I am trying to pass middle school first." Says Olivia. "Eva, are you done yet?" Says Nina. Eva turns around with one bag and the rest that she had packed up and she picks up the ones that she is not using and puts them in the trunk. Eva closes the trunk with all her sport stuff. "Okay mom you can go now." Says Eva. "Thank you, also can you shut the car door please." Says Eva's mom. "Oh, right sorry." Says Eva. Eva closes the car door. As soon as Eva shuts the door her mom drives away. Then everyone was at Nina's house for the night, and they all walked up to Nina's bedroom. Nina shuts the door behind them and then walks over to Emma. "Hey Emma, do you have your notes?" Says Nina. Emma looks up to see that everyone was looking at Emma. "Yeah, right here?" Says Emma. "I just want a little help with the assignment that is all. To be honest, I think everyone wants your help in the group." Says Nina. All the girls look away in shame for a second then they all look back at Emma in her eyes and Emma knows what those looks are on there faces. "Okay, you all need to write more notes down and pay attention in Mrs. Gates class. I love having you guys as friends, but at this point I feel again that you are using me for my smarts." Says Emma. "I am sorry that you feel that way, but its not true Emma. I just like to work as a team sometimes. I am not good on my own lots of times. I am good on my own when it is about fashion, but when I must do these kinds of assignments. I am lost." Says Nina. Emma pauses for a second. Emma realizes that Nina was telling the truth because every time there seemed to be an assignment Nina would come to Emma for help all the time. Emma just did not know why, but now Emma knows why. Because Nina is not fully independent. Emma then puts down her notebook in her bag and walks toward Nina, to hug her. "Hey, Nina you are smart in your own way. It's just. I think that you are scared to do something that you are not interested in doing, that is why you don't like doing these kinds of things." Says Emma. Nina just stands there looking at Emma, as if she has never seen the world before and just found something amazing to be inspired about. Nina then starts to tear up a little bit, because of what Emma said. "Don't worry these are happy tears. I just need to think about what you just said to me. Because this might help me. I am going to think about trying on a new skirt or shirt or something that looks ugly. So, I am going to try working on my own and reading the questions. If I don't like the price, I will find a better price for my decision." Says Nina. "Wow you just made a very good opinion for your side of things, that is amazing." Says Emma. "I did. I DID." Says Nina in a loud happy voice. "Well, think I want to try to get far in the assignment what do you guys think?" Says Nina. "I thought we were going shopping or whatever you wanted to do?" Says Olivia. "Yeah, but that can wait. I am amazing at shopping, but I got to try what Emma does." Says Nina. "Okay, I was just wondering if I was talking to a different Nina, or something because she never says no to a flash sale." Says Olivia. "I will never say no to that, but school does not last forever, so I want to get this done first before shopping. If that is okay with everyone." Says Nina. Everyone does not argue with what Nina wants to do, so they get their notebooks and start studying for this new assignment that Mrs. Gates gave to them today.

An hour later, everyone except for Emma. Was not done. Everyone was still working hard and then there is Nina rocking the page with words and thinking faces that she makes. Everyone was surprised, even Emma was. Emma walks over to Nina to see how she was doing. Emma could almost not believe it. Nina had one more question to do, she was going to be the second one done out of everyone else. Emma was proud of Nina doing something all by herself. It looked amazing what Nina was talking about. Nina was talking about her passion for fashion and how it all helped her with her life choices. Emma walks away from Nina and walks toward the other girls sitting down on couches with there laptops out and notebooks out to. Emma hears something by Nina's workplace area and Emma sees that Nina was laying down and her pencil was in the air, as well as her hands were as well. Emma walks over to see what was wrong. "Nina, what's wrong?" Says Emma. "Emma, don't you see I did this all by myself. Aren't you proud Emma?" Says Nina. "Yeah, I am proud. Of course, I am proud of you for doing something on your own." Says Emma. "Are you guys ready to go shopping?" Says Nina. Everyone throws there work back in their backpacks. "Yeah, I think they are ready to go shopping. I think?" Says Emma. Eva pulls down her hair. Amy has never seen it down before, so Amy had a face of surprised of how beautiful Eva was with her hair down. 'Okay, I am ready to go now." Says Eva. "Girls Eva put her hair down, that means she is serious." Says Nina. "Yeah, I want to look nice. Why is this a surprise to everyone?" Says Eva. "Because you never put your hair down for anything." Says Jade. "Yeah, so. I just like my hair up in a ponytail lots of times. But when I go shopping at the mall, I like my hair down." Says Eva. "Eva we are not judging you. We are just surprised that is all." Says Nina. Eva looks around the room and sees that even Amy is surprised to see it down. "Okay let's just go." Says Eva in a laugh. "Yeah, we will be going with the ponytail less Eva tonight." Says Olivia in a laugh. "Okay, I am going to start wearing my hair down more, because this is weird that all of you think it's a surprise that I have my hair down." Says Eva. "I would love to see that more." Says Olivia in a smile. "Jasmine. Can you get our driver ready to head to the mall, my favorite Mall?" Says Nina. "Yes, Lady Nina. I will go get him right away." Says Jasmine. Jasmine walks down the stairs to go find the driver that drives Nina around a lot. Nina and the group hear a car honking outside of the house. "Okay everyone the driver is ready. Let's go." Says Nina. Nina and the girls grab some money, well mostly Nina. Everyone walks out of Nina's bedroom and walks toward the front door downstairs. Nina and the girls meet up with Nina's regular driver, but since there was more than one person going into the car, the car that they were getting a lift by was a limo. The girls were mind blown for what they are seeing today. Nina's driver opens the limo car door for them. As he opened the limo door, they all basically ran into the limo fast. Everyone sat down in the limo in comfy seats. Then the driver shuts the limo car door then walks toward the front seat of the limo. The driver opens the window connected between the drivers and passengers in for the back seat of the car. "Where to Lady Nina?" Says the driver. "My favorite Mall, Mark." Says Nina. "Alright. Let's get going shall we." Says Mark the driver. Mark closes the window in between of the back seat of the limo and the driver's seat. Mark then starts the car. In the back seat of the limo the girls are talking about the mall. Nina was very excited to pick out new clothes for Emma, and the other girls.

An hour later they arrived at the mall that Nina was talking about. It is 9pm and the Mall is still open. Nina says it stays open till 12 in the morning that is why Nina loves this mall. Nina and everyone get out of the limo, Mark walks up to Nina. "Lady Nina I am just going to go to park the limo in a safer area. I will be back." Says Mark the driver. "Alright, but you can go do something that you like." Says Nina. Nina gives 50 bucks to Mark. "Go enjoy yourself Mark." Says Nina. "Wow you don't have to do this Lady Nina." Says Mark the driver. "Mark, you can just call me Nina, you don't have to call me Lady Nina." Says Nina.

"Why are you being so nice?" Says Mark the driver. "You deserve it. You drive me everywhere for me. It's the least I could do, for you." Says Nina. "Thank you, so much." Says Mark the driver with a smile on his face, and about to hug Nina. Nina hugs back. Mark let's go of Nina and gets back in the car to find a better parking space. Nina walks back toward her friends to show them around the mall. "Well, what do you guys think?" Says Nina. All the girls except for Nina were mind blown about how big this mall was and there were many people in the building shopping in many of the clothing stores. Some were also buying dinner with there children then the other half was leaving for the day. "So, what do you guys want to do first." Says Nina. "I think we should eat." Says Olivia. "Yeah, I am sort of hungry myself." Says Jade. "Alright we will eat first then we will go SHOPPING!" Says Nina. The girls walk toward Nina's favorite fast-food area to eat some food before shopping. Nina pays for everyone's food because she knows that most of them don't have money. The girls go take a seat in the food court to eat some dinner, as they do that everyone talks about how excited they are. Most of the group has never been in the mall before besides Nina because her dad is rich and wealthy. 30 minutes later the girls were done eating, they threw out the garbage in the trash bins from there food. "What store do think is the best to go in first?" Says Emma. "That store right there." Says Nina. As she was pointing at a store that sold clothes. They walked toward the store. When they got inside the store, the theme was very luxurious. But also, very modern. "Wow this place is amazing." Says Eva. "I know right, this is the store that I brought these earrings and my clothes basically." Says Nina. "I still can't believe this is the place that you hang out." Says Olivia. "Well, I am going to go look for something for me to wear tomorrow at school." Says Nina. Nina walks away from the girls to look at her favorite area in the store. "So, where should we go look first." Says Jade. "I have no idea; I am sort of worried about Emma right now. Because she has never shopped like this before." Says Eva. "I have shopped like this before." Says Emma. "Really when?" Says Jade. "I shopped like this once with my mom, but I never really touched any of the clothing." Says Emma. "Well, I am going to go try on something." Says Eva. Eva walks away and finds the interesting part that she likes, there was sporty wear to the left of the store. "Yeah, I am going to go somewhere in the store. I am looking for something to have as a dress maybe." Says Olivia. "I never pictured you wearing dresses." Says Jade. "Well, I wear them." Says Olivia. Olivia walks away toward the same direction that Nina went toward to. "I am just going to go find Nina, I guess, she can show me what to do with this place." Says Emma. Emma walks away from Jade and Amy. Now it was just Jade and Amy deciding where they are going to go. "Well, where do you want to go, Amy?" Says Jade. "I have no idea, there is many things to look at." Says Amy. "I agree with that, but I am looking for farming stuff. Maybe there is something in here that can work." Says Jade. Jade looks around the store to search around if there was any trousers or Plaid shirts. At some point Jade saw something that looked like what she was looking for. Jade walks toward the thing that she thinks that is what she is looking for. Amy stands there looking around, she does not really need anything, but she just starts to wander around looking at random clothes. Then Amy spots something that looks nice. Amy picks it up and it was a skirt of some sort. The skirt was black and white. It also sort of looked plaid themed it looked beautiful. Amy went looking around to finding a changing room, but instead she found Nina looking at boots or shoes. Emma was looking at what Nina was doing. Amy heard that Nina was saying to Emma that she needs to grab something that she likes. Emma was looking around lost like a puppy. Then Nina picked up some shoes that looked like Emma's kind of shoes. Emma than sat down and tried them on. "So, what do you think? Do you like them?" Says Nina. Emma stands up to walk in them, it was a little hard for Emma because the shoes were heels and Emma was the kind of girl that does not really wear fancy shoes or heels in general. "Nina I can't walk in these; they are not what I am used to." Says Emma. Emma then starts to fall over a bit, Nina catches Emma as she was about to fall on her face. "I got you, it's okay. I had a hard time with heels to but look at me I am great at it now." Says Nina. "Nina I am not you. I will never be you. You are beautiful." Says Emma. "Emma, I was about to give up on walking in these kinds of shoes, but I never gave up because I really liked my first heels and I always wanted to wear them everywhere I went. Even at school, but I don't wear heels at school anymore because they make my feet hurt." Says Nina. "But Nina. I can't walk in these kinds of shoes. I am bad at something that I never tried before. I was born smart. Not born pretty." Says Emma. Emma sits down. "I must tell you something no one knows this about me, but my family does know about this but. I was you once. I was smart, well not as smart as you. Maybe when I was a baby, but when I was in grade 1. I got the best mark in math and science in the class. Then when my dad divorced my mom, I was depressed, and I became not smart anymore. Then a year later my dad got married again to my stepmom I don't like my stepmom, but she made me like this. She made me not smart; she made pretty and available to walk in heels than she trained me to run in high heels, then I became a pro in heels, but they still hurt my feet a lot, but that did not stop my stepmom from teaching me to be like her. I had my smarts from my real mom. I never see my mom anymore, so I only know how to be like my stepmom, she does not like smart people like you. She likes smart fashion ladies, and to be honest I would love it if you could teach me to be like you or my real mom again. Because I know that my real mom is not coming back. That is why I can't do anything that you do. Because I am not used to it anymore. I was when my real mom was around, but she was not around long enough for me to keep that gift that I had in grade 1. I miss those smarts because it was the only thing that I had left of my mom, but it walked away and never came back." Says Nina looking sad. Emma moves a little closer to Nina and hugs her. "Nina. It's okay. People still love you no matter what. You are perfect the way you are, it does not matter if you are not smart. I still get inspired by you. You never give up on something that you are bad at. That is the thing that keeps me going. When I first met you, Nina. I thought you were always into your looks and having popular friends, but then when you asked if I was okay that time when bullies pushed me and called me ugly, and you told them to stop bothering me. That is when I was wrong the first time in my life. You are my first real friend. Nina you are my best friend, and I am happy that you are in my life." Says Emma. Nina tears up a little bit when Emma says that. "I never had a best friend before. All my friends just leave me at some point." Says Nina in a sad voice. Nina then hugs Emma tight. Emma then hugs Nina tight. Amy walks away she does not want to ask a question from Nina right now, cause Emma and Nina were having a moment. Then

Amy found the changing rooms. Still Amy could not believe that she just eased dropped on Emma and Nina. They were very close as friends. Amy could not stop thinking about what Nina said about herself that her parents got divorced at a young age. Then her stepmom changed Nina completely into a popular girl instead of a smart girl. Amy puts on the skirt and looks at herself in the mirror. Amy then twirls around a lot. Amy likes the skirt a lot on her. Amy takes off the skirt and looks down at it and says to herself that she can not afford this. Then Nina was right outside of the changing rooms. "Hey Amy, what's up." Says Nina and Emma was behind her. "Nothing just trying on this skirt and about to put it back. Because I can't afford it." Says Amy. "I can get it for you, I have enough money to spend on you and the girls. I have maybe 10,000$ with me in my bank and in cash." Says Nina. "Wow that is a lot of money, I will pay you back, sometime." Says Emma. "No, it's fine I will buy it. on the house from me. Is there anything else you want to get?" Says Nina. Amy looks around to find something else that is to an interest to her, but she finds nothing. "No not really. I just like the skirt." Says Amy. "Okay, whatever works for you." Says Nina. "Emma, do you want me to help you find a look, remember I am giving you a make over tonight." Says Nina. "Oh, right I forgot." Says Emma in a sarcastic way. Nina laughs at Emma's eye roll and sarcastic voice. "There is so much more to look at I promise you." Says Nina. "Oh boy, I am in for a treat am I." Says Emma. "Yeah, you are girl. I am going to make sure that you look fab tomorrow for class." Says Nina. "Okay, I will do it your way tomorrow, but I am going back to my way on Friday." Says Emma. "Okay, deal." Says Nina. Nina grabs Emma's hand to show where Nina usually shops and buys her stuff. Jade comes toward Amy. "So, you found something I see." Says Jade. "Yeah, I found this skirt. I already tried it on, and it looks great on me." Says Amy. "Well, that is nice. I can't find anything in this store. I only found this that looks decent." Says Jade. Jade shows Amy that she found nice boots. "Yeah, those look nice, have you tried them on?" Says Amy. "Yeah, I tried them, that is how I decided that they look nice on me." Says Jade. "Good point." Says Amy. "Well do you want to go find where Olivia and Eva are?" Says Jade. "Sure, what the heck. Hey, Jade." Says Amy. "Yeah, what's up?" Says Jade. "Do you know what Nina and Emma's deal is?"

Says Amy. "Well, all I know is that they were the first smart and popular girl to be friends within our school. It is sweet that they are friends though. I think they don't know it, but I think they are a great team together." Says Jade. As Jade and Amy look at them looking at clothes together. Nina was putting a lot of shirts and shoes and pants in the cart that they just grabbed. "I think they are going to buy out the store to be honest." Says Jade. As Jade starts to laugh. "But I mean it. They were friends before I came in their lives. I just moved here just about four years ago, and they let me in their group, or I don't know they just started wanting to hang out with me. Well, more likely that Nina wanted to hang out with me, Eva, and Olivia then we were a group of friends that did not have friends. And that is where you came in our lives as well." Says Jade. "Well, that is cool. Where did you live before this place?" Says Amy. "I lived in the USA. Then my parents wanted to get away for awhile then we moved to Canada or in BC." Says Jade. "Wow you, came far." Says Amy. "Yeah, and I am happy that we moved out of the USA. I was starting to hate it there, but now I am going to have to go there to visit my family in spring break." Says Jade. "Oh, I see. I don't know where my parents lived before BC, but I am pretty sure that we were always in Canada." Says Amy. "Oh cool. Well, let's go find Olivia and Eva shall we." Says Jade. Amy and Jade walk around to find Eva and Olivia. Amy and Jade find them looking in the same area. They were looking at sport stuff that Eva was looking for. Surprisingly Olivia was just watching Eva try on some sweaters or pants that showed her bum a lot. Olivia would just start laughing at Eva a little. "Eva, stop making me laugh. Every time to try something on your butt looks huge." Says Olivia. "Well, I am sorry that I do squats everyday." Says Eva. "Are you trying to get a big butt or something?" Says Olivia in a laugh. "Olivia can you just go look for your dress that you said you would be looking for." Says Eva in a laugh. "I already found one that I like." Says Olivia. "Ahh, I found something that I like." Says Eva. Eva throws the pants at Olivia face to shut her up. "Hey, don't throw things at my face. You jerk." Says Olivia in a laugh. "What is going on here. Did you guys get into the sugar again." Says Jade. "No, we are just like this to each other." Says Eva. Eva and Olivia stare at each other as if they were looking for something, but then they turned away from each other and looked back at Amy and Jade. "So did you guys find anything that you like." Says Olivia. "Yeah, I found this cute skirt." Says Amy. "Oh cool. I wish I could wear skirts like that." Says Eva. "Why can't you wear skirts like that?" Says Olivia. "I just don't like wearing skirts and my mom does not like me wearing anything like that." Says Eva. "Oh, I get that, because your mom has a smile on her face all the time when she sees you in pants and not wearing anything like I do." Says Olivia. Nina and Emma walk up behind them. With Emma covered in clothes that Nina is buying for herself and Emma. "Hey guys. What up." Says Nina. "Nothing just talking. You buying the whole store or something?" Says Olivia in a sarcastic joke way and funny way at the same time. "Again, why do you do that?" Says Nina. "It's funny." Says Olivia. "Well don't you think it is getting late?" Says Jade. "Yeah, the stores are going to close, so we should probably go pay for this stuff." Says Nina. Eva puts back the pants that she threw at Olivia's face and runs up to the group. "Eva did you want those pants?" Says Nina. "No, I just wanted to throw something at Olivia's face." Says Eva in a laugh. "Oh." Says Nina in a laugh. Nina walks up to the cashier. "Amy give me that skirt, I will pay for it." Says Nina. "Okay, thanks. I owe you one." Says Amy. Amy hands over the skirt to Nina so she can pay for it. "Did you find everything tonight good?" Says the cashier. "Yeah thanks. I love shopping here." Says Nina. "I can see that." Says the cashier. As the cashier scans all the clothes that Nina is buying. Nina's total is five hundred dollars for all the clothes and the shoes that she brought for herself. "Okay that is five hundred dollars for you. You have a great night." Says Nina. "You to. Come again." Says the cashier. "Okay, Nina we got shopping done. Now what?" Says Jade. "We are going to my house, this mall likes everyone out by 11:30. It gives time for the workers to close shop, so we should get out of this place." Says Nina. Nina leads the girls to the exit of the mall back to where Mark the driver is. Mark was just across the street, Nina and the girls started walking on the road to the other side. They make it, but then Nina realizes that something dropped out of her hand. Nina puts the bags on the ground, and she runs toward it, then suddenly as Nina was picking up the bag. Nina hears a car ramming toward her, and the car was not stopping, Nina froze in spot. Then out of nowhere Emma pushes Nina out of the way. Then Emma got hit by the car instead of Nina. Nina was on the ground. Nina got one scrap, but Emma was in worse shape than Nina was. Nina then leaps over to Emma to see if she was alright, but Emma was blooding a lot and her leg looked broken. "EMMA, WHY DID YOU DO THAT?" Says Nina. "Because you... are... my... best... friend." Says Emma. Eva grabs her phone out of her pocket and calls 911. Emma passes right out after seeing that Nina was above her. Crying on her chest. Is all Emma could hear was Nina screaming and crying before passing out. Jade walks over to see if Nina was okay, Jade has never seen Nina cry before. Jade hesitates to ask if she was alright, but Jade says it. "Nina is everything okay." Says Jade. Nina keeps looking down at Emma and tears just keep forming in her eyes, dripping down onto Emma's chest. "Nina the ambulance is here." Says Eva. But still nothing no movement from Nina, she was just looking down at Emma. "Where is the kid who got ran over?" Says the paramedics. "Over there." Says Olivia. The paramedics runs toward Emma on the ground. "I am sorry, but you are going to have to move out of the way." Says the paramedics. Nina still does not move, then Jade walks over to Nina to grab Nina away from Emma's unconscious body. "Nina, come on. The paramedics need room to help Emma." Says Jade. Nina gets up finally. Jade walks her over to a seat with Nina under her arm. Amy walks over to see what was in the bag that Nina was trying to grab. Amy was sad it was her skirt in the bag. Nina then says to Amy. "I hope you are happy with the skirt that probably killed my friend." Says Nina in a mad voice. "Nina I am sorry." Says Amy. "You better be because if you where not here Emma would be fine right now. Cause that skirt dropped out of my hand. This is your fault." Says Nina getting up, getting in Amy's face. Jade stops Nina from pushing Amy to the ground. "Nina stop this is not her fault it was an accident." Says Jade. "Sure, it was. Jade, this is your fault to because you let her in our group. I don't ever want to see Amy again." Says Nina. Amy then starts to cry walking away from Nina and then running away from everyone. As Amy was running away Amy felt her power coming out. "Nina, what the heck was that. This is not Amy's fault." Says Jade. "It feels like it... you know why." Says Nina. "Why does it?" Says Jade. "Her skirt was the one that I went after, and she is new in this group. You invited her in our group. If she was not here this would have never happened to Emma." Says Nina. Jade stares at Nina in angry. "I can't believe that this is Amy's fault she did nothing but come in our group and stand there watching you almost get ran over." Says Jade. Nina walks away angry. Then Emma's unconscious body gets in the back of the ambulance car. The paramedics close the back doors of the ambulance vehicle and drive away back to the hospital. Everyone in the group except for Nina is wondering where Amy is.

Amy keeps running and running in the forest far away from where she was and then finally Amy stops in the dark forest in the middle of nowhere. Amy leaded against a tree and started crying and crying more in the dark forest alone. Her power was taking control right now. Amy lite on fire crying flames out of her eyes. Then finally Amy screamed out so loud that birds flew away in the dark sky.

CHAPTER 12

THE PRESENT DAY

"Morning Jack." Says Grim. "Morning, I was just about to summon your uncle." Says Jack. "Well, you should eat first. Let me show you where." Says Grim. "Oh, you don't have to. I just want to get this summoning over with." Says Jack, as Jack's stomach growls. "After that sound I am going to definitely take you." Says Grim. "Alright, I guess I am stuck with you for a bit." Says Jack. Jack and Grim walk toward the café for some breakfast. "Well, here is the café where everyone eats." Says Grim. Jack sees that were many, many tables taken, but there were still tables open for people to sit at for breakfast. "So, Grim when did you start doing this entire thing?" Says Jack. "I started awhile ago. I started because I need answers. Wait why do you want to know?" Says Grim. Jack pauses for a second. "I am wondering of what kind of answers your looking for. I just want to know what my friend Grim has been doing this entire time." Says Jack. "Well, it is a long story. I opened this base up because I want to know why or what I am. Exactly." Says Grim. "Oh, I see, but we know already. You are a man who, is the decent of the Grim reaper." Says Jack. Grim looks at Jack for a few seconds. "Yes, I am the decent of the reaper, but why am I?" Says Grim. "Grim I think that you are thinking too much." Says Jack. "No, I was never meant to be this person. My parents cursed me from saying my own name. You were there for that, Jack." Says Grim. "Yeah, I was and felt bad for you, but I think you need to accept who you are Grim. I know it sucks to not be able to say your name but make the most of it. You can make people fear you, because they don't know your name." Says Jack. Grim looks at Jack for a few moments then he looks at the window outside and he sees grass and trees all around them. Grim wants to be able to say his name to the world. He does not want to sound scary or be feared by anyone. He just wants freedom. "Grim, I know you hate that you can't be yourself, but just think about what I said, alright." Says Jack. Grim says nothing. Grim and Jack continue to eat their breakfast, but in silence. Jack knew that Grim was mad at what Jack said. "Well, thank you for eating breakfast with me Grim." Says Jack. Grim responses surprisingly to Jack. "No problem." Says Grim. Grim walks away after that. Jack walks to the room that Grim lend to him, for Grims Uncle skull. To summon him, to chat business to getting Reaper Skull. Getting his Shadows angels off Jack's back.

Jack walks into the abandoned room. Jack pulls out his candles and his chalks to draw a pentagram to make the summoning spell stronger. Once Jack was done drawing the pentagram on the ground he got in the center of the star. As soon as he stepped in the center the candles lit flames without Jack even near one. Jack grew horns out of his head. The pentagram started glowing. Jack did not even have to say any enchantments for the summoning spell. Suddenly a dark cloud was in Jack's face with red eyes. Then the dark cloud turned into a man with a dark black cloak, and he was holding the reapers staff. It was Reaper Skull. Jack's body floated back to the ground to face Reaper skull. Jack blends down and bows to his lord. "Reaper Skull my lord. It is a pleasure that you answered my call." Says Jack. "What do you want?! Jack." Says Skull. "I am just giving you an update of our deal. I am in your nephew's base area." Says Jack. "Good." Says skull as breathing fresh air. "Mmmm, nice air." Says Skull. "Reaper Skull, sorry to disturb your moment, but what do you want me to do now?" Says Jack. "I smell power that can GET ME OUT OF THIS CURSE, that my sister put me in of the help of Gretel the Witch." Says Skull as taking a deep breath. "What is it that you smell?" Says Jack. "I can smell my niece Amy's blood somewhere in this building." Says Skull. "Why does the person concern you?" Says Jack. "Because they are my other way out of this form. They can set me free from the realm. FIND THEM." Says Skull. "Wait." Says Jack. "What!" Says Skull. "Do we have a deal still about you getting your Shadow Angels off my back?" Says Jack. "Fine I will command them to stop. But if you mess up or fail, I will make them hunt you again, and they will kill you this time!" Says Skull. Jack gulps at how Reaper Skull said that. He feels pressure a little more. To please his Lord even more. "I will not fail. My lord, I will capture whoever I find that has your niece's blood and bring her to you." Says Jack. "Good, plan. I know who you are I see you mess up a lot. This is the one thing that you can not mess up. Jack. Now go find information. there should be information somewhere around here." Says Skull. "I am on it my lord. I will not mess this mission up." Says Jack. "Alright, I am leaving it to you now." Says Skull. Reaper Skull disappears out of nowhere. Jack's horns vanished off his head and he turned back to normal human version. Not even a trace of a demon form around.

Jack put all his candles in his secret spot then uses a spell to ease the pentagram off the floor. Jack closes the room that Grim allowed Jack to use for summoning his uncle. Jack walks in the halls around looking for his first clue and who this girl is. Jack bumps into a girl solider. As Jack got up, he noticed that she had a key card to go everywhere he would need to find answers. Jack froze time to duplicate the girl's key card and took the real one with him. As soon Jack was far away from the girl solider time unfroze. She picked up the duplication key card and she went on with her day. Jack put his key card in his pocket and walked to his guest room that he was staying for a couple days. Jack walked in to find that Grim was standing in his guest room. "Hey, what are you doing in here?" Says Jack. "I was waiting for you. How did the deal go with my uncle?" Says Grim. "It went great, the Shadow Angels are not after me anymore." Says Jack. "Jez, I think my uncle has a soft spot for you or something, because he would never let go of a demon's soul." Says Grim. "It was not that easy as you think, Grim. Me and him sort of argued for a bit, but of course I annoyed him to get him to get his Shadow Angels off me." Says Jack. "Well, you better feel lucky because my uncle does have some issues with breaking his deal at the end. So be careful. Is all I am trying to say." Says Grim. "I will. we made a great deal and he said he would back off." Says Jack. Grim turns to look at Jack in the eyes. Grim senses that Jack was a little nervous and off since the last time he seen Jack. "Are you okay?" Says Grim. "I am fine. Why are you asking me?" Says Jack. "Because you seem nervous or something."

Says Grim. "Well, I am not maybe I am just wanting a nap or meditate." Says Jack. Grim looks at Jack again. "Okay, I will come in to tell you when dinner is ready, I got to check on my niece Hazel." Says Grim. Before Grim could even get out of the door. Jack stopped Grim with a door closing spell. "Wait. You have a niece." Says Jack. "Yeah?" Says Grim. "Why is she here? Is she apart of your cult?" Says Jack. "No, she is not apart of my group. She is helping me get rid of my curse unlike what you said." Says Grim. Jack looks at Grim. Trying to not look suspicious. "How can she help you with that?" Says Jack. "We are still trying to figure out how exactly. Why are you asking this many questions?" Says Grim. "I just want to know who or what I missed in your life Grim, why is that so much to ask." Says Jack. Grim looks at Jack in the eyes. Grim sees empty eyes nothing, but fear and curiosity. "Well, I should probably go check on her. I will see you later Jack." Says Grim. Jack's door spell vanished as soon as Grim walks up to it then Grim walks out of the room. Closing the door behind him. Jack looks at the door for a few moments then realizes that he found a clue. Jack jumps up with joy. Jack walks over to his bed. As soon as he closes his eyes a third eye popped right onto his head and his horns appeared again. They were so red and at the tips they were black. Jack started meditating, is all Jack could see was black then suddenly a girl was there in his head surrounded by darkest. Jack walks up to her. "Polly, I need you to find me and meet me where I am. I need to talk to you." Says Jack. Polly turns around to see Jack. Her face did not look happy to see him. "What, Polly?" Says Jack. "Not even a hi?! Its all about business for you now. Ever since you meant Reaper skull you always wanted to be under his wing. Now you are, but you always come to see me when you need me to help you with his dirty work for him. What does he want you to do now?!" Says Polly. "He wants me to help him free him. From where he's been ban vanished to." Says Jack. Polly looks at Jack angrier then ever. "ARE YOU INSANE! Jack. There is a reason why he is ban vanished in that realm. He is more powerful than you Jack. He will take your soul. He only cares about himself. He does not care about anyone who helps him. DON'T HELP REAPER SKULL. He will make this world worse than it is." Says Polly. "Polly why can't you just help me capturing someone?" Says Jack. "What for? To help Reaper

Skull gain full freedom. Power as well." Says Polly. "Yes, but I will give you something in return and why do you care suddenly about this world getting destroyed by a dark demon lord." Says Jack. "Because the humans do not deserve that. Skull was like a father figure to me once, then I saw him kill an innocent person for more soul power. He just stud there and laughed at the human trying to defend himself. Demons are not supposed to interact with the humans. They can fight witches and other creature, but the one thing that is in the law book for us. WE don't touch humans. They are harmless and they just live and wither away. When Reaper Skull made me lose faith in him, I left to be a peaceful demon. I meant you because you were in trouble and wanting friends. I had a secret crush on you, and I let you in to only find My lord's picture's. You were wondering who Reaper Skull was and you wanted to meet him. Then when you meant him, I lost you as a boyfriend and a friend. Because you were slowly turning into him." Says Polly in a sad voice. Jack looks at Polly, walking toward her. "Hey, Polly, I still love you." Says Jack in a smile. Polly and Jack hug. Polly cries a little bit. Then Jack whispers under his breath a spell that Polly would be forced against her will and in mind control. Polly's arms let go of Jack. She stud there looking in the distance. Her eyes flickered green. "Polly, are you going to help me?" Says Jack. "Yes, I will. Help you free Lord Skull known as Reaper Skull." Says Polly still looking in the distance. "Good choice you, won't regret this. Reaper Skull will be happy to see you again." Says Jack. Jack touches Polly. Suddenly Polly and Jack were back in Jack's room in Grim's base. Jack puts Polly in the closet tied up like a person being trapped in a cage paralyzed as if someone has died in their life that was special to Polly. "Polly sit down." Says Jack. Polly sits down on the ground in the closet. Jack puts tapes on her month. "Don't make a sound, the last thing we need is someone knowing about you Polly that you are in here. But Polly sweetie I am going to shut this door, okay. I will see you tonight to plan our evil heist once I know where this Hazel is. I am going to go find her." Says Jack. Jack pushes Polly to the back of the closet and puts stuff in front of Polly to hide her. "I love you, Polly." Says Jack. Before Jack shut the door, he made a soundproof spell in the closet so just in case if the mind control spell wore off, then he thought that it would be a good idea to put another spell on the door to the closet. He casted a door knocking spell on the door as he shut the door. Jack began to realize that he forced his girlfriend to help and possibly lost her as a friend and a girlfriend, but Jack keeps moving on. He shimmered disguised himself as a solider of Grims soldiers. So, no one would ask questions of why he is in the computer room. Jack walks to the computer room. Luckily there was no one in this computer room, he opens the door with the key card that he stole from the girl solider. Jack types in Hazel. Then Jack finds lots of flies about her. Jack found out that Hazel is a project that Grim was looking for, for awhile. Then a couple days ago everyone found out that Hazel is not the guardian that they were looking for, but Hazel was something that Grim was wanting to find, but he did not know that he wanted to find her. Jack kept digging for info there was dream realm journals or files, sound clips, and more. Jack went through it all. It took a long time, but he finally knows that Hazel is possibly the decent of Reaper Skulls niece Amy. Hazel is a powerful being. Jack was running out of time for him standing in the farthest side of the computer room. So, Jack touches the computer to take this information with him in his brain. Jack finds that her room is far from where he is, but it was close to the room he was staying in. Jack walks in disguise as a Grim solider toward Hazel's room that she was staying in. Jack finally arrives of where Hazel's room is. Jack looks in the window and sees that Grim is sitting on a chair with his eyes closed. They were alone in that room, then Jack sees Hazel laying down on a flat table connected to lots of machinery. Jack closes his eyes trying to concentrate on what is in the room. Jack notices there are cameras everywhere in the room where Hazel is in. Jack thinks about how a little challenge this will be, but Jack thinks of a plan he could turn off the cameras in the room for a limited of time. Also turn off the alarm system. Jack opens his eyes again. Jack looks in the door window again, Grim was awake this time. Jack moved his head away from the window. He heard Grim coming toward the door. Jack walks away from the door so, it does not look like he was watching or spying on him. Jack walks back toward Hazel's room when no one was around to see him or ask questions. Grim was gone to out of site as well. Jack walks into the room looking around. He was not going to do anything bad to Hazel, but he was going to go in the room without cameras and look at anything that possibly was different to what he has already. He saw that there was a specker to the room, he did not touch anything, but looked the machinery to see if he could control any of the cameras. He found all the camera options available to him. He looked at the settings for the cameras times and he found exactly what he wanted, and this would make his job so much easier. Jack had an evil grin on his face then he watched when he walked in the room. Jack removed that memory of him walking in and he has a setting on to make the cameras blank when he walks out of the room. No one will know that he was in the room. Jack turns the setting on and walks out of the camera room, but before Jack could leave Hazel's room Jack just stared at Hazel while her body was suck in a trance. "I am coming, to get you later." Says Jack. Then Jack walks out of Hazel's room.

Jack was back in his guest room, and he shimmered back to his real self. There was a knock on the door. "Come in." Says Jack. Grim walked into Jack's guest room. "Hey, so your awake then." Says Grim. "Yeah, I have just been reading some books for awhile then I cleaned up after myself." Says Jack. Grim looks around to see that the guest room were clean then he looked back at Jack. "Well, you sure learned how to clean after yourself." Says Grim in a smile. "Why are you happy?" Says Jack. "I am happy I am getting close to getting myself free from this curse. I can feel it." Says Grim. "How are you getting close?" Says Jack. "I think Hazel my niece is telling me that I need to kill my Uncle Skull in his real form." Says Grim. Jack looked shocked and terrified of his lord getting killed he must warn Reaper Skull about Grims plan to end Skull's life. Grim then looks at Jack. "Hey, you okay. Jack?" Says Grim. "I just some fresh air I will be right back." Says Jack. "Wait, I also came to tell you that dinner is ready." Says Grim. "Thanks, but I think I will catch up with you later. Grim." Says Jack. "Oh okay." Says Grim. Jack opens the door and closes it behind him then runs to where he can summon Reaper Skull. Jack opens the door to the summoning room that Grim gave jack to summon Reaper Skull. Jack grabs the candles, and he draws a pentagram again on the same spot. He walks in the center of the circle. Jack floats again, but before he let Skull get summoned by Jack. Jack put a locking spell on the door to the only exit.

Jack let the summoning continue commencing. Once again there was a black cloud turning into a man like last time. Of course, it was Reaper Skull. Skull looked mad. "WHAT, this better be good Jack. I was in a meeting with important demons." Says Skull. "Trust me it is good news, but also bad news." Says Jack. "Okay, go on with it." Says Skull. "Well, okay so. I went around Grims base and found everything that seemed useful. I found who's blood you were smelling to." Says Jack. "Whose blood is it. I can still smell it." Says Skull. "It is Grims niece, her name is Hazel. I am capturing her tonight with the help of my girlfriend Polly." Says Jack. "That sounds promising, what is the bad news?" Says Skull. "I think Grim knows how to kill you?" Says Jack. Skull starts to laugh a little. "Jack I can't die. I only can die by the purest of heart and Grim my nephew he is not pure he has killed before. So, you don't have to worry about Grim touching me. I won't die or get ban vanished again from anyone. I am finally going to finish my mission." Says Skull in an evil grin. "What is your mission my lord?" Says Jack. "I am not going to tell you. You will have to get me out of this place first." Says Skull. "So, be it. I will get you out of there tomorrow." Says Jack. "Good. You will need to go to an evil secret place, but also pure place for me to get out of this place." Says Skull. "What kind of place would that be?" Says Jack. "At nightfall in a forest surrounded by evil things, such as blood, candles, a pentagram, a cave for me to waken in and a mirror for me to walk out of." Says Skull. "I know the perfect place." Says Jack in a smile. "Good I will see you later then." Says Skull smiling. "Yes, my lord." Says Jack. Skull's man form, forms back into a dark cloud then vanishes out of nowhere. Jack floats down as his horns fade from his head. Jack cleans up completely, leaves no trace of any dark magic. He puts all his stuff in the bag and this time he brings it with him since he won't need it anymore in this room. He is going to need all this stuff for the cave and the forest he is going to send Polly there to get everything ready. Jack walks back toward his guest room. Opens the door. Jack walks toward the closet where he put Polly. Jack opens the door closet to find Polly in the same spot behind the boxes that he put her behind. He moves the boxes with his powers. Jack picks up Polly and removes the tape on her face then unties her. "Polly, I need you to find a mirror and the location where we meant and fell in love. Go there and make it evil, but also pure. So, we can free our lord, Skull." Says Jack. "Yes, Jack I will go to the forgotten forest." Says Polly. Jack gives Polly the bag full of his stuff which is candles and chalk. Polly then uses her ability of teleportation to get there. Jack gets changed into different clothes and walks toward the café for supper.

Jack arrives at the café to find Grim sitting alone near where they were sitting this morning. Jack walks over there with a food tray. Jack then sits down across from Grim. "Hey. Sorry I am late." Says Jack. "It's okay, dinner takes a long time to get made. We make it the most favorited meal of the day, so we just basically started eating." Says Grim. "Of, but I thought you said that dinner was ready the last time I saw you?" Says Jack. "Yeah, I thought it was to, but the chefs took a nap and was late making dinner." Says Grim. "Oh alright. As long food is ready. I am hungry." Says Jack. "Well, I am glad that we have got food for you on time then." Says Grim. "So, Grim what were you doing all day?" Says Jack. "I was doing my job as a leader. I was making sure that we are on top of things, I visited my niece in her dream realm I talked to her about my sister for a bit. I think we are getting somewhere. Tomorrow me and Hazel are going to go deeper in her library brain." Says Grim. "Oh, I hope you guys can find what you are looking for." Says Jack. "Yeah, I want to be out of this curse then I am going to find away to awaken Hazel out of her coma that she is in." Says Grim. "Well, I hope it works out." Says Jack. "Yeah, I just want to see my niece in the flesh. Instead of in her dream land." Says Grim in sad voice. "Since when you care if you have family?" Says Jack. "I changed or Hazel has changed me. I don't know what happened for the past week now." Says Grim. Jack looks at Grim and he notices that his soul and his eyes have changed since the last time that he saw Grim. But it did not make Jack change heart for his lord he is still going to capture Hazel, Grims new joy in life. Jack sees that Grim has gone soft as well. Jack and Grim continue to chat and eat their supper in the café.

"Well, that was good food. I guess it was worth the wait then." Says Jack. "I told you my chefs here know exactly what there doing." Says Grim. "Yeah, you were right." Says Jack. "So, what are you going to do for the rest of the night?" Says Grim. "I am going to sleep early tonight. I think I might leave tomorrow morning." Says Jack. "Oh, you're leaving." Says Grim. "Yeah, I should probably go find Polly tomorrow since those Shadow Angels are not after me anymore." Says Jack. "Oh okay. Whatever works for you. I am going to miss you though." Says Grim. "Thanks for everything Grim." Says Jack. "Yeah. No problem always here to talk. I am your friend. Well, I am going to go say night to Hazel." Says Grim. "Do you think that Hazel might just want some sleep, or however she sleeps." Says Jack. "Are you saying, I should not go say good night to Hazel before bedtime." Says Grim. "Yeah, that is what I am saying. You should let her get rest." Says Jack. "Hmmm. That might be best. Hazel always seems tired. I do have some things to check on before bed to." Says Grim. "What things will you be checking on?" Says Jack. "I think in my office?" Says Grim in voice that he was suspecting something from Jack. "I was just wondering. I guess I am just curious of where you are going." Says Jack. "Are you okay, Jack? Is there someone hunting you. Cause you never care where I go." Says Grim. Jack has a slight panic in his heart. "I guess I have changed a little to." Says Jack in a smile. "Oh okay. Well, I sort of like it, but you seem paranoid." Says Grim. "I am not. I am just getting too excited that I found one of my friends after all these years." Says Jack. "Oh okay. Well, I should get going and do the rest of my night chores for a bit. Good night, Jack." Says Grim. Grim gets up from the table and walks out of the café away from Jack. After when Grim was out of the café. Jack gets up and uses his ability to see the entire base. He sees that pretty much every solider is sleeping in their quarters, but Grim was still walking toward his office. Grim then walks in his office and shuts his office door behind him. Jack walks to his guest room quietly. Once he walks into his room, he senses that an hour or so later that Grim fell asleep at his desk. Jack closes his eyes to see if anyone else was awake. He sensed that everyone was sleeping in their quarters. Jack moved in on the target. Jack transformed into his demon form. So, no one would recognize him. He was floating in his guest room. Then he decides to fake his death for Grim again. So, he duplicates himself bloody. He picks up two pillows and transforms a copy of Jack in the bed bloody and a knife stabbed right in the throat. He then floats right outside of his room and floats toward

Hazel's room. Jack goes through his pockets and finds the key card in his pocket uses it on the door to allow him in the room. Jack teleports to the alarm system to turn it off before it could even notify Grim that someone was in Hazel's room. Jack floats up to Hazel and cuts her lose off her restraints and disconnects her from the machinery. As soon as Jack heard the door open again Jack teleports himself away.

Suddenly Polly was standing in front of Jack in the middle of the forest where they first meant and fell for each other. Polly was dressed in her black cloak. Polly was looking up at Jack in his demon form. Jack then looks around to find that there were candles pentagrams everywhere and a mirror. Everything was ready for the summoning to be tonight. Jack walks over to a flat surface to put Hazel down on the flat table. "Polly is there anything you can do to get Hazel to free Skull?" Says Jack. Polly looks up at him. "There is nothing you can do, you just let it happen. See it is already happening." Says Polly. The pentagrams were starting to glow red, black and blue. Then the mirror glowed. Someone was walking out. It was Reaper Skull. Polly and Jack bowed to there Lord. "I AM FREE. Finally." Says Skull in a deep breath of fresh air.

CHAPTER 13

FREEDOM AND THE AWAKEN
OF THE LOST SOULS

"Welcome back my lord." Says Jack. Skull looks at Jack and Polly. Skull then turns around to see his great niece on a flat table. "My great niece, I am here now." Says Skull in an evil grin.

It was still night fall, Grim wakes up sensing trouble. Once he opens his eyes to see that he fell asleep on his desk again. He looks at Hazel's room camera. Grim sees that she was not there. He watches the camera video to see what happened. Grim saw a demon floating in all the hallways to Hazel's room it was big and red. The demon had big horns out of his head, the horns were red, but the tips of the horns were black. The demon also had an eye on his head that glowed light blue. Once it walked into Hazel's room, he pulled off the restraints off Hazel, like they were nothing. The demon disconnected the wires as well like they were nothing. The ending was when the demon picked Hazel up and disappeared out of thin air, as if he was never there. Grim throws papers at the walls in frustration. Suddenly someone says hello. Says Skull. Grim looks up and sees the impossible. "Hello Nephew, ready to join the end of the world." Says Skull in an evil grin. Grim gets up from his chair. "No, how are you here?!" Says Grim. "I am here because your friend Jack betrayed you. He is that demon who took your niece. Now I have her, I am going to awaken her. Oh, and say hey to Robert for me." Says Skull. Before Grim could run at him, Skull disappeared out of nowhere. Grim was screaming in angry. The scream from Grim was so loud that everyone in the base woke up. One solider came walking in. "What's wrong sir, I heard a loud scream." Says a solider. Grim looks at the solider in much angry, not at him though, but at his stupidity. Grim could not believe that he could trust his friend Jack. He has lost faith in his old friends. All of them, but he has not lost faith in one family member. Grim looks for his phone book that he has for important emergencies. He picks up his phone, types in a number. "Hello?" Says Robert. "Brother, it's Grim. We need to chat." Says Grim. "What, how did you get my number?" Says Robert. "I have it written down. I have some scary and horrible news." Says Grim. "Okay?" Says Robert. "First, I am sorry for everything. Robert. Uncle Skull is back." Says Grim. "WHAT, HOW." Says Robert. "He somehow got to convince my old friend Jack to capture…" Says Grim. "Who did Jack capture?" Says Robert. "Your daughter Hazel. She was apparently powerful enough to let him out of the realm he was suck in for years and now he is going to possibly do horrible things." Says Grim. "POSSIBLE, He has my daughter. Grim. I have not seen my daughter for two weeks because you captured her. I thought I could trust you." Says Robert. "YOU CAN. JUST GIVE ME A CHANCE." Says Grim. Grim hears a sigh from his brother Robert. "Fine, I will give you a chance. Just don't get Hazel killed." Says Robert. "Thank you, Robert." Says "Grim. I am coming back to your base. I am bringing Hazel home." Says Robert. "Dad, who are you on the phone with?" Says Luna. "Okay, I will send you the address where I am." Says Grim. "Okay thanks." Says Robert. "I got to go, right now though. I will see you soon Robert." Says Grim. "Yeah, see you soon Grim." Says Robert. Robert hangs up the phone. "You were on the phone with Grim?" Says Luna. "Yeah. I was." Says Robert. "What is going on, heard something about Hazel getting captured by someone." Says Luna. Robert sighed. "Yeah, Hazel was captured by my uncle Skull. He is way more dangerous than Grim." Says Robert. "What is Skull going to do?" Says Luna. "What he always wanted." Says Robert in a feared voice. Robert and Luna arrive in their town an hour later. They drive into the driveway at there house. Luna gets out of the car running inside to pack to get ready to leave to get Hazel back. "Luna where are you going?" Says Robert. "I am coming back with you, to save Hazel. From Skull." Says Luna. "NO, you are staying here. Look after Lee for me. Please." Says Robert. "DAD I AM COMING WITH. I am not leaving Hazel again in the dark." Says Luna. "No, Luna my

uncle is way to dangerous to deal with. Me and Grim will handle this."
Says Robert. Robert walks out of the house starting the car and driving
away faster than he has ever before. Robert put the address that Grim
sent to him in his phone track app and started driving there.

Lee wakes up hearing yelling from downstairs. It sounded like Luna
and dad were home. Lee walked downstairs, finding Luna hitting the
wall with her hand. Lee was confused about what was going on. "Luna,
what's going on?" Says Lee. Luna looked over at Lee on the stairs. "Oh,
nothing just dad did not take me with him to go get Hazel back." Says
Luna. "What are you talking about?" Says Lee. Luna sighed. "You see
Hazel was captured by Grim and dad's uncle." Says Luna. "Oh. Dad
will get her back I know it." Says Lee. Luna just walked away from Lee.
Luna was not in a hopeful mood. She just wanted to know that Hazel
was going to be okay. Luna just walked up the stairs not saying anything
else to Lee. "Alright, I guess I will go see Sam. Make sure she is alright."
Says Lee. Lee looks around. Lee walks into the kitchen making food,
going up the stairs packing some stuff to head to the hospital to go see
Sam. Once Lee was done eating food and packing his stuff and heading
to the hospital to see Sam.

Once Lee arrives at the hospital. Lance was there of course, Lance
noticed Lee walk in. "Hey, Lee." Says Lance. "Lance, I don't mean to
be rude or anything, but Sam told me not to talk to you." Says Lee. "I
was just going to tell you that Sam had stitches last night, I thought you
would like to know." Says Lance. Lee's face changed. Lee then ran down
to the hall to Sam's room. Lance thought about chasing Lee, but Lance
just let Lee go. "Doctor, can I see Sam?!" Says Lee. "You are Lee, right?"
says Doctor Collins. "Yeah, I am. I heard Sam had stitches last night. I
just want to make sure she is okay." Says Lee. "Yeah, for sure. I will lead
you to her room." Says Doctor Collins. Doctor Collins leads Lee down
the hall to Sam's room. Once Lee saw Sam laying down on her bed.
He ran to her. "Are you okay?" says Lee. "Yeah, I am fine. Why are you
here?" Says Sam. "I am here, to make sure you are alright." Says Lee.
"Well. I am fine." Says Sam. "Are you mad at me or something?" says
Lee. Sam just looked in the distance, not saying anything. Lee looked

over at Doctor Collins. "Is she okay?" Says Lee. "Yeah, she is just tired. Sam did not get any sleep last night." Says Doctor Collins. Lee looked back at Sam. "Sam, are you doing, okay?" says Lee. Sam looked back at Lee. "I am just tired. That's all." Says Sam. As Sam continues to look into the distance again looking at nothing. Lee just put his hand onto Sam's hand. "I will leave you guys then. I have some patients to catch on." Says Doctor Collins. "Sam, talk to me" says Lee. Sam just kept staring into the distance looking into nothing. "I don't know how to talk to you, right now." Says Sam. "What does that mean. Are you mad at me?" says Lee. "I just said no, I am not mad at you. I am just tired. Maybe it's best if you leave me alone for the day…" Says Sam. "I am not leaving you alone. After I heard you had stitches last night. I want to make sure you are alright." Says Lee. "Lee, I am fine, I just want to be alone. Also, those stitches were from a long time ago… My dad gave those stitches to me." Says Sam. Lee looked at Sam funny. "What do you mean, your dad gave you those stitches a long time ago." Says Lee. "Lee, he just stabbed me in my side okay. Now you know, can you leave me alone. Please…" says Sam. Lee just stared at Sam. Not knowing what to say. "I am sorry. Sam, I had no idea…" says Lee. "Of course, you did not. You just met me." Says Sam. "Sam, I want to be here for you." Says Lee. "Lee, can you please leave me alone…" says Sam. Lee got up and walked out of the room. Not knowing what to do now. Lee just went into the waiting room for a bit.

Luna walks down the stairs. "Lee, are you still here?" says Luna. There was no response. "Okay, I guess I am going to work then." Says Luna. Luna gets ready to head over to work. As Luna gets her coat on and starts walking to work. Luna starts to think about Hazel and her dad. Luna was worried, about Hazel. As Luna walks into her job. Eva saw that Luna opened the door wearing her work uniform. "Eva." Says Luna. "Luna, you are okay." Says Eva. "Yeah, I am okay." Says Luna in a sigh. Eva looks at Luna. "Are you sure?" Says Eva. "Yeah, I am fine I am just worried about somethings." Says Luna. "Do you want to talk about it?" Says Eva. "No, I should not. It would be hard to explain." Says Luna. "Give me a try I am sure that, I can try to understand." Says Eva. Luna looks up at Eva. Luna could see curiosity in Eva's eyes, but also

175

the one person that would not understand. Luna changes the subject. "So, what do you want me to do today?" Says Luna. Eva knew that Luna was changing the subject, but Eva gives Luna a task to do for work today. Luna walks over to the sign in machine, so she can get recorded into the system. As Luna started to arrange flowers for the showing area, so that people can see what kind of flowers the store sells. When Luna was just about to finish. She hears her name being called. Luna looks around to find no one around calling her name. Eva was in her office ordering flowers for her shop. Luna continues working on the stage for showing the flowers in the window for Eva's shop. But then Luna hears her name again. "Luna, it's Hazel." Says Hazel. "Hazel, You are okay! And how are you talking to me?" Says Luna. "I am fine, I am just weaker. This Lord Skull guy is, making me weaker. I feel like something is being taken away from me." Says Hazel. "What do you feel?" Says Luna. "I feel empty, but very weak." Says Hazel. Suddenly Luna gets a vision of something. Telling what happens or what did happen. "Luna are you still there?" Says Hazel. "Yeah, sorry. I think I might know what happened to you." Says Luna. "What happened to me?" Says Hazel. "Something is telling me that maybe Skull took your soul, and he is trying to switch your soul and you to the evil side." Says Luna. There was nothing, but silence until. A scream loud in Luna's ears that Hazel screamed about. Oww. Hazel that hurt. Says Luna. "Sorry, something pinched in my heart." Says Hazel. "Skull is getting closer to getting you on his side. Where are you!!" Says Luna. "I don't know I can't see anything, but my realm that I have been in a coma since." Says Hazel. "Right, Hazel try to concentrate to the outside world. I know you can hear them, but you need to try to focus on what you can see." Says Luna. "Okay, I will try." Says Hazel. Luna could hear a deep breath from Hazel in her ear. Suddenly there was nothing, but silence from Hazel's side. Luna was starting to think that it worked or that Luna might have got Hazel in trouble even more. "Hazel, are you still there?" Says Luna. "Yeah, I am just trying to see." Says Hazel. Hazel could see candles everywhere, pentagrams, a forest, and a cave. "I can see outside my head. How did you know I could see outside my head?" Says Hazel. "I just had a feeling." Says Luna. "Well, what else do you have feelings about?" Says Hazel. "I have no idea." Says Luna. Hazel then sees someone walking toward Hazel's coma body. Hazel saw that her eyes were still closed, but there was huge scary red person coming toward Hazel. The red person picked Hazel up and took her toward two other people. A woman and another man. Hazel could hear what they were saying. "Place her down right on that flat table." Says Polly. The red person places Hazel down on the flat gray table. Hazel could see now that her body was placed in a cave where there were more candles, pentagrams all over the wall, and a mirror. There were green vines, a hole in the cave leaving it big enough for the sun to be right on Hazel's face. The woman puts something on Hazel's wrists to keep her pinned, they also put the same on her ankles. They were strong throne vines, she just put them on with power that Hazel has barely seen before. "Hazel are you still there?" Says Luna. "Yeah, I am still here. My body is restrained to a flat gray table that is in a forest somewhere, and we are near a cave." Says Hazel. "I am coming to find you, Hazel." Says Luna. "But how are you going to find me? We don't even know these people. I think I might not want you to come find me. Stay where you are. Where is dad?" Says Hazel. "He has gone to Grim's base, to try to get you back." Says Luna. "Text dad to tell Grim not to come. I don't want anyone else to die." Says Hazel. "What are you talking about? Who else died?" Says Luna. "Doctor Whales." Says Hazel. "Yeah, but he was letting Grim in the hospital. If Grim that Doctor Whales really wanted to protect, he would have, but him letting Grim in the hospital to just take you. Shows me that he did not care, and he just wanted power." Says Luna. "You are right, but Doctor Whales was still a person." Says Hazel. "I am coming, I don't care what you say, or dad says. I am coming to get you out of this." Says Luna. Hazel does not say a word to Luna. Mostly because Hazel can't stop Luna from coming to get Hazel out of this mess. "I just have to tell Eva about this. I am not going to say what I am doing." Says Luna. Luna finishes the task that she was asked to do. She gets out of the show stage display area for Eva shop. Luna walks toward Eva's office. "Hey, Eva are you off the phone." Says Luna. "Yeah, I am done ordering flowers. There is a big sale day tomorrow. Are you done with what I asked you to do?" Says Eva. "No, I am done I just wanted to ask you a question." Says Luna. "Oh okay, what is the question?" Says Eva. "You can fire me, but I need to take three weeks off. I am sorry, but there is something going on and I need to help." Says Luna. "Wow, Luna. I am not going to fire you. I just thought you were coming back." Says Eva. "Yeah, I was, but I can't be normal right now. My family is no longer normal." Says Luna. "Well, okay if that is how you feel, I will let you take as long as you need. I want you to feel a little normal. Once you get your issue fixed with your family. I will be happy to let you come back here to work. You are always welcome here." Says Eva. Luna stares at Eva in happiness. Luna did not expect Eva to say this was okay. Luna finishes saying goodbye to Eva for awhile. Luna started walking back to the house. "Hazel what is happening now?" Says Luna. "I feel something in my heart. Wait there saying something." Says Hazel. "Lord Skull, why do we need Hazel. Why don't we kill her." Says Jack. "We need Hazel because she is my great niece. Hazel. She could help make my plan work better and easier." Says Skull. "How could she make it better she is in a coma?!" Says Jack. Skull's eyes glow red even brighter with rage that Jack was basically saying that Hazel was useless. "What did you say, about my family's blood!?" Says Skull. Jack stops talking. "Sorry, my lord for disagreeing with you." Says Jack in a feared voice. Skull looks back at Polly. "So, Polly can you do anything to awaken my great niece?" Says Skull. "I could probably go into her head and see her in her dreams." Says Polly." Good, get to that than." Says Skull. "Okay, I will go into Hazel's head." Says Polly. Polly walks toward Hazel and puts her hands on Hazel's head. Then closes her eyes. Hazel lost connection to Luna. Polly was then in Hazel's dream land. Hazel also loses connection on the outside world. Polly walks over to Hazel. Hazel is for some reason terrified of what is about to happen. Polly stops right in front of Hazel's face. "Hello, Hazel. I am here to help you get out of your coma." Says Polly. Hazel was trying to get out of Thorne vines just like the ones that they have her restrained on the outside world. Polly puts her hands on Hazel's head to relax her from struggling too much. Once that was done. Hazel was relaxed and Hazel could feel something awaken in her again. But something different was awakened inside. Hazel's eyes closed then. Polly concentrated all her power to get Hazel out of her coma. Then there was a glow of light blue in Hazel's realm. Hazel was in the restraints on the gray flat table in the cave. She did not see purple mist anymore. She was free from her coma. Hazel's eyes then opened fully. Polly then walks away from Hazel's awakened body. Hazel can feel the thorns stabbing her in her ankles and her wrist. Then a big man walks into Hazel's view not the red guy, but the black-haired guy and the red eyes. That was Lord Skull. Hazel tries to struggle to get out of the thorned vines, but she could not get out of the vines. "Why are you struggling my child?" Says Skull. Hazel just looks at the people around her looking down. Skull notices the black wings that he helped Amy got as well, Skull noticed that Hazel's wrist was glowing blue. Skull grabbed her wrist. "You have the same as my niece Amy. Your wings as well." Says Skull. "I am struggling because you have me pinned to a gray flat table." Says Hazel. "Yeah, because I don't want you to run, and we got you out of that coma that you have been dying to get out of." Says Skull. "Yeah." Says Jack. "What do you want?" Says Hazel. "I want you to help me with my beautiful plan that I wanted to do for many, many years. You have the power to help me. That is why I have taken you, for myself." Says Skull. "What are you talking about?" Says Hazel. "I am talking about, that you have my favorite niece's power. Sadly, she died by my sister Cynthia. But I am glad that the power went to a beautiful girl like you." Says Skull. Skull caresses Hazel's hair. "I am going to awaken the lost souls. MWHAHAHA. Finally." Says Skull. "Wait you want to awaken the lost souls. DO you know unsafe that is!" Says Jack. "Jack you should know I am the Grim reaper I need souls to capture, and the lost soul army wants to grow. I can team up with them." Says Skull. "How can you make a deal with them? They ask for the most expensive prices." Says Jack. "Yeah, they do, but if we work together, they can have bodies to be inside of, in return they all can be my army to rule the universe. We are going to have to prepare for the summoning of the lost soul's kingdom. I want to talk to there king tonight. They like it when it's dark." Says Skull. Hazel tries to get connected back to Luna to warn her about the lost soul's army. "I need a quiet place to find the spell to summon them. I am going to need this place to have light magic forcefield up." Says Skull. "I will make sure, that no good magic will be used in here in coming in." Says Polly. "Good. I hate light magic it sickens me." Says Jack. Hazel loses the ability to do anything. She can't do anything now. since there will be a forefield of light magic going up around everyone in here. Hazel was the only light magic creature in this area. Skull walks back over to Hazel. "Hazel, don't fight become with evil. It will come to you because. I took your soul, but you still have rights." Says Skull as he was holding Hazel's soul in his hand with a cage around it. "Do you want your soul back? If you want your soul back, you are going to have to let me teach you the dark side, of magic." Says Skull. Hazel looks at her soul, then looks back at Skull. "NO, I don't want my soul back. I will figure out away to get out of this alone." Says Hazel. "If you say so, good luck trying to get out of demon or evil witch vines. They are super powerful and slowly draining your life force and giving more life to a dream witch." Says Skull. Hazel looks at Polly, she was glowing. Hazel was giving Polly more time to live in this world. Hazel thinks again. If Polly can get Hazel out of comas. Hazel started to think what if Polly could get people suck in comas or death. Hazel was only making Polly stronger by every little second. Skull starts to walk away. "Wait." Says Hazel. Skull turns around to see what Hazel had to say. Hazel a shameful face. But she could not just let a dream witch get stronger. "I want to help." Says Hazel in a sigh of shame. "Good, choice my child, but if you betray me, I will make sure the lost soul that goes into you suffer more." Says Skull. "Let her out of your vines Polly." Says Skull. Polly makes the vines go away off Hazel's wrists and ankles. "Now come with me, my great niece." Says Skull. Hazel gets up from laying down on the flat gray table. Skull reconjures Hazel's soul in his hand. Skull puts Hazel's soul back into her body. Hazel feels less empty inside. "Does that feel better?" Says Skull. "Yeah, it does." Says Hazel. "Good now. I need you to help me with betraying the lost soul group. I want you to be the soul control. I get to feel the souls in and apart of me, but you get to make sure that they will not know what I am doing to them." Says Skull. "What are you going to do to them?" Says Hazel. "I am going to put the lost soul army into my slaves for eternity." Says Skull. Skull and Hazel walk toward a place where Skull can concentrate on finding his spell book to summon the lost souls king.

As Lee sits in the waiting room. Texting his family to see if they are alright. He gets no messages back. Lee did not care for some reason. He was just sad that Sam was dealing with some stuff, and Sam was kicking Lee out of her space. To be alone with her thoughts. Lance walked over. "Hey, Lee. Why are you not in Sam's room?" Says Lance. "She does not want me around right now…" Says Lee. "Why?" Says Lance. "I don't know she just wanted to be alone." Says Lee. "Well, me in my opinion you should be in that room with her. No matter what she says. She used to do that to me." Says Lance. "She used to push you away?" Says Lee. "Yeah, she did it all the time. Yeah, she hated it when I would stay anyway, but she seemed fine after awhile." Says Lance. "Hmmm. Thanks Lance." Says Lee. "No problem." Says Lance. Lee gets up from the chair in the waiting room, then he walks down the hall to Sam's room once again today. Sam was laying down on the hospital bed, looking into the distance, not noticing that Lee walked in the room. Lee grabbed a chair and sat down next to Sam on the chair. Lee held her hand. Lee did not except this to happen. Sam grabbed hold of Lee's hand and pulled him close to her. Lee felt tears on his clothes. Lee said nothing, but just kept hugging Sam. As she kept crying and crying. "I am sorry. I was rude to you. I just have bad luck with people caring about me." Says Sam. "Shhh, It's okay. I am not mad at you. I am still here for you." Says Lee. Sam pulled Lee on the bed making it easy for them to hug. "Please don't leave me." Says Sam. Lee hugged Sam tight. Not too tight since Sam had stitches. Sam lifted Lee up. Sam and Lee just stared at each other. Sam put her face close to Lee, then Sam kissed Lee on the lips. Lee kissed back and pulled Sam in closer to make out with her. "I have been waiting to do that for a week now." Says Lee. "Oh?" says Sam. "I will always be here with you Sam." Says Lee. "GET OFF, Of my daughter boy." Says Sam's dad. Lee and Sam look over at the door. Sam's dad was standing at the door. "Come on, let's go Sam." Says Sam's dad. Lee felt his phone vibrating in his pocket. Someone was calling him. Lee chooses to ignore it. Sam struggles to get out of bed. When Sam got to her dad, Sam stud up looking into Sam's dad's eyes. "You are not allowed to ruin my life anymore." Says Sam. "What do you mean. Anymore." Says Sam's dad. "I am not going with you, that's what that means." Says Sam. Sam tries to walk away, but Sam's dad grabs Sam's arm and drags her out of the room. Lee gets up from the bed, following Sam. "Hey, let Sam go. She said that she does not want to go home with you." Says Lee. Sam's dad looks at Lee.

"Boy, this is not your concern. GO home and leave my daughter alone."
Says Sam's dad. Sam's dad continues to drag Sam in the hospital toward
his car, Sam was trying to get out of his grip, but he was just too strong.
"Let go of me." Says Sam. "Get in the car!" Says Sams dad. "NO." says
Sam. "What do you mean no. Girl." Says Sam's dad. "I mean no. I had
enough of you. I want to start my life from the beginning. I want to
move on from you. I want nothing to do with you." Says Sam. Sam's
dad lets go of her arm. Sam and her dad just stared at each other. Finally,
Sam's dad grabbed her arm and pushed her in the car. Sam sat down.
Wanting to cry, but she was done crying. She wanted to show strength.
"Why were you with that boy." Says Sam's dad. "Cause he actually cares
about my well-being. Unlike you." Says Sam. Sam's dad looks behind
him and stares at Sam. "What has he done that made you go against
me." Says Sam's dad. "WHAT. ARE YOU TALKING ABOUT!" says
Sam. "I am your father." Says Sam's dad. "YEAH, MY DAD THAT
BEATS ME, STABS ME, ABUSED me my entire life. I don't want
anything to do with you. Why did you come here, you don't even care
about me. Then there was Lee, he cared for me, he brought me into his
house to support me." Says Sam. "IF YOU SAY THAT NAME ONE
MORE TIME, I WILL GROUND YOU FROM EVER SEEING
THIS WORLD AGAIN." Says Sams dad. Sam just sat there in the
back seat of her dad's car. She kept holding tears back. Sam's dad then
looked at the front of the car. As Sam sat there in silence. Sam's eyes
glowed black, her hair started to float in the air. Sam screams so loud
that it blows out all the windows in the car. The glass targeted Sam's
dad. Sam was not harmed. Sam passes out in the car in the back seat.
Lee runs toward Sam in the car. Before Lee could get to Sam. There
was someone standing right outside of the car where Sam blew out all
the window's glass toward her dad. The person opened Sam's door, he
tried waking her up, but Sam was out cold. Lee got to the car, walking
up to the man. When the man touched Sam on the shoulder, he felt her
blood boiling inside of her body, the man picked her up out of the car.
"Hey, put Sam down!" Says Lee. The man looked at Lee. Lee saw that
the man was wearing a white cloak. In his other hand he had a staff
with a moon and stars all over it. The man stomped his staff on the
ground. Then a portal appeared in front of them. The man was walking

toward that portal that he summoned with his staff. Lee tries get to the man before going into the portal, and he makes it just in time to follow them into the portal. Wherever they were going, it was not earth. As they flew through the wormhole, Lee, the man, and Sam were surrounded by purple mist. Suddenly the transportation stopped in a beautiful place. Surrounding Lee with water flowing down in a colored blue when he looked around a lot of buildings were white, the sky was bright, there were stars in the sky. There were people dressed in white cloaks. Lee lost where the man went. That captured Sam, Lee walks around looking around, but then two people came up to Lee. "How did you get here?" Says a celestial guard. Lee looked at them with fear of what he is going to say. "I found a man carrying my friend Sam, and I am now looking for her." Says Lee. "I am sorry, but we are going to have to lock you up because we can not have outsiders knowing about this place." Says the celestial guard. The celestial guards take Lee to a castle where there sat a woman. Dressed in beautiful pastel white colors, her eyes were very bright blue, her hair was white as well, and Lee notices that she has a crown on her head. With a moon and the sun on it. "My queen, Nelia. We found a human that clearly does not belong here." Says the celestial guard. Queen Nelia gets up from her throne to get a close look of Lee. Queen Nelia looks deep into Lee's eyes it seems like she might only see that Lee is an enemy to them. "Look Queen Nelia I just came here to get my friend Sam back from a strange man that just picked her up and brought her here. I don't know any of you, but when I find Sam. I will take her home and not say anything to anyone about your home." Says Lee. Queen Nelia looks deeper into Lee's eyes he was full of strength, and he was committed to leave wherever he has stumbled upon. The man who took Sam was right behind the Queen of this unknown world. "Where is Sam!?" Says Lee. The man looks at Lee. "Leave us celestial guards. I want to have a little chat with this boy." Says Queen Nelia. The celestial guards leave the room, to the man and the Queen. "So, you just want to take your friend Sam home?" Says Queen Nelia. "Yeah, I will not say a word about this place." Says Lee. "Well sorry. Whoever you are. We need your friend Sam. We have been looking for her for." Says Queen Nelia. "What do you want with Sam?" Says Lee. "We want with her to be home here in our homeland. Her mother was a celestial Witch." Says Queen Nelia. "She's a celestial Witch. Why did she not tell me? And what is that, mean?" Says Lee. The man walks toward them. "She did not know. Her mother Lucy was pregnant with Sam when she just got rid of her power. Then Lucy died after two years being away from her homeland. Lucy was a warrior she was a legend here." Says the white cloak man. "She did not tell us that she had a daughter ever. Because she thought she would have gotten in trouble. Which she would have. But we still honor her to this day. We do miss her." Says Queen Nelia. Lee was looking at both people that were saying that Sam has always been like this for most of her life. "Sam just did not know that she was a celestial. So, you just kidnap someone that probably has no idea what you want from them. Sam does not like being lied to, to be honest. If you wanted to be on her good side, I would tell the truth." Says Lee. "We will when she wakes up, and we will be letting you go home. You don't belong here. In this world." Says Queen Nelia. "I know I don't belong here. I want to leave, but I want to leave with my friend Sam." Says Lee. "Well to bad. She is not leaving. She needs to stay here, to control her power" Says Queen Nelia. "Well, Sam is human." Says Lee. "I know, but she was also born to be here instead of in your world." Says Queen Nelia. Lee stands there looking defended more than ever. "I am going to go home with Sam. I don't care what you say. I will find her." Says Lee. Queen Nelia looks at Lee admiring of how brave he is to be standing up like this, but Queen Nelia must do what must be done. "GUARDS." Says Queen Nelia. The celestial guards walk in the room. "Yes, my queen." Says a celestial guard. "Take this boy to the dungeons." Says Queen Nelia. "Yes, my queen." Says a celestial guard. One of the celestial guards grab Lee by the arm, taking him to the dungeon. "What should we do about this boy, my queen?" Says The cloaked man. "We are going to keep him alive, just keeping him in the dungeon." Says Queen Nelia. "What are we going to do with Sam? My daughter?" Says the cloaked man. The queen looks over at him. "We will train her to become like us." Says queen Nelia. The cloaked man looks at the Queen worry. "I must go, now." Says the cloaked man. "Alright see you around, my sorcerer." Says Queen Nelia. The sorcerer walks toward Sam's room where she is staying in right now. Lee was being walked downstairs at this moment. Then finally they arrived down at a place. A dungeon. Finally put Lee in a cell locking him in there. The celestial guards walk away as they locked the door. Lee walks over to the bed sitting down then he put his head down on the pillow thinking about where Sam might be. In sadness.

The sorcerer walks in the room where they put Sam in for rest, to get her energy back slowly. The man with the white cloak looks down at Sam in worry. He thinks about what he is going to say to Sam when she wakes up. Suddenly Sam's eyes open slowly. Sam sees that there was a man looking down at her sleeping. Sam jumps up scared out of her mind. "Who are you !?" says Sam. The white cloaked man looked at Sam in fear, of what Sam would think about him being her father. He just says his name. "My name is Cole. I am the sorcerer here in the celestial realm, where everyone is a Day Witch/Wizard and a Night Witch/Wizard. It's a lot to take in. But you will understand soon." Says the white cloaked man. "How did I get here?" Says Sam. "I picked you up from your stepdad." Says the cloaked man. Sam looks at the man confused when he said stepdad. "Why did you just call my dad, stepdad?" Says Sam. The man looks at Sam convinced that he should tell her the truth. "I am... your... father Sam." Says Cole. Sam's jaw dropped when he said that. "NO, you can't be my father. My father was a dick. He beat me and forced me to stay in the dark from other people. You are not my father I don't know you." Says Sam. Cole looks at Sam, not blinking. Cole looked into Sam's eyes, seeing Lucy through them. Sam pauses looking at Cole. Cole looks at Sam not knowing what else to say because this was to much information toward his daughter. That did not even know that her real father is a Wizard and not a screw up like Sam's thought real father. "Sam, I know this is a lot to take in, but Queen Nelia would probably want to be talking to you right now." Says Cole. "Who is Queen Nelia?" Says Sam. "Queen Nelia is one of your mom's best friends. Well, was one of your mom's best friends." Says Cole, looking down at Sam. Sam gets up from the bed that she was resting on. Cole and Sam walk toward the throne room area. Cole opens the door to find Queen Nelia drinking some tea. "Queen Nelia. Sam Bows has wakened up from rest." Says Cole. Queen Nelia puts her tea down on the side table that she had and stud up from the throne chair.

"Morning my child." Says Queen Nelia. Sam has no idea what to say to a queen, she was nervous to say anything, so she just says nothing, but waves. Queen Nelia was a little confused, but then Queen Nelia realizes how much it is a lot to meet a queen, so she lets it side that time. The room was silent until Queen Nelia speaks. "Sam Bows, we have been looking for you for along time, we have finally found you. I want to welcome you to the celestial realm, where all the celestial Witches and Wizards live in harmony away from humans. We, well I don't like being apart of the humans. But also, it is safer for the humans to stay away from us because we control time and space. Well, we help with time and space. That is what the Time Witches do is make sure that time and space are safe and are balanced." Says Queen Nelia. Sam looks at Queen Nelia confused. Sam has never been this confused her entire life. "What does this have to do with me, I am human. Why am I here?" Says Sam. Queen Nelia turns around to look at Sam in the eyes. "You don't know that you have our abilities, do you?" Says queen Nelia. Sam looked at the queen even more confused than last time. "What are you talking about? I don't have any powers and I am not a Witch. I am human just trying to get away from my dad." Says Sam. "Well, you sure did that well." Says Queen Nelia. "What are you talking about?" Says Sam. Queen Nelia walks up to Sam and touches Sam's head. Sam then sees a vision of Sam scream and yelling then there was glass and the car's window's shattered and all over Sam's "stepdad like Cole said he was". The vision was over. Sam looks up at the queen. "So, what if it was something else." Says Sam. "It was not something else. It was your ability to defending yourself. That is the ability that I use when I am angry at someone. In fact, your mother taught me that ability." Says Queen Nelia. Sam looks up at Queen Nelia. "What you knew my mom?" Says Sam. "Yes, we were best friends. She was the most loved woman here. Everyone loved your mother, Lucy. She was beautiful, but also very fierce as fire. She moved gracefully but fast as the wind. She was everyone's hero here." Says Queen Nelia. Sam just keeps the most eye contact with the queen. She looks closer and Sam had a feeling that Queen Nelia was not lying about her mother. "What else was my mom?" Says Sam. Queen Nelia looks down at Sam. "She was always wanting to be the protector of our realm. Of course, she always impressed the previous queen of this realm before me." Says Queen Nelia. "I just want to know why. Why did she decide to come to my world, why did she not just stay here? Did she love it here?" Says Sam. "Of course, she loved it here, but she was also very curious of what other worlds were out there. She might have been also a little bit of a book worm and she also did get herself into trouble a lot." Says Queen Nelia in a sigh of laughter. "That sounds like me." Says Sam. "I am glad that some of her traits went to you. It will be fun training you to be available to control your power. It is very important to be in control of your night side and your day side, but here is the catch. You can not lose balance between yourself. You need to keep both sides of your dark side and your light side balanced. If you get one more over than the other. You will be out of control, and it will be hard for you to stay in control of what you are doing around your loved ones. That is why you are here as well. To learn how to not kill someone. Either on purpose or on accident." Says Queen Nelia. "Like I did on accident to my "stepdad" says Sam sadly. "Why do you sound so sad? I thought you would be happy that he is dead. After all we have been watching what he does to you. He did not deserve you. I wonder what Lucy saw in that man, but Lucy should have never gone to that world. I should have tried harder to keep her here in our realm. Because I knew it would have been a bad idea letting her go meet humans. It was and will always be against the law for us to travel to the other world. Your world Sam that you were raised in is just a normal world where nothing good happens." Says Queen Nelia. "That is not true. I meant someone that cares about me. His name is Lee White. He is the most caring boy I have ever meant, and I care about him." Says Sam. Sam then thinks about what Lee is thinking right now. is Sam alright or is she not okay. Sam is now wanting to go find Lee to tell him that she is fine. "I need to go back to the other world. The one that I came from." Says Sam. "Why?" Says Queen Nelia. "I want to see Lee. I want to tell him that I am okay." Says Sam. Queen Nelia turns back to look right in Sam's eyes. "I think that is the boy that followed my sorcerer in his portal to get here." Says Queen Nelia. "Wait, are you saying that Lee is here?! Where is he?" Says Sam. "We have him in the dungeons where he belongs." Says Queen Nelia. "NO, HE does not belong there. You don't even know Lee." Says Sam. "I do know that he is a foolish boy who is in love with a Celestial Witch." Says Queen Nelia. "I want to see him now." Says Sam. "No, you are not seeing this Lee that you have named out to be a human." Says Queen Nelia. "TAKE ME TO LEE, RIGHT NOW. OR I AM LEAVING WITH LEE IN THE MORNING." Says Sam. Queen Nelia sighs at Sam. "Fine I will take you to his cell in the dungeons." Queen Nelia walks Sam to the dungeons cell rooms. Finally, they arrived at Lee's cell. Sam looks in the cell. Sam sees that Lee was laying down on the bed looking at the ceiling. "Lee!!!" says Sam. Lee turns toward the cell door and sees Sam standing right in front of his cell door. "Lee are you alright?" Says Sam. "Do I look fine. I am locked in a cell, and I have no idea who you are anymore. I am just confused that's all." Says Lee. "I am confused as well, but I will get through this. I will get you out of there soon. I promise." Says Sam. "I hope so. Hey Sam, I am always here for you." Says Lee. "I must take Sam away from this human, so she does not get out of control." Says Queen Nelia. Queen Nelia grabs Sam by the arm and drags her up to the upstairs out of the dungeon. "Where are you taking me?" Says Sam. "I am taking you to your room that you are staying until I will consider letting you go home with your friend down there." Says Queen Nelia. "Let him out." Says Sam. "NO, come with me right now Sam. This is why humans are dangerous." Says Queen Nelia. Sam looks at Nelia. She was wrong about humans being dangerous. After all she was human to. Sam and Queen Nelia walk in the halls to finally enter the room, where Sam is going to be staying for awhile. "This is going to be your room for awhile. Don't try anything." Says Queen Nelia. Sam walks over to the bed and lays down feeling like she is going to cry, but she holds back her tears. Moments later she falls asleep on the comfy big king-sized bed.

Skull was sitting down on a rock meditating for hours Hazel was looking at a man with his eyes closed. Hazel was bored now, but she was happy to not be in that coma anymore. She must admit that Hazel is grateful that they got her out of her coma, she felt more powerful than usual. It was sort of scaring her. She felt that she could kill someone with her power, but she holds back on those emotions on feeling like killing someone for fun or to feel more power coursing through her veins. Suddenly Skull opens his eyes finally after hours of waiting to see what he was looking for. Skull stands up with a book in his hand. It looked old and the color of the book was brown, and it looked ripped and trashed. As if it was through a lot of fire and water. "Ahhh, this is my spell book I missed you." Says Skull as kissing the book. "Alright let's see here." Says Skull. As the pages in the book start to flip by itself without Skull using his hands. Suddenly the pages stopped flipping and it stopped on one. Skull puts it on a table. Hazel walks over to the table to see what the books pages turned to. It was a summoning spell for the lost soul's army and King. Hazel gulped at the title of the page. Hazel feared what Skull really wanted to do with this lost soul's curse. Is all Hazel knowing that whatever Skull was doing it was bad news for everyone in this world? But Hazel just stayed calm. Watching Skull closely at every move that Skull made and spoke. Skull looks at Hazel looking like he was going to ask her to do something for him. "Hey, Hazel." Says Skull. "Yeah?" Says Hazel. "I need you to do me a favor. I need you to make sure that we have everything set on this list. By tonight. Which is in three hours." Says Skull as Skull gives Hazel a list of stuff to have and do. Hazel looks at the list. She did not know half of the stuff that said on the list, but there was a feeling inside of Hazel. That feeling was telling where to find the stuff that she does not know about or heard of. Hazel walks around getting all this stuff on the list and bring it back to Skull. For his ritual for tonight.

Once Hazel was done getting all the stuff off Skull's list. Hazel could hear something in the darkness lurking. The noise got closer and closer. There was a dark figure walking toward Hazel in the brushes. Before Hazel could want to throw a fire ball at the dark figure it came into the light when Hazel conjured a fire ball in her hand. Luna was right in her flames light space. "Luna!? How did you find me." says Hazel. "I found you because you are my sister and I have been sensing somehow that you were over here or in this forest." Says Luna. Hazel runs at Luna to hug Luna tight. Luna puts her arms around Hazel to. The moment of Hazel and Luna's reuniting moment. Hazel could hear Skull yelling for her. "Luna leave now. While you still can. I must go." Says Hazel. "I am not leaving you. We are leaving together." Says Luna. Luna grabs

Hazel by the arm running away, but before Luna and Hazel could run away together. There was suddenly a fire ball just missed Luna's head. "Where do you think you are going?!" says Jack." Lord Skull I found Hazel." Says Jack. Suddenly Skull was right next to Jack with his red eyes glowing in the dark forest and the moon was bright they could see his black dark hair. Skull walks over to Hazel and Luna. Suddenly Luna was in a cage in a tree. Skull looks at Hazel. "I thought I could trust you. I guess not." Says Skull. Skull takes the items that Hazel got for Skull's ritual, gives them to Jack, then looks back at Hazel. "I do need one more thing for the ritual to work properly. I need a pure heart to hold the portal between me and the lost soul's army. I was just going to go find another pure heart like you Hazel, but you proved that you can not be trusted, so I am using you as the power source for keeping the portal open between the lost souls and me." Suddenly Hazel was hooked up to Polly's vine again. Hazel was squirming at the vine's thorns in her wrists again along with her ankles. "Draw pentagrams Jack." Says Skull. "Yes, my lord." Says Jack. Skull puts all the items in a certain order on the tips of the pentagram that Jack drew on the caves floor. Hazel was hanging off the ceiling in the cave. "Polly come here." Says Skull. "Yes, my lord." Says Polly. Polly and Skull whisper at each other. Suddenly Polly connected herself to Hazel and started using Hazel's energy as a portal source to keep it open for as long as they want, but it will only close if Hazel ends up dying. Skull stands in the center of the pentagram. Skulls eyes glow even redder brighter than blood. Skull started to float in the air as Hazel was feeling much pain in her blood and it felt like her live source was being sucked away out of her body. A bright green and blue portal opened right in front of Skull; it took a second to realize that the lost souls were being summoned finally there was a shape coming out of the portal.

CHAPTER **14**

QUEEN NELIA AND THE CELESTIALS TRUTH

Cole was walking down the halls of the castle, making his way to Queen Nelia's throne room. Cole stud in front of the door just staring at the door, fearing of what he was going to say to Nelia about him being a dad, and was in a relationship with Nelia's best friend. Finally, Cole has the guts to open the door. Once Cole saw Nelia, she was sitting on her throne, drinking her tea. "Hey Nelia, do you have a moment?" says Cole. Nelia looked up from her book and looked at Cole. "Yeah, I have a minute, Cole. What is it? You look nervous." Says Nelia. Putting her book down. Cole said under his breath. *Here goes nothing.* Cole looked Nelia in the eye. "Nelia, I... I have... a... Daughter. Lucy gave birth to her in the other world." Says Cole. Nelia sat there sitting on her throne, almost dropping her tea. "What! Was that you said that Lucy and you were dating? And you have a daughter, I know you have Nixie as your daughter, but I did not know you had another daughter." Says Nelia. Cole stud there saying nothing. "Yeah, Nixie is my daughter as well, but Nixie is not Lucy's daughter. I met my other daughter before. Ruby told me about her, years ago. Just been keeping it a secret." Says Cole. "When did this happen?! Why did you not tell me that you were talking to Ruby about this." Says Nelia. "Almost 20 years ago. Me and Lucy were dating in secret, then she broke up with me, and ran away with her being pregnant. I think that is what happened. I mean that is what Ruby said anyway." Says Cole. "You know that is against the rules. You should have told me about this." Says Nelia. "I know that is against the rules, that is why I said secret. We wanted to get married, but then one day, in just about four years in our relationship. She got up and ran away one day. She must have been running away with my child when she was pregnant. I did not tell you because, I wanted this to be secret, mostly to forget Lucy. But I can not keep this to myself anymore." Says Cole. Nelia just sat there, putting her tea down on the side table. Nelia got up from her chair. "Cole. You must go get your daughter. She does not belong in the other world. As much as I am so close to throwing you in the dungeons right now. I need you to clean up your mess. Go get your daughter, right now." says Nelia. Cole looked at Nelia and nodded his head. "Alright Queen Nelia. I will leave today, then. I shall be back with my daughter." Says Cole. Cole turned to leave Nelia's throne room. Walking back to his house.

Once Cole got to his house, his daughter Nixie was home playing with her mother's bow and arrow. Cole walked up to the house's door. Once he walked into his house, he heard the door open downstairs. Cole looked out of his room and saw that Nixie came in the house. Cole continued packing his stuff for the trip to the other world getting Sam. To the Celestial realm. Once Cole walked down the stairs, he went in his front closet getting his staff. "Dad where are you going?" says Nixie. Cole turned to look at Nixie in the eye. Cole had no idea how to explain this to his daughter Nixie, about having another daughter. That he has been keeping from everyone. "Dad are you okay?" says Nixie. "Yeah, I am fine. I... Just don't know how to tell you this..." says Cole. Nixie looked at Cole as if he had three heads. "What are you talking about?" says Nixie. Cole stud there looking at his daughter. Cole sighed. "I have to tell you at some point..." says Cole. "What, do you have to tell me?" says Nixie. "Here goes nothing." Says Cole. "Dad, just say it. You are freaking me out." Says Nixie. "You have a sister." Says Cole. Nixie stud there looking at her father. "Hmm, what, what are you talking about?" Says Nixie. "I know, it's hard to believe. I have been keeping that from everyone. I just had to tell Nelia today, she was not happy about this either." Says Cole. "Dad, what are you talking about. I always wanted a sister. Can I meet her. I want to come with you." Says Nixie. "Oh... No, you are staying here. The other world is far to dangerous for you." Says Cole. "What. How can another realm be dangerous. Who is the mother, Was it my mom. How old is my sister??!! I have so many questions?" Says Nixie. "Well, I can answer a few. No Sam is not your mother's daughter... Sam is your half sister. She is older than you to, I don't know when her birthday is. The mother is Lucy Barns." Says Cole. "Wait, the hero. Lucy Barns that were the best day Celestial in the realm... What happened to her, you two were in a relationship." Says Nixie. "Oh, celestial queen, I might not be able to answer your questions Sam. But yes, Sam is the daughter of Lucy Barns." Says Cole. "YOU, have to let me come with you now! Please!!" Says Nixie. "No, you are staying Nixie. I don't want you getting hurt." Says Cole. "I won't get hurt. I promise. Just please let me come with. I want to meet, my sister." Says Nixie. "I am sorry but Nixie. I want you to stay here in the celestial realm, there is a reason why no one leaves to go to the other world, its big and full of humans." Says Cole. "I love an adventure, please let me come... Please." Says Nixie. "NO, Nixie, end of this discussion. I will be back before you know it. I promise. I love you, Nixie." Says Cole. Cole hugged Nixie bye. Cole walked out the house. When Cole shut the door behind him, Nixie grabbed her sword and ran out the door closing the door behind her. Nixie followed her dad down the river. Luckly Cole's portal was open just enough time, for Nixie to jump into the portal and follow her father to the other world. Finally Nixie and Cole, still Cole not aware of his daughter following him to the other world from the Celestial realm. Cole looked around him, Nixie panicked. Then Nixie went into cloak mode, using one of her abilities. Then Nixie's dad went walking toward some trees. Nixie followed him for awhile, finally they both find themselves walking into a city, on road. Nixie was curious about this world. She wanted to explore this realm. But she had to stay focused she had to keep following her father. Finally, Cole walked up to a street, Cole was watching a girl walk up to a house, looking sad. Suddenly the girl stud looking at the front door of the house. The girl knocked on the door. The door opened. A man stud before the girl. "Finally, you are home. Where have you been Sam." says the man. "I was at school. I told you I was leaving this morning." Says Sam. "Well, you know that I am tired, and I was drinking last night. I don't remember you saying that." Says the man. "I am sorry, dad. I will make sure I write down a note for you. Next time." Says Sam. The man smacked her in the face. Sam just stud there taking the smack from her dad. Cole put his staff in the brushes, then he acted like he was walking by, as if he was a normal human being. "Is there something wrong, here?" says Cole. The man looked at Cole. "No, there is nothing wrong. Keep going on your day." Says Sam's dad. "Why are you hitting your daughter then?" says Cole. "This is none of your business. Move on old man." Says Sam's dad. "I make it my business, when someone's parents hit their own child." Says Cole. The man stud there looking at Cole, then back at Sam. "What is your name?" Says Cole. "My name is Connor. Why do you want to know?" Says Connor. "I want to remember, how much of a better father I am, than a shitty father you are. To your own. This kid deserves better." Says Cole. "What do you know about having kids?!" Says Connor. "I know because I have two children. But one kid of mine does not know I am their father…" says Cole. As Cole looks at Sam. Cole looked at Sam's eyes. Sam had Lucy's eyes. Cole saw in them, were fear and sadness. Cole wanted to take Sam home so bad, but he could not just take Sam away right now. Cole needed to get Sam to trust him as a person. "Well, I bid you fair well. Have a great day." Says Cole. Cole started to walk away, but Cole saw Sam walking up to him, on the street, and Connor went inside his house. "Hey, I am sorry about my dad. Thank you for defending me…" says Sam. "It's fine. I deal with lots of people like that." Says Cole. "I don't mean to be noisy, what's your name?" Says Sam. Cole stud there looking down at Sam as a little girl. "My name is Cole." Says Cole. Sam just stud there looking down at the road, Cole saw that Sam was tearing up. Cole wanted to hug her, but that would be weird, so he pulls back. "I just want to see my mom again. I miss her so much…" says Sam. Cole leans down to Sam, so he could look her in the eye. "Everything will get better, soon. Just be patient. Something will come one day to change your life." Says Cole. Sam just cries in Coles arms. "GET OVER HERE SAM, RIGHT NOW." Says Connor. "I should go now… Thanks Cole. Bye." Says Sam. Sam walked away from Cole and back into her house. Cole wanted to get Sam out of that house right now, but. He had to wait, for the right moment. He hated the fact that he had to leave his daughter with this man, abusing his daughter. Cole walked away from the house, walking back to the brush getting his staff back and he tapped his staff on the ground. He was heading back to the Celestial realm. Nixie ran after him, Nixie just made it in time. Before the portal closed, leaving

Nixie behind in the other world. Nixie snuck up behind her father. "Why did you not get my sister there. To bring her home?" says Nixie. Cole turned around looking at Nixie. "You followed me!? Nixie, I told you to stay here." Says Cole. "Yeah, I followed you. I wanted to meet my sister. Who was that man, hitting my sister?!" says Nixie. Cole just stud there looking at his daughter. "I wanted to take her, back here. But I looked her in the eye, and I saw that she needed to stay there a little longer to fill her destiny. She will come here one day, but today is not the day. Oh, and never follow me again. Understand. I could have been doing something more dangerous." Says Cole. "You looked sad when she left and went back into that house…" Says Nixie. "Nixie. I would have loved to take her with me, but again she needs to be there for awhile now…" says Cole. "We could have helped her, instead you left her with that man." Says Nixie. "Nixie, just drop it. Sam is where she should be, I can't get her yet. I will be picking her up one day, but for now. Let's drop it." Says Cole. "I can't believe you would leave your own child like that, in a situation where she is getting hit by that man. She is my sister to. She is not just your daughter; she is my family to…" Says Nixie. "I know you see me as the bad guy right now, but please Nixie, drop it. Sam will be home with us in the future, just give it time…" says Cole. "Fine, have it your way "dad" I am going to go get to know my sister." Says Nixie. "What! No, you are staying. That world is dangerous." Says Cole. "Yeah, for my sister. Apparently. You can't stop me." Says Nixie. Nixie picks up a potion and drinks from the bottle. Nixie then disappeared out of thin air. Cole tried to stop her, but it was too late. Nixie was now missing from Cole's sight. Cole tapped his staff on the floor, but every time he tried teleporting to Nixie. Cole would be in a different realm.

Nixie was in a city that looked unfamiliar, but that did not stop her finding her sister. Nixie wandered around the streets, and it was starting to get dark. Nixie realized she is more powerful at night. So, Nixie uses her tracking power to find Sam her sister.

Hours later she finds a trashed house. Nixie walks up to the house's door. The lights were on in the living. The rest of the house's lights were off. Nixie used her other ability, X-ray vision. Nixie saw that someone was upstairs, a little girl crying in bed. Nixie levitated herself to the window. Then Nixie knocked on the window to Sam's room. Nixie saw that someone was getting up from the bed. Sam looks out the window and sees that Nixie was floating outside in the darkness. "Hey. Let me in. I want to come in and make sure you are alright." Says Nixie. Sam opens the window. Nixie could sense that Sam was scared, and she is thinking what she is doing letting Nixie in her bedroom. "Hey, I know this is weird, but thank you for letting me in your room. Sam." Says Nixie. "How were you floating just now, and how do you know my name?" says Sam. "I know your name because we are dreaming right now. I am in your dream." Says Nixie. Nixie hated that she lied to her sister about her dreaming, but it was good cover, so Sam could not have the urge to yell or scream or freak out. "I am dreaming?" Says Sam. "Yeah you are dreaming." Says Nixie. "How did you get in my dream I don't know you?" Says Sam. "Yes, I know you don't know me, but I know you. You are Sam, a girl that just wants to be free from her dad that she is living with now. What if I told you that you can be free? You just got to let me show you. What you can do." Says Nixie. Sam wiping her tears from her face, and she was intrigued of what Nixie was saying to her. "How can you show me?" Says Sam. Nixie puts her hand out toward Sam. "Give me your hand Sam. This is how I can show you." Says Nixie. Sam gives Nixie her hand. Suddenly Sam was floating, her hair was floating in the air as well, and her eyes were completely black. Sam was seeing visions in her future, mostly that can see what will happen to her and what she can do. Sam was amazed of what she saw in those visions. When the visions stopped for Sam. Her hair was back to normal, her eyes were the normal color, and she was back on the ground. Sam looks at Nixie. "What was all of that?" Says Sam. "You saw the moon and the sun, right?" Says Nixie. "Yeah, I saw that I could do things that you are doing right now. Who are you? And where did you come from?" Says Sam. "I am from the celestial realm I live there, and my name is Nixie a night Witch." Says Nixie. "Wow, my mind is blown. How is this a dream. I wish, I had these abilities." Says Sam sadly. Nixie suddenly had a headache that was hurting her. Sam was confused of what was happening to Nixie. "Nixie are you okay?" Says

Sam. "I must go, now I am sorry. I will see you soon Sam. I promise." Says Nixie. Nixie grabs a potion out of her other pocket and disappears away from Sam. Nixie was sad to leave Sam like that, but she had no choice. Nixie had used another portal potion, but she was not home that time. Nixie was in a forest still in the other world and it was dark still. Nixie ran out of potion to get her home again. Nixie mad at herself, but at least she got to meet Sam and show her who she is. But now Nixie had to figure out to get herself out of this situation on her own. There was something coming right at her. Nixie froze in spot and got shot by an arrow in the leg. Nixie felt sleepy. Before Nixie fell asleep, she could hear someone yelling "I got her" and running footsteps toward Nixie's paralyzed body.

CHAPTER 15

THE ALLIANCE

Robert was driving long distance. He kept looking at the app on his phone. The destination that Robert was trying to get to what Grim sent him. That destination was an hour away from where he is right now. He was so tired and stressed about getting to his brother Grim. Robert just wanted this problem to be solved, he wanted to make sure that Hazel was safe from Uncle Skull. Skull is a dangerous Reaper; Robert knows that Grim is the next Reaper in line. But Robert knows that Grim does not want to be in line. Grim just wants answers and an exit out of this destiny that Grim has. Robert feels like it is time to help his brother finally. Make an alliance with Grim. He does not like the idea of teaming up with Grim, but there was no other way. Suddenly there was a weird message on the app that he is using to get to Grim's destination. It was a message from unknown person. "Hello?" Says Dad. "Hey, Robert is that you?" Says Grim. "Yeah, this is Robert? Who are you?" Says Dad. "Robert its Grim. I found your phone number, but Robert, I can't text you for long on this phone, because I don't want this phone grabbing attention from the FBI, but anyway. Are you almost at the destination that I sent to you?" Says Grim. "Yeah, I am an hour away right now. Grim I can't text and drive at the same time. I will talk to you soon in person." Says Dad. "I know, I just wanted to make sure you were coming. If you are wondering why I can't text you from my phone because someone broke it. My old friend Jack, I am going to kill him." Says Grim. "Oh okay. I will see you soon. What did Jack do?" Says Dad. "Yeah, he is the one who betrayed me and took your daughter away from me. That is probably how Uncle Skull got out of his dimension that he was banished from. I did not know that Hazel could have been another way out for him. I have no idea who is our family anymore. I want to make things right for this family." Says Grim. Robert does not say anything. Because he could tell that message was Grim. Robert did not really want to care right now about what Grim is feeling, but at this point Robert needed to be apart of Grim's life right now. It has been difficult for Grim the most. Grim has been just trying to figure out who he is and just wanting to change, but Robert did not trust that for a second. Robert had to see what Grim has to say and do for this family. "Grim, it's going to be alright… I don't trust you, but when it comes to saving my daughter from Uncle Skull. I am going to do things that are pretty much unexpected. I know somewhere in that heart of yours Grim. You care just a little bit." Says Robert. "Thank you, Robert. I appreciate what you are doing for me. I am going to let you go, so you can focus on driving, but before I let you go. Robert. I must say something." Says Grim. "What is it?" Says Robert. Grim stops for a second. Grim thinks again and changes his mind. "Never mind. I forgot." Says Grim. Okay, see you soon." Says Robert. "Yeah, see you later." Robert goes back into the app to see how long of a straight it is now. Now it says Robert is just about 30 minutes away from the destination. Robert is happy that he was getting close to where Grim's address is, but for the mean time Robert puts on some loud rock music for the rest of the ride there.

Finally, Robert arrives at Grims destination. Robert gets out of the car walking to the back of his truck to get a weapon of some sort. He still did not trust Grim at all one bit, so he did not want to take any chances. He grabbed a pistol and put in a gun hoister underneath his jacket. Robert closes his truck and walks to the front door. This time there was guards everywhere. One of the guards walk up to Robert confused and he was putting up a gun at his face. "Who are you?" Says a guard. "I am Grim's brother, did he not say that he was excepting someone?" Says Robert. The guard looked confused. Then his face expression changed. "Oh right, come with me. I am sure that boss will see you now." Says the guard. Robert and the guard walk inside the building in the hallways. Finally, they were at an elevator. The guard pushed a button that had the number 7 on it. They were going up. The elevator door opened to an office and Grim was standing at a window front view, staring into space. "Sir Grim, he is here." Says the guard. Grim turns around to look toward Robert and the guard. "Leave us Fred." Says Grim. The guard Fred leaves the room to go down the elevator back to the main floor. Grim walks toward Robert as the guard left the room. Robert and Grim both stared at each other in uncertain feelings. Finally Grim says. "I see you made it than." Says Grim. "Yeah, I made it to this place. Of whatever you call it." Says Robert. "Its my home, that I have never had before." Says Grim. Robert looks at Grim for a few moments and lost words of what he could say to that, but he could not find anything to be the truth. Because Grim has spoke the truth to Robert, that Grim never had a home. Grim just had to go on his own to make his way around the world and that worked out better for him. Robert just wanted to get this over this, so Robert continues asking the one question that will for sure start this war between Uncle Skull with Grim and Robert between each other. "So, what is the plan with taking down Uncle Skull." Says Robert. Grim stands there looking at Robert. Grim feels the weight on his shoulders once again, but this time it was Grim's mess to clean up. A big mess he made between Uncle Skull a long time ago. Grim was determined to end this once and for all. "The Plan is to find where Uncle Skull is hiding and what he wants with this world and why did he capture my niece and your daughter. We got to figure out why, Hazel was valuable." Says Grim. Robert has no idea how he is going to tell Grim the truth. Robert should have known to not let Hazel be alone. Robert just was too busy to realize that Hazel was in trouble with the evil side of the world. "Grim I have to tell you something that I should have told you a long time ago." Says Robert. Grim looks at Robert concerned. "What is it?" Says Grim. Robert takes a deep breath. "I know why, Hazel was powerful enough to be Uncle Skull's source." Says Robert. Grim looked at Robert closely. "Why? Is she powerful enough and what do you know?" Says Grim. "You are probably going to be mad at me, but it has something to do with Amy our sister. Mom told me a long time ago, that she had a daughter or a kid way before us. She was powerful. Mom told me everything about her, but I thought she was lying all these years. I guess my daughter Hazel picked up Amy's power." Says Robert. Grim tried to stay calm, but Grim changed face expressions in angry, but on the other hand Grim could not be mad at his brother Robert. He can only be mad at his mother once again. "What did mom tell you?" Says Grim. "You are not going to freak out at me for knowing something for my entire life?" Says Robert. "No, I just want this problem gone. Maybe put my mom in the past finally. I never want to speak of her again." Says Grim. "Alright. I will explain everything." Says Robert. Robert explains that their mother said that Amy was beautiful, talented, she was a troubled kid, but one day when she meant this boy named Grayson. She become obsessed with him. Amy wanted nothing to do with there mom anymore. Cynthia was trying to convince Amy to stop hanging out with Grayson the boy that she meant, but of course she ignored her and kept going to see Grayson every night. Cynthia knew that this boy Grayson was bad news and their mother was right. One day Cynthia over heard Grayson saying that he was just using Amy for sex and her body. Cynthia ran to warn Amy about what she heard, once she got there. Cynthia told everything to Amy, but then Amy did not believe her at all. The only thing that Cynthia could do was kill the boy that was lying to her daughter. One night when Amy and Grayson were done having sex. Grayson got up and put his clothes back on. Amy was laying down in bed sleeping. Grayson got up and walked outside in the cold with his clothes on, but he had no shirt on. Little did Grayson know that Cynthia was following him in the forest. Cynthia was questioning why he just got up and started walking in the forest alone. When Grayson stopped in the middle of the forest. A cave appeared in front of Grayson, there was a man in a red cloak just sitting on a rock. Grayson walked in the cave and sat right next to the man in the red cloak. Grayson suddenly turned into a demonic creature with horns and glowing eyes color white. "What took you so long?" The demon said that mom heard says Robert. "Anyway, continuing the story. I took long because I was depositing in a woman." Says Grayson. "I hope that child will carry in that girl that you are doing it with" Says the demon. "It will because Amy told me she has abilities. That is why I choose her." Says Grayson. "Good, we need more demons like us, or we will go extinct." Says the red cloaked demon. I hope the next child I am depositing in this girl. Is going to be a girl because I want a demon that can hold their own child. I am getting tired of doing all the work." Says Grayson. "I can tell you look tired." Says the red cloaked man. Cynthia finally wanted to make a move to get this over with, but now she had to kill another demon. Cynthia found out that Grayson and this other man were demons. "HEY!" Says Cynthia. Grayson and the man in the red cloak looked over at Cynthia in angry. "You were followed!" Says the red cloaked man. "I assumed that I was fine, but I guess not. This will be fun." Says Grayson. "No this will be fun for me." Says Cynthia. Cynthia runs at Grayson picking up a good fight. Until Grayson uses one of his abilities, but he misses Cynthia. Cynthia slashes Grayson's side. Grayson started bleeding on the left side of his torso. Cynthia does not hesitate to cut off his head. Grayson's head was on the ground. Cynthia's sword was covered in blood. The stones underneath her was covered in blood. Cynthia looks at the demon in the red cloak. But before Cynthia could even think about killing him to. He was gone. The cave was gone as well. Cynthia turns back and walks back toward the house. Once Cynthia gets back in the house. Amy was up on the couch. "Hey, mom? Have you seen Grayson?" Says Amy. Cynthia pauses and looks at Amy. "I knew I was right about that boy of yours. He was a demon. He was using you, Amy." Says Cynthia. "What did you do?!" Says Amy. "I did the right thing. That's what I did." Says Cynthia. "Answer my question. What did you do?" Says Amy. Cynthia paused for a moment looked down then up looking Amy in the eyes. "I killed him." Says Cynthia. "WHAT!??" Says Amy. "He was using you once again. He was trying to get a deposit demon in you." Says Cynthia. Amy looks down starting to cry. Then looks back at Cynthia. "IT DOES NOT MEAN YOU HAVE TO KILL ANYONE TO PROTECT ME." Says Amy, raising her voice. "No, its my job to help you stay alive and not make stupid decisions because you were in love." Says Cynthia. "IT DOES NOT MEAN YOU HAVE TO KILL FOR ME EITHER." Says Amy. "I was just trying to protect you." Says Cynthia. "Well don't, anymore. I hate you." Says Amy. As Amy walks away Cynthia stabs Amy right in the heart. Cynthia realizes what she has done. Cynthia removes the sword out of Amy's chest, but Amy was dead before Cynthia could help her do anything to help Amy stay alive. Cynthia leaned over, Amy's body and started to cry. The next day Cynthia takes Amy too the witch Cynthia trusts the most out of any Witch out there. Cynthia takes Amy's body to Gretel and the sword for the evidence of Cynthia ever killing Amy in the first place. After that day she never saw Amy again. Grim looks at Robert angrier than ever before. "So, our mom killed our sister, and took her to my best friend, Gretel. Then Amy was gone?" says Grim. "Yeah, that does suck. Now I understand why you hate our mom." Says Robert. "Well, I am glad that you realized that this year, when she is dead." Says Grim. Grim walks over his bookshelf and grabs a box in a hidden compartment behind his bookshelf. Grim puts the box on his desk full of books and papers already. "What is this?" Says Robert. "It is our mom's journals about Amy or other people that were in our mom's life." Says Grim. "If you hated her so much, why did you keep her journals?" Says Robert. "I just thought this stuff would be useful and would be helpful." Says Grim. "Read most of this stuff that mom wrote. It is all true because it was happening to Hazel. So, Hazel is some what the same as Amy which is our sister." Says Grim. "Yeah, but how can we stop Uncle Skull that is our real task." Says Robert. "Yeah, I know that is our real task." Says Grim. Grim then changes expressions on his face. He goes through the box that he pulled out. Grim picks up another journal that he saw, but he never wanted to open it because Cynthia was writing about Uncle Skull. So Grim opens the book, the first page it literally had him scared because Cynthia his mom was moderating her siblings there was even one about Aunt Emerald. But he wanted to read the one about Uncle Skull. Grim opens the book and a few pages went by, and he found something that might help. "Robert come here." Says Grim. Robert walks over to Grim looking over his shoulder. Grim and Robert look at each other. "Skull does not have a weakness. The only way we can stop him is banishing him again." Says Robert. "Well, nothing can be easy can it." Says Grim. "Yeah, but this is easier than you think it is. But I think we are going to need help..." Says Robert. Grim looked over the book. A few moments later Grim remembered who banished him. "Robert, Gretel. She is the one who banished Uncle Skull in the first place." Says Grim. "Yeah, you're right. She did. I remember that day, that day was stressful." Says Robert. "Now, we have to go looking for Gretel." Says Grim. "Yeah, on it." Says Robert. "Where are you going?" Says Grim. "I am going to go to Gretel's house." Says

Robert. "You clearly don't know Gretel, do you. She is not going to be home. She is possibly going to be somewhere where no one can find her. Expect me." Says Grim. "Okay, what do we do then Grim? We don't have much time to play games." Says Robert. "I am not playing any games. I am telling you the truth." Says Grim. "I believe you, its just we don't have time to play these games with Gretel, is there away we can find her faster?" Says Robert. "I think so." Says Grim. "Really, how ???!!!" says Robert. Grim walks over to his desk and opens the drawer and shows Robert the piece of paper. "What is this?" Says Robert. "It's a piece of paper, a spell that she gave to me, if I ever needed help. I could summon her." Says Grim. Robert had a look of relief on his face. But I need something expensive. Since our family was and still is an asshole to everyone and Gretel." Says Grim. Robert looks at Grim and eye rolls. "You know why Gretel is nice to you and likes you better. Because she has feelings for you." Says Robert. "That's what Uncle Skull said, but I don't think that is true, because I am the only one in this family who actually paid back for the deal, I made with her." Says Grim. Robert rolls his eyes again and gives up mostly because he has no time to argue with Grim at this point. "Okay, Grim let's just get this over with. What is the expensive item?" Says Robert. "I know just the item." Says Grim.

The shape came out of the portal looking around excepting worse, but as the shape came out of the portal. It turned into a man with a crown. As soon as he came out of the portal. Skull bowed to the king of Souls. Skull looked over his shoulder and saw that Polly and Jack were not bowing. Skull yelled at them to bow to the king of Soul. Polly and Jack then bowed to the king of soul. "My King. I am very sorry if you were doing something, but I need to chat with you." Says Skull. "What, do you want? Do you want me to bring back someone you love most, that is going to coast you!" Says King of Souls. "No, I do not want to ask you to give me a soul. I just want to chat, make a deal with you." Says Skull. The king looks intrigued. "I am listening." Says King of Souls. "I am thinking of making an army out of the undead. I want your souls to help me make that army possible." Says Skull. The king of souls looks at Skull. "Why do you want to terrorize this world?" Says King of Souls. Skull gets up and looks at the King. "Don't you see these people and creature are sources for you and me, but they are. Worthless to you and me. If we work together, we are for sure going to be available to make everything right. I can collect souls from other worlds, and you can put that soul in a body that is a live and we can rule this world. Together." Says Skull in a smile. The king looks at Skull with an evil grin. "Very well then. I will think about your invite to this. I just want to know the purpose of your thinking. You want to do?" Says King of souls. "I want to do this because the humans deserve it and mostly that I am hungry for something else. I am hungry for chaos and destruction." Says Skull. The king thinks again about what Skull was saying. The king would think about it as soon as he said chaos and destruction. The king walks over to Skull putting out his hand. "What do you want me to do?" Says Skull. "I want you to shake on that we agree to our terms. We share souls. You take the souls and capture them, and they turn into mindless zombies that bow to us. We take them around the world, the universe to make more mindless zombies that bow to us all in this cave." Says King of Souls. Skull shakes to that. "I agree, with you King of Souls. Call me King Hall, Skull." Says King of souls. "King Hall. How did you know my name?" says Skull. "I knew your name. You are a grim reaper." Says King of souls. "Yeah, in fact. I have taken a lot of souls." Says Skull. "Good then you know that souls are fun to play with. You can put them in anyone's body, and the soul won't be messed up it will only have freedom, but it won't know the difference between being in someone else's body, but also not noticing that they don't belong in that body." Hazel was staring down at them, thinking about what they are talking about. "You are wrong, about souls you know." Says Hazel. The king looks up at Hazel. "Excuse me but are you the queen of souls. No, you are not. Shut up." Says King of souls. "Hey, don't talk to my great niece that way." Says Skull. King of souls rolls his eyes. "Fine, whatever, but I still know what souls enjoy and not enjoy." Says King of Souls. The King of soul's notices something in Hazel's Souls. He walks up to Skull. "We need to talk in private." Says King of Souls. "Alright." Says Skull. Skull and king of Souls walk into another area in the cave. "You need to kill that niece of yours. She is powerful enough to stop me and you." Says King of souls. "Sorry, but that is not about of our agreement." Says Skull. "Well, then I can't do this plan. And that was going to be your payment for the alliance with me." Says King of Souls. Skull looks at him and then looks at his great niece. "Wait, I will figure out away to make us both work together like this as a family. With Hazel still alive and us working together." Says Skull. The king looks at him. "Fine, do what you must, but if you want to do this you are going to have to get Hazel to stay away from me and you." Says King of Souls. "Fine I will away. I always do." Says Skull. "Alright, I will be back. Just summon me again by calling on the King of souls. AKA just say my name then I will be here." Says King of Souls. "Alright." Says Skull. "Bye for now." Says King of Souls. As the King of Souls walks back in his portal. "Polly let Hazel down, I need to chat with her more a few moments." Says Skull. Polly puts the charger out of Hazel. Hazel drops down to the ground. Weak and still not free from being imprisoned by her great Uncle Skull. Skull carries Hazel to a more private area for them to talk. "So, King of Souls does not trust you at all. He thinks that you are going to kill me and him." Says Skull. Hazel gets a little more of her strength back, but only just enough to stand. "You said you wanted me to take over him? What. Are you not going to do it anymore?" Says Hazel. Skull looks at Hazel with much greed and a little confusion. "I don't know anymore, but If I want this to work you are going to have to stay out of my way with this part." Says Skull. Hazel looks at Skull in no words. Skull suddenly looks at Hazel with a different expression that Hazel has never seen on him before. "I am sorry, but I must make this plan work with the King." Says Skull as he puts up his hand. Suddenly Hazel's soul was out of her body again. "Polly come over here." Says Skull. "Yes, my Lord." Says Polly. Polly walks over to where Skull was. Hazel was on the ground without her soul again. Skull picks up Hazel and puts her on the gray flat stone table. "Alright, Polly vine her." Says Skull. Polly spawns the vines again on Hazel's wrists and ankles once again. Hazel could feel the pain in her ankles and her wrists. Once again Hazel was vined to the table where she started. "NO." Says Luna. "What's wrong don't like to see your sister struggling for life." Says Skull as he walks away. Luna can't do anything because she was in a cage hanging from the roof top of the cave that they all were in. Luna looks at Polly. Luna notices that Polly is under a control spell. Luna could probably figure out how to get through to this woman who is being forced against her will by doing these bad things to people. Mean while Luna is stuck in a cage still. Jack is still trying to get Skull's approval of trying for Being Skulls apprentice of wanting to be a Grim reaper. Skull walks toward his space to be alone and writing down some notes of what is going to happen next. Skull still sort of wants Grim to be on his side for the plan, but Skull knows that it won't be this easy to get Grim to work with him in the plan. Little did these people know that someone, that is a no one is watching them in the forest in the shadows. While everyone was getting ready to head to sleep the unknown visitor comes walking around their camp as everyone was sleeping except for Luna of course. The unknown person would throw up some food toward Luna. Luna would try to ask what their name is, but they don't talk at all. Luna has not even since there face ever before. As the stranger walks away again in the darkness of the forest. Luna starts to lose hope, but then suddenly the stranger came back, but this time prepared to do something useful. It looked like the stranger was going to help get Luna out of the cage off the ceiling, but the stranger did it quiet as possibly to not wake anyone. Moments later, the cage was on the ground for Luna to be available for Luna to just walk out without her, her hurting herself. Finally, Luna was in a good enough distance to see that the stranger who saved Luna from being in that cage any longer. Finally, Luna says to the stranger. To help Luna Hazel out of those vines, but the stranger shook her head no, to helping Hazel get out of that vine. The stranger spells out that we are not to interfere with the hero. "What are you talking about!? Hazel can help us. She is my sister I want to help her." Says Luna. The stranger pulls out her arm. There was a symbol on her arm. The symbol looked time a clock on her arm. The Stranger says that we must not interfere with time. "Are you a Time Witch?" Says Luna. The stranger nods yes. The stranger symbolizes that it's time to go. I came here to save you not anyone else. The stranger grabs Luna's arm and runs fast than Luna can let this stranger hold on to her arm like this. Luna kept up with running away. Luna felt bad leaving Hazel again with the villain.

Sam was just wandering around the realm that Lee and her stumbled upon. Sam was changed into clothes that she does not really like to wear, but Sam was being forced to wear the cloak. She did not like it, but she had no choice. Someone came behind Sam, while Sam was trying to relax in the garden or just to get away from everyone. "Lady Sam, the Queen wants you to come back for another study session." Says a Celestial Guard. Sam sighs wishing that Sam was with Lee right now. "I am trying to relax right now. Can I go later?" Says Sam. "No, I am afraid that you must come now. The queen does not like to wait." Says a celestial guard. Sam looks at the guard and rolls her eyes. Sam gets up from the bench. The guard escorts Sam to the castle. Where the Queen and the sorcerer is. As Sam walks in the room with the guard by her side. The Sorcerer was chatting with the queen about something, that Cole was talking about Sam. Sam was wondering what her "Father" was talking about her to Nelia. "Hey, is there something I need to know about you or something. Cause every time I hear my name a lot from your mouth Sorcerer. Says Sam. The queen and the man look at each other. The queen whispers in his ear. "Okay, that is a enough. If you are talking about me. Just say it out loud. You have my friend in your dungeon. You can at least tell me what you are talking about. It is rude in my culture to talk about someone behind there backs." Says Sam. Sam's "Father" and the queen look at Sam. "You do have a good point, but you can't know yet." Says Queen Nelia. "Okay, I guess I am going to go get Lee and leave. Since you guys won't just tell me, so I can trust you." Says Sam. As Sam begins to walk away. Sam's "father" yells. "Wait. I am sorry I just don't know how to say that you are my daughter, and I am so happy that I found you finally. I just wish that your mom did not keep you a secret from me. I could have raised you in this world, and Lucy... would probably still be here. But of course, she had to be the hero, and move to the other world and marry that horrible man. Giving you a home, then her dying in the process. Then Sam realized something, this man, was the man that came to her one day, when she was just coming back from school. "That was you... Wasn't." says Sam. Cole just stud there, not saying anything. "Yes, that was me... I was at your house; I saw that man that you lived with "Connor" That Lucy married and left you there with him. He was an abusive father; I can't believe that Lucy liked that man." Says Cole. Sam just stud there looking at her "Father" Cole, Sam had no idea what to say now... "Sam,

I just want you to know that I love you. Very much, even though I did not know that Lucy hid that away from me... I am now here for you, not that stepfather of yours. "Says Cole. "Yeah, because he is dead." Says Sam. "Maybe that is best..." Says Cole. "How could you say something like that. I know he was a bad man, but he is still a person." Says Sam. "Don't tell me you were okay, with him abusing you like that. Sam." Says Cole. "I was not in a good place with him. I will agree with you on that, but he was still a person." Says Sam. "You have Lucy's kindness..." says Cole. Sam just looked at her "father" "I want you to know, "Father" I don't trust you." Says Sam. "How can I make you trust me... then..." says Cole. Sam stud there looking at Cole. "Tell me your name..." says Sam. "My name is Cole." Says Cole. "Why were you there that day..." Says Sam. Cole stud there not saying anything. "I wanted to meet you, I wanted to take you home here... But you were young to just switch to different lifestyles. So, I left you there..." Says Cole. Sam stud there saying nothing. "You may have stopped him once from hitting me, but you did not stop him from... other things." Says Sam. Cole had no idea how to keep this conversation going, they were just getting more far away as being a family than ever before. "Sam, I am sorry that all happened to you, but you are home and safe. From him, he is gone, he can't hurt you anymore." Says Cole. "That does not heal the scars that he left, I waited for you. To come back and talk to me." Says Sam. "I am here now." Says Cole. "Yeah, you are, but still again. You left me with that man. I know he was my stepfather, but he was a mean man. I did not want him to die though." Says Sam. "Well, Sam what happened, is what happened. I would have probably made it a bit different for you, but I knew it was not the right time." Says Cole. "What do you mean, it would not have been the right time." Says Sam. Sam lifts her shirt showing Cole and Nelia her scars. "Where were you for those scars. "Father" WHERE WERE, when I needed you." Says Sam. Cole looked the scar. Heart broken. "That man did this to me; I was going to die that night. All because of a beer being dropped on the ground. Where were you then?!" Says Sam. Sam puts down her shirt. Sam starts to walk away from Nelia and Cole. Walking toward back to the gardens. Cole did not bother following Sam. He walked away himself walking toward the dungeon. Little did Cole know that Sam was heading, trying to go visit Lee, in the dungeons, but a guard was stopping Sam from going down. Cole walked over the guard. "Let her go down, I will go with her." Says Cole. Sam looked over at Cole, she did not say anything. Sam walked down the dungeon, and Cole followed Sam down to the dungeon. Once they go to Lee's cell. "Cole, can you leave me and Lee alone. I just want to talk to him in peace." says Sam. "yeah, I will just be over here, I guess." Says Cole. Cole walked away to let Sam talk to Lee alone. When Sam knew that Cole was gone, Sam opens the cell door and walks into the room, falling right into Lee's arms, for a hug. "Sam, you alright?" says Lee. Sam just kept crying in Lee's arms. Lee said nothing after that Sam started crying, Lee just hugged Sam, giving her comfort. Moments later, Lee realized that Sam, fell asleep in Lee's arms. Lee picks up Sam and puts Sam right now top of Lee letting Sam sleep on top of Lee. Lee pets Sam on the head kissing her head and wiping her tears off her face. Finally, Cole came back to check on them. Cole walked into the cell. "Is she alright..." says Cole. "I have no idea; she just fell asleep." Says Lee. Cole sighed. "I will take her up to her room, to get some rest." Says Cole. "Whatever you did to Sam, you need to apologize for it, otherwise she will not forgive you..." says Lee. "I will, we just need sometime." Says Cole. "No, I think that you guys need to figure it out now, before it's too late." Says Lee. "I know when the best time will be... It just takes time." Says Cole. "Well, don't take to long. It won't go well this you and her. Relationship wise." Says Lee. Lee gets up and gives Sam to Cole, and Cole picks up Sam, Lee giving Cole the key to his cell, then Cole left the dungeon and put Sam into bed, in her room. As Cole put down Sam onto the bed, he looked down at her, feeling sorry for abandoning her. Cole looks at the scar that Sam had on her side, it looked painful to sleep on. Cole then thought of an idea. But he was going to wait for Sam to wake up, so he could ask, if could heal the scar on her side. Cole walks out of Sam's room to give her some space for sleeping. Then he closes the door and walks toward his house. Once he got to his house. He sat down on the couch in his house, and he made eye contact with a picture of Nixie. "Where are you Nixie, where are you?" says Cole. Cole lays down on the couch hugging the picture of Nixie, falling asleep himself. On the couch.

CHAPTER **16**

WHERE IS NIXIE?

Nixie wakes up in a moving vehicle chained to the floor in the vehicle. Suddenly the vehicle stops in spot. Someone opens the back door of the vehicle and grabs Nixie up the arm chaining her arms and legs. Nixie started to be dragged across a dirt path. Nixie was still half sleeping by that arrow that the man shot her in the leg with. Suddenly someone was right in front of Nixie chained as well. She was more chained though, more than Nixie was. "I got a Celestial witch here." Says a figure. "Put her with the other Celestial witches in the separate rooms. Like everyone else has been." Says a voice of a woman. Nixie was being dragged again, Nixie could feel wood scraping in her pants that she was wearing. Nixies vision was back. Nixie could see her surroundings. The people that were dragging her, threw her in a small room with a bed and the walls were iron bars. Nixie could see other people in the same kind of situation that Nixie was in. Nixie was scared for sure, she stayed tough to not show fear. Mostly Nixie was confused of how these people knew about Celestial Witches or Wizards. Suddenly a door opened. Nixie could see that there was another girl getting dragged into a room next to Nixie. Nixie heard what the person said that was throwing the girl in the room next to Nixie's room. He said that. We deserve to be in these cells. Then he slams the cell door behind him and walks out of the cell block area. "Hey, are you okay?" Says Nixie. The girl looks scared. She was not trying to hide her fear of being in the room, but then something unexpected happened. The door opened again, but this time there were armed people walking in the cell block area. They walked to one of the cells, opened the door to a room. They dragged out a Celestial wizard and took him with them in chains. The Celestial Wizard was yelling NO, not Me, not me. Says the scared Wizard. Everyone in their cells feared the worst. Even Nixie as well. Nixie still had a brave face of saying to someone. "Where are they taking him?" Says Nixie. No one answered until the girl next to Nixie that was recently thrown into the room next to her. The girl walks to the iron bar. Nixie tries to understand what the girl was saying, but she could not speak sign language. "Sorry I can't understand you." Says Nixie. The girl walks to her bed grabbing something underneath her pillow. Pieces of paper. The girl writes down on the piece of paper. "They took him to the arena, for fighting." Says on the paper. Nixie looks at her. "What is the arena?" Says Nixie. The girl writes on another page. "A dangerous place where no one usually comes back from... I just got back from it just now... I been to the arena a lot already. So, I know what to do... And know what to except..." Says on the page. Nixie notices on the girl there was a scar on her arm. That looked fresh. "What happened to your arm?" Says Nixie. The girl hides the scar away from Nixie so that Nixie could not see it. The girl writes on another piece of paper. "Sorry, I just don't like talking about that scar. But I am going to say, I got it from the arena." Says on the piece of paper. Nixie respects the girls wishes about the scar on her arm. Nixie and the girl that can't talk, but the girl just keeps writing down words on the paper to communicate with Nixie. Nixie could tell that the girl was getting frustrated that she could not talk. She wanted to be a warrior and be like everyone else, but she kept her angry to herself that she did not have a voice. Suddenly the door that keeps opening every hour and people getting picked up to be taken to the arena. Finally, Nixie was chosen to go to the arena. She was picked out of her room of the cell block. Nixie was cuffed in chains Nixie could not get out of the chains even if she tried. The chains that were put on her were Celestial weakness. Which was the opposite power that Nixie had which was the Sun. Nixie was a night Celestial. Her weakness would be the sun. Nixie could stand in the sun, but Nixie was weaker in the sun. Nixie at this point was under house arrest. Finally, Nixie and the armored guards made it to an elevator that went down to a big open hole deep under ground. The guards dragged Nixie on an elevated platform that went deep under ground. Finally, Nixie meant up with more armored guards. They dragged her to a door that led her to big open space that was in fact an arena that Nixie saw that there were weapons to Nixie's left side of her view. When Nixie looked straight, she saw there was huge door that was opening. Nixie grabbed a weapon from the stand. Since she was unchained, she could also use her night abilities, but her power won't be at her fullest. Nixie looked up around her. She noticed that this was a test of power and becoming a weapon. Nixie did not like this place at all, she wanted out, but there was no escape. The door was fully open. What came out of the door was a small creature that had wings. It was a baby dragon. She did not want to kill a baby dragon. Nixie just stud there looking at the poor creature that was imprisoned by this horrible place. Nixie threw the weapon on the ground staring at the baby dragon. There were boos in the crowd that was watching Nixie down below. Nixie heard a door behind her open. She felt a hand grabbing her very hard dragging her back in the elevator area then she saw that they shot the dragon in the head with an arrow. There was blood spewing out of the dragon's head. Nixie was sad that the dragon was shot right in the head, because she would not kill the dragon. Nixie did not know where they were taking her now, but she was chained again, and they were dragging her somewhere else. The armed guards put Nixie on a chair and restrained her to the chair. The armed guards grabbed a needle, walked over to her. And injected her with the needle. Nixie screamed in pain. Also, she felt more powerful, but she was still screaming in pain. Nixie stopped screaming. A lab coat doctor came in the room with a clipboard writing down notes. The armed guards left the room, leaving Nixie with the lab coat doctor. The lab coat doctor walked up to Nixie looking at her deep into her eyes. She felt a sudden chill down her spine. Nixie saw that the doctor's eyes glowed green. The last thing that Nixie remembers is that the doctor said. This will only hurt for a few moments. Nixie saw that the doctor had another needle in his lab coat. The doctor connected Nixie to a machine. Nixie felt the doctor cutting into Nixies arm and felt something plastic inside of her blood stream. Nixie felt a tingle inside of her blood stream. She felt something like liquid going inside of her veins. She was still awake through this all. The doctor was surprised, but they kept going with there experiment. Someone else walks in the room. "How is it going? Doctor mimics?" Says the woman. The doctor turns around to make eye contact with the woman. Nixie hears that they were talking about her. Of how she is still awake from the liquid that was being injected inside of her blood stream. The woman walks over to Nixie looking at her in the eye. Nixie heard out of that woman's mouth was. "Interesting. I like this one." Says the woman, as the woman was touching Nixie on the face grabbing her jaw. "I think I want to keep this one, with the ones that can handle the sleeping injections. This one failed the first task, but I will make sure to make this one not fail next again." Says the woman as she let's go of Nixie's jaw. The Woman walks back toward the doctor, forcing him to write Nixie down to a new cell block. Nixie was now more scared than she has ever been in her life. Nixie was trying to call her dad for help in her mind, but something was blocking her power. The doctor walks back over to Nixie. The doctor puts out the liquid tube. He turns off the machine as soon as he pulls out the tube out of Nixie's arm. Nixie passed out after that.

A couple hours later she woke up in a different area. Nixie was in different clothing and this time she had a number on her clothes. 2048. There were windows with bars, but the windows were high up. Nixie could feel the night fall in her blood stream. She felt powerful currently. She tried to use one of her abilities, but she could not do anything now. She did not know why, but then she saw a mirror in her room that she was in. There was a neck collar thing on her neck. Nixie kept trying to use her abilities, but she could not do anything, but walk in her cell with the neck collar on. Nixie was missing home more than she could ever imagine in her life. Nixie had no idea where she was. She feared what might happen next. Nixie thought of how quiet it was. Nixie thought it was weird it was this quiet. The only thing that Nixie could hear was the outside of wind trees swaying back and forth from the outside where she could not see. She felt fear in her blood stream, of what might happen next to her. Suddenly the door opened to her cell in the block. Nixie got up off the floor and looked right up at who just came into the cell room. "Hello night Celestial Witch. We have put you in here because you have proven to Lady Wolf that you are strong enough to be in this cell block, but I must warn you that this cell that you are in is soundproof. We made that a reason for this cell block, because we like this cell block more secured and quieter, so everyone in this block can get the proper sleep, but I must warn you. If you stay up late and have no reason. You will be punished." Says the armored guard. "Now you must eat, for tomorrow night. You are going meet some of your opponents and lady wolf. Get some sleep." Says the armored guard. Before the armored guard could leave the cell. Nixie got up and ran at him. The guard was prepared to knock Nixie to the ground. The guard knocked Nixie down. Nixie felt a headache. Nixie then right away regretted what she tried to do. Because then the guard touched a button on his wrist. Nixie felt electricity through her body. She was paralyzed on the ground. With a headache and felt a shock through her body. The guard put her food on the ground in her cell then shut the door and left. Nixie got up a few moments later. Looking at the food. Nixie picked it up then started eating the food. Once she was done with the food. Nixie put it in the corner of her cell. Nixie got up and looked up at the iron bared window that was up high from Nixie's view of the moon. Nixie felt the moon giving her power, but Nixie could not use that power. She felt helpless. Her tongue was gone. She was frustrated of her situation. She wanted to go home and hug her father again and make sure that Sam is safe from the stupid humans that she was living with. Nixie always wanted a sister. Now since Nixie has one, she wanted to get out of here to get to know Sam way better. She closed her eyes just letting the quiet cell block smoothing her to sleep for the day light to come. She then fell asleep. As the day light was about to a peak for her. The cell that she was in being kept in. Her cell flooded with sun light all over her sleeping body.

CHAPTER 17

GRETEL

"So, what are you doing?" Says Robert. "I am doing the thing that Gretel likes when I summon her for when I want to see her." Says Grim. "What is it that she likes, when you do for her?" Says Robert. "I grab… Never mind." Says Grim. "What, what is wrong?" Says Robert. "Nothing is wrong I just don't feel comfortable with telling you anything about my relationship with Gretel. We are best friends; I had not seen her in years." Says Grim. "Okay, fine I don't want to know anyway." Says Robert in a sarcastic voice. Grim looks at Robert and rolls his eyes. "Fine, she makes me go mining for these kinds of gems. Called love stones." Says Grim. Robert laughs. "What, what is so funny." Says Grim. "Gretel makes you mine gems, called love stones. You know those are stones that get fumes in your nose, right?" Says Robert. "No? I don't know that. What kind of fumes?" Says Grim. "The kind of fumes that you can make someone fall for you." Says Robert. "What, no I feel great mining them. They are not a problem to find most of the time." Says Grim. "Grim do you have a nose and a computer?" Says Robert. "Yeah, I have both of those." Says Grim. "Well, search it up if I am right about the fumes." Says Robert. Grim sighs. "Fine I will search it up. Then we are off to the mines." Says Grim. "Alright. Whatever you say." Says Robert. Grim searches up love stone. As he looks at the info about love stone. Grim looks right at Robert in an eye roll. "Fine you are right. They have fumes, but I don't know why I feel nothing, When I mine it? I have no idea why it does nothing to me." Says Grim. "I am sort of thinking that Gretel makes you mine it because you don't get affected by love stone." Says Robert. Robert and Grim look at what love stone does and Grim looks at Robert as if he has seen a ghost. "Gretel likes me?" Says Grim. "I guess so. Uncle Skull was right about you." Says Robert. "Let's just get this mining over with. I don't care if Gretel likes me or not. I just want our uncle skull to be gone back into his world." Says Grim. Robert looks at Grim for a few moments. "Hey, Grim. It's okay if you like her. Everyone has feelings for someone in their life." Says Robert. Grim ignores him and gets his pick out of his closet from his office. "You stay here. I don't want you acting weird." Says Grim. "Okay, I will stay in your office then." Says Robert. "Alright I will see you in a couple hours." Says Grim. As Grim walks out of his office. Robert sits down in Grims office chair, but then he gets up from the chair and looks around, looking at what Grim has in his office. Robert stops in spot looking at a picture of Cynthia which was their mom. Dead mom. Robert picks it up and sits down on the office chair. Just looking at the picture.

The girl that saved Luna wakes Luna up for breakfast. The girl gives Luna a plate. "Can you talk? Don't mean to be rude or anything I am just wondering?" Says Luna. The girl shakes her head no. "Thanks for the food. What's your name?" says Luna. The girl looks at Luna. Not knowing how she is going to tell her name. Then she finds a stick and there was dirt everywhere. The girl that can't speak picks up the stick and writes down a name. The first letter was S. Then the rest of it spelled out Scarlet. "So, your name is Scarlet?" Says Luna. Scarlet nods yes to agreeing what her name is. "That's a pretty name." says Luna. Scarlet erases her name off the dirt. Scarlet writes thank you on the dirt. "No problem, Scarlet." Says Luna in worry. Scarlet erases off the dirt that was saying thank you. The girl writes in. "Why do you look worried?" The writing in the dirt says. Luna looks up at Scarlet, Luna does not know how to explain that Luna was annoyed that they just left Hazel in the night suffering painfully wrapped up in deadly vines that is sucking Hazel's energy away out of Hazel's body. "I am worried about Hazel, the girl that we left last night to suffer. I hope there is a good reason why, to do that Scarlet. Leaving Hazel behind." Says Luna. Scarlet erases the sentence that Scarlet wrote in the dirt. Scarlet writes down. "Trust me, there was a good reason why we left her, Luna. I know you don't like to leave your family behind, but that was a time that you needed to leave." Scarlet writes in the dirt. Luna was still worried about Hazel. Luna did not know why Scarlet came to save Luna but decide to leave Hazel behind. Scarlet erases her big sentence in the dirt. Scarlet writes down "we must go to Time Witch Ruby." Says Scarlet's writing in the dirt. "Wait a second. You know Time Witch Ruby?" Says Luna. "Yeah. She is the one who taught me how to be a Time Witch in the first place, and she is also the one that sent me here to get you out of that situation you were in. That you are not supposed to get involved yet." Scarlet writes in the dirt. "Fine, I want to meet this, Ruby. That told you to abandon my sister." Says Luna. Scarlet erases her other sentence. Scarlet writes down in the dirt. "Alright let's go meet up with Ruby in a private place where no one is going to find us. While we are in her dream land with Ruby." Scarlet writes down in the dirt. "Her dream land?" Says Luna. Scarlet writes down. "Yes, it's the only safe place that we can talk to her. She can't come in our world. Cause she is busy doing stuff in the Time Realm." Scarlets writes down in the dirt. "I have many questions. Right now. The dream realm and the Time Realm? Are they the same?" Says Luna. Scarlet writes down on the dirt. "No, Ruby makes her dream realm for talking that is how we Time Witches talk to each other." Scarlet writes down in the dirt. "So, anyone of a Time Witch can call each other?" Says Luna. Scarlet erases her sentence once again. Scarlet writes down. "Yes, that is how we all communicate. In different times or realms or space." Scarlet writes down in the dirt. "Wow. Why am I A Time Witch?" Says Luna. Scarlet erases her answer. Scarlet looks at Luna. Then looks down at the dirt. Finally, Scarlet moves her stick again writing. When scarlet was done. The answer on the dirt said. "I don't know why. Some people are just chosen to be a Time Witch. In their blood or something. I don't know. Ruby would know more because she is the leader of the Time Witches." Scarlet writes on the dirt. "Well, then I am just going to have to ask her myself." Says Luna. Scarlet writes down for the last time. "Let's go get ready then." Scarlet writes in the dirt. Scarlet gets up throwing the stick away out of her hand. Grabbing her stuff out of the tent. Luna gets up and helps pack up the tent and all their stuff. As they were finished packing all the stuff. Scarlet walked east toward a forest, deeper in the forest there was a cave waiting for Scarlet and Luna. To have a secret private talk with Time Witch Ruby.

As Luna and Scarlet arrive deeper in the forest. Scarlet sees a cave open and not full of bears or anything that would disturb them. They walk into the cave and set camp in there. Scarlet sets up her tent magically. Luna sets hers up with her hands. Once they were done unpacking and getting firewood. Scarlet sets up a safe area for Luna and Scarlet to call Time Witch Ruby for help and to ask what is next for them to do. Luna puts down all the firewood that she collected in the forest. Luna sat down drinking some water. Scarlet walked over to Luna writing down on a piece of paper that she had in her backpack the entire time. Scarlets writing said. "Come with me, I am ready to call Ruby." Says on scarlet's paper. Luna gets up, following Scarlet to where she wanted Luna to come with. Scarlet grabbed out another piece of paper writing down. "Sit down on this chair." Scarlet's writing said. Luna sits down on the chair. Luna was wondering why the chairs were this close together. But Luna just sat down with no questions asked. Suddenly Scarlet grabbed out another piece of paper writing down. "Don't let go of my hand in the Dream Realm." Scarlet's writing says on the piece of paper. "Okay. I won't I promise." Says Luna. Scarlet grabs hold of Luna's hand. Scarlet closes her eyes, saying words. Luna was surprised because Scarlet can't talk, but let she is speaking in a different language. Suddenly Luna's eyes closed. Luna could not hear scarlet's voice saying something in a different language, but Luna and Scarlet had their hands interact, holding together. "Alright let's meet up with Ruby." Says Scarlet. Luna looked at Scarlet surprised. "You can talk?" Says Luna. "Yeah, but not on the other world. It was very frustrating writing all those words on the dirt for you. Was going to just give up at some point, but it is worth writing for a Time Witch." Says Scarlet. Luna has a look on her face. Of saying I have many questions about you Scarlet. But Scarlet did not want to waste time talking about her. Scarlet needed to talk to Ruby to see what Scarlet must do next. "Okay, Luna. Do not let my hand go." Says Scarlet. "Why?" Says Luna. "Because you will get stuck in somewhere, we can't help at all for you. Even Ruby can't help. So, no matter what you do, do not let go of my hand." Says Scarlet. "Okay. I won't." Says Luna. "Okay, let's summon Ruby." Says Scarlet. Scarlet leads Luna to where she needed to go to summon Ruby in Scarlet's dream realm or getting Scarlet to come into Ruby's dream realm. "Alright we are here." Says Scarlet.

Scarlet closes her eyes thinking about Ruby. Suddenly there was a phone ringing sound in Scarlet's head. Luna heard something or someone answering Scarlet's call. Luna heard a voice. "Give me a second, Scarlet. I am just in another call, just wait right there." Says the voice. Luna looks over at Scarlet's face. Her eyes were still closed. Luna was standing there not knowing what is about to happen. Suddenly there began glowing shapes around them both of Luna and Scarlet. It was a beautiful purple glow and red. Suddenly Luna and Scarlet were in a different place. Luna sees that there were stars all over in the sky. Then there was a chair a big chair. Someone was sitting on the chair. It was a woman who had red hair as the blood moon. The woman got up and walked toward Scarlet. "Hey, Scarlet. Did you bring Luna with you?" Says the woman. "Yes, my lord Ruby." Says Scarlet. Luna looks at the woman. "Luna I am finally meeting you for the first time. I am happy that you have made it this far in being a Time Witch." Says Ruby. "What do you mean I have made it this far in being a Time Witch?" Says Luna. "Well, Luna don't you see. You have the heart of being a Time Witch for the time you were born. But since your parents knew that you were a Time Witch. They knew who they could talk to, to making your destiny later in your life. Because their lives were already complicated, so they asked me if I could... Take your power till your parents died or when you became 18 years old. But since your parents died, I came to you in your dream when you were 8 years old and alone. Your powers awoken when your parents passed on, but now you are safe from all the complications that your parents had in their life. You are no longer involved." Says Ruby. "What does all this mean, that now I am involved in the Time witch thing?" Says Luna. "You are involved in between Time and Space. It's your job and my job to keep Time and Space fair for everyone and to also make sure that everyone got their destinies sorted out." Says Ruby. "So, it's my destiny to become a Time Witch and to I don't know let my sister deal with an insane person which his name is Skull." Says Luna. "Yeah, I am afraid that you are going to have to wait till the end of the battle between the saviours." Says Ruby. "Well, when can I get in the action? I am not a kind of person that stands around waiting for my turn." Says Luna. "I know you are that kind of person, but you must not interfere with Hazel's destiny. It is her destiny to become evil for a bit then you come in. You Luna. You are the one who is going to save the world. That is your destiny and Hazel's destiny for the time being." Says Ruby. Luna suddenly feels better in her veins that in a point of time Luna is going to be the one who is the only one that can stop Hazel for destroying the world. Along side of Reaper Skull. "Alright. Lord Ruby. I need to know what is next for me?" Says Scarlet. Ruby turns to Scarlet. "You must. Make sure that Luna success her destiny to saving Hazel in the battle. It's getting close to the end of the beginning." Says Ruby. "THAT'S ALL I HAVE TO DO. For the next rank!" Says Scarlet. "Yes, that is all you must do for Luna. She is the saviour in this story. Right now, we must talk about the future for Luna." Says Ruby. "What are we talking about me?" Says Luna. Ruby looks over at Luna for a few moments then looks back over at Scarlet. "We can't talk right now though." Says Ruby. "Why?" Says Luna. "Because Luna this is a private tale that you must not know. Scarlet we will talk about it later, but for now. You guys have much to do." Says Ruby. "Wait, Ruby. Can I have the ability to talk in the other world? Just for a bit." Says Scarlet. "I can't control who you are. I am sorry Scarlet. I believe that you can do this. Without a voice. You got Luna here without a voice. I am very proud of you Scarlet. You have become a great Warrior as a Time Witch, but I must go now. I believe in you Scarlet and you to Luna." Says Ruby, as she disappears out of thin air. Suddenly Scarlet and Luna were back in the other world that the Time Witches are calling it right now. Luna looks around in the cave, still worrying about Hazel. Of what Skull is doing or what his plan is to destroy this world.

Grim walks in the room with the love stones in a bag. Grim looked like a wreak. He was covered in dirt. Grim also looked tired. "What happened to you?" Says Robert. Grim puts his pickaxe away in his closet. As Grim closed the closet door in his office. He walks toward Robert like he was a zombie. "The mines are what happened to me. What do you think happened to me?!" Says Grim. "Okay, sassy sue." Says Robert. Putting his hands up in the air as if he had a gun pointed at his face. "Well, I am sorry that the mines are difficult to focus and it's hot down there." Says Grim in an exhausted sigh. As Grim sits down for a few moments. Robert grabs out of the fridge a bottle of water.

Robert walks over to Grim to give him the bottle of water. "Thank you?" Says Grim. "What. What is wrong with me giving you a bottle of water?" Says Robert. "Nothing is wrong I just did not except you to give me a water. That's all." Says Grim. Grim drinks the water. Robert gives Grim a few moments to feel fine to answer some questions about what they are doing next with the love stones. Finally, Robert gets up and sits right next to Grim on the couch in his office. "I know that face of yours Robert. You want to know what is next in getting to meet up with Gretel. Is that what you are fishing for?" Says Grim. "Yeah, how did you know I was going to ask something about Gretel." Says Robert. "Because you have mom's face when she is waiting for someone to finish relaxing a little bit. But since you want to know now. The piece of the puzzle, the final piece of the puzzle is on my desk. But I have to do the last step." Says Grim. Robert walks over to Grims desk to see that there was a box with Gretel's name on it. Robert picked up the box walking over to Grim with it in his hand. Robert gives it too Grim. Grim takes it out of Robert's hand. He opens the box and there was a piece of paper in the box. He picks it up and reads it in his head. Moments later Grim felt not exhausted anymore. He felt determined to be meeting up with Gretel and putting his Uncle Skull away forever in his realm for the rest of Grims life. "Come on we got a place to find that Gretel likes to be summoned. I want her in a good mood when she gets summoned. Because she can be rude when she gets summoned somewhere that she does not like at all." Says Grim. As Grim walks out of the room, Robert followed Grim wherever he was going.

A couple hours later Grim and Robert were in a beautiful part of the forest there was a waterfall, and pond connected to the waterfall. There were flowers every where, and there was an open spot for the sun coming in the forest when you would look up in the sky. You could see many clouds popping in front of the sun. It would still hurt your eyes when looking up. But Grim looked happy to be here. "This spot is perfect." Says Grim. "Question. Why does it matter if Gretel likes where she is summoned?" Says Robert. "There was one time when I summoned her. It was bad. She screamed at me. For summoning her in a village full of people. Then there was this other time I summoned her in a sticky Barn, and she was not in a great mood to help anyone that day. But anyway, we should get everything set up for the night." Says Grim. Grim gets out the piece of paper that Robert was reading earlier about Gretel. Grim said to Robert to just let him do all the work. So, Robert just sat there watching Grim get the summoning ready for Gretel at nighttime. Which that was in three or two hours later.

"Ahhh, get me OUT OF HERE. GET ME OUT." Says Polly in her head. Someone appeared in her head. It was Time Witch Ruby. "Polly, what's wrong?" Says Ruby. "You know what is wrong. Every Time Witch knows what is going on with everyone. Especially you, you are the lord of Time Witches." Says Polly. Ruby looks at Polly. "Oh, right you are being mind controlled by your boyfriend Jack. Or Ex-boyfriend, right?" Says Ruby. "Yes, JUST GET ME OUT OF THIS SITUATION PLEASE. The headaches hurt." Says Polly. "Well, I am afraid that you need to do this yourself. Polly you are strong and independent Witch. I believe in you. That you can get of this situation on your own." Says Ruby. Before Ruby could teleport away out of Polly's head. Polly grabbed Ruby on the arm begging Ruby to help Polly. "Polly I am sorry, but I can't help right now. If you want help call Nelia, she is happy to help an old friend." Says Ruby. "I hate her and besides you were always a better friend than her. You always were there for us both. Please help me. I will tell you anything." Says Polly. "Polly its against my law to help anyone with this kind of stuff. I only can watch. You know that." Says Ruby. "Yeah, but why can't you just help me once and I will do you anything you want. I just want out of this situation." Says Polly. Ruby looks at her old friend in suffering all Ruby can do is just watch Polly be in pain. By her own thoughts of helping evil instead of the good. She hated helping Jack. Polly hated it more because she could not fight back, or she felt like she could not fight back in the first place. "Polly, I can't help you. I believe that you can fight this nightmare that you are having. All by yourself. I always thought you were the strong one in this group. So, that is why I believe that you can do this own your own." Says Ruby. Ruby fades out of Polly trapped dream land. Polly screams louder after Ruby leaves. Polly tried to relax, but it only got worse in her head. Polly was listening to the words that were negative on her side. Polly could only crumble to the ground crying and believing what the words are saying about her being weak and pathetic, but somewhere in that heart of Polly's she did not believe what the words were saying to her.

"Jack, get me ready for the summoning of the undead tonight." Says Skull in an evil grin. "Yes, my lord Skull. Come with me Polly darning." Says Jack. "I am coming." Says Polly. Polly and Jack leave Lord Skull alone with Hazel on the gray table still underneath all those vines that were sucking her life force away out of her body and into Polly. Giving her more strength of living longer. In this lifetime. Skull got up from his throne that Skull got Jack to make for him since he was going to be the new king of souls. He wanted all the souls to himself. Skull looked over Hazel smiling in evil. "Hazel, you and I are going to rule this world. I would love it if it was my Amy, but you will be just as good and good enough like Amy your auntie. That you never will and ever meet. I miss her. She was so beautiful and smart. She was my favorite niece. Even though she had Cynthia foolishness, but I still loved her as family. She was the only one who did not betray in this entire family line." Says Skull. Hazel was trying to say something, but she was just too weak to say anything with the vines taking her life force away from her slowly. Hazel felt something else besides her life force being taken away from her. She felt like laughing and wanting to join her great uncle Skull on his journey of becoming the next king of Souls. She wanted or felt like joining his team in evil. But there was also this other side of Hazel. Was fighting staying on the good side, but it felt like Hazel was falling off the good side and going to the dark faster. Is all Hazel could do was let it happen. Hazel, let the evil course through your veins. "Let the evil take over and be your buddy. Evil always wins at the end." Says Skull. Hazel looks up at Skull finally having the strength to say something. "No, good always wins. You will see. I may be turning on your side, but evil will always have light to fight and light will always have evil to fight. That is how it works in this world." Says Hazel weak. Skull looks down at Hazel. "Why did your sister not take you away then, if good always wins? Isn't your sister supposed to save the light." Before Hazel could say anything. Skull continued talking. "Don't you see Hazel she gave up on you. She could only see a weak and dark little girl. That is too late to save for the light. Let the evil course through your veins. My child. You will understand one day that evil is the light. That keeps light moving. The only reason why light is real, because darkness was here first. And that is why darkness wins all the TIME. The light should be thanking the darkness. We made the light; we made the hero's a person a symbol of hope. They are the weak ones. They fight because they get themselves involved and light just wants more attention. Light takes the spotlight. Darkness and lightness. We fight each other because both sides never stop fighting each other. One the light will know their dark time. Which might be tomorrow." Says Skull in an evil grin. Hazel can't say anything mostly because she does not know what to say to that and Skull is right about that. Darkness was here first, and light is life they came second. Hazel looks up at the sky which there is the sun, trees, birds chirping. Then there was Lord Skull standing before Hazel right above her. Staring down at Hazel. Expecting Hazel to say something back. Hazel was too weak to say anything. She was also speechless for what Lord Skull has said to her. "That is what I thought. I am going to leave you now to think about what I just said. I am going to make the vines to the work. There working just fine. You will see what I mean soon. Hazel, my great niece." Says Skull in an evil grin. Lord Skull walks away from Hazel, walking toward his throne sitting there watching as Hazel suffers the consequences of being good.

Polly and Jack were walking in the forest alone. Basically, near nightfall. Polly stopped right in spot staring into space. Jack was collecting the stuff that Lord Skull needed for the summoning of the undead army. Jack then noticed that Polly was just standing there looking in the distance doing nothing. Jack walks up to Polly staring right into her eyes. Polly was still thinking of what Ruby had said to Polly. That she can fight the mind control that her boyfriend was put on her. Inside Polly's head there were words that weren't true, but some of them were. Polly sat there in her head for a couple minutes realizing what Ruby did when she left the inside of her head. Ruby helped a little bring the spell weaken the negative words. Polly listened to the words of what Ruby said before she left. Then suddenly the negative words were lowering down a bit. Polly's headache was fading a little. Polly just kept thinking about what Ruby

225

had said and that made her stronger for some reason, but Polly did not think to much of why this was working well. Suddenly Polly stud up and yelled in the void of inside of her head. "I CAN DO THIS. I AM NOT WEAK. I AM NOT STUPID. I AM ENOUGH." Says Polly. Suddenly Polly punched Jack right in the face getting out of his mind control spell. Polly runs away from Jack into the forest, she keeps running away far from Jack before Jack could do anything to Polly again. Polly just keeps running without thinking of where she is going to end up.

Jack wakes up from being punched in the face by Polly. All Jack can think was about what Lord Skull was going to do to Jack he was terrified of Lord Skull being angry at him. Jack opens a bag and collects all the stuff on the list that Lord Skull needs for the summoning of the undead souls that Lord Skull is planning to gain control of. Couple moments later. Jack had all the stuff in the bag that Lord Skull needed for the final summoning of the undead souls. Jack walks back toward where Lord Skull is sitting on his throne waiting for Jack to drop off all the stuff. As Jack arrives back to Lord Skull. Lord Skull sits up from his throne walking up to Jack taking the bag out of Jack's hand. Lord skull walks up to Hazel. With a bowl in his other hand. Lord Skull placed the bowl next to Hazel. Lord Skull opened the bag grabbing out all the stuff, that Jack worked hard to get. In just under an hour. Lord Skull smashes all the items in a ball, stirring them in the bowl making a potion. Lord Skull picks up the bowl. Making Hazel drink the potion. Then Hazel had enough strength to scream in pain. Hazel's scream was loud that birds all over the forest flew away across the sky. Lord Skull looked up at the night sky looking at all the birds flying across the sky. Hazel's wings grow back on her back. They were strong enough to destroy the vines off her wrists and ankles. Hazel flew up in the night sky. It was hard to see Hazel in the night stars, but Lord Skull was excited to have Hazel on his side and her knowing what it is like to have the evil flow in her veins. Hazel flew down to bow to her Lord, which was Skull. "Yes, my child, you finally understand who you are meant to be." Says Lord Skull.

"Grim, what is the hold up here?" Says Robert. "I can hear her coming." Says Grim. "Okay, but please tell her to hurry, the world is at shake right now." Says Robert. Robert hears a scream in deeper in the forest. Robert thinks it sounded like Hazel. Robert was getting more worried now. Suddenly a woman came out of the woods with a dark cloak on. Her hair was hidden, but you could see her eyes glowing in the darkness. That was Gretel. Gretel's eyes always glowed in the darkness. Gretel walks out of the bushes walking toward Grim. Gretel notices that Grim and her weren't alone. "What is he doing here?" Says Gretel. "Gretel it's okay, Robert is working with me. We need your help putting Uncle Skull back in his realm for eternity. I don't want him to have another way out ever again." Says Grim. "How did he get out?!" Says Gretel. "He got out because my niece is powerful apparently like my sister that I have never meant. Apparently, you know who my sister was to? Why did you not say anything?" Says Grim. Gretel stud there looking at Grim in the eyes. Looking worried. "I could not say anything. Your mom told me not to tell anyone about Amy." Says Gretel. "But I trusted you. Gretel. You were my only real friend, the day you cursed me with my uncle I have questioned my friendship with you and now figuring out that you did not bother telling me that I had a sister. I have lost many trust in you. But we still need your help. I need your help." Says Grim. Gretel stud there expecting Grim to yell at her, but all Gretel got was I need your help to put my uncle away again. "Grim, I will help you with that. I am great at putting your uncle away. I always have the perfect items to lock people into realms that they can't get out of." Suddenly all three of them hear someone coming running toward them in the darkness. Robert prepared his gun at the brushes in the forest. Suddenly Polly came running out of the forest as Robert was about to shot Grim stopped Robert shotting Polly in the head. "No, don't. Don't shot Polly. She is a friend." Says Grim. As Polly stops in spot terrified of a gun pointed right at her face, but Robert puts the gun away. "Sorry, I thought you were someone coming to attack us." Says Robert. Polly was out of breath. Polly just sat down sitting on a rock right next to Robert's rock that he was sitting on. "Polly, what happened to you. Why were you running in the forest in the dark?" Says Grim. Polly finally catches her breath. "I was running away from Jack; he was mind controlling me." Says Polly. Grim looks at Polly and walks over to her sitting next to her. "Hey, Polly it's okay. I thought Jack was dead?" Says

Grim. "No, he is not dead. His demonic form is out right now because he is with his king right now. Lord Skull. Which is your uncle." Says Polly. "Wait, What Jack was the one who kidnapped Hazel in the first place." Says Grim. "Yeah, he did. He was trying to convince me to help do that, but I said no. Then he put me under a spell, and I was under his control for a couple days, then here we are talking to me running away from Jack and Lord Skull. Wait what are you guys doing here in the forest in the darkness?" Says Polly. "Wow, you might as well have the permission to kill Jack in. And we are here at night summoning Gretel my old friend that trapped Lord Skull, which you are calling my uncle now apparently. But anyway, we are trying to trap him again in his realm. Are you going to help us get Lord Skull out of this world forever?" Says Grim. Polly sits there for few moments thinking about what Grim is asking of her to help with. Suddenly Polly nods her head yes. "I will help you, bring that Damn jerk down in back in his hell. I am in for a battle." Says Polly. Grim smiles. "Good, let's plan out what we are doing then." Says Grim. Suddenly they all see the clouds in the night sky turning greenish and bluish. Robert thinks to himself. What is happening. Gretel was more scared than anyone around her. Cause Gretel knows what Lord Skull has done. "I can't believe he has done the impossible." Says Gretel. Grim looks at Gretel confused. "What is going on?" Says Grim. "Your uncle just opened a vortex from the world of the undead. Known as the lost souls. He probably made a deal with the Soul King." Says Gretel. "Yeah, that was and is his plan. He wants to control all the souls in that realm and become the soul king himself." Says Polly. Everyone turns their heads toward Polly. Looking mad, but then they eye roll. "What!" Says Polly. "Why did you not tell us about my uncle wanting to do that?" Says Grim in a sigh. "I am sorry." Says Polly. "Polly, it's fine. But we know his plan now. that is all that matters." Says Grim in a smile. "Why are you smiling brother? This is not good." Says Robert. "I know it's not well, but we had a person in the inside of our uncles' operations and a witch that has trapped him before. I think we are in a good spot. To say that we are in the clear of winning this fight against Uncle Skull." Says Grim in a bigger smile. "You are right we got this." Says Robert. Gretel was standing there looking at the clouds, not saying a word.

CHAPTER **18**

THE BAD DAY

Amy woke up in the forest alone. Amy feels like she deserves to be alone at this point after what she has done to Emma. Amy still could not get Nina's face out of Amy's head. Amy was afraid to go to school or home again. So, she decided to stay in the forest. Amy's powers were still out of control as well, she was trying to control herself, but every time she tried. Amy could not get the words out of Amy's head of what Nina said to her the night when Emma got ran over. Amy just sits down on a log looking up at the gray clouds excepting rain to drip all over her. But nothing comes down. Just Amy looking up at the sky.

Jade woke up in Nina's room. Noticing Nina was not in her bed. Eva and Oliva sleeping on there couch still. Jade walks toward the bathroom and as she opens the door to the bathroom. Jade sees that Nina was standing outside on her balcony just standing in space. Looking at the dark clouds. Jade walks toward Nina outside to her balcony. Jade taps Nina on the shoulder to make sure Jade would not scare her by walking behind her. Nina turns around with tired sad eyes. Jade was still mad at Nina for yelling at Amy and blaming her that Emma got ran over by a car, but Jade ignored that feeling. "How are you this morning?" Says Jade. "I am fine, I am just tired, sad and angry at Amy still." Says Nina. Jade looks at Nina and rolls her eyes at Nina. "Are you rolling your eyes at me, because I am mad at your friend "Amy"." Says Nina. "Yeah, because I think it is a dumb reason to be mad at her for you dropping her skirt on the road. This is your clumsy hand's fault!" Says Jade. Nina's eyes look at Jade angrily than ever before. "Did you just say it is my fault that I dropped Amy's skirt? I never drop anything, I am great at carrying bags, but I guess this was the one thing that did not want to stay." Says Nina angrily. Jade realizes what she said. "Nina I am sorry that I said that this was your fault, but it's still not right that you are blaming my friend, that I let in this group." Says Jade. "Jade, I have something to say to you. I never trusted you or ever liked you. And I still feel that way, but since you think this is my fault. I don't want you in the group anymore. I was going to give you a chance, but you show me every time to not give you another chance." Says Nina. "Fine, I don't want to be in this group anyway." Says Jade. "Good, then leave. NOW." Says Nina. "Fine, I will." Says Jade. Jade leaves the house with her stuff. Before Jade uses the bathroom before Jade leaves. Eva and Olivia were awake looking at Jade as soon Jade came in. "Jade, were you fighting with Nina?" Says Olivia. "Yeah, because she still blames Amy for Emma getting hit by a car." Says Jade. "Jade, I know you are sticking up for Amy and that is good of you, but right now Nina just needs support and patience, for that kind of thing. Remember Emma is in the hospital." Says Olivia. Jade goes to the bathroom, thinking of what Olivia said. When Jade came out of the bathroom. Olivia was gone off her couch. Jade knew what it meant for Olivia to be dealing with this kind of thing again. Olivia has dealt with this kind of pain before. Olivia's grandma was ran over by a car and her grandma did not last, she passed away right after that car rammed her. All Olivia could remember from the driver. He did not care at all about an old lady that died by him Olivia's grandma. He only cared about the dent in his car. The man had an enough money to repair the dent, but when that man found out when Olivia's grandma died. He started laughing and he said good, I am happy that old person died. She deserved it. So, Olivia knows how it feels, for someone that you love gets ran over by a car. Olivia wanted to hurt that man for laughing. At Olivia's grandma's death. Olivia hated that man. Jade sees that Olivia was outside hugging Nina. Nina was crying with tears on her face. Jade just stud there looking at her and sighed. Jade walked back to her couch that she slept on. Jade grabbed her phone out of her backpack. She messaged Amy. "Hey, Amy. I am worried about you. Can I come find you?" Says Jade. Jade waited for Amy to message back, but there was no message back. Only that Amy read it. Jade was more worried about Amy. Someone knocked on Nina's bedroom door. Eva answered the door. "Hey, sorry to bother you guys, but someone is on the phone for Nina." Says Jasmine. "Okay, I will get her." Says Eva. As Eva leaves the door open, she walks out to the balcony of where Olivia and Nina were talking. Eva opens the balcony door. "Nina, Jasmine is here to tell you that someone is on the phone for you." Says Eva. Nina looked at Eva in many tears. "Eva, I don't think it's the best time for Nina to answer the phone." Says Olivia. "No, It's fine. I will answer the call." Says Nina. Nina walks out back into her bedroom walking toward Jasmine. "Who is on the phone for me currently?" Says Nina. "I have no idea, but here." Says Jasmine. Jasmine gives Nina the phone and Jasmine walks away from Nina. "Who is this?" Says Nina. "Hey, I am at the hospital with my daughter Emma." Says Emma's mom. "Oh, hey Emma's mom. How is Emma doing?" Says Nina. "I am sorry to be calling you at this hour, but I am going to come and pick her stuff up at your house." Says Emma's mom. "Oh okay, but how is Emma doing?" Says Nina. Nina could hear a sigh in the call from Emma's mom. "Nina, to be honest I want to say it will be okay, but I am not sure right now." Says Emma's mom. Nina looked down at the floor about to cry more, but Nina stud strong for Emma. "Okay, I am on my way to your house right now to get Emma's stuff. I want to be gone right away, so please have her stuff ready for me right away." Says Emma's mom. "Yeah, I will make sure all Emma's stuff is ready to go. See you soon." Says Nina. "Yeah, I will see you soon." Says Emma's mom. Emma's mom hung up on the phone Nina walked to Emma's couch she was going to sleep on, but since her mom was coming to pick her stuff up. Nina had to pack it up, Eva and Olivia helped get her stuff into her backpack. Once they were done with packing up all her stuff, Nina walked out of the room downstairs with Emma's stuff. Eva and Olivia were looking outside the window where Emma's mom's car pulled up a few minutes later, as Nina gave all Emma's stuff to Emma's mom. Emma's mom drove away fast before a wave that Nina was going to give. Nina closed the door and walked back up the stairs to her bedroom where everyone was not making eye contact with Nina. Nina just crawled into bed putting her head down on her pillow. Eva walks toward Nina to her bed. "Nina, do you want us to go home to give you some space to process all what happened last night?" Says Eva. Nina looks up at Eva with tired sad eyes. "I don't care what you guys do, but you must go home then you are more than welcome to head home. Especially Jade" Says Nina. Nina puts her head back on her pillow. Eva just looks around trying not look like she wants to go home bad. Eva walks out of the room to go to the bathroom. "Fine I will go. Bye I don't want to be here anyway." Says Jade. Nina looks up at Jade in angry. "Good LEAVE THEN." Says Nina. "Okay, bye." Says Jade. Jade leaves the room, slamming the door. Nina looks at the door as being slammed but lays her head down once again not caring. As Jade leaves the room. Nina's dad was walking toward the door of Nina's bedroom door. "Is she okay?" Says Nina's dad. Jade did not know how to answer honestly. "Sorry, I can't answer right now. Me and your daughter are having a fight right now." Says Jade. "Oh, okay? do you want some breakfast. We have a great chef here." Says Nina's dad. Jade looks at Nina's dad. "I should go." Says Jade. "Oh okay, that is fine. I will go ask if Nina and the other girls wants something to eat." Says Nina's dad. Nina's dad walks into Nina's room. Jade could hear him talking to Nina, Olivia, and Eva about some food. Jade walks out of the house. Jade felt like everyone was being unfair about how Amy just ran into the forest and that it mostly was Nina's fault that Amy thinks that it is her fault that Emma was ran over by a car. That was still unfair for Nina to just blame Amy for an accident that was not even Amy's fault. Jade walks out to the gate and pushes the open button. The gate opens Jade runs before the gate could close again. Jade was outside of Nina's property. Jade starts walking away from Nina's in angry walking toward her house, then to the forest Jade goes.

Troy and Cynthia wake up next to each other. Troy wakes up tired, but he is ready for the day ahead of him. Cynthia was still sleeping. Once again Troy gently pushes Cynthia off Troy's chest and gets out of bed. Troy walks quietly in their bedroom getting dressed. Once Troy was getting into some morning clothes for the outdoors. Troy goes downstairs to a quiet kitchen where Amy was not home, and Cynthia was sleeping upstairs still. Troy walks toward the kitchen making some food. Troy turns on the TV in the kitchen watching the news for the morning. Troy was cutting up some tomatoes for breakfast. Suddenly he heard and turned to look at the TV. Troy heard right. Some kid was ran over by a car last night. So far, they are not doing good. They have a huge chance of dying in the hospital. But Troy notices someone that looked like Amy running into the forest alone. Also, a girl that looked like Jade trying to stop her from running into the forest. Troy was a little worried now. Troy grabs his phone off the counter, messaging Amy. "Hey, Honey. Where are you right now?" Says Troy. Troy was standing there. Amy was not answering his messages. Troy was done making breakfast a few moments later. He was done waiting for a response from Amy, so Troy got up and ate the food he just made and cleaned up. Once he was done cleaning up in the kitchen he went out to where the car crash was last night. It took a couple hours driving there, but Troy made it. Troy looked at the forest where Troy thinks that Amy ran in there alone in the nighttime. Troy locks his car and walks toward the forest. Before Troy could continue walking into the forest alone. Troy found Amy's necklace on the ground. Troy picked it up and continued running in the forest looking for his daughter. Suddenly Troy could hear crying. Troy ran toward the crying and then there she was. Amy was crying on a stump in the forest near a pond. Amy was just sitting on a log. "Amy." Says Troy. Amy turns around to see that her dad was there, just looking at her. "Dad? How did you find me here?" Says Amy. "I saw you running in the forest alone on the news this morning. Why did you run in here alone?" Says Troy. "I ran in here because I deserve to die in this forest." Says Amy. "Why do you think that?" Says Troy. "It is my fault that Emma got ran over last." Says Amy. Troy looks at Amy. Troy whips her tears away off her face. "Hey, Amy. It's not your fault that Emma got ran over. It was an accident." Says Troy. "No, my skirt that Nina brought for me dropped out of Nina's hand and she went to get the bag off the road. Then Emma pushed Nina out of the way." Says Amy. Troy hugs Amy. "Amy it is still not your fault. Nina made that choice to go and pick up your skirt that she brought you. Don't blame yourself for what happened." Says Troy. "I was not blaming myself, but Nina was blaming me for what happened." Says Amy. "What, did she say?" Says Troy. Amy got the strength to stand up and tell Troy what Nina said to Amy. Troy was mad a little, but then said. "You should not listen to people like that. They are just the kind of people that bring you down. Amy, you are a good person, and you deserve people that won't blame you for those kinds of things." Says Troy. Amy looks up at Troy in sadness. "Amy, you look hungry let's go home." Says Troy. Amy get's up off the log and follows Troy back to the car. Suddenly Amy felt someone or something watching them. Amy yells out. "WHO IS THERE!!" Says Amy. Troy looks at Amy in confusion. "Honey let's go home. I got to get you home." Suddenly there was a gun shot. Troy went in front of Amy and fell to the ground. Amy just stud there looking at Troy frozen in spot. "DAD!" Says Amy. "Honey it's okay, just call on my phone or yours to call the hospital. It's okay, just stay calm." Says Troy. Amy grabs her phone calling the hospital. Amy tells them where they are. A few moments later the ambulance vehicles arrived. The paramedics ran toward Troy. Picking Troy up gently and putting him on a gurney. "Little girl is this your father?" Says the paramedics woman. Amy was just still paralyzed staring in space processing what just happened. The ambulance drives away with Amy in the back right next to Troy's unconscious body. They arrive at the hospital later; they guide Amy to the waiting room. They rush Troy's body to the emergency room. Amy was just sitting there looking at nothing and only imagining Troy holding Amy's hand than suddenly. Bam, Troy was on the ground bleeding out on the street. Amy was convinced that the world was trying to tell her that she does not deserve to live or be happy with anyone. Amy loses her mind. Amy trying to control her emotions in the hospital suddenly there was fire flickering in her hand. Amy was scared to do anything. Amy could not move one bit. Someone saw Amy just sitting alone in the waiting room. So, they sit right next to Amy. "Hey, what's up?" Says unknown. Amy looks over to see that it was a man talking to Amy while she was losing her mind again. "Hey, Amy. It's okay. I am here for you now." Says unknown. Amy looks at the man. "How do you know my name?" Says Amy. The man suddenly rolls his eyes. "Your mother didn't tell you did she." Says the man. "No? what did she not tell me?" Says Amy. "I am your uncle Skull. I volunteer at the hospital sometimes, but right now I am just visiting my father's grandma." Says Skull. "Why? Have I never heard of you before?" Says Amy. "I have no idea why. I guess Cynthia is still mad at our parents for abandoning her when she was pregnant with you." Says Skull. Amy looked at Skull for a few moments. "So, why are you here?" Says Uncle Skull. "My dad just got shot." Says Amy. "Oh, that is why you are staring in space looking sad. Amy, I believe that Troy will be fine. Your dad is a strong man. He can fight a shot." Says Uncle Skull. "How do you even know my dad? We have never seen each other in real life. Until now." Says Amy. "Yeah, because your mother does not want anything to do with her parents after when they abandoned her." Says Uncle Skull. "But why did they abandon my mom because she was pregnant with me?" Says Amy. "Your mother was 17 when she had you and our parents did not approve of Cynthia having kids at that age." Says Uncle Skull. "Oh. I get it. I guess everyone hates me." Says Amy. Skull looks at Amy. "You are not hated Amy. You just came at the wrong time, but I am happy you are here. I am sure that your dad was happy that he had you in his life to, and your mom I bet she loves you." Says Uncle Skull. "Yeah, you are right, but the world just hates me." Says Amy. "I know that feeling." Says Uncle Skull with a sigh. "What happened to you that made you think that you were not good enough?" Says Amy. "How did you know I was thinking that?" Says Uncle Skull. "I don't know. I just guessed from your sigh." Says Amy. Skull sits there turning away from Amy for a couple seconds. Finally, Skull told why. "I accidently killed my dad's sister. She was my favorite aunt. I was trying to heal her, but my powers were not in control of themselves. I tried to heal her, but I killed her instead. I watched my favorite aunt turn into ashes in front of me. Then my dad came to find his sister in ashes in front of me. My dad hated me, and he still does hate. He left my mom because of me." Says Uncle Skull. "Wow, that is horrible." Says Amy. "Yeah, it is horrible. I can still hear my aunts screams in my head. So, you are not the only one who the world is hunting ever. The world is probably screwing someone else right now." Says Uncle Skull. "Yeah, you are probably right." Says Amy. Skull looks in the distance still just sitting down on the chair in the waiting room. A doctor called Amy's name. "Is there an Amy here?" Says the doctor. Amy walks up to the doctor to see if dad was alright. "I am Amy." Says Amy. "Alright. I think you will need a seat for this." Says the doctor. Amy sits down. "Amy, I am so sorry, but your dad. He did not make it. Your dad passed away on the operation table." Says the doctor. Amy started crying hard, probably harder than ever before. Uncle Skull walked up to them to see what was going on. "Hey, what's up?" Says

Uncle Skull. "Her dad passed away just now. while we were trying to give him blood, but he lost to much of blood and the bullet was deep. I think it was to late to save him. The bullet was right in the heart." Says the doctor. "GET OUT OF MY NIECE'S face." Says Uncle. The doctor stud there looking at Amy. Then he walked away. "Amy, its okay." Says Uncle Skull. "How is it okay, my dad is dead!" Says Amy. "I know, I know, but I should probably take you home to your mom." Says Uncle Skull. Skull holds Amy's hand and drives her back to there house. Amy did not know how Uncle Skull knew where they lived, but Skull arrived at Amy's house. Amy stares into space not noticing that she was home. Skull shook Amy out of space. "Hey. Kid we are at your house." Says Uncle Skull. Amy gets out of Skulls car without saying a single word. Amy just walks toward the front door. Skull went inside to see Cynthia and to explain what happened to Troy. Skull shuts the front door to the house behind him. As Skull walked into Cynthia's house. Amy was crying hard in Cynthia's arms. "What happened?" Says Cynthia. Skull walks into the room. Cynthia looks up at Skull realizing that he dropped Amy off. "What are you doing here?" Says Cynthia. "Don't get mad. I am just here to drop off your daughter and tell you what happened." Says Skull. "Fine, shot your bullet. Skull." Says Cynthia. Skull explains that Troy was shot and passed away on the operation table in the hospital. Cynthia then put herself down on the chair that was behind her. Cynthia sat down looking at nothing just like what Amy was doing in the waiting room at the hospital. "I know it's a lot to take in, but Cynthia you have to stay positive for Amy there. I really think that kid can not deal with another parent right now sad or dying. Amy is a good kid. I wish our parents gave her a chance to be in their lives." Says Skull. Cynthia still has no words to be said right now. "Skull where did you find Amy." Says Cynthia. "I told you she was in the waiting room where I volunteer at the hospital. That is where I found your girl just sitting there alone." Says Skull. "Skull I am thankful that you brought back my daughter, but I think you should go for now. Me and Amy need some space just for a bit." Says Cynthia. Skull nods. "Okay, I will give you a week. But I will come check up on you guys once a day after that week is over." Says Uncle Skull. "Okay." Says Cynthia. "Okay. I should go it's getting late." Says Uncle Skull. Skull leaves the house. Shutting the door behind him and drives away from the house out of the driveway. As Skull leaves the driveway. Cynthia breaks down crying. Cynthia's hands were on her face. She was crying hard in her hands were covered in tears. Amy walks in the living seeing her mom cry. Amy holds Cynthia's hand. Saying it will be okay and it will get better. But Cynthia lost her mind for a second. "NO, IT'S NOT. Going to be fine. Amy." Says Cynthia. Cynthia realized what she has done. Amy starts crying again. Cynthia stops crying. Cynthia tries to comfort Amy, but nothing works. Amy runs toward her bedroom crying and slamming her door behind her. Cynthia looks down at the floor feeling bad for what she said to Amy. Cynthia walks toward Amy's bedroom. Of course, Cynthia hears crying in her bedroom. Cynthia opens the door. Cynthia walks into Amy's room to hug her trying to calm her down. Finally, Amy just hugs Cynthia. Suddenly Amy fell asleep in her mother's arms. Cynthia gently tucked Amy in bed. Cynthia got up and turned off Amy's bedroom lights. Cynthia shut the door behind her quietly. Cynthia walked into the living room turning off all the lights in the house. Cynthia then walked up the stairs to her bedroom where her boyfriend was not there of course. Cynthia crawled into bed. Tossing and turning in her sleep. Cynthia tried every single way to falling asleep then suddenly she had one more thing to try that also helped. Cynthia tried sleeping with music on. Just sleepy music. Cynthia started falling asleep crying.

Jade was walking around alone in the dark. It was taking awhile to find Amy in the forest. Jade was starting to think that Amy just went back home. So, Jade started walking home. Before Jade started going to start walking back to her house. Jade got a call from Eva. "Hey, Jade where are you?" Says Eva. "I am looking for Amy right now in the forest where she ran in alone. Like you guy's care." Says Jade. "Oh wow, Yeah Nina was saying rude things about you. What did you and her fight about?" Says Eva. "I don't care what she says about me. Me and Nina are fighting because she still blames Amy for Emma's accident." Says Jade. "I know she is blaming people for what happened to Emma, but I think you would do the same if Amy got rammed down by a car. How would you react if someone that you cared about got rammed down, and they were in a coma or something worse?" Says Eva. "I would not do what

Nina is did to Amy. I would be saying it's not your fault or not saying anything." Says Jade. "Well, Jade just remember everyone acts different in the game of life. Life is not a game, but it's chance and choice." Says Eva. Eva can hear a sigh coming out Jade's mouth. "Jade just remember. That Nina had worse than us. She has been dealing with lots of stuff." Says Eva. "I know the queen of the group has many more problems than anyone new in the group." Says Jade. "Jade, that is kind of unfair." Says Eva. Jade hangs up on the phone and continues to walk back home in angry at everyone in the group. Jade walks away in the darkness toward home thinking about the words that were said with her "friends" today.

CHAPTER 19

TROY'S FUNERAL

It's been a few days since Troy passed away by a gun shot in the heart. Amy blames herself a little, but Cynthia and her uncle Skull convince her that it was not her fault that Troy was shot in the heart. Amy did not to go to school anymore after that, so Cynthia let her go back to being home schooled for awhile, but since Cynthia had to go find another job. Uncle Skull was teaching her simple math, science, English, history, and philosophes. Amy got to get to know more of uncle Skull as well. Skull was a traveller he loved going around the global to see mountains, beaches, oceans, etc. Amy was inspired to learn more. Amy was learning a lot from her Uncle Skull. Amy wanted to go on a trip with him once day. Uncle Skull said that he was planning on going to Hawaii this spring and Amy was begging him if she could come with him. Skull said "Yeah, of course you can. You just have to ask your mom first." Says Uncle Skull. Amy went to run to see what Cynthia was doing. Of course, Cynthia was busy putting Troy's Funeral together. Amy than changed her mind about asking now. Amy thinks that Amy should wait till her mom is alright talking about things that Amy wanted to ask. Amy walks back in the kitchen with Uncle Skull. "I am going to wait to ask mom, about it when dad's funeral is done and over with. I don't want to talk about me going away for awhile to mom. Also, that Hawaii is a happy place. Maybe you should ask if mom wants to come with us?" Says Amy. Skull looks down at Amy. "Maybe you are right. I should ask if your mother wants to come to Hawaii, she probably hates this cold weather. Maybe possibly get away from home for awhile." Says Uncle Skull. "Yeah, it is sort of sad because dad built this place out of love and hard work. He sometimes worked on this house day and night.

I miss him. Oh, and he was also making this garden down by the pond he made stairs to go down. He was making that garden for mom and me." Says Amy. Skull looked around the house seeing that, this house was beautifully made. Skull did not know it was made by Troy himself. Skull thought to himself. Wow I would have loved to know Troy a little, then he did. Skull walks back to the kitchen toward Amy. "Okay, Amy, I need you to get this done for me. It is History. It is probably the most interesting thing you are probably going learn about." Says Skull. Skull gives Amy the papers to read and gives her a book to read to finding the answers. "Uncle Skull?" Says Amy. "Yeah, my niece." Says Skull. "Why aren't you a teacher." Says Amy. "I guess I like to keep a low profile. I do like sharing knowledge to you, but to be honest I think I just like sharing to one person. I really have enjoyed teaching you all the stuff I know about what I have taught you for a couple days." Says Skull. Before Skull could walk out of the room to give Amy some space. "Wait, Uncle Skull." Says Amy. As she runs up behind Skull. "You are my favorite uncle. Thank you for teaching me all this stuff. It is all interesting." Says Amy. As Amy hugs Skull. Skull feels a tingle in his heart. The one that he has not felt in years. Since his aunt was alive before he accidently killed her. Skull hugs back Amy. "Okay, Amy study girl. I will be back in your mom's room. I need to chat with her." Says Skull." Okay." Says Amy. Amy walks back to her seat. Skull walks up the stairs to find Cynthia laying down on her back tired, but so sad. She was totally not in shape to have Amy around for around here. "Cynthia. I need to chat with you." Says Skull. Cynthia gets up from laying down on her bed. "Yeah, what's up?" Says Cynthia. "I think I might want to take Amy for awhile. I think you need some time to yourself. I think?" Says Skull. "Why, do you think that." Says Cynthia. "Amy hates seeing you sad. But now that Troy is gone, you are always sad. I don't want Amy to feel anymore pain. I think I might take Amy to Hawaii. She was asking if you wanted to come, but I think you need time to process all this what is happening and how you are going to deal with it." Says Uncle Skull. Cynthia stands there thinking about what her brother is saying. First time in a long time Cynthia agrees with Skull. "Okay, I will tell you what. I think you are right, but I really do still love Amy, but like you said I might need some space. So, I will agree with that." Says Cynthia.

Skull was surprised that she agreed to letting Amy come with Skull go to Hawaii. "Amy can go with you after when the funeral is done. The funeral is in two days from now. She can go for spring break if that is okay with you?" Says Cynthia. "Yeah, that is what my plan was to do anyway." Says Skull. Before Skull could go back downstairs. Cynthia stopped him. "Thank you, Skull, I really appreciate it, for offering to let my daughter go with you on vacation. To be honest I think she needs an escape as well." Says Cynthia. "I don't blame her she has been through a lot with friends and just losing her father. That is a bit much for a child like Amy." Says Skull. "Yeah, I agree." Says Cynthia. They both stare at each other for a few moments. "Well, I better get back to picking stuff for Troy's funeral." Says Cynthia in sadness. "Yeah, I will leave you to do that. I just wanted to get that out of the way." Says Skull. "Thank you, Skull I am thankful that you are doing this much for Amy. Even though you barely know her." Says Cynthia. "Cynthia she is family I do anything for family, and beside I am the favorite uncle." Says Skull in a smile. Cynthia laughs at how Skull said that. Skull leaves the room, as he does that Cynthia smiles. At how Skull likes Amy a lot. Cynthia did not know why Skull liked Amy so much, but she was happy someone else likes Amy a lot besides Cynthia and her friend Jade, that has not been talking lately to Amy, mostly because Amy was busy learning about what Skull is teaching her for school.

"Is a Nina here?" Says a nurse. "Yeah, I am right here." Says Nina. "Okay, you wanted to see Emma. Right?" Says the nurse. "Yeah, is it possibly if I could?" Says Nina. "Yeah, sure right this way. I am just going to tell you, that her family is in there." Says the nurse. "Okay, that is fine with me." Says Nina. As the nurse and Nina walk down the hallway to Emma's room in the hospital. The nurse and Nina arrive at the door of Emma's room. The nurse opens the door to the room, and Nina walks in to see Emma's mom and dad looking over her while she was still in a coma. The nurse shuts the door to the room as Nina walks in and grabs a seat. "How, is Emma doing?" Says Nina. Emma's dad looks over at Nina in much worry. "She is just in a coma that is all we know about Emma's condition." Says Emma's dad. Her mom was more quiet than usual. Her mom loved Emma very much, but she was more sensitive toward her family. If something ever happened to one of her daughters or sons. Emma's mom would go crazy on them, but this time it was just a face of silence and hard to read. The only thing that Nina could tell by Emma's mom's face was sadness, Nina felt bad for Emma's parents the most right now. They don't deserve to be seeing there Emma in a hospital bed. No parent deserves that. Nina and Emma's parents were just sitting there, being there for Emma for support. Hoping that something magic will happen, but nothing happens in those moments of visiting Emma in the hospital.

Jade messages Amy. "Hey, Amy how are you doing. Back in home schooling. I miss you a little." Says Jade. Amy messages back. "I miss you to. And I am loving it. My uncle is teaching me the most interesting stuff I have ever heard of. He is teaching me History and lots of other stuff." Says Amy. "Well, I am happy that you are happy." Says Jade. "Thank you. How are classes in person?" Says Amy. "They are fine, but I still miss you." Says Jade. "How is everyone?" Says Amy. Jade just looks at the text not knowing what to say to Amy at this point, because Jade was still mad that Nina and the group did not feel any symphony for Amy running in the forest alone in sadness and fear. "I am not talking to them right now; they are busy and I getting space from them for awhile." Says Jade. "What happened. I thought you liked your group a lot." Says Amy. "I do like my friend group, but right now they are being unfair to me right now." Says Jade. "Wait why are they being unfair to you right now?" Says Amy. "They were blaming you for the dumbest thing." Says Jade. "Jade. A lot of stupid stuff happened to me the past week. I miss you guys a lot, but I am scared to be in the same room as Nina. Because I feel like she is going to make a scene." Says Amy. "Oh yeah Nina would totally do that, but at this point I said meaner things to her than you did." Says Jade. "What did you and her fight about anyway?" Says Amy. "I started a fight with her about you. Because I think it is stupid that she just blames you for getting Emma hurt." Says Jade. "Well, Jade that is not my business, but don't try defending me anymore. I think you are better off with them anyway." Says Amy. "I don't think so. You are a nice person and Nina is just saying that her dropping your skirt is a sign of unlucky. I don't know it's just annoying stuff." Says Jade.

"I know, but don't fight with friends. Bad things happen fighting with friends." Says Amy. "Yeah, no shit." Says Jade. Amy or Jade don't text till awhile. "Hey, Jade it's okay to be worried sometimes, but don't let that worry affect your decisions." Says Amy. "I know, but Amy I must go. My classes are starting. I will talk to you later." Says Jade. "Okay see you around." Says Amy. Amy puts her phone back in her pocket. Amy gives all her attention back to her homework that her uncle gave to her. Amy sits there reading and writing down everything that she wanted to know or needed to know about the assignment. Uncle Skull sees her writing down a lot on that piece of paper. Skull was impressed by how she was compassionate about learning all the things that she could. So, Skull just went out for a walk around the house. Skull went to go find that garden that Amy was talking about that Troy was making for Cynthia. Skull wanted to see what Troy was working on, that made Amy smile. When Amy was telling Skull about his garden for his beautiful rose Cynthia.

Two days later. The funeral. "Amy get dressed we got to get going." Says Cynthia. Amy moves out of bed sad. Today is the day that they put Troy to rest, properly. Cynthia walks into Amy's room checking if she is getting dressed for the day. "Are you dressed yet?" Says Cynthia. "Almost, done." Says Amy in sadness. "I know this a sad day, but we got to be on time for this kind of thing." Says Cynthia. "I know, It's dad's funeral today. I guess I don't like to be remembered." Says Amy. Cynthia stands there looking in the distances just staring at nothing. Cynthia gets out of that phase when Amy walks out of her closet changed into black clothes for the funeral. "Good you are dressed now I am just going to turn off the lights then we can go." Says Cynthia. Cynthia turns off all the lights in the house. Amy and Cynthia get out of the house after when Cynthia turned off all the lights in the house. As they both got out of the house, there was a car waiting for them just outside in their driveway. Cynthia walks up to the car wondering who it is. "Cynthia it's me." Says Skull. "Skull what are you doing here?" Says Cynthia. "You said last night to me. Can you drive me and Amy to the funeral for tomorrow?" Says Skull. "Oh right, I forgot. I was drunk last night, when texting you." Says Cynthia. "Wait, why were you drinking? You don't like drinking." Says Skull. "Now I do." Says Cynthia. As Cynthia and Amy get in the car. Cynthia starts drinking rum out of the bottle. Amy was asking what Cynthia was drinking then. Skull took the drink out of Cynthia's hands and hid it from Cynthia. Once they arrived at the burial grounds. Cynthia went up to Skull gesturing that she would like her rum back. Skull shock his head no. They were at burial grounds not a party. Skull locks the car door, so Cynthia can not find the rum in Skull's car. Skull and Cynthia walk toward the grounds where Cynthia chose where Troy is going to be buried. Amy was standing looking at the gravestone. Amy could not believe that a nice man and amazing father has pasted on to the afterlife. Amy was sadder to see her father's gravestone in person. Amy thought she would be fine doing this, but Amy could not do this. Amy stayed strong, and she stayed for mom. Amy, Cynthia and Skull sat down on chairs when the ceremony started. Cynthia did not know that more people would come to Troy's funeral. Cynthia felt better that many people cared a lot about Troy to miss there day and pay respects for Troy. Half of them looked like workers that worked with him on the field of work of construction. Then Amy's friends came to see Amy for Troy's funeral. Then someone came out of a car and walked toward the burial area of Troy. Cynthia was wondering who that was. When the person came closer it was Troy's parents. Evelyn and Edward. Cynthia barely knew them, but Cynthia was happy that more people came to come to the funeral for Troy. As everyone was there. A priest walked toward the area starting the ceremony. As the ceremony started everyone sat down listening to the priest of what he had to say about death, life, and acceptance. Cynthia grabbed a tissue out of her bag. To cry in softly, but quiet. Cynthia did not want people to know that she is crying. Amy zones out most of the time looking at her dad's gravestone, but she can still hear what the priest has to say, but all her attention was on her dad's gravestone. Skull sits there looking around at the area. Skull feels bad that he barely knew Troy his brother in-law. Skull loved the way he built his house out of love and his garden was beautiful. He was a hard worker. Skull liked that about him. Once the priest was done talking, he was inviting the pray of silence. As he was done, Cynthia came up to the stand. Cynthia said a speech about Troy and how he was a great man. Also, that Cynthia will never find a better man to replace him. Even if Cynthia is in a new relationship. It will never be the same. Cynthia gets off the stand. Then there was music playing for Troy. A band of Troy's favorite. Everyone was listening to the quiet music letting all this news and tension sink in. Troy's parents went up to Cynthia talking to her about him, and that they heard that he passed away on the news. Also, that they were looking for him for awhile. They were worried about Troy a lot, but now they know that their son has passed away. They wanted to find him alive, they were sad that they found him like this, but at the same time they were happy to see that he was happy with Cynthia and his daughter. They left after talking about him to Cynthia. They felt bad for being like they were to Troy, but still they were happy to see him grow up to be an amazing father.

Skull drives them back after a long day at the burial grounds. Amy was still sad and felt the guilt running through her veins. Amy still thought that this was her fault that Troy died from a gun shot in the heart. Amy got out of the car slowly, hiding her feelings for her grief of her dad passing right in front of Amy's eyes. Amy ran into her room. Got dressed into her PJ's. Cynthia went up to her room to go to bed. Skull left to go to the hotel he was staying in. Amy was crying in her bed for at least three hours about her dad passing. Amy only can see her father's face when he died in her arms. Amy turned off her lights in her bedroom and puts her blanket on top of her. Amy continues to cry for awhile finally then falling asleep imaging her dad reading her a book to sleep, like he always did before bedtime.

Cynthia was upstairs laying in bed looking at Troy's side of the bed. Cynthia grabs the Scotch out of Troy's drinking drawer downstairs. She continues looking at the house around her. Cynthia can only see in this house was happiness, but now it is a memory that Cynthia will never make more with. It is just a house that Amy and Cynthia lived in now. Cynthia felt nothing, but sadness and grief. Cynthia felt all the love that was built in this house, was all… gone. A good person died in vain, protecting their daughter, but now Cynthia feels alone again. She feels like the first time that Cynthia meant him when Cynthia was 15 years old. Now he is gone, and she was alone for sure this time, she hated being alone in this world, but Cynthia must accept it. Still, she hated this feeling. As she was walking around Cynthia kept drinking the scotch out of the bottle, then finally arrives in her bedroom once again. Cynthia crawls in bed looking up at the skylight. Remembering why they wanted one in their room, but now Cynthia felt sad remembering why they wanted it. To look up at the stars together and sleeping under the night sky. Cynthia hated all the things that were making her remind her of Troy. It was just painful to think about all the things that they wanted to do together, but never had the time to do any of them. Cynthia looks up in the sky light trying to find peace, but she finds nothing, but darkness in the sky. Cynthia continues to drink her scotch in her hand looking up at the dark night sky. Cynthia feels sick drinking this scotch, but Cynthia drinks it anyway. Suddenly Cynthia heard something like singing. Cynthia looks around to see Troy as a white angel. Troy as an angel walks toward Cynthia. Grabbing the scotch out of her hand putting it away in Troy's drinking drawer. Troy closes the drawer. He walks back toward Cynthia putting her underneath the covers on the bed. "You should not be drinking, my beautiful angel." Says Troy. Cynthia looks at Troy crying begging him that he is alive and about to crawl in bed with Cynthia, but Troy sits down next to Cynthia looking at her in worry. "Don't cry Cynthia. I am in a better place, don't drink." Says Troy in worry again. "I want you to be here with me." Says Cynthia in sadness. Troy sits there on the bed just looking at Cynthia. Cynthia. "I know you want me here, but I have passed away. I can't come back." Says Troy in a sigh of sadness. Cynthia stares at Troy in tears, many tears. Troy wipes the tears off Cynthia face and hugs her softly. Cynthia felt a warm heated hug like she has always felt, but it was not the same. Cause Cynthia knew that she would never feel that hopeful hug ever again, this was her last time getting a hug from Troy. Cynthia sat there letting Troy hug her in bed. Troy tried to let go, but Cynthia did not want him to let go of her. Cynthia tears up again. Cynthia's tears were washing up against Troy's shoulder, Troy lets her hug him as long as she wants. Troy realized that Cynthia was starting to fall asleep in his arms. Troy puts Cynthia's weak body down to sleep. Troy get's up from the bed, tucking Cynthia under the covers making sure that she was warm. Troy looked over Cynthia and kissed her on the forehead. "I love you, my beautiful rose. I will always be here with you and for Amy. I love you both so much." Says Troy. Troy kisses Cynthia on the lips one last time. Cynthia felt a tear on her nose as the beautiful light of Troy's angel body disappeared in the darkness of the room. Cynthia began to cry again, but even louder in the darkness. Cynthia was crying so much that her eyes were red, and her face was covered in tears. Cynthia closed her eyes in pain of a lost lover, that Cynthia will never forget and get over.

CHAPTER **20**

HOPE AND FIGHTS

"Jade breakfast is ready." Says Jade's mom. "Okay, I am coming." Says Jade. Jade walks down to the dinning room to some breakfast. Once Jade was done eating breakfast Jade did some chores in the barn, it was six am in the morning Jade was cleaning the horses den arena. Jade loved horses and animals, but she mostly loved horses. She wanted to ride a horse one day around the forest, so she was saving up to buy a horse one day to do just that. Jade loved just waking up to a cool morning that would make her hair flap around in her face sometimes. Once she was done cleaning the stalls out, Jade would sit down outside on the hill and read or maybe sketch in her drawing book trees in the distance of the hill that she would sit on under a tree that was bigger than her future that is why she loved it. She tended to draw it so many times. It would come out differently every time when drawing the tree. Jade would draw the tree repeatedly until she got sick of it, but Jade knew she loved this tree for a reason. There was no way that Jade would ever get sick of this tree. Jade sat down underneath the tree just drawing it differently.

Jade realizes what time it was after an hour looking at the tree and listening to music. Jade gets up off the grass and runs home to get ready for school. Jade makes it on time for the bus for a ride to school. As Jade sits on the bus. Olivia walks over to sit with Jade on the bus. "Hey, Jade. What's up?" Says Olivia. Jade was listening to music not aware of Olivia sitting or talking to Jade. Olivia taps Jade on the shoulder. Jade jumps at the touch of Olivia's hand on her shoulder. Jade drops her pencil on the bus ground. "Yeah, what's up?" Says Jade. "I am sorry I scared you, but I just wanted to make sure that you were okay, because Eva and Nina seem to not want anything to do with you right now for some reason." Says Olivia. "I know they want nothing to do with me. Eva called me in the forest last night saying that we should be okay with Nina yelling at Amy for Emma's car accident." Says Jade. "Jade, I know this is hard to hear, but. Maybe Nina and Eva are right about them being worried about Emma. Because she got ran over by a car and now Emma is in a coma." Says Olivia. "I know it is bad to get ran over by a car, but it does not mean you must get mad at someone because of there clothing dropped where Nina picked up Amy's skirt." Says Jade. Olivia and Jade continue chatting or arguing about how unfair this entire situation is. As the bus stopped at Eva's house or stop to pick her up. Olivia looked at the bus door to see that Eva walks on the bus tired like always, but this time Eva was looking at Olivia in the eyes angrily that Olivia was sitting with Jade on the bus. Eva walks over to sit where Olivia and Eva sit all the time. "I am going to go sit with Eva. I will see you later in class or lunch." Says Olivia. "Yeah. Okay." Says Jade. Olivia gets up and walks toward Eva to sit right next to her on the bus. Jade puts her music back in her ears. As they stop at Nina's house Jade dares not to look up from her seat on the bus. Jade could feel Nina looking at Jade from a distance. Jade looks around, Jade sees that Nina was giving Jade the death stare. Nina, Eva and Olivia were sitting together talking about something. Jade already knew what it was about though. As the bus went by stops to pick up people for school. The bus finally arrives at the school. Jade still has her music in listening to Rock music. Jade packs up her drawing book and gets up from her seat and walks off the bus. Jade could still feel Nina and Eva looking at Jade deathly. But Jade kept going toward her locker than class. As Jade opened her locker. Jade grabbed all her books for her classes for today. Jade felt like not coming back to her locker today. As Jade walks to class, Jade was still listening to music. Jade walks into her class not knowing where to sit down. Jade did not feel like sitting with the girl's today, so she sat in a different seat at the back where Amy uses to sit before, she went back to home schooling. Class started with everyone paying close attention even Nina for once in her life. Jade was looking up at the board seeing what Mrs. Wallace was writing. Jade still had her music in her ears, but Jade was still paying attention to Mrs. Wallace.

As class ended after an hour later Nina and Eva were looking at Jade in the eye. They were watching every move that Jade made around them. Nina was most mad at Jade right not for saying basically it is Nina's fault that Emma was ran over by a car, Eva was a little frustrated with Jade because Jade was not helping Nina be positive. Eva just wanted Jade to understand that people go through a lot to just keep a person that they care so much about, Eva was just frustrated with Jade because Jade was not being a good friend right now. As Jade walks out to the bathroom. Jade accidently ran into some boy. "Sorry. I did not see you there." Says the boy. Jade puts off one of her ear buds. "It's alright I did not see you there either." Says Jade. "My name is Dylan." Says Dylan. Jade stud there in spot not knowing what to name but say her name. "My name is Jade. Nice to meet you, Dylan." Says Jade. "It was nice meeting you. I should possibly get back to class." Says Dylan. Dylan walks back toward to his class. Jade continues walking toward the bathroom. Jade only thinks about the cute boy that she just accidently ran into. On accident in the halls. Jade can only think about Dylan Jade never thought about someone like this before. Jade walks back in class looking around in the room to only seeing Nina and Eva talking. Olivia was just sitting there listening to them argue. Jade just walks by sitting down in her seat trying to ignore them. "Can Nina Goods come to the office?" Says the speaker in the school. Nina gets up from her seat wondering why she was sent to the office. As Nina leaves the room class continues.

Nina arrives in the office waiting room. "Nina Goods the principal is ready to see you." Says the person sitting at front desk. Nina gets up from the chair that she was sitting on and walks into the principal's office. As Nina opened the door, she saw that there were two police officers in the office. Now Nina was worried. "Are you Nina Goods?" Says one of the cops. "Yeah?" Says Nina. "Someone is out to kill you right now. That is why your friend Emma is in a coma right now. Since Emma pushed you out of the way from the car that was trying to hit you. The driver that hit your friend, they meant to hit you instead, but they failed. So, we are going to be driving you home tonight after school is over and we are going to be watching over you." Says one of the officers. "Who is trying to kill me?" Says Nina. "We are not sure yet, but right now. We must keep you safe from the driver that tried to kill you." Says the officer. "Okay. Can I go back to class?" Says Nina. "Yes, but we are picking you up later to take you home. So don't go on the bus we are driving you home." Says the officer. "Okay, I guess I will see you later." Says Nina in a sigh. "I know you don't want to be drive home by the cops, but its safer for you Nina." Says the officer. "Okay. we will see you later." Says the officer. Nina walks out of the office back toward to her class. Nina was not concerned about her. Nina was more concerned about Emma in her coma. As Nina walks back to class, Nina thinks about why the other officer did not say much, Nina thought it was weird that one officer was talking, but not the other one to back up their opinions about what they should do. But Nina dropped it and opened the door to class and paid attention in class for the rest of the day.

Lance walks over to his brother Dylan. "What, do you want?" Says Dylan. "I just wanted to know if you had a great day school." Says Lance. "It was fine, it was normal. Like any other school day." Says Dylan. Lance notices something strange in Dylan's voice, as if he meant someone. "Did you meet someone at school or something? I can hear it in your voice." Says Lance. Dylan looks around his room at there house. Dylan has never meant anyone that cute of a girl before. Dylan still looks at Lance blushing. "You did meet a girl. So, what is her name?" Says Lance raising his eyebrows. "I think her name is Jade?" Says Dylan. Lance stands in spot for moment as if he has heard that name before. Lance continues to hear out Dylan here. "So, what does she look like?" Says Lance. Dylan describes Jade to look as if she was sort of a goth girl, but she was still pretty. Lance now definitely has meant Jade before. Lance was Jade's ex-boyfriend. They were happy together until Lance got his powers and than the priest of light got involved, than Lance had to leave her and break her heart. Lance never wanted to break Jade's heart, but he also had a duty to do. "Lance, why do you look down now?" Says Dylan. "The girl you meant today. Treat her well Dylan. Treat her well." Says Lance as walking away from the conversation. Dylan had a confused look, but he did not think of it was a real problem or a concern to himself. Dylan continued doing his homework on his desk.

The bell rings for lunch period. Jade walks up to the door to the outside of the classroom. Jade walks toward her locker getting her lunch. As Jade walks toward the café, she pulls out her phone texting Amy asking what she is doing right now. Jade finds her own table to sit at before it gets crowded.

Dylan was walking toward the café, noticing that all the tables were full. But he noticed that Jade was sitting alone. Dylan walks up to that table. "Hey, can I sit down here. All the tables look like they have been taken." Jade looks around and notices that he was right there were no more tables to sit at. "Sure, you can sit here. I am sitting alone anyway." Says Jade, still sending a message to Amy. Dylan has no idea what to do right now. Dylan thinks that he likes Jade a little. "Hey, who are you texting?" Says Dylan. "Just my friend Amy. She was going to school here than she went back to home schooling." Says Jade. Dylan than notices that Jade had more friends than just Amy herself. "Jade, do you have other friends. I swear you look like you hang out with Eva, Olivia, Nina and Emma. Or am I just making this up right now?" Says Dylan. Jade puts her phone down for a moment. "Yeah, they were my other friends, but right now we are in a fight." Says Jade. "I know this is none of my business, but what kind of fight." Says Dylan. "Well, let's just say that Nina was being unfair toward my friend Amy." Says Jade. "Okay? How so?" Says Dylan. "They were being unfair because they were blaming Amy for Nina dropping her skirt in the middle of the street at the mall. As we were walking out of the mall. Nina dropped Amy's skirt that Nina brought for Amy. Then Nina drops it on the road and blames Amy for Emma getting rammed by a car." Says Jade. "Wow, I did not except that to be honest. I did agree to that. But maybe Nina was just emotionally scared for Emma getting rammed by a car. I am not saying that I am on there side, but I know emotions. I have blamed someone like that before. But it turned out to be fine and we are still friends, and we are good." Says Dylan. "What was your accident?" Says Jade. Dylan looks at Jade for a moment. "I can't say, sorry, but all I can say is that I almost lost my friend by fighting about it so, I am saying don't fight with friends." Says Dylan. Jade and Dylan sit there talking about what they like and not like for awhile. Jade and Dylan give each other their numbers, just so they can get to know each other better or when someone just wanted to chat with someone for awhile to waste time or in general just wants to chat. "I better get going my next class. I will see you around then Jade. It was nice having someone new to chat to." Says Dylan. "Yeah, thanks for sitting with me at lunch time. I think I needed a chat from a new person in my life. I think I will think about giving Nina some time to herself." Says Jade. "Good. I am glad. I will see you around." Says Dylan. Jade and Dylan wave at each other goodbye for now. Jade walks back to her locker dropping off her lunch bag putting it back in her locker. Jade walks back to her classroom.

"Okay, Officer Davis. We have to get ready to pick up Nina Goods soon because her school day is almost over." Says Officer Jim. "Officer Davis are you listening to me?" Says Officer Jim. Officer Davis looks up at Officer Jim in black eyes. Officer Davis was grabbing something out of his pocket a knife. Officer Jim grabs out his gun trying to defend himself, but it was already too late to try shotting at Davis. Officer Jim was stabbed right in the heart, then Davis grabbed out the knife out of his chest then stabbed Jim's eyes out. A shadow was over Davis holding his shoulders whispering in his ear. "Good work, now go pick up the girl yourself." Says the shadow over Davis's head. Davis cleans up his officer outfit then he throws Officer Jim's body out in the furnace. Is all you could hear in the furnace was screaming out of Jim. Davis kept walking though ignoring the screams. Davis walked outside toward a car to drive to the school.

As school was done for the day. Nina walks out to the parking lot looking for the cop's car. As Nina was about to give up and not listen to the cops and take the bus. The cop's car drives right in front of Nina. Nina gets in the car and shuts the door. Nina notices a couple minutes later that the cop is driving the wrong way to her house. "Hey, cop you are driving the wrong way to my house." Says Nina. The cop turns around looking right at Nina in the eyes. Nina saw that the cop had pitch black eyes. Nina went for the door, but it was locked and there was no button that she could open the door so she could escape the not cop guy. So, Nina just sat there frozen in spot in fear. The cop kept driving further away from Nina's house. Nina then thought of something. She had her phone on her. But the cop noticed that she was texting someone or doing something on her phone. The cop turns around again looking toward Nina. He grabs her phone and throws it out the window. Now Nina was panicking.

An hour later Nina and the cop with pitch black eyes arrive at unknown place in the middle of the forest at a cave. Nina was scared. The cop gets out of the car, walking toward Nina's seat. The cop grabs Nina out of the car, dragging Nina in the cave. Nina was screaming for help in the forest. "No one can hear you." Says Davis. "I guess I will keep trying. HELP." Says Nina. The cop covers her month and keeps dragging her into the cave. Eventually the cop arrives deep in the cave there were candles everywhere around the cave, there was a gray flat table with candles surrounding it as well. The cop placed her down on the table tying her to the flat gray table. Nina was trying to get herself out of the ropes, but the ropes were too tight. The cop stands there looking down at Nina. Then the shadow appeared over the cop's shoulders again. "I got her." Says officer Davis. "Good, good. Now grab that little sculpture. That is sitting on the podium over in the corner of the cave." Says the shadow over the cop's shoulder. The cop walks over to the podium in the corner of the cave picking up the sculpture. The cop seemed to know what to do with it because the shadow was doing most of the brain work for the cop. Finally, the cop popped off the head of the sculpture, suddenly there was a dark cloud coming out of the sculptures head then it transformed into another shadow. The other shadow was going toward Nina. The shadow was forcing Nina's months to open to let the shadow in her soul. As the shadow was gaining control over Nina's body, Nina's eyes turned pitch black like the cop's eyes. The shadow gained control over Nina's body, and she ripped through the ropes in Nina's body. "Perfect body brother." Says the girl shadow. "I picked it myself. I have been watching Nina for three days. Welcome to the world of humans, they will be ours soon enough." Says boy shadow in an evil grin.

Jade arrived at her house at 4:30 pm just in time for dinner. Jade went up to her room to put her school stuff away. "Honey. Dinner is pretty much ready, don't be long up there." Says Jade's mom. "I won't I am just putting my stuff away from school." Says Jade. Jade walks up to her bedroom with her backpack on her back. Jade opens her bedroom door putting her backpack near her desk in her bedroom. Before Jade walked out of her bedroom. Jade heard her phone go off. Jade picks up her phone, it was a message from Dylan. "Hey, did you get home okay?" Says Dylan. "Yeah, I did, I am sorry, but I must go my dinner is ready." Says Jade in message. "Okay, I have to go to. My dinner is ready as well. Talk later?" Says Dylan in message. "Yeah, talk later." Says Jade in message. Jade puts her phone on her desk. Jade closes her bedroom door and walks down the stairs walking toward the kitchen.

"Jade before you go do your homework or whatever you do upstairs. I need you do the dishes quick. I know it's my turn, but I must go somewhere." Says Jade's mom. "Oh okay, but you are doing them tomorrow." Says Jade. "Deal, thank you so much beautiful." Says Jade's mom. Jade's mom walks out of the kitchen walking toward her bedroom. Jade starts washing the dishes. Before Jade just put all the dishes away when she was done. Jade's mom came out of her bedroom dressed up beautifully. "Mom. Is it you and dad's Annie or something?" Says Jade. Jade's mom looked nervous that Jade asked her that question. "Honey. No, it's not my Annie with your dad today." Says Jade's mom. "Why are you dressed like you are going out on a date?" Says Jade. "I thought you were fast at doing the dishes." Says Jade's mom. "Mom what are you doing tonight?" Says Jade. Jade's mom looked down at the floor depressed. "Honey, can we talk after I am done tonight." Says Jade's mom. "Mom, are you cheating on dad?" Says Jade. Jade's mom's face kept changing every time Jade asked a question. Then finally Jade's mom fell to the ground crying. "Yes, I am cheating on your dad. Because I don't feel in love with your dad anymore." Says Jade's mom. "So, you are just going on a date to solve the problem and acting like this is helping me and dad. With your solution that you don't love dad anymore. I thought you were better than that, but I was right about you being honest. But never imagined you cheating while you are married." Says Jade. "Honey, I know you don't like what I am doing right now, but please don't tell your dad about this because this is my last date out with this guy. I really like him, but if this date makes me feel bad or not a good person, I going to call off dating this guy, but this is the decision. I am making please accept my decision. I know it is bad of me to do this, but I must do this to make sure that there are other paths I can do in my life. Instead of your dad. Don't get me wrong I feel awful about cheating behind your dad's back, but please just give the sword to decide my life for once. Instead of being the sword, I want to be the one holding the sword of fate this time. Just once." Says Jade's mom. "Fine do what you must, but make sure that you want that for sure. Don't just do it because you don't feel anything in your heart for dad. Do what is right. If you don't love dad anymore leave him now. Then go for the new guy, but don't hurt dad's feelings." Says Jade. Jade puts the rest of the dishes away, then slams the drawer walking up the stairs in shame in her mom. Jade felt so betrayed that Mom was going out on dates behind dad's back. Jade just wanted to text her dad this, but Jade also wanted mom to be happy and available to make her own decision her mom was a big girl she can handle herself. Jade puts her head under her blanket with her phone in her face. Jade feels like crying, but instead she messages Dylan. "Hey Dylan. Are you there?" Says Jade in message. Dylan was replying. "Yeah, I am here. What's up." Says Dylan in message. "I just want someone to chat with right now. I feel like shit." Says Jade in message. "Why do you feel like that?" Says Dylan. "I feel like that because my mom is cheating on my dad." Says Jade in message. Dylan sends GIF that has a cartoon with a surprised face. "Why is she cheating on your dad?" Says Dylan in message. "Because apparently, she is not in love anymore with him." Says Jade in message. "Oh. Sorry I don't know what to say to them Jade." Says Dylan. "Dylan its, I am just mad at my mom a little." Says Jade. Dylan sits there on his bed holing his phone feeling bad for Jade, that her mom is cheating on Jade's dad. "Jade just let me know if you need someone to be there for you. I can be there for you. I got your back with what is happening right." Says Dylan in message. "Thank you. But for now, if you want to be there for me. I need you to just talk to me and not say anything about what is going with my mom and my dad. I just want a distraction from everything, just for now." Says Jade in message. "Yeah, I can help with being a distraction for a bit." Says Dylan in message. As Dylan sent that message, he felt he was lying. He wanted to ask Jade out on a date or something, but it was a bad time to ask her out. But Dylan wanted to support her because Jade has basically no friends right now. Except for Amy, Dylan does not know why Jade told Dylan about her mom cheating on her father. Dylan just thought it was an opening to earning Jade's friendship. So, Dylan continues just being there for Jade, like a shoulder to cry on. Finally, they hit 12 am in the morning just chatting away. Jade was not answering Dylan's messages. Dylan amused that Jade fell asleep. So, Dylan sent good night to Jade, then Jade messages back "sorry I am falling asleep. I think it is best if we both go to sleep." Says Jade in message. "Yeah, I am tired myself. See you tomorrow, Jade." Says Dylan in message. "Yeah, see you tomorrow. Oh, and thank you for talking to me this late." Says Jade in message. "No problem. I am here for you." Says Dylan in message. Dylan saw that Jade's status is offline. Dylan puts his phone on charge and turns his bedtime mode on, which was sleeping music. As soon as Dylan did that, he fell asleep.

CHAPTER 21

THE PLAN!

"Gretel so what is the plan?" Says Grim. "I just need my notebook for the instructions to getting the spell back for your uncle Skull." Says Gretel. "Okay, where is your notebook?" Says Grim. "It is all the way back home, but you are lucky I can think about it, and I can get it in my hands, I hope." Says Gretel. "Alright do it then." Says Grim. Gretel closes her eyes thinking about her notebook. Gretel then starts floating in the air with her hair flowing through the air. Grim stands there looking at how powerful Gretel can be. Robert walks up to them. "Hey, what's going on here?" Says Robert. "Gretel is trying to receive her notebook." Says Grim. "Oh, I see. I think that Gretel is powerful enough to beat our uncle on her own." Says Robert. "I know she looks powerful, but you should know that our uncle has an army of dead souls, and he has the king of souls on his side. That makes him more powerful than Gretel." Says Grim. "I know that. Still, I think Gretel could beat Skull on her own, even with all the dead army he has and the King of souls." Says Robert. "Yeah, that is why the only option is to banish him again in the realm where he came from." Says Grim. "Yeah, I agree." Says Robert. Gretel went back down to the ground and her hair was back in a normal way. Gretel's was in a portal, getting her out a notebook out of her house. "I got it, Grim." Says Gretel. "Awesome, so what do we need to do, to put our uncle back." Says Grim. Gretel opens her notebook; Gretel was flipping the pages repeatedly. Finally, she found the page that she was looking for. "So, what do we need?" Says Grim. "We need something to put him in, like a jar or a vase that has a lid on it." Says Gretel. "Oh, that is easy. What else?" Says Grim. "A place that I can focus and curse that vase or jar, whatever you find that has a lid on it. I also need candles." Says Gretel. "That sounds so easy. I literally have so many jars at my base. And things with lids. Are you sure that is the right spell?" Says Grim. "Yeah, it's the right one." Says Gretel. "That is amazing. Alright, let's head to my base shall we. Let's get my uncle in a jar." Says Grim. "I will go get Polly then." Says Robert. "What do you want? What is going?" Says Polly. "We got the plan; we are heading back to my base." Says Grim. "Oh, okay. Let's go then." Says Polly. Polly and everyone pack's up everything and starts walking back toward to Grim's base. Grim was happy to be on his brother's good side once again in his life, even through Grim feels like Robert is just on his side because he wants to get Hazel back and see that Uncle Skull gets once again trapped in a world that Skull is trapped for the rest of his eternal life.

"Lord Skull, what can I do to help?" Says Jack. "You know, what you can do Jack. Just sit there and wait till I have something for you to do. By the way Jack, I probably won't need you, you are just a piece of my plan." Says Lord Skull. "Oh really, what kind of piece?" Says Jack. "A useless piece. You already let me out and got my great niece for me. Now I don't need you anymore." Says Lord Skull. "What! You don't want me to help anymore." Says Jack. "Yeah, because you are just a demon that wants a leader and needs a leader. You just wanted me to be out of my realm so I can lead, but here is the thing, Jack. I don't want to be your leader." Says Lord Skull. Jack seemed to have his look on his face changed when Lord Skull said that Jack is a useless part of his plan now and not wanting him around anymore. Jack felt rage then. "SO, LORD SKULL I JUST GOT YOU OUT OF THE REALM THAT A WITCH PUT YOU IN. AND THIS IS HOW YOU REPAY ME. YOU ARE WORSE THAN I THOUGHT." Says Jack. Lord Skull made a serious angry face at Jack. "Yeah, but Jack thank you for getting me out of that realm, but I want you to leave before I change my mind to sparing you your life." Says Lord Skull. "You are sparing me? Wow you are weak." Says Jack. Lord Skull gets up from his throne. "What, did you just say." Says Lord Skull. "I think that you have become soft since you have meant this Hazel girl." Says Jack. "You are going to regret that, Jack." Says Lord Skull. "Oh, well." says Jack. "I am not in the mood to dance with a worthless demon." Says Lord Skull. "DON'T CALL ME WORTHLESS. I am the one who got you out of that realm you were stuck in. If you think I am worthless, what about you. Skull who needed help from me, getting out of that realm." Says Jack. "Fine, you may have helped me with getting out of the realm, but you are just a piece of the puzzle to ruling this world. I am going to make sure that you and everyone else bows to me." Says Lord Skull. "What are you talking about? I will never bow to you. You lost me when you said today that I am worthless." Says Jack. "Like I said you demons just want leaders, leading you to do this and that. I am not a leader for weak demons like you." Says Lord Skull. "Fine, I guess you just don't understand what I want from you. I will leave like you wanted me to do in the first place. Bye Skull." Says Jack. Jack turns around to walk away in the forest, not looking back to Lord Skull. Lord Skull sat back down on his throne. Waiting till Hazel came back from his favor.

Grim opens the door to his base. Everyone behind him follows inside. "So, where are all these jars or vases you were talking about?" Says Gretel. "They are in my office. Down that way up the elevator." Says Grim. "He is right, his office is up there, and now I just realized that I was touching a lot of the vases and jars up there." Says Robert. "You were touching my stuff?!" Says Grim. "Yeah, I was waiting for you for awhile. I thought you died in the caves when you were looking for those love stones." Says Robert. "The one thing I did not want you to do was touch my stuff. But whatever we have bigger problems right now." Says Grim. Grim and everyone walks up to the elevator. Grim pushes the button that goes to his office. As he pushes the button the doors for the elevator closed. Once the elevator opened again, they were up in Grims office area. Grim and Gretel walked in first. Gretel was looking around trying to find the perfect jar or vase to trap Lord Skull in. Finally, Gretel picks up a vase that had flowers all around the base line. "This is perfect." Says Gretel. "That was fast." Says Grim. "Yeah, will all of them could honestly work, but this one caught my eye more." Says Gretel. "Well, do you need the room to yourself." Says Grim. "Yeah, I probably will need the space to concentrate on cursing this vase." Says Gretel. "Okay, we will leave you alone then. I must go check on somethings anyway. I have

not been at the base for a day now, so I got to go check on my group."
Says Grim. Grim leaves the room going down the elevator, leaving
just Polly and Robert in the office with Gretel. "I am going to go find
a place to try getting my energy back." Says Polly. Polly walks around
the office, Polly opens a door to another room that had books all over
the place. Polly shuts the door behind her with just a wave of her hand.
Robert sits down looking at things in Grims office once again. Robert
does not know where he could go. Robert gets up off a chair and walks
toward the elevator looking at buttons in the elevator. Robert pushed
the main floor one. The elevator door shut fast to when he pushed the
button. Robert gets out of the elevator and walks around the main floor
for awhile then noticing there was garden outside that Robert has not
noticed yet. Robert walks out to the garden, at this point Robert was just
walking around Grims base looking what his brother has been doing all
these years. Robert notices how beautiful that the flowers were arranged
in the flower bed. Then the one thing that caught Roberts eyes was a
tree the biggest tree that was in the garden. Robert walks up to the tree.
Once Robert got closer to that tree. He noticed there was something
carved into the tree. It looked like someone carved their initials in the
tree. There was a heart that had the letters G+G. Robert was thinking
about who the first word of there name G+G. Robert's face turned into
a thinking face. Then Robert realized that it could be Grim and Gretel.
"So, I see you found my garden in my base." Says Grim. "Where did
you come from?" Says Robert. "I came from the inside of the base.
Why are you out here?" Says Grim. "I am just wandering because I
have been curious of what kind of man you have become." Says Robert.
"Well, you see now. That I have become a gardener that mom would
have never imagined me to become like that." Says Grim. "I know,
Mom never thought you would become anything to be honest." Says
Robert. "Well, she was right about one thing. I never became a father
or a grandpa." Says Grim as he was looking at the carved tree. "I have
a question." Says Robert. "Yeah, what is it?" Says Grim. "Did you and
Gretel date or something no one just writes a carved initials down in
a big tree in the center of there garden and tend their garden making
it look nice." Says Robert. Grim sat down on the bench. "Don't tell
Gretel. But I liked her a lot back then." Says Grim. "Oh wow. I so, did

not hear that at all." Says Robert in sarcasm. "Don't get sarcastic with me, Robert I have crushes. Sometimes." Says Grim. "Are you sure this plan to getting Uncle Skull back in his realm is going to work?" Says Robert in nervousness. Grim looks over at Robert having the same face expression. "It worked last time, didn't it? But I am still worried about that part." Says Grim. "Yeah, we are going to have to prepare if this plan does not work." Says Robert. "I will do that myself. This is my responsibility that our uncle got out of his realm. I will handle it." Says Grim. "Are you sure?" Says Robert. "Yes, I am sure." Says Grim. "Okay, that is okay with me. I guess I will let you focus for a bit." Says Robert. "Yeah, thank you." Says Grim. Before Robert leaves to leave Grim alone to thinking about a plan B. He turns around looking at Grim in the eyes. "Grim, just please don't hurt yourself. I am just starting to trust you and consider letting you visit my family, and I am sorry for not being there for you. I should have been a better brother." Says Robert. Grim looks up at Robert. They both were looking right in each others eyes it was the most contact that they have made in awhile. "I will make sure that I stay alive. Robert. Thank you for trusting me and being there for me in these times. I would like to apologize to losing your daughter and being blinded by an old friend that I once trusted, and they for sure lost my trust." Says Grim. Robert walks back toward Grim, going in for a hug. "Grim, it's alright that you lost my daughter, I am not mad at you anymore for that. I am just mad that, I did not bother getting to know you at all, and I am sorry for that. I just hope we can still get to know each other." Says Robert. "We will Robert, we will." Says Grim. Robert hugs Grim for a few moments. Robert turns around getting up from the bench and walking out of the garden giving Grim space to think about his plan B, but Grim looked like he already had a plan, If the plan did not work.

"Hazel are you ready to open the gates of death and freedom." Says Lord Skull. "Yes, my Lord." Says Hazel as bowing down to Skull. "Alright then let's call upon the Lost Souls King. Earn his power for me that I must and want to weald for I am going to be the new king of the souls. And you Hazel you will be the queen of Souls, and my warrior whatever you want." Says Lord Skull. "I will be honored to be anything you want me to be. My lord Skull." Says Hazel still bowing down to Lord Skull. "Hazel, you remind me of my niece Amy, she was and will always be on my side of the fight. You know why because I earned her trust all these years, then I turned the tables on Cynthia. I made Cynthia Amy's mom hate Amy for who she was. When I found out that Amy had power. I wanted that on my side. I wanted a family, then Cynthia had to take that family away from me. I am going to make sure that you Hazel. That you don't get taken back to your father Robert or your uncle Grim. I want you to be safe." Says Lord Skull. Hazel gets up from bowing. Hazel walks up to her Lord Skull. "Nothing will stand in between us Lord Skull. You will always be my Lord and I will make sure that will be official." Says Hazel. "Then let's get the chaos started. I CALL UPON THE LOST SOULS ARMY. I CALL UPON THE LOST SOUL KING. I CALL UPON THE UNDEAD SOULS. I AM GIVING THE LOST REALM A PURPOSE TO MAKE THIS REALM NOT SO LOST. I CALL UPON FOR FAMILY AND HELP." Says Lord Skull. As Lord Skull was floating up in the air. The clouds and the skies turn green and blue. Then suddenly the sunlight disappears in thin air and the world around them was dark. Then there was a strike of lighting around where Hazel and Lord Skull were. There stud the king, before them. There with no portal or chain on his waist. The King looked more than ready to be family for Skull. Finally, Hazel got up and bowed to her false King, while her arm was glowing blue. The king looked down at Hazel. The king did nothing but look at the world around him. The kings face changed into an evil grin then he started laughing at the sight of the other world so dark and doomed. Then there were vortexes in the ground. There were particles coming out of the vortex. Then there were souls flying all over the place. It looked like there were souls going into the storm above in the clouds. There were blue orbs all over the world going into people's bodies, so that the lost souls can be in anyone's body at anytime. Besides Lord Skull and Hazel. Lord skull let the souls rattle up in the sky for a few moments then his plan to be able to control the lost soul army he took his chance and succeed. Lord Skull grabbed the lost soul's staff and grabbed his Lost soul crown. Then he trapped the Lost Souls King in a cage. Since he had no power now, he was just a false King and an old man that was looking for his power box again. Once Lord Skull put the crown on his head. Lord Skulls eyes glowed black and white off and on. Finally, they turned black completely. Lord Skull was now the King of the lost Souls. Skull raised up the staff up to the clouds. There were more lighting strikes once Lord Skull did that. Suddenly most souls came to Lord Skull and bowed to him. The lost soul army bowed to there new king. "What shall we do? King." Says one of the lost souls. "Chaos, find all humans and terrorize them for there last moments of being human. Go inside them and be not lost anymore. I SUMMONED THE LOST ARMY TO ENJOY FREEDOM AND BE WHATEVER THEY WANT. TO BE A HUMAN AGAIN." Says Lord Skull. The souls were surprised what Skull was saying to them, they never got this kind of freedom before. The souls flew up in the sky doing what they were told. Skull was laughing in an evil smile. Hazel has never seen so much evil.

Polly looks outside the window in the library that she went in. Polly was paralyzed of what she sees out there. Polly saw was green and blue skies. Lighting strikes. And floating blue blackish orbs all over the sky. It also looked dark out, out there to. Gretel did not notice because she was still trying to concentrate on cursing the flower vases. Polly ran into the office next door where Gretel was. Polly started freaking out at Gretel. Asking Gretel to look outside. Gretel stopped for a few moments and looked right at Polly in frustration. "Polly I am trying to concentrate on getting this vase cursed." But the corner of Gretel's eye. Gretel saw what Polly wanted Gretel to be looking at. "Everything is going to be fine Polly just let me concentrate." Says Gretel. Gretel goes back to concentrating on making it possible for the vase to trap Lord Skull into there. Polly runs out of the room rushing toward Grim and Robert. Polly pushed the button to the main floor. Polly was very impatient at this point. So, she made the elevator go faster. Once the elevator got down to the main level, she basically was running in the halls looking for everyone. She finally finds Robert in a room alone. "ROBERT. ROBERT." Says Polly. Robert turns around to see that Polly was yelling Robert's name. "Yeah, what's wrong." Says Robert. "Look out a window NOW." says Polly. Robert and Polly walk out of the room that Robert was just sitting in alone. Once they got toward a window Robert looked and noticed that the clouds and the sky were very dark, blue and green. Now Robert was worried about why is the sky that color again. Polly and Robert go look for Grim in his base. They find Grim in the garden still just laying there with his eyes closes. It looked like Grim was meditating on the ground. Robert walks up to Grim tapping him on the shoulder. "What, is it Robert?" Says Grim. "Open your eyes." Says Robert. Grim opens his eyes and gets up off the floor. Grim looks outside the window. Grim sees what everyone else has been seeing for awhile now. Grim had a worried face, but then his face turned into a brave, but still feared face. They all stud there looking at the window outside. Grim moved and started walking toward the elevator it looked like anyway. Robert and Polly followed him to up the elevator. Once they went into the elevator again. Grim pushed his office button. The elevator door closes right in his face. Once the elevator stopped in his office. Grim, Polly and Robert walked into the office looking for good news about the vase. Before Grim could say one word of what the update was. Gretel opened her eyes and floated back down to the floor. The vase was glowing for a few moments the color white and black. Once the vase was done glowing the final color was white. "It's ready to trap Lord Skull. Forever this time." Says Gretel. Grim and Robert stud there looking at Gretel in faceless expression they just wanted to get this over with. Gretel held the vase in her hand saying one more word to the vase. Gretel made the vase shrink small, so it could go into her pocket. Everyone in that room looked more serious in their lives in a long time. Gretel, Grim, Robert and Polly were ready to trap Lord Skull in a vase. All of them went down to the main floor. One of the soldiers that is apart of Grims group calls out Grim. "Grim sir, there is someone at the door for you." Says the guard. They all walk together toward the door. To just see that it was Jack, standing outside the door. Still in his Demon form looking like he wants to come into the base.

CHAPTER **22**

WHO IS SKULL REALLY?

"Hey, are you Gretel?" Says A women. "Yeah, who is asking?" Says Gretel. "I am a mother of two children, but my little boy has a power that I don't want him to have. I heard that you could do anything what your customers askes for a price." Says the mom. Gretel looks at the woman with the child in her arms. The mom gives her the child. Gretel sees death and life inside of this little boy. Gretel looks at the woman as she was holding the baby. "So, you want me to get the power out of who?" Says Gretel. "Oh right, this is my child Skull. He has the power of death and life, but I don't want him to have that power." Says Skull's mom. "Fine, I will do as you wish. But you must give me extra the pay. Since the child is a baby." Says Gretel. "Fine, whatever you want I just don't want him to have this power." Gretel places Skull on a podium surrounded by candles. Gretel draws a circle around her feet with a star in it. Gretel starts saying words in a language that skulls mom did not understand. Gretel begins to float in the air taking Skull's power away and Skull's power was being put in a jar. Before the ritual was done Gretel's hair was floating in the air, and her eyes were glowing black and white. Once the ritual was done Gretel returned to a normal state on the ground, her hair was normal once again and her eyes were no longer glowing white or black. Gretel looked weak after the ritual was done, but Gretel picked up Skull and gave him back to Skull's mom. Gretel was gesturing to pay her the price. The mom gave her the price that Gretel was wanting. Skull's mom said thank you and left Gretel's store and went back home. Skull's mom arrived home an hour later to find that Cynthia was waiting on the couch for mom to come home. Cynthia hoped up in joy to see that her mom was back with her little brother Skull. Cynthia held Skull on the couch. Cynthia noticed that Skull seemed different, but Cynthia did not really care so she just continued playing with her little brother Skull.

"So, Skull is normal like us then I amuse." Says Skulls father. "Yeah, I paid Gretel what you thought that she liked, and Gretel took the stone. Gretel looks like she needs to retire helping the people with our problems." Says Skull's Mom. "I agree, but Robin it was worth it. Our son is normal like everyone else. Once he goes to school no one will want to bully him, and no one will get hurt." Says Skull's Father. "Yeah, but I still feel bad for not giving Skull a chance to grow with that power that he had. Before we decided to make it possible for the powers to be taken away from him." Says Robin. "I know I know, but it is best for Skull to be normal like us." Says Skulls father. "Alright Cynthia I got to put Skull down for the night. It is getting late for the little guy." Says Skull's father. "Aww man. I was just getting comfortable with hanging out with Skull." Says Cynthia. "I know, but your little brother needs rest. He is just a baby. Also, you need to go to bed to." Says dad. "I am not tired though." Says Cynthia in a wine. Skull's dad picks up Skull taking Skull to his bedroom to put down for bedtime. It took 30 minutes to calm him to sleep. Robin at this point put Cynthia to sleep as well. Robin and dad turned off all the lights in the house and walked toward their bedroom basically crawling into bed. Robin was more tired than dad was. "Robin do want to do something tonight." Says dad in a naughty voice. "William I am tired." Says Robin. "I know, but I thought you like it when you are tired." Says William. William throws off his clothes tossing them across the room. Robin was laying down with her eyes closed. William was reading Robin right. Robin opens her eyes and sees nothing, but candles and the lights were off Robin got up from laying down on the bed Robin was throwing her clothes across the room where William threw his clothes. Robin and William kissed each other literally everywhere. William kissed Robin on the neck. As William was kissing Robin's neck. William put himself on top of her. William still kissing Robin on the lips and neck. As time went by both were tired. Robin laid down on her back sweating. William put his head down next to Robin. Robin put herself on William's chest. Robin closed her eyes falling asleep on his chest.

11 years later. Skull was 13 years old. Cynthia was 17 years old. Cynthia was sneaking out all the time. Once Skull caught Cynthia kissing a guy and Skull heard noises from her room. Skull in voided Cynthia's room because Skull did not want to know what was going on in that room and that Cynthia did not like it when other people would go into her bedroom. One day Cynthia did not come home for a couple days, it felt like a month. Skull and Skull's parents found out that Cynthia was pregnant with the guy that Skull caught Cynthia kissing one night. Skull's parents went to the hospital to lose their minds on her. Once they came back home, they basically were pushing Skull to pack their stuff. Skull asked where we are going. "We are going far away from your sister. Your sister got pregnant and now is a mom. She must do that on her own." Says William. "But what if she needs help. Dad." Says Skull. "NO, SHE IS LEARNING THIS ON HER OWN. Now go pack your stuff we are leaving. NOW." Says dad. Skull runs to his room to start packing his stuff for the move, even if Skull did not want to move. It looked like Skull did not have a choice.

It took awhile, but Skull was completely packed to go right away. Skull looked inside Cynthia's bedroom. He never saw what was in there before, but he just saw a room that is his sister's room. Skull had a feeling that he did not want to leave Cynthia alone in this world with a baby. Skull tried to tell mom that he did not want to go without Cynthia and her mystery boyfriend. But Robin said no to bringing Cynthia with them. "Your dad is right. Your sister must learn her lesson on her own with her boyfriend to not bring a baby in this world when she is her age. She needs to know the consequences." Says Mom. Few hours later Dad and Mom were collecting everything that could fit in the car. Then they called a friend to ask to borrow a trailer. A trailer came an hour later. All the stuff that they were moving out with was already outside of the house. Dad and Mom were collecting all the stuff and putting it all in the trailer. Mom put Skull in the back seat of the car, so Skull did not have a chance of running. Skull sat in the back seat of the car wanting so badly to run to the hospital to meet Cynthia's baby, but Skull could not run cause the car would have gone off and he would have gotten caught. So, he just sat there waiting for Dad and Mom. An hour went by. Mom and Dad were done loading up the trailer. Mom went in the house one last time. It looked like she had a paper in her hand. Once she ran out, she did not have that paper anymore. Mom just got in the car. As soon as Mom got in the car Dad started the car and drove off fast. Skull started basically crying inside, because his own parents left Cynthia his big sister alone and never got to say bye and never being allowed to see his childhood home ever again. As Skull was sitting in the car for most of the ride just watching the trees move in the car window. Mom and Dad were arguing in the front seat of the car. Mostly arguing about Cynthia. Skull just tried to ignore them in the front seat of there car. Finally, many hours listening to Mom and dad argues about stuff in the front. Skull get's out of the car and sees that they arrived in the middle of nowhere with a house in the mountains. Dad and Mom never took us here before. "Skull can you pick up your stuff in the car or just some stuff and put them in the house." Says Dad. "Where are we dad?" Says Skull. "We are at my dad's mountain cabin. He gave it to me if I needed somewhere to live or escape for awhile. Now, can you get most boxes flowing inside of the house." Says Dad. Skull opens the back left seat of the car and starts picking up boxes out of the car and bringing them inside of the house. After hours of grabbing heavy boxes and stuff that belonged places in pacific rooms. Skull grabbed his stuff and Dad directed Skull to his room. Skull continued going up and down the stairs putting his stuff in his new room. Skull stud there looking at the room that had an open window area. The house was completely empty. Mom and Dad unpacked downstairs first for the kitchen so mom could make some dinner from the long trip. Mom had to drive awhile to get to a grocery store, but there was one near by, but an hour away from there new home. Dad was now unpacking the living room stuff putting blankets on the couches. Skull continued unpacking his boxes. It took Skull an hour of re decorating his new bedroom. Skull laid down on the floor with his blankets on the floor. They have not gotten Skull's bed up the stairs yet; Skull thought the bright side is that his room. He kind of likes his new room he thought to himself. There was open window space and there was a nice skylight on the ceiling he could see everything like the stars, the clouds and the sun and rain drops. He liked it, but he still missed his big sister Cynthia.

Hours later. Mom came home with groceries. Mom puts them away and leaves out what they are having for dinner. Dad puts Skull's bed upstairs all by himself. But Skull does help with putting it upstairs in his bedroom. "Wow son you look like you are happy in here. I mean I am happy that you are happy to have moved here." Says Dad. "I am not happy with the move, but I do like this room." Says Skull. "Why are you not happy?" Says dad. "I am not happy because we did not take Cynthia with us." Says Skull. Dad sighs at that name. "Why, can't you just forget about your sister." Says Dad. "What. How can I just forget about Cynthia she is my big sister, she probably raised me! Then you ever did." Says Skull. "Excuse me, but that is not how you talk to your dad about how I raised you. Skull. I know your sister means a lot to you, but you are going to have to learn about not having your sister around okay." Says Dad. After Dad says that he leaves the room slamming the door behind him. Skull crawls in bed crying at the sight of the stars. When Skull was younger Cynthia would take Skull out of the house showing him the stars at night. They would name stars with there imagination. Skull started crying at the fact that he thought of that. As he was looking up in the clouds. It was getting darker and darker. He could see the one star that Cynthia told him about the brightest one. She spoke. "If you ever feel alone Skull and I am not there. Look at that star. The brightest one in the sky. I will be that star, maybe you will see a shotting star with it on the side. I call that one star. Hope." Says Cynthia. Skull stared at that one star for an hour it felt like. Finally, he saw something shiny glimmer through the sky. Skull made a wish. Skull hoped that his wish worked. Skull closed his eyes thinking about his wish, he was hoping that one day Skull would be allowed to meet Cynthia's child one day and seeing her once again.

CHAPTER **23**

THE NEWS!

One year later Skull was 14 years old. Skull found out that his parents were pregnant again. Skull wanted to know where Cynthia was now. Because Cynthia had to know that she was going to be a sister again. To a boy or a girl. Skull did not know yet. What gender it was going to be. Skull grabbed his phone and messaged the phone company where Cynthia his sister was living of course they could not tell Skull that cause he was only just a boy, but Skull was determined to find out where his sister was living. Skull gave up on his phone a little. He searched up where there was a bus stop near him, there was one three hours away from him. But he did not care, so Skull got his bike and rode it down to the bus stop and waited at the bus stop for awhile. Finally, he made it just in time to make a bus stop pick up for people that were waiting there more probably an hour. Skull picked up his bike and brought it on the bus with him. He went up to the bus driver. "Hello, what do you want?" Says the bus driver. "Can you take me to this address? I will pay you extra." Says Skull as he was holding 500$. "Yeah, sure kid. It will be three hours, but I will get you there." Says the bus driver. "Thanks, so much." Says Skull. Skull sat down by himself to the back of the bus with his bike. As everyone was getting off there stops. Skull could feel that it was his stop next. He was excited. He did not think about how he is going to get home, but since he found away out here. I am pretty sure that he can find away back home. Once Skull's stop came. Skull went up to the bus driver. "Thank you so much for this." Says Skull, Skull gives the bus driver a personal tip of a hundred dollars. "No thank you. Are you sure you don't need this money for yourself?" Says the bus driver. "No, you take it. You were so nice to me for driving me here. Cause I know this is not your route you don't drive around here." Says Skull. "You are right kid, I don't drive around here, but I will take your tip. You have a great day." Says the bus driver. As skull got off the bus. The bus drove fast away from where Skull just got dropped off. But Skull had to get to the end of this driveway. To get help looking for his sister. Finally, Skull got to the end of the driveway. Skull saw that there was house. It looked abandoned, but there was a car in the driveway. Skull put his bike on the ground, Skull ran toward the door knocking on the door repeatedly. Finally, the person who answered the door did not look happy. "What do you want?" Says the man. "Can I please come in. I need to know where my sister lives." Says Skull. "Fine come in." says the man. Skull goes into the messy ratty house. "Sorry about the mess, but I don't get visitors or feel like cleaning my house, but anyway what do you want from me?" Says the man. "I want your help to find my sister Cynthia. Are you Hunter search." Says Skull. "Damn it I knew that show would come and bite my ass." Says Hunter. Hunter rolled his eyes then started walking toward somewhere. He turns around looking at Skull. "Well, are you coming?" Says Hunter. Skull walks behind Hunter then they finally hit in a room. Where hunter uses to find people around the world. "Alright let's see here. Ahh here we are. Is your sister's name Cynthia Thorn." Says Hunter. "Yeah! Did you find her?" Says Skull. "No, it's going to take me awhile to find her with this junk. Kid just go home I will find your phone number and let you know what I find. But kid before you leave, I want money for this. Cause I retired." Says Hunter. "Yeah, I will pay you lots." Says Skull. "Okay, get out of my house." Says Hunter. Skull leaves the house. Beginning to have hope again. Skull arrives home late like super late for supper.

"Where were you. We were worried about you. I thought we lost our only kid." Says Mom. Skull looks at right at them. "I AM NOT YOUR ONLY CHILD. I heard you are having another baby. Second you have Cynthia as the older one and you to pretend that she is not real." Says Skull. "DON'T TEST US KID. WE GAVE YOU A HOME." Says dad. "YEAH, YOU GUYS ALSO FORCED ME TO COME WITH YOU AND I LOST EVERYTHING WITH MY SISTER. So YEAH, I GUESS YOU ARE THE BEST PARENT'S I HAVE

EVER WANTED. I HATE YOU BOTH." Says Skull in much rage. Skull turns around trying to walk away up to his bedroom, but Skull's dad grabbed him by the arm and turned Skull around and snapped him right in the face. Skull got back up and pushed him in the nose. Skull's dad was on the ground bleeding. "GO UP TO YOUR ROOM RIGHT NOW." Says mom. "FINE I WILL. I can't believe you are on his side mom. I can't believe you." Says Skull. Walking away from the scene.

Few months later. Hunter and Skull were basically best friends. Skull was still scared by that day when Skull's dad hit him in the face and Skull punching his dad on the nose. But that did not make Skull feel bad for a moment. Skull was grounded from his phone so he could not get any messages on his phone so, he just sent secret letters Hunter. Skull hopes that he will be able to send messages to Cynthia one day. He just hopes it's soon. Skull and Hunter become like pen pals. Skull knows that Hunter hates that name, but he liked Skull as a friend. Mostly because he was lonely out in that house alone. One Day when they sent a letter to each other. Skull got a letter saying that Hunter found Cynthia in Canada just when he turned 15 years old. Yesterday. Skull was excited he did not even care if his parents did not get anything for his birthday. He just wanted to be with Cynthia, but Skull knew he had to wait for awhile to be available to move there for awhile to see Cynthia. As Skull was writing down Cynthia's address where she was living at this point in their lives. Skull started writing a letter to Hunter saying thank you for sending me her address. It means the world to me. Then Skull was done writing his letter to Hunter for the thank you and Skull starts writing a letter to Cynthia saying.

Hey, can you let me know if you got this letter. If you did not, you should know not to read this letter whoever got it. but anyway, if you got this Cynthia, this is Skull your little brother. I just wanted to say that I miss you. Oh, and mom was a bitch. And dad was a dick leaving you behind like that. But Mom is pregnant I just thought you would like to know about that. Please send me a letter back. I need to know that you are alive and well. Please.

Ps Skull

Skull wrapped both of his letters to Cynthia and Hunter. Then Skull went back up to his room to go to sleep. Before Skull could go to sleep to his bedroom. He heard something fall upstairs. Skull went upstairs to see what it was. It was mom, she was laying there. Skull ran downstairs to the phone to call for help. Once he ended the call the help came 30 minutes later. They went upstairs to see if it was prank because a kid called, but when they saw his mom laying down on the floor, they took her in. Putting her on a Gurnee. Mom was in the back of the ambulance's vehicle. And they drove away fast. Skull went back inside of the house seeing the lights in the distance. An hour later dad comes home. "Robin where are you?" Says Dad. "I called you, that mom is in the hospital." Says Skull. "Well, I did not get that because son I am a miner. I have no network down there. What happened?" Says Dad. "Mom fell, when I got up there, she was laying down on the ground barely breathing." Says Skull. "Fine, but I am going to the hospital without you." Says Dad. "Good, because I don't want to come." Says Skull. "Okay see you later kiddo." Says Dad in sarcasm. Dad walks out the door driving toward the hospital. Skull goes up to his bedroom to go to bed. Skull wants to send a letter to Cynthia with a picture of Emerald. Skull remembers that mom and dad left Emerald alone in her bedroom. So, Skull goes to her room to check on Emerald to make sure she was alright. Skull sees that Emerald was in her crib looking hungry and sad. Skull picks her up out of Emeralds crib. Skull takes her downstairs to the kitchen looking for baby food. Skull finds some in the fridge. Skull feeds Emerald food, once she was eating Skull cleaned up her mess, went back upstairs in Skull bedroom playing with Emerald. Emerald was finally getting tired. Skull picks Emerald up and bounces Emerald to sleep. Before Emerald closes her eyes and falls asleep. "Skully." Says Emerald. Skull looks down at Emerald hugging her tight basically crying about how Emerald knew how to say Skull his name. Skull put Emerald back in her crib and went to bed himself.

CHAPTER 24

THE FIRST LETTER OF HOPE

Skull goes through the mail to see what was up today. Skull could not believe his eyes. Skull recognizes that address. It was from Cynthia. Skull opens that one first looking what it has to say.

> *Skull, It's okay. I understand that dad and mom did not want me to have a child at the age 17, but I am sort of happy that I am not in there life anymore. I can do it myself and not have to worry about them judging how I take good care of Amy. Yes, that is the name of my child. Her entire name is Amy Amber Thorn. She is my little precious bean. But anyway. Why did you want me to send a letter? Oh, I am going to send you a picture of me Amy and Troy together. We are so happy. Troy built a house so; we could live all the way out here on our own. Troy is my boyfriend that got me pregnant, but Anyway I am talking about myself to much. What is going on with you? I miss you to Skull.*
>
> Ps Cynthia

Skull was happy that he could talk to someone else for once in his life. Especially since it was Cynthia. Skull missed her so much. Now Skull has Cynthia's address. So, Skull can literally send her any letter anytime he wanted. Skull went up to his room. Once he walked in the door there was dad looking right at Skull. "So, is there any mail for me or your mom?" Says Dad. "No, there is nothing for you just me." Says Skull. "Who in the hell sends you letters? It just does not make sense. Can I see who you are talking to?" Says Dad. "No because you took my phone in the first place and now, I have to wait to write back to them. Sometimes I wait days to just get a response sometimes I even forgot what I said to them, but anyway you and mom don't get to read who I am talking to." Says Skull. Skull tries to walk away from, but dad grabs Skull by the arm. He hesitates to slap him again, but all he does was let him go. Skull walks away not looking back. Skull walks up to his room writing down letters to Hunter and Cynthia. Skull kept writing journals or re reading the letters that he gets. Then he throws them into his mailbox in his closet, when he was done writing the answers that people were looking for in his letters. Skull loved writing for some reason, he did not like it when he did had to do it before, but now he loved writing to his friends and his family across the globe. Once Skull was done writing his letters to Hunter and Cynthia. He walks back in the house to notice that Skull's dad was sitting on his chair looking down still. Skull is going to regret this decision. "Dad, what's wrong?" Says Skull. Dad looks up at Skull in sadness. Your mom had a heart attack that last night when you called for help. Says Dad. "Oh." Says Skull as he sits down across from dad. "I don't know what to say." Says Skull. "Well, I am going to say that she is still alive, but if we want to keep her going. I am going to need to work harder for my job. That means you are going to have to take care of Emerald for us." Says Dad. Skull looks at dad in his eyes realizing that they have not made eye contact for awhile. Because of all the fighting that they have been doing. Maybe that is why mom is having heart attacks, but Skull thought about this. It was their fault. Where they are right now is there fault especially with there own son. "Okay. I want to go check on your mom at the hospital so can you look after Emerald for us please." Says Dad. "Yeah, I will dad, I am doing this for Emerald not for you guys." Says Skull. Dad gets up from his chair grabbing the keys off the kitchen counter and dad looks back at Skull. Then dad turns around looking toward the outside in the sunlight. Is all Skull could hear was a car starting outside of the house. Then dad driving away from the house toward the hospital. After hours and hours making sure that Emerald was okay. Emerald had food, they played for a bit watched some TV kid shows though. Skull did not enjoy watching the shows, but he loved it when Emerald was happy, her smile got Skull to smile. Emerald was probably the only thing that Skull is going to miss when he leaves. When he is old enough to go on his own. Skull eventually was starting to get tired him self. Skull got up to set up Emerald play pen, so maybe Skull could have a nap for awhile, but once he placed Emerald in the play pen she started crying. Skull picked her up. Emerald stopped crying once she was in his arms. Skull wanted to have a nap, but he also did not want to deal with Emerald crying so Skull had a solution. Skull would hug Emerald making sure that Emerald could not get out of Skull's arms. Skull was on his back starting to close his eyes then finally skull fell asleep with Emerald in his arms. Eventually Emerald fell asleep in his arms.

"Skull, where are you?" Says Dad. Skull woke up from the yelling of his name being called. "What, what is going on." Says Skull. "I was calling the house phone number just wanting to check up on you and Emerald, I was getting worried that something happened to both of you." Says dad. "Sorry, I was just napping I have been here all day looking after Emerald she is a cute baby sister, but she is a handful." Says Skull yawing. "I know babies are like that Skull. You were that once. Your big sister on the other hand was quiet. Cynthia just liked being hugged and played with. You were all about getting the attention as well. You were always a feisty baby to. Man, I sort of miss those days." Says dad in a sigh. "Why did we leave Cynthia to be alone?" Then. Says Skull. "We left her because your mom wanted to teach her a lesson to not getting pregnant at her age. That she was. She is possible 20 now." Says Dad. Skull looks at his dad sad. Skull sits up wanting to say something. "Dad." Says Skull. "Yeah, son." Says Dad. "If you want to know who I have been in contact with. I have been in contact with Cynthia and this guy that helped me find her in the first place. Cynthia is in Canada where she always wanted to be, with her family." Says Skull. "She is in Canada. Yeah, she always wanted to move in Canada didn't she." Says Dad in a sigh. "Dad is mom coming home or what are we having for dinner?" Says Skull. "We are going to order some food to just chat for awhile. I want to spend more time with my son and my youngest daughter." Says Dad. Skull smiles at how dad wants to spend some time with his kids. It was sort of nice knowing that dad was still around caring about his children I don't think Skull's mom is still not happy with Cynthia. Maybe mom was the problem and not Skull. As dad orders some food from a pizza fast restaurant. Dad gives Skull the remote to pick a TV show on the TV. 30 minutes later the food arrived at there house hot and ready for dinner. Dad pays for the food. Then the delivery guy was done at there house, then he left the front door area and drove away on his motorcycle into the darkness. Dad walks into the living room with the pizzas. Dad and Skull sit down on the couch and eat the pizza watching the show Skull picked out for them to watch. They were done eating pizza; they could not have spare pizza for tomorrow because they did not know if mom was coming back tomorrow. So, they ate all the pizza. And drank all the pop from the pizza place. After when they were done eating. Dad put Emerald to bed in her crib than came back downstairs to watch more of what Skull chose. While they were watching that TV show they were talking. Skull could not believe what was happening tonight. Skull thought that his own dad hated him, but Skull was happy to have the night to himself with dad. "Son, it's getting late I must get ready to head to sleep. I have a job tomorrow to go to." Says Dad. Skull's dad gets up from the couch walking toward mom and dad's room. Skull sat there for a couple moments. Then realizing that he should say good night. "Hey, dad." Says Skull. "Yeah, son." Says Dad. "Good night and thank you for hanging out with me." Says Skull. "No problem son. I love you. Go to sleep soon." Says Dad. "I will, after this episode." Says Skull. As Skull's dad walks into mom and dad's bedroom Skull could feel the eye roll at him, but it was a playful eye roll. Skull finished up his episode and turned off the lights in the house and went to bed in his bedroom.

CHAPTER **25**

THE FIRST GRIM REAPER!

A year later. Skull was 16 years old now. Skull's dad has been working more than him. Skull had a job being a librarian at the closest and farthest library out there. Skull loved working with book. He never thought that he would be a book person, but since he was not doing school, he wanted to learn things on his own. So, every time he went to work, he would read about history, it's like Skull would be making his own class. Skull grabs all the books that interest him. He would grab History, Salem books with the time of Witch math, art, art culture, psychology, medicine, English, science, and geography. He loved making his own notes and tests. He would study himself. He was possibly one of the smartest kids that were not in school. There was always a weird connection to the witch Salem times. He felt like he was supposed study it so he would be ready for something, but he did not know what he was preparing for. So, Skull kept studying all the knowledge books. Once Skull was done his shift for his job at the library, he would ask his boss if he could take some books home, to read and write some notes down. "Of course, you can Skull. Skull, can I talk to you before you go home?" Says the librarian. "Yeah, sure. Mrs. Green. what's up?" Says Skull. Mrs. Green and Skull walks to the back room. "Skull. I would like to promote you to. Assist Librarian." Says Mrs. Green. Skull's face went bright red. "Oh my god really. You are going to make me assist." Says Skull. "Yeah, you have proved yourself to be able to look after the library for me, thank you so very much. Skull. The day that you came to apply for a librarian job. I was going to laugh at you, but I have been eating my laugh for a month. You have proved me not to judge anyone by there face cover again." Says Mrs.

Green. "Why, did you think it was funny I applied here." Says Skull. "I thought it was funny because you are a boy, or your name was deadly. But I was wrong to have judged like that. But anyway, you have proved me wrong about everything I was laughing about." Says Mrs. Green. "Well, I am glad I was being judged because I would have never gotten this far. Thank you. So much for giving me this job I needed it, and I am grateful that you promoted me." Says Skull. "No problem, Skull." Says Mrs. Green. "Well, I will see you tomorrow." Says Skull. "Yeah, we will see you tomorrow." Says Mrs. Green. Skull leaves the library driving his car back home. Skull loved the way his life was. Skull arrived home just about 30 minutes later. "Mom dad I am home." Says Skull. "Why are you in a good mood?" Says Dad. "Well, I just got promoted to assist Librarian." Says Skull with a big smile on his face. "You're still doing that girls job." Says Mom. "Yeah, Because I love that job. I can read literally any book I want." Says Skull. "Well, just saying you probably would have more money, by now if you were working in the mines with your father." Says Mom. "Well, we talked about this. I don't like the mines. I would rather be in the books. I don't know what it is, but I love reading and writing." Says Skull. "It's okay son. I am just glad that you are happy." Says Dad. "Thank you, dad." Says Skull. "Why are you letting him have this job, we need money. You are always working, and I never see you anymore." Says Mom. "Yeah, because I need to pay my beautiful blossom her medicine and her hospital bills." Says Dad kissing mom on the cheek. "Fine, whatever." Says Mom. Mom walks away from Skull rolling her eyes. "Don't let your mom get to you Skull. I am proud that you are working in a book environment. I never thought you would be working in that kind of environment, but I am still proud of you." Says Dad. "Thank you so much dad. I am going to go read my books." Says Skull. Skull walks up the stairs to his bedroom reading about the Salem times for Witches and Wizards. He felt like he was supposed know about this stuff coming up in his life. So, he kept studying for the Salem times the most. An hour went by. Skull went to go see if there was any mail in the mailbox. He walks downstairs to the front door walking out of the house and seeing if he had any letters. He had two one from Hunter and Cynthia. He was and excited to see how Cynthia was doing. Skull walks back up to his room and reads the letter that Cynthia had written to him. He had another picture of his niece. She was beautiful just like her mom. On the back of the picture, it said that Amy is four years old now. Skull began to write a letter to Cynthia. Skull heard his name being called from downstairs. "Dinner's ready Skull." Says Mom. "Alright I will be down in a few." Says Skull.

12 am at night. Skull was still writing a letter to his sister. Skull does not know why it took him a long time to figuring out what to write to his sister, but he finished telling Cynthia that he got promoted at his job. And that Mrs. Green was the nicest old lady that he has and will ever work for. Skull got up from his chair to put his letter away in the mailbox outside again, but this time Skull was tired, and he just wanted to go to bed. Before Skull went up the stairs Skull saw his mom on the floor barely breathing. Skull runs to the kitchen, but the phoneline was out. Skull did not know what to do exactly but try to give her CPR. But Skull mom was dead before that. She has been dead for 5 minutes. Skull sat down crying on his mom's body. "Sorry I was not there on time. Sorry mom." Says Skull still crying on his mom. Skull felt a sudden cold dark soul in the room and the lights started flickering in the living. The lights stopped flickering Skull turned around to see a floating black figure scythe. Skull looked closer at the figure; the figure looked familiar. it kind of looked like the grim Reaper. Then the dark figure came closer to Mom's dead body. The figure put his hood down. "Who are you?" Says Skull in tears. "I am the grim reaper." Says the grim reaper. The grim reaper looked right into Skulls eyes. The reaper saw something that Skull has not had in a every long time. "Skull, have we seen each other before?" Says the reaper. "No?" Says Skull. "Your eyes look very familiar like my eyes when I was just your age." Says the reaper. The reaper walks up to Skull touching him on the shoulders. The reaper was right, Skull had a power that he had when he was a boy. The reaper closes his eyes concentrating on who took his power. "I have a quest now. I want to help you get power, your power again." Says Reaper. "What are you talking about?" Says Skull. "A witch named Gretel took your powers away because of your parents. I will be taking your moms soul with me to my realm." Says Reaper. "Wait, leave my mom's soul out of this." Says Skull. "Why she is the one who agreed to

giving your gift away to a witch that has it in a jar in her store. I won't kill anyone, but I will if this Witch gets in my way." Says reaper. Skull looks up at the reaper. "I am coming with you. I am only coming because I don't want you to hurt anyone anymore." Says Skull. "Good, that is what I wanted, I wanted you to come because you are meant to be a reaper just like me." Says Reaper. "Oh, okay. Whatever." Says Skull. "You are meant to be my apprentice or my replacement. I can sense the power that you have in you. I am wanting to give back your gift. Please let me just do that, for you Skull." Says Reaper. Skull feared this reaper, but he had to go to see what he was talking about. Seeing if this man was telling the truth about his parents giving or making sure that Skull would have never had power before. Skull knew he was missing something in his life. "Alright hold my hand we will teleport there." Says Reaper. Reaper holds out his hand toward Skull. Skull hesitates for few moments, then grabs hold of the Reapers hand. Then they were at a store in the middle of the forest. Skull looked around and saw nothing, but forest and a store. The Reaper was walking up waiting for Skull to come follow him. Skull followed the Reaper up to the store. Reaper opens the door without knocking on the door. "Hello, is anyone home?" Says Reaper. A woman comes out from the back. "Are you Gretel?" Says Reaper. "Yeah, and you are the grim Reaper. What brings the Grim Reaper to my shop in the middle of the forest." Says Gretel. "I brought myself because you stole something from this boy, when he was just a little baby boy." Says Reaper. Reaper moves out of the way, so Reaper could show who he was talking about. Gretel's facial expression changed right away when she saw Skull's face. "Your, Skull, aren't you?" Says Gretel. "Yeah, I am Skull. Do I know you?" Says Skull. "It's a long story, Skull." Says Gretel. "Gretel why don't you tell him the truth. Give him his power back and we will be on our merry way." Says Reaper. Gretel looks down at the floor confused of how this is going to go out, but Gretel gestures to Skull to follow her in the back room. Skull followed Gretel to the back room, but Reaper stayed where he was standing, so Skull could figure what the truth on his own. Gretel led Skull to a locked glass briefcase, there was a jar inside of the briefcase. Gretel opened the case. "What is in this jar?" Says Skull. Gretel looks down afraid of telling the truth. "It's your power Skull, that I took from you when you were a baby. Your parents did not want you to have this power, but I don't really care anymore. I mostly wanted to say no to taking your power away. From you when you were just a kid. But your parents were a different story." Says Gretel. Gretel opened the jar. Suddenly a glow of white and black rose out of the jar. Flying toward inside of Skull. Skull was paralyzed by this feeling in his veins. He did not want this to be true, but Skull always felt there was something missing in his life, he just did not know that it was this to be exact. Reaper walked into the back room where everyone was standing. Reaper walked in smiling. "Thank you, Gretel we will be on our way now. I will see you around another time." Says Reaper. Reaper grabbed Skull's hand and they were back in Skull's parents living room. "Well, Skull I did my quest. It was easier than I thought, but I most go now. I will be back checking on you some other time." Reaper waves out his hand toward. Skull's mom. Suddenly Skull's mom started to glow blue, then an orb came toward Reaper's hands. Reaper breathes in and out. Like it was a refreshment to take Skull's mom's soul away from them. Then Reaper waved his hand toward Skull. Skull fell to the ground asleep. Reaper then teleported away leaving Skull for grieving and powerful.

CHAPTER 26

THE TRUTH OF DESTINY

Skull woke up the next day. Feeling off. He woke up on his mom not breathing. Skull started yelling and screaming for dad. "DAD, WHERE ARE YOU?" Says Skull. "Boy, I am trying to sleep." Says Dad. "Did you not notice that I was in here sleeping on top of mom's body? She died last. I could not call the phone lines, because they were unavailable." Says Skull. "Well, yeah, I did not see you guys, right there." Says Dad. "How, did you not see us here?!" Says Skull. "Skull, don't I just go to bed right away when I got home. I was tired because I work in a mine for hours. Probably the entire day till 12 am in the morning. Of course, I am going to go to bed right away." Says Dad. "Look dad I am sorry, but I am just still traumatized of what I was dreaming about and scared of who I saw." Says Skull. "What happened last night for you?" Says Dad. "The Grim Reaper. Happened to me last night." Says Skull. "What, the Grim Reaper is not real." Says Dad. "Then why did I have the power to be like the Grim Reaper." Says Skull. Skull's dad's face changed as soon as he said that. "You have your power, don't you?" Says dad. "Yeah, I do in fact. I mean I don't know because I thought it was a dream, but mom is not breathing and then I went somewhere else. The Reaper gave me my powers back. Then there was this Witch who had my power in a jar. She opened the jar and there white and black coming out of the jar and it flew toward me. Now I feel like dead and alive at once." Says Skull. "Skull please. Let me take you back to that witch and our lives will be normal again." Says Dad. Skull looks at him. "No, I am not going back to that Witch because she gave me a chance to know myself again. I always thought I was missing something in my life, and now I got the chance to know who I am going to become. Dad you are not going to make my decisions anymore." Says Skull. Skull's dad's face turned angry. "SKULL, you don't understand what you are getting yourself into. You had those powers you had when you were born. I tried to forgive you, for what you did. But you killed my sister when you were in her arms. Is all I can remember you when you were a kid. Are your eyes turned black, then suddenly my sister was turning into ash right beyond my eyes! When I found out that there was a Witch that could make you normal just like me. I wanted to do that, for you, but I guess I should have seen this coming." Says Dad in much angry. "Well, you still did not have the right taking my gift away from me. I am sorry, that I killed your sister. I was a baby I could not control what I was doing. Are you really going to hate me for the rest of my life now?" says Skull. Dad looks at Skull realizing, "yes, I am going to hate you because of your power. I am never going to forgive you. Skull, so I am going to leave it up to you of where you are going." says Dad. Dad leaves the room angry and leaves his son behind forever. Skull knew in his heart that his dad was never going to come back to him ever again. So, Skull decided to leave his dad alone in this house, but he decides, if Skull's dad did not like him. He gets to be completely alone that means. Skull takes Emerald with him. Skull picks up Emerald. "Skull where are we going?" says Emerald. "We are going away for awhile." Says Skull. "Okay!" Says Emerald. Little did Emerald know that her mom was dead, and her dad hated Skull for who he was, so Skull took Emerald with him to go find Cynthia to be with one another again. Skull wanted Emerald to meet the good side in the family. And Skull was finally getting that chance. Skull grabbed Emerald and put her in the backseat of the car in her car seat. Skull buckle's Emerald in the car seat and closes the door walking toward the front seat of the car. Skull starts the car and drives away from the house and does not look back ever again.

CHAPTER 27

THE PRESENT DAY FOR SKULL

Skull was sitting on his throne looking a upon the stars. Thinking of the people who have left him or have died in vain for him. Skull missed both of his sisters. He was doing this for them. Skull asked a soul guard if there were any souls by the name of Cynthia Thorn and Emerald Bars. The guard said yeah there were souls like that, but they are trapped in the soul prison. "What, did you just say. About my sisters." Says Lord Skull. The guard looked at him in fear. "We can get them out. Its just they were bad souls, and they had much love and other good feelings. So, we put them in that section." "I want them alive again, but I know that will take longer to get them here, so I am just going to accept them dead for awhile." Says Skull. "Okay, so do you want us to let them out?" Says the soul guard. "Yeah, I would like that. Thank you." Says Skull. Skull Went into the portal with the guard and the guard led him to where they were being kept.

"What do you want?!" Says Grim. Jack stands there looking down at Grim. "Grim, I am sorry. I went on the wrong side of the world. I just wanted a leader." Says Jack. "You don't have a right to be here right now." Says Grim. "Grim, please let me in. I will show you that I won't betray you again please just let me in." says Jack. "So, you could betray me again. You stole my niece, and you gave her to the devil himself." Says Grim. "I may have given whoever your nieces name is, but Grim I can tell you what your uncle's plan is officially. I want to help you." Says Jack. Grim grabs Jack by the arm dragging him in the base. "Okay, what is your bullet. Are you going to shot me with betrayal again or are going to help!?" Says Skull. "Grim, you don't have to grab me by the arm." Says

Jack. "Well, you took my niece away and you may have destroyed this world. I have a right to kill you right now, but I won't." says Grim. "You won't?" says Jack. "No because you deserve to be in a jail cell. Guards take this one to the cells." Says Grim. Grim throws Jack in their arms. The guards start walking toward the cell block area. "Grim, why would you do that?" Says Robert. "Because he is not to be trusted. I trusted him already and he threw that out the door." Says Grim. "Polly what's wrong?" Says Robert. "That was also Polly's ex- boyfriend I think?" Says Grim. "Yeah, he is my ex-boyfriend. Why did you throw him away like that? Grim." Says Polly. "I just said he is not to be trusted right now. He is hard to read these days." Says Grim. "Yeah, but you could have gotten me to talk to him." Says Polly. "What so he can control you again forcing you to be under mind control again." Says Grim. Polly looks at Grim as if she realized why she was here in the first place. Then looks down in sadness. "That's what I thought." Says Grim. Then Polly runs after Jack. "Did you have to be so harsh." Says Robert. Robert goes after Polly. Leaving just Gretel and Grim again.

"Polly, wait. I am sorry about Grim. He has always been that way." Says Robert. "I know that, but I must see Jack." Says Polly. "So, you are not mad at Grim?" Says Robert. Polly sighs "I am not sure; I just want to chat with Jack to ask him if he knows anything about the green and blue sky?" Says Polly. "Yeah, I was sort of wanting to ask the same since you knew that he was on Lord Skull's side also known as my uncle." Says Robert. "You can come with me, if you want?" Says Polly. "Sure. I will come with you then." Says Robert. Polly and Robert walk together toward where those guards went to put Jack away in the cell block.

Skull and the soul guard arrive at the soul prison in the dimension of the lost souls. Skull and the guard walk toward the front desk. "Hey, bud. The new King of souls is here to pick up some souls here today." Says the soul guard. "What for?" Says the front desk. "I am picking them up for a show, what I call is revenge for them to watch." Says Lord Skull. The front desk looks at Skull for a moment then realizes that he was new king of Souls. So, the front desk had no reason to say no. Because the way Skull was looking at him looked like he was not asking for a favor, but he was giving a command. The front desk leads them to the cell block of where Emerald and Cynthia were in. Skull looked around to notice that the cells were boxes. Big boxes. Finally, the front desk person or ghoul opened one of the cells and then another cell. "There you can put their souls in anything you like, but if you want to put them in anything you are going to need a jar or something that you can carry them in." Says the front desk. "I know, I am a Grim Reaper to, you know." Says Lord Skull. Skull grabs from his side of his waist two jars. One for Cynthia and one for Emerald. Once Skull opened the boxes one at a time. He opened Cynthia's box first, then there was a blue soul that tried to get away, but Skull caught Cynthia before running away. He put one of the jars back on his waist. Then Skull walked into Emerald's cell. The soul tried to run as well, but Skull caught the soul before Emerald could run as well. Skull had both of his sisters right beside him now. He wanted to leave this place to bring them back where they lived before. Up in the otherworld. "Thank you, front desk ghoul I appreciate what you have done for me. Thank you." Says Lord Skull. "King of souls." Says the soul guard. "Yes." Says Skull. "Do you want to see your throne in this dimension?" Says the soul guard. "No, I just want to leave and claim my destiny." Says Lord Skull. "Oh, alright. We will go back to the otherworld then." Says the soul guard. The soul guard escorts Skull back to the otherworld.

Once they got out of the lost soul dimension. Skull took a breath in and out heavily, but in a victory way. Hazel walks up to Lord Skull. "Did you find what you were looking for." Says Hazel. "Yeah, I did. They are here to watch. There nephew die and son as well." Says Lord Skull as he was holding up Cynthia's and Emerald's jars up in the air. "Hello, Skull. I see you have grown into…" says the voice in the brushes. The figure came out of the brushes looking over Skull up and down. "You have grown into a king I see." Says the figure. "Reaper, what are you doing here?" Says Lord Skull. "I am here to help you with your plan." Says Reaper, as he was gesturing the sky. "What are you going to do now?" says Skull. "I am going to help you with taking over the lost realm. That realm needs you Skull. You need to rule that realm first, before you rule the otherworld." Says Reaper. "Who is this guy? Lord Skull." Says

Hazel. "He is my teacher. He taught me how to use my power correctly." Says Skull. "Yeah, that is right. I am here to teach you the final lesson of ruling worlds. You don't just have the power to ruling the world, you need the smarts for it. It's like you becoming president, but you could that sit. Now you must be smart about this, Skull my favorite and only student." Says Reaper. "I only was your student because I needed help. But now I don't need help from an old teacher, I worked by myself to get here. You don't get to just earn a spot in my throne room." Says Lord Skull. Reaper smells Cynthia's and Emerald's souls. Reaper breaths in and out. Those souls smell familiar. "Cynthia and Emerald, your sister's. You brought them back with you, so you can feel more rage and strength, that is good for you. Maybe you don't need much of my help." Says Reaper. "I don't. Stay away from my sister's." says Skull. "I can't touch them anymore, because you are the king Skull. You chose who can touch what is yours and who can take what is yours. That is why the king of souls made us. The Reaper who steals dead souls and the lost ones that need to be guided. You get to chose who I am going to be in this world. Or about of your dimension, that you must learn more about before ruling this world." Says Reaper. "I will show you that I don't need to know anything about the lost realm. I will rule this world before anyone even gets to stop me." Says Lord Skull. "You have always been cocky like that, haven't you?! But you are the king I can't stop you anymore. You have grown into a man with a staff and a crown." Says Reaper. "Yeah, I am a man and a King of the realm that I always researched when I was just a boy. I always thought there was something missing in my life." Says Lord Skull. "Well, good luck because you are going to need it. King of Souls." Says Reaper. Before Reaper left Skull to be alone. He turned around to notice the wings on Hazel. Reaper's face changed right away to fear. Reaper was afraid to say anything, so Reaper just walked away and never looked back at Skull or Hazel.

Polly and Robert walk into the cell block area, but before they could continue, they were stopped by a guard. "Hey, you two can't be back here." Says the Grim guard. Robert looks at him. "I am your boss's brother and the man that you just put away was her ex-boyfriend and we would like to chat with him." Says Robert. The guard looks at Robert

rolling his eyes. "Fine, you may pass through the cell block area." Says
The Grim guard. The Guard opens the gate to the cell block area where
they could see down the hall where Jack was. Jack pretty much was the
only prisoner in the cell block area. Polly and Robert walked down the
hallway toward Jack's cell. Jack could almost not believe what he was
seeing in front of his eyes. "Polly?" Says Jack. Getting up from his bed
in the cell. "Yeah, it's me. Polly the one that you forced to help capture
Hazel the girl, but now look where you are and look where everyone
else is in the world, we are screwed. All because you helped get a crazy
uncle that wants revenge on what the world has done to him. I have
may questions for you. First one, why?" Says Polly. Jack looked at Polly
sad. "I just wanted a leader to lead me and my family to safety, but Lord
Skull was right I was to weak and pathetic to have a leader like him."
Says Jack. "What is going on with your family?" Says Polly. "My family
is being screwed by these other demons right now, and they are probably
suffering. Cause I am not around right now." Says Jack. Polly looks in
Jack's eyes. Polly grabs hold of Jack's hand and closes her eyes seeing if
he was telling the truth. Polly saw was in Jack's mind was death, blood,
screaming, and pain. Jack was telling the truth. Jack was just trying
to find a good leader to teach him how to defend his family from the
demons that were terrorizing them. "Jack, I am so sorry." Says Polly.
"It's okay. I am just worried that something more horrible is going to
happen all because I wanted a leader." Says Jack. "We can fix what you
and I started." Says Polly. "Polly, you can say this is my fault. Lots of
things are my fault. I can handle this being my fault, because I am the
one who helped Lord Skull get out of the realm that Gretel sent him
to, then I lied to my friend Grim, and finally I forced you to help me, to
getting Hazel for Lord Skull." Says Jack. "Yes, you may have done those
things, but Jack, you still have time to change everything that you have
done for this world. You can help us fight Lord Skull and get him back
in the realm forever." Says Polly. "Are you sure, because it did not look
like Grim wanted my help anymore?" Says Jack. "I know, but he is just
mad because it was you who betrayed him. Bros don't except their best
friends to betray them. Jack, tell me what you know, and I will convince,
Grim to let you out of this cage." Says Polly. "I know that Lord Skull has
put Hazel in an evil spell. Also, that he is the King of the lost realm, he

has his shadow angels, and a plan that he has been working on for years and more years. To work. So, he is excepting you guys going after him." Says Jack. "So, the question is what is he not going to expect?" Says Polly. They all think of one thing that Lord Skull would never expect. Which was Grim giving up himself and imprisoning Robert. To Lord Skull. Everyone looks at each other. Polly opens the cell door. Grabbing Jack by the arm and running out of the cell block with him. Polly, Jack and Robert running back toward Grim and Gretel.

"What is he doing out?!" Says Grim. "We have a plan Grim. Please just hear him out, for a minute." Says Polly. Grim sighs at his friend. "Fine, do tell." Says Grim. As Grim and everyone listens Jack's plan. Grim thought it was stupid, but then the last part of Jack's plan was a surprise. "So, that is your plan?" Says Grim. "Yeah, it is. The idea is to make it look like you Grim to change your mind about being on the good side, but then you decide that you want to be on the bad side with your uncle." Says Jack. "It would work if it was the other way around. Which me as the prisoner and not Robert. Did nothing to piss off our uncle. You see I killed his sister Emerald, and he is still pretty pissed at me about it." Says Grim. "Okay, so then it will be Robert changing his mind about being on the good side and Grim being the prisoner. That works way better than I thought." Says Jack. "Then I come in while he is not paying attention to anymore guests?" Says Gretel. "Yeah, then you go in with your trap vase and say the command and he should go right in the vase." Says Jack. "Yeah, that sounds about right." Says Gretel. "So, that is the plan." Says Polly. "Yeah, are you alright with-it Polly?" Says Jack. "Yeah, it's great for you guys, but I want in this. I want to fight Lord Skull." Says Polly. "Maybe you can. Stay here and make sure that every solider that Grim has, is safe." Says Jack. "Wait, are you suggesting that I stay here at Grim's base?! To baby sit." Says Polly. "Yeah, Polly. You can only go into people's dream's up close. Skull knows that and I don't want you to get hurt." Says Jack. "I won't I promise." Says Polly. "You're staying here. I know you don't like not being apart of this, but you must not come Polly. Please. I am just trying to keep you safe." Says Jack. "Well, I don't want to be saved. I want to be apart of this battle. If you want me to forgive you, you are going to have to let me come with you guys." Says Polly. "No, you are staying I am sorry, but this is for the best." Says Jack. Polly turns around looking the other way. Polly looks back at Jack and gets up walking away from the table. Everyone continues to sit in silence. "Sorry, about that, but I can't take Polly with us. She is not powerless, but her power must be close to her enemy." Says Jack. "I know. Your right it was just hard to listen to that." Says Grim. "So, anyway. Let's leave in an hour I know where Skull is hiding, and I know the perfect spot where we can all hide out for awhile." Says Jack. "Alright, let's get going then." Says Robert. Grim walks up to his sword case. Looking for a sword that his uncle gave to him before Uncle Skull hated Grim. Grim looks at the sword that he wanted to take. He looks closer at it and remembers Skull saying. "That this sword that I am giving you is, powerful and any dark creature or light creature can die right as the blade hits their heart or anywhere on there body." Grim grabs his sword hoister and puts the sword into the hoister. Grim looks around his room looking for anything else that would be useful to bring with, but he found nothing but the sword. Grim just had a feeling that he would need this sword for some reason. Gretel walks in the room grabbing her bag and putting the vase in the bag. With her potions. Gretel turns to notice that Grim looked nervous. "What's up, Grim?" Says Gretel. "Nothing I just feel like I must say something to you, if anything bad happens to me." Says Grim. "Nothing bad will happen Grim. We will come back here together in victorious of us winning against your uncle Skull." Says Gretel. "I hope you are right. I am bringing this sword just in case. I need it." Says Grim. "Yeah, whatever you are bringing is smart at this point." Says Gretel in worry. Grim looks back at Gretel. "Why are you worried?" Says Grim. "I am just worried that. I don't know I just have a feeling of something." Says Gretel. "Oh?" Says Grim. Suddenly Jack and Robert walk in the room. "Okay, let's go. It's four pm right now and we will be there at eight pm." Says Jack. Everyone walks out of Grims office toward the exit. Starting to walk toward inside the forest.

Luna was just sitting on a log wondering what the blue and green clouds mean. Luna looks up at Scarlet. Just sitting getting firewood on the firepit. "Scarlet, why do you think the clouds are that color right now?" says Luna. Scarlet lifts her shoulders. Her shoulders were saying that, she does not know. Scarlet then grabs out of her bag grabbing a piece of paper. Scarlet gives Luna the page of what Scarlet just said or was wanting to say. "I think that Lord Skull got what he wanted, but nothing was happening. So, he just wandering around the lost realm and doing nothing yet or that he is just wanting for the good, best moment." Says Scarlet's writing. "So, Skull is the king or something." Says Luna. As Luna gives back Scarlet's paper. Scarlet wrote yes on the page. "What is he the king of?" Says Luna. Scarlet writes down on her paper. Giving it back to Luna. "He is the king of the lost soul's realm right now. Did you feel someone walking in the forest?" Says Scarlet's writing. "No? wait, I feel something, the footprint in the grass." says Luna. Luna's eyes close as Luna sees Grim and everyone walking alone in the forest in just about time when it starts to get dark. Luna sees that Grim and her father were walking with two other people. Luna's eyes open again. Luna jumps up looking around the forest for her father. "Scarlet, we got to go look for my dad and Grim." Says Luna. Scarlet nods to that like Scarlet is just going to let that happen. Scarlet and Luna start walking toward Robert and everyone.

Skull sits there on his throne talking to the jars that were Emerald and Cynthia. "My sisters I will get my revenge for you. By killing Grim." Says Lord Skull. Hazel walks up to Skull sitting on his throne. "Lord Skull, are you hungry?" Says Hazel. "Yes, in fact. Thank you. Hazel." Says Lord Skull. Skull eats some chicken that Hazel clearly killed and cooked up for Skull. Hazel eats as well with Skull. "So, my lord Skull what is your next step in your plan." Says Hazel. "I am waiting till my friends make the move, I am waiting till your father and Uncle come around to try to kill me or possibly trap me again. Then I will kill all of them." Says Lord Skull. Hazel laughs evilly at what Lord Skull said. But in the inside Hazel was crying. Basically, yelling for help. "What do you want me to do?" Says Hazel. "I will probably need you for back up maybe." Says Lord Skull. "I am here by your side always Lord Skull." Says Hazel. "Good, but for now. Let's enjoy some of the chicken that you brought for us." Says Lord Skull. Skull and Hazel raise's a glass to that and drinks the wine in their hands. Skulls chugs that wine in his hand. One of his shadow angels were guarding or just flying around their lord Skull. Hazel in the inside was crying and was in pain. Hazel in the inside was feeling. Hope somehow and calmed down a little from crying. Inside Hazel's mind someone came in her head. Saying it's going to be okay. Hazel just listened to that woman with red hair, and she was floating. She sort of looks like an angel.

Jack stops in spot where there was a firepit. "We are here." Says Jack. "Where are we?" Says Grim. "We are just at me and Polly's base area, where we would sneak around somewhere around west around here. We would come out here to watch the stars." Says Jack. "So, which way is my uncle?" Says Grim. "He is north from here, just 10 minutes away from here." Says Jack. "Okay, works for me." Says Grim. Jack and everyone unload there bags and sets out there tents and Gretel went to go get some firewood. Jack heard someone running toward them. "Who is there?!" Says Jack. Luna walks out of the brushes out of breath and Scarlet was also out of breath. "Luna! Why are you here. I thought I told you to stay home." Says Robert. "You know these two?" Says Jack. "Luna is my daughter, but I don't know who this is?" Says Robert. "Dad." Says Luna out of breath. "This is Scarlet me and her are friends. She saved me from this guy named Skull?" Says Luna. Robert looks over at Grim in fear and then looks back at Luna. "What. You were near my uncle." Says Dad. "Yeah? Wait Skull is your uncle?" Says Luna. "Yeah, he is the one who made the sky green and blue and wait how long have you been in this forest." Says Dad. "Scarlet told me that it was Skull that turned the sky blue and green, so I already knew that, and I have been in this forest probably three days or a week at least." Says Luna. "Why don't you ever listen to me?" Says Dad. "Because Hazel was in trouble, I felt it and was talking to her from work in my head." Says Luna. "Why didn't you text me?" Says Dad. "Because I know what you would have said. You would have said no, for me coming." Says Luna. Robert looks down. "Yeah, you are right I would have said no. But it does not mean that I am happy to see you." Says Robert. "Fine, but I am here to help and wonder why you are here?" Says Luna. "We are here because we are going to save the world from Lord Skull." Says Jack. "So, what is the plan exactly?" Says Luna.

CHAPTER 28

THE CELESTIAL SWORD

Jacks yells out in the campsite while everyone was still sleeping. "Breakfast is ready, everyone. Get up, get up now." Says Jack. Grim gets out of his tent, yawning, and looking at Jack. "Why are you up this early." Says Grim. "Because we have a big day for all of us." Says Jack. "Oh right, today is the day we bring down Lord Skull. Wait, Jack how do you even know that it is daytime?" Says Grim. "I just feel like it, it is daytime." Says Jack. "Alright." Says Grim. Grim grabs a log so he could sit at the table that Jack made yesterday before they all went to bed. Luna and Scarlet wake up on the floor smelling the food. "Hmm, what is that beautiful smell." Says Luna. "I made breakfast for everyone." Says Jack. Everyone who was still in their tents. Everyone came out of there tent and joined the table. Eating breakfast.

"Hazel, go find something for the king to eat." Says Lord Skull. "But aren't you King?" Says Hazel. "Yeah, but I am just trying to remind everyone that I am king now and that loser in the cage is no longer King." Says King Skull. "Alright, I will go get him something to eat then." Says Hazel. Hazel flies in the forest just above the base of where everyone was hiding out. Hazel was looking up, so she did not notice that they were down there.

"So, remember the plan everyone. We are going there in four hours, so be ready. I want to make an amazing quick goodbye to Skull." Says Jack. "Sounds great to me." Says Grim. As Grim and everyone was eating their eggs and bacon. Luna and Scarlet were talking with paper. Robert thought it was strange, but he let it happen. Jack was eating so much bacon, and he was drinking his favorite juice, in fact he made that juice himself.

A few hours later everyone left the stuff that they could clearly pack up later, but Grim and everyone packs up their stuff for the battle or their death. But they believed that they were going to win. Jack draws where everyone is going to be standing and running in. Of course, "Robert and Grim and going in first. Grim is going to be tied and Robert, you are going to act like you have turned on his side of evil. Then Gretel, you are going to run behind Skull to open the jar and say the spell." Says Jack. "What about Hazel. She is the wings and the eyes above." Says Grim. "Good point. Jack putting on his thinking face. I can distract Hazel." Says Luna. Robert and everyone looks at Luna. "Luna, no you are not getting involved in this at all." Says Robert. "Dad, you need me here. I know what to do for Hazel. I got this. Everything is going to be fine." Says Luna. "Fine, but if you get hurt, I won't be able to forgive myself for that." Says Robert. "Dad I will be fine. Just trust me, please." Says Luna. Robert looks at Luna in the eyes. Robert saw fear but knowing Luna. She was the best shot for Hazel not being apart of this fight. "Okay, fine. You do that Luna. I am believing in you right now." Says Robert. "Thanks dad." Says Luna. Luna gets up from the chair and runs to where Hazel would be staying. Where Luna would want her to be staying. As Luna runs away. Scarlet was following Luna in the woods wherever Luna, was going Scarlet needed to know. Luna stopped in spot. She was watching Skull sit on his throne. Finally, a figure flew down right in front of Lord Skull, which was Hazel, Luna could recognize those black wings from anywhere. "Scarlet, why did you follow me." Says Luna. Scarlet writes on her page. "I followed you because me and you need to stick together." Says Scarlet on the page. "Fine, but just be careful. My sister Hazel is under a spell right now, and my attempt of getting her back is today." Says Luna. Luna closes her eyes trying to get Hazel to come over where she was thinking. Scarlet sees that Hazel was pressing her hands against her head. Then Hazel flew away. Luna opened her eyes and then started running toward the spot. Hazel was there waiting for Luna. Luna walks out of the brushes with Scarlet beside her. "Hazel are you in there." Says Luna. Hazel turns around looking right at Luna.

Robert ties Grim in a rope. "Okay, is that tight enough?" Says Robert. "Yeah, that is perfect. Skull is so going to believe this for a second." Says Grim. "Okay, is everyone ready?" Says Jack. "Yeah, I got my vase ready." Says Gretel. "Looks like our prisoner and capturer is ready for encounter. Okay, let's do this." Says Jack. Robert and Grim walk toward where Skull sat down on his throne. Gretel and Jack were walking two minutes behind. Gretel had the vase ready for impact and Jack had his magic power ready. Finally Grim and Robert make it to where Lord Skull was sitting. "Robert what are you doing." Says Grim. Trying to get out of the ropes that Robert tied. "What are you to doing here?" Says Skull. "I am here to give you Grim as a gift, for what he has done to our family." Says Robert. "What, I can't believe you, are doing this to me." Says Grim. "Give him to be me." Says Skull. As Skull got up from his throne. Gretel walked behind him and opened the vase saying the words. Before Gretel could finish succeeding. A shadow Angel swoops in protecting his master. Gretel tries to catch the vase, but it breaks in pieces. Skull looks behind him looking right at Gretel. Robert untangles. Grims ropes. As he does that. Jack ran into the battle, cause the plan was falling apart early. Skull freezes everyone in spot. Jack, Grim, Gretel, and Robert were frozen in spot and suddenly Hazel came flying with Luna in her arms and Scarlet knocked out. Skull looks at everyone frozen in spot. "Wow, you tried and failed good effort everyone. Hazel put these fools in the cage in the cave." Says Lord Skull. Hazel uses her power to make everyone float and throws them in the cage, but for some reason Skull stopped Hazel from putting Grim in the cage. Skull cuffed Grim to the floor with his more powerful magic abilities. "What, are you going to do with everyone?" Says Hazel. "First, I am going to Kill Grim, then I guess I will kill everyone else. Except for the Witch Gretel." Says Skull. "Hazel, please snap out of it. We are here to help you and defeat Lord Skull." Yells Dad. "I don't want to be snapped out of it. I love this side of the light." Says Hazel. "Well, Grim I am going to make your family watch you die in front of them. This kill will be worth the wait for many years." Says Skull. Hazel grabs Skull's staff for him, there was a stump in front of Grims head. Skull puts his staff down next to his throne. Skull grabs his axe. "Oh, right I want everyone to watch. Hazel, do what you do best." Says Skull smiling. Hazel picks up Skull's new staff making just cages for Everyone to watch Grim die first. Hazel floats everyone in their own cells. "Alright I am ready now." Says Skull breathing in and out. Skull attempts to chop off Grims head, but suddenly a arrow hit the axe out of Skulls hand and dropped on the dirt. "WHAT WAS THAT!?" Says Lord Skull. "I am here everyone. With back up." Says Polly. "How did you know that we were going to need you?" Says Jack. "I just knew. Attack Grim guards." Says Polly. The Grim guards attack the Shadow Angels in the sky while Lord Skull is distracted Polly runs to the cages that Jack, Robert, Gretel, Luna, and Scarlet were in. Polly broke all the locks. Hazel was distracted as well by attacking the Grim Guards. "HAZEL OVER HERE. I WANT TO CHAT." Says Luna. "Well, hello their Uncle Skull." Says Grim. "Damn it, I did not except this. I will kill you now, I guess." Says Skull. Before Lord Skull could chop off Grims head, Robert ran up at Skull with a sword hitting Skull right in the face. Just enough time for Robert to chop off the rope that was holding him down. Skull ran toward his throne and picked up the staff yelling in angry. Skull had blue fiery eyes and a sword spawned in his hand. "I will fight Skull. You just make sure that Polly and everyone else is alright." Says Grim. Robert runs away looking back at Grim. Grim pulls out a sword like Skull did. "So, we are sword fighting again?! This time, you are losing. I am not your uncle anymore. See those jars right here on waist." Says Lord Skull. "Yeah?" Says Grim. "Your mom is here and your aunt that you killed. I am getting their revenge for them. TODAY." Says Lord Skull. Skull runs at Grim this his sword in the air. Skull tries to go for the head, but Grim puts his sword above him. Skull tries to sneak for the ankles, but Grim was still fast at sword fighting. Robert fought off the Shadows angels as well for awhile since there was just about 20 more. Gretel was on a roll with making sure that everyone stays alive. Gretel was using her magic abilities fast, but graceful. Jack sees that Grim is having trouble with keeping up with Skulls slashes. Jack goes to help Grim sword fight Skull. "Jack what are you doing?! Go help someone else." Says Grim. "Gretel basically wiped-out half of Skulls death angel." Says Jack as they both were trying to get slices off Skull, but Skull was fast as well. Grim fell for a second, then Skull threw his blade right at Grim on the ground. Jack ran in front of the blade that Grim was about to get hit by. The blade goes in Jack impaling Jack right in the chest. Jack falls to the ground. Polly turns around to see that Jack was on the dirt dying. Polly runs toward Jack. Polly sides underneath Jack. Polly puts Jack on top of her kneels. "Jack, please stay, stay with me." Says Polly in a sob. "Polly. I have, one thing to say to you." Says Jack in a dying voice. "No, save it for later. I promise please. Save your energy." Says Polly. "Polly. I am sorry for making fights all the time. I love you." Says Jack. Jack's eyes close. Polly puts her on his chest making sure that he was still alive, but he was dead. "NO, NO, No. You can't die. Jack please I can't be without you. I love you, to. JACK, JACK." Says Polly in a cry. Polly laids her head down on his chest crying her eyes out. Polly's eyes turned red. Jack's chest was full of blood, tears, and dirt. Grim stands there looking at Jack's body. Then Grim looks at his uncle. Grim runs at Skull with his sword high in the air. Grim stabs Skull right in the chest. Skull stands there laughing pulling out the sword out of Skull's chest. Skull stabs Grim in the heart. Then everyone turned toward Skull and Grim. They both we're glowing like fire. Skull and Grim were screaming. There bodies turned right into ash right away, then the sword exploded flames all over the place. Almost hitting Jack's body with fire, Polly made a forcefield around her and Jack's dead body. Suddenly all the shadow Angels disappeared. Because Skull was gone. Then the sky was turning back to normal. Everyone went down to there kneels and breathed heavily. Hazel fell on to the ground with her black wings, but her eyes were back to her normal color. Green and hazel. Luna sees that Hazel's arm was glowing blue. Luna watched a symbol disappear off Hazel's arm. "Huh, what happened." Says Hazel. "HAZEL, YOUR BACK THANK GOD." Says Luna. Luna hugs Hazel tight. Hazel was confused, but she did not argue about getting a hug. Hazel hugs back Luna. Luna was hugging Hazel tighter than Hazel was hugging Luna. Robert walks over to Lord Skull's and Grims ashes. Robert stands above his brother's ashes and accepts his fate of losing his brother in battle. Grim turned out to be hero. Robert was happy that it turned out that way, but he wished that Grim survived. Robert picked up the jars that were on Skull's waist before he died. And he let out the man that was in the cage that was off the ground. The man got out of the cage limping. He looked very weak and tired, but he walked toward Skull's throne and picked up the staff. The man walks over to Skull's ashes and the man picks up the crown again and he starts glowing blue and green just like the sky was. "Thank you for defending that Skull lord dude. I am lost Soul king again thanks to your battling thank you, but I must go back to my realm. I have much to do." Says the King of Souls. The king of souls summons a portal for him to go back home to. Before the king leaves. He looks at Hazel one last time. "Thank you, Hazel., I did not trust you, but I should have never trusted a man like that. I hope to see you all again." Says King of souls. As the king of souls walk in his portal all the strange things float into the portal with the king. Robert looks at the labeling on the jars, they said on the name tags were. Cynthia and Emerald. "Wait, King of whatever you are." Says Robert running toward the portal. "Does my mom and aunt belong in your realm?" Says Robert. The king of souls stops right in the middle of the portal between his world and the otherworld. The king looks at the souls. "Robert, I know your name, but to be honest I don't think your mom or Aunt belongs here. You keep them, my realm is all about suffering and souls being lost, but it seems like your aunt and Mom know where they are now. They just wanted to be with one of there children again. And I think that is you. Robert." Says The king of souls. The king of soul's pats Robert on the shoulder comforting Robert. "Wait, can you say hey to my brother Grim in there if he is in there now?" Says Robert. I will. Now you Robert don't die for a long time. I hope to see you as old and wise, not young and wise. Now I must go, thank you again for saving my throne." Says the king of souls. As the king of souls walks into the portal it disappears right behind him. Robert walks toward Grims ashes. "I will make sure that this world is safe brother. I hope you are safe. I should have a better brother. Thank you Grim." Says Robert. Kneeling noticing that Skull had a ring on his ashes. Robert picked up the ring in the ashes. Robert puts it on his finger and notices that he could open the ring. So, Robert picks up some of his brother's ashes and puts it in the ring. "You will be with me for the rest of my life now. That sort of terrorizes me to think about that, but I am proud of the brother you have become brother." Says Robert. Gretel walks behind Robert then magical puts the vase back together. Gretel puts the vase down, then. Gretel uses her magic picking up all Grims ashes into the vase. Robert did not know what to do with Gretel putting his brother's ashes into the vase, but Robert was sad and happy that Grim was the hero once again. Robert got up and looked at everyone who survived the battle between Lord Skull. He was dead. And everyone brought back Grim's ashes in the vase, back to base.

As Gretel and everyone walks into Grims's base. Gretel places down the vase full of Grims ashes. Polly was carrying Jack's body still crying. Polly was covered in blood, but she seemed to not care at all. Because Her boyfriend died today. Hazel had a massive headache Luna and Scarlet were talking with paper once again. Hazel was confused of what was happening, so Luna explains of just happened. All the Soldiers were gathering around Grims's vase and saying their peace with him and then saying thank you for protecting everyone last of us. Robert was still paralyzed of what just happened today. He lost his brother, and he earned his mom and Aunt's souls back. Robert did not know what to do with his life now. Gretel came up behind Robert. "Hey, Robert. I don't mean to ask you this at this timing, but what are you going to do with your mother's soul and Aunt's soul? There are a few ways to give them a peaceful afterlife. Or you can keep them and put them in necklaces…" Says Gretel. Robert turned to look at Gretel, he would no words to say. "I think I might have to let them go. Cynthia my mother, my aunt Emerald deserve rest finally, after what they went through. I want to let them go into the afterlife with Grim." Says Robert. "That's a good idea Robert. We will let their souls be free from being lost souls. Give them to me, I will make sure that they are free from being lost." Says Gretel. Robert gives Gretel, the jars. Robert then walked away from everyone, walking toward the garden.

Hours later everyone went to sleep. Robert crawls in bed touching Skull's ring and his brothers' ashes at once. Robert hopes the days will get better. Without Grim around, but what was he thinking. Robert still feels guilty for never being there for his brother. Robert closes his

301

eyes thinking about what Grim would say. And he laughed to himself, that Grim would say. "You idiot. Why are you thinking about me? You are the one that never wanted me to be around, but look at me know I am not around, and yet you were wrong." Robert felt worse in a second. Robert falls asleep thinking about Grim.

CHAPTER 29

THE HERO'S FUNERAL

Gretel wakes up in the car near where Robert was driving to. Robert Luna and Hazel were finally home together again. They were all hoping to find Lee home, but no one has been home for days. The house was a mess, So Robert and Everyone cleaned the house. Scarlet was getting frustrated that she still could not talk anyone, like everyone else like always. But Luna could still have the patience talking to Scarlet. Everyone else did not really trust Scarlet because she couldn't talk for some reason. "Luna, when was the last time you saw Lee?" says Dad. "I am not sure, because I have had quite the journey like you did." Says Luna. Hazel looked at the house up and down. Hazel thought for sure, that she was never going to see this place ever again, but Hazel is safe once again. Gretel was carrying Grims vase around the house of where Robert, Hazel, and Luna lived. Once every was done cleaning the house around. Robert led everyone to the guest rooms, which they needed was only three bedrooms open. Robert led Gretel to the one guest bedroom that was next door to Robert's bedroom. Gretel went inside that bedroom and set down Grim on the dresser. Robert led Polly to the couch in the living room because there is a pull out in there. Polly sat down. Finally, Scarlet just shared a room with Luna on the floor in her bedroom. Robert walks toward the phone to check messages. Robert totally forgot about his job. There were 30 messages from work. He was screwed. He listened to them all, the last one was yesterday. It said that Robert was fired, but his boss sounded disappointed that he ended up firing Robert in the end. Robert accepts it, because he was not really in the mood to be working right now anyway. Robert went to his room to sit down and sink into what happened this week. Robert was exhausted from the journey that he had for over two weeks.

"Luna, we need to talk." Says on Scarlet's paper. "What's up?" Says Luna. Scarlet's begins to write a large message on her page. *"Me and Ruby want you to come back with me to train, so you know how to use your abilities and to be connected to time and space. That means you must leave with me tomorrow or whenever is the funeral. I know your family has died a little, we will wait for you, but I am not going to stay, I will come and pick you up when you are ready. Just think of my name in your head or do what I showed you when we called upon Ruby. Just close your eyes and think of the time Witch you want to chat with. I will be ready to get you. Take your time to grieve, don't rush sadness and loss."* Says Scarlet's writing. "Why aren't you staying?" Says Luna. Scarlet writes on the piece of paper. "Because I was called a couple hours ago in the car when your dad was driving back to his house. I did not want to just vanish out of nowhere in the car, so I stayed that long, but anyway I got to go tonight. Ruby was to chat with me before you come in our dimension. I will see you later. Luna." Says Scarlet. "Scarlet, before you go. I just want to say. Thank you for helping my family. I appreciated it." Says Luna. As Scarlet writes down her last page for Luna to read, Scarlet throws it on the ground. Closes her eyes making a portal. Scarlet was gone. Luna walks toward the page on the ground that Scarlet wrote for Luna one last time. "Luna, I was honored to have fought with your family, so no problem it was fun meeting you and Luna keep your spirit and keep your sister Hazel close. Hazel looks tired and confused. I would talk to your sister for awhile. She needs you before you leave, make sure that you do that. Then you call upon me." Says Scarlet. "I will Scarlet and thank you." Says Luna.

Hazel sits down on her comfy bed. Hazel was tired and exhausted from being kidnapped like three times. Hazel also realizes that Hazel missed half of her year of high school, her last year in fact. Suddenly Hazel feels a vibration on her bed. Hazel looks over at her phone, suddenly 100s of messages pop up on Hazel's spare phone. Cause her other phone was stolen by her dead uncle Grim. But there were more messages from

Mackenzie and Brittany's chat with Hazel in it. It was just saying that they were worried where Hazel was all this time. Hazel texted back in that chatroom. "Hey, guys I am alright. In fact, I just got home today. Do you guys want to come over." Says Hazel in the message chat. Immediately Mackenzie and Brittany texted back. "Yeah, we will be there soon." Says Mackenzie. "See you then. Oh, and there might be a couple people. Here, we just met a lot of people and my uncle died yesterday and one of his friends." Says Hazel. Mackenzie messages back. "Oh, Hazel I am very sorry for your loss." Says Mackenzie in message. "It's okay. I just need you guys right now for talking. Come over." Says Hazel. "We are on the way." Says Brittany. "Good. I am glad." Says Hazel also sending a smiley face.

An hour later. There was a knock at the front door. Hazel gets up to the front door and answers it. As Hazel was walking toward the front door, she noticed that the house was quiet, and Polly was sitting there crying more than ever. She looks sort of broken. Hazel opens the front door. Seeing that Brittany and Mackenzie were standing right in front of Hazel at the front door. "Come in." says Hazel. Brittany and Mackenzie walk in the house feeling the energy what Hazel was talking about. Hazel looked down at her arm. Hazel noticed that the symbol was gone. Hazel was confused about who she was. Then Brittany and Mackenzie notice the wings on Hazel's back. "Hazel, what happened to you exactly cause am I just seeing those wings in my imagination." Says Mackenzie. "No, they are who I am now. I am still trying to figure out who I am really? I am sort of lost right now." Says Hazel. "Hazel it's okay we are still your friends. I think they are pretty." Says Mackenzie. Hazel looks up at Mackenzie. Hazel walks up to Mackenzie hugging her. "Thank you." Says Hazel as she forms a tear a little. Hazel's tear glowed beautifully out of her eyes. Brittany comes in for the group hug. Hazel starts forming more tears on her friend's shoulders. Hazel could not feel anything, but pain in her body. Hazel felt weak and a lost girl in the world. Hazel did not feel like she was like everyone else. Hazel felt alone in this world, but then when her friends listened to her talk about what happened on her weird journey finding out that she was some kind of Witch? Hazel felt different and lost even more after that journey. She will never feel the same after this journey. That Hazel had. Luna was looking above at Hazel and her friends hugging. Luna was moved by how Mackenzie and Brittany acted toward her little sister. Luna walked down the stairs, walking up to Hazel and her friends. "Hey, Hazel. I need to chat with you. In private." Says Luna. Mackenzie and Brittany walk in the kitchen giving Luna and Hazel some space. "Hazel., I know it's hard to have gone through this mostly alone, but you are safe now. I am here. But I need to chat with you. I want to know if you are alright." Says Luna. "Can we talk about this in my room?" Says Hazel. "Yeah, whatever makes you comfortable." Says Luna. Luna and Hazel walk up the stairs toward Hazel's room. Hazel closes her door behind Luna. Hazel sits down on her bed and Luna stands up talking to Hazel.

"Mackenzie, what do you think happened to Hazel exactly she looks worse then usual?" Says Brittany. "I have no idea Brittany, but I hope Hazel will heal from her process of whatever happened to her." Says Mackenzie. For the rest of the day everyone ate some food. Mackenzie and Brittany left a couple hours later after dinner. Because Hazel wanted them to stay for awhile. Hazel fell asleep on her bed as Mackenzie and Brittany were talking to her then they looked away for a second. Hazel's eyes were closed. Mackenzie and Brittany put a blanket on top of Hazel and turns off her light, then shuts the door behind them quietly. "We should go home." What Mackenzie said before they left. Gretel was having a hard time sleeping. Gretel was dreaming about Grim and her kissing again. Gretel did not know that she loved him. So, Gretel gets up from the bed and walks outside to get some fresh air to breath in and out the night sky. Gretel felt something like a vision was about to pop out of her mind. Gretel sees that Amy was still alive and she was flying in the night sky, with news horns on her head. Gretel did not know what that vision meant to her, but she thought about telling Robert about Amy his sister. Gretel wanted to tell Robert that his sister was still alive. Because of Gretel.

Robert was having a hard time sleeping as well. Robert was having a dream. Him realizing that he could not save Grim, and he kept watching repeatedly about Grim's scream crying for help, but the dream was that he was stuck in spot. The only thing that Robert could do was watch his brother die repeatedly. It was painful for Robert to see again. Finally, something pulled him out of the dream that he was having. Robert sat on his bed for a moment. Robert turned on his lamp in his bedroom and got up and opened a drawer. It was a picture of Grim and Robert together before they started fighting all the time. Robert formed a tear onto the picture of them playing in the water. Robert put that picture on his night stand he no longer hated his brother. He trusted him with all his heart. Robert turned off his lamp again and closed his eyes trying to get some sleep, but of course he was still having that dream of Grim dying repeatedly.

Luna was up for some reason. Luna just was sitting there mediating on her bed with candles all around her. She was still confused of who she was to. But Luna was not dealing with loss, she was dealing with change. Everyone around her lost someone special to them. Hazel has been through a lot these past weeks. Hazel needed support, but at the same time everyone needed all the support that could be given.

Polly was sitting in the dark, in the living. She never felt this much pain for a long time. The last time she felt this way, Polly lost her brother sometime. When she was only 11 years old, Polly still misses her brother, but losing a boyfriend was more tough for her. Because Jack and her ended things not what she expected the way it would go. Polly cries and cries thinking about what Jack's last words were. "I love you, Polly. And I am sorry." Every time she hears that word love you, she cries even heavier than before. The difference was how Jack died in Polly's arms and how Polly's brother was found dead by bandits that killed him cold blood. I guess Jack's death hurt way more because she witnessed Jack's death and died right in her arms.

Morning. Everyone was super tired still. Hazel was still looking sad than ever. Luna was mostly the only one that did not feel grief because she again did not lose anyone, but she was sad that everyone else was sad. Luna walked up to Hazel. Hugging her. "Hazel it's going to get better, I just know it." Says Luna in a smile. Hazel ignores her and sits at the dinning room table. Dad brings out food for everyone looking tired than ever. Polly is to depressed. Luna tries to help Polly eat and get out of her bed in the living room. "Luna, if Polly does not want to get out of bed. Then just leave her alone. I know that you did not deal with any lost or grief, but don't push others to be okay. Give us time. The funeral is today, maybe some of us will feel better about saying good-bye to Jack and Grim. They were heroes and they are heroes till this day." Says Dad. Everyone eats their food in silence. Polly does not get out of the living room and get up to eat food she sits there crying basically the entire time. Finally, Robert gets up asking if anyone was done with there plate. Robert picks up the plates that were empty and brings them to the kitchen.

An hour later Polly finally got up, but she did not eat anything. Polly got dressed and just waited till everyone was dressed for the funeral. Once everyone was dressed, Gretel grabbed Grims vase and brought it with them to the funeral site. So that they could bury his ashes in the ground. Robert arrived with everyone at the burial site just waiting for the priest to arrive at there burial area for Grim. The priest finally arrives at there site looking tired, but Robert did not care because he lost his brother in battle. Gretel gives the priest the beautiful vase with flowers all over the vase. "I have two more, people to put to rest." Says Gretel. The priest wondered what was inside the jars, they were souls. Cynthia's and Emerald's soul. "What am I supposed to do with these?" says the priest. "Put them to rest like the other two. I have my own ceremony for them." Says Gretel. "Alright, whatever you say." Says the priest. Gretel leaves the jars up there with the priest and takes her seat. "Thank you. I am so sorry for your loss. Let's start with praying to God about lost and grief is the most important thing in life." Says priest going on and on about it. Hazel was looking down at the grass and sitting down crying about Grims's death because after all Hazel was just starting to like Grim her uncle. Robert listens to the priest but looks around and noticing that Polly was crying again way too much every time that the priest said Jack's name, Robert walked over to Polly hugging her. Polly hugged tight back to Robert. Before everyone left and put flowers on Grim's and Jack's coffins. Gretel got up from her chair, and she did the soul ceremony. Meaning that she was putting Cythina and Emerald to rest, the priest watched the soul ceremony, he was the most shocked of what was going on, with so many orbs, lights, shapes. The two souls then finally floated up to the sky and disappeared in thin air. Robert looked up at the sky. "Rest in piece, Grim, Cynthia, and Emerald. Rest well." Says Robert. Once the funeral was over, and watched Gretel do the soul ceremony for Cynthia and Emerald everyone got up from there chairs, grabbed a flower and threw flowers at Grims coffin and Polly puts 10 flowers in for Jack. Polly looks down at Jack's coffin. "Jack, I love you so much. I wish we did not fight a lot. Because I would have totally been your girlfriend. Jack why did you jump in front of Grim. Why." Says Polly crying. Robert holds Polly, taking her to the car. Everyone started to follow. "Hazel." Says Luna. Hazel looks over at Luna looking sad more than an hour ago. "I think you have to deal with this grieving on your own. I can't decide to make you all happy again. I think that was my test from Scarlet and Ruby. I must go. To their dimension for awhile to figure what who I am really. I am very sorry if this is bad timing for me to leave, but I need to figure out myself out more." Says Luna. Hazel hugs Luna. "Luna, I think it's best if you go find answers about you. Just please visit me. I will miss you." Says Hazel. "I will miss you to Hazel. I am sorry that I must leave now, but like I said I think all of you guys need to do this on your own. It's my turn to leave for awhile." Says Luna. Luna sits down on the ground closing her eyes thinking about Scarlet. Suddenly behind Luna there was a portal, Luna got up and walked in the portal. As Luna walked in the portal it disappeared right in Hazel's face. "Bye, Luna, I miss you already." Says Hazel walking toward dad's car.

Sam wakes up in her bedroom that she was staying in for a couple days. Sam gets up and gets dressed and makes it in time for breakfast. "Sam. How are you this morning?" Says Cole. "I am fine? Why are you asking?" Says Sam. "I just want to chat with you for a second. Sam., I want to ask you something?" Says Cole. "What is it now?" Says Sam. "I was just going to ask if you wanted me to give that scar a healing?" Says Cole. "What, do you mean healing?" Says Sam. "I was thinking that you wanted me to get rid of the scar on the side of your rips." Says

Cole. "No, I don't it's apart of me. If you want to gain my trust let Lee go. Or at least let him out." Says Sam. Cole looks at Sam. Sam looks at Cole. Sam gets up angry and walks outside to get some air. "Cole stop trying hard to gain Sam's trust, it takes time for that kind of trust." Says Queen Nelia. Cole sits there not talking about anything. Cole just sits there thinking. Queen Nelia sighs. "I think I know how to earn a little trust for Sam. If you are that interested in wanting Sam to trust us. We are going to have to let Lee out of that cell in the dungeon." Says Queen Nelia. "Are you sure?" Says Cole. "Yeah, she won't trust you or me. So that is basically the only option right now." says Queen Nelia. "If it's alright with you, then let's do this." Says Cole. Cole and Queen Nelia go down to the dungeon, to let Lee out of his cell.

"What's up?" Says the celestial guard. "We are here to let Lee out of his cell." Says Queen Nelia. "Alright." Says the celestial guard, as he gave them the key. Queen Nelia and Cole walked to the back of the Dungeon. Lee was just sitting on the bed. Lee looked up and realized that the Queen and Cole were standing right in front of Lee's cell. Lee stud up for them. "What are you doing down here?" Says Lee. "We are letting you go and see Sam for awhile." Says Queen Nelia. Queen Nelia opens the cell door letting Lee out of the cell. Lee, Cole and Queen Nelia walk out of the dungeon. Lee was nervous to say anything, so he choses not to say a word in front of both, mostly Lee was nervous because Lee thought they would change their mind if he said anything, but they said nothing either. Queen Nelia, Cole and Lee arrive in the garden where Sam seems to always be, in this dimension. "Sam." Says Lee as he was running toward for a hug. "What, how did you get out?" Says Sam hugging Lee. Over Lee's shoulder, Sam saw that Queen Nelia and Cole were looking. Sam "let's go of Lee. So, you let my friend out?" Says Sam. "Yeah, we let him out." Says Queen Nelia. "Thank you." Says Sam.

Hours later Sam listens to what Cole and Queen Nelia. Sam finds out that Cole was in fact telling the truth about him being her father. Sam, and Lee hang out for days. Sam let's the Queen teach her some abilities that the celestials can use, and Sam was amazed of what her abilities can be. Sam was getting taught by Queen Nelia and her father Cole the sorcerer. Sam was still confused about all this stuff, the Celestial realm. Sam and Lee grow a bound that has not been around in this realm in a long time. Human and Celestial Witch together in a relationship. Lee was happy to have been with Sam with entire time, but he was still sort of worried about his family back at home. Sam could sense that Lee was thinking about his family, and he was trying to hide his true emotions from Sam, but officially it was not working. Days still have gone by. Lee was feeling completely depressed for no reason. Sam was starting to get worried about Lee, and Sam was thinking about Lee's feelings. Sam put her hand on Lee's chest as they were cuddling in Sam's bed. Sam felt pain and deep depression, but it was not from Lee being with Sam. It was other people's feelings Sam was convinced that Lee should go back home for awhile. See what is going on. With his family. "Lee, I think you should go back home for a few couple days. I will be fine here, I know you are staying for me, but please don't if you are feeling home sick or depressed." Says Sam. "Sam it's not me who is depressed, I know you been touching my chest to keep checking on my feelings. Sam, I don't want to leave you here alone." Says Lee. "Well, you are leaving. Please I just want you to check on your family." Says Sam. "I don't want to leave you here Sam. I want to stay with you. The first time I told you that I cared for you, having a crush on you. Was hard, especially when you pushed me away, but Something always made me pull through to get to you. There is no way I am leaving you here alone." Says Lee. "I know you do, but it's time to think about you right now and your family. I am sorry for that by the way... I care a lot about you, to just keep staying here for me, I want you to be able to see your family, that is why I think you should go home for awhile, see your dad, Luna, and Hazel. You have been worried about them for awhile now. I can feel it, in your chest." Says Sam. Sam gets out of bed with Lee, but Lee grabs Sam by the arm, and pulls her down on Lee, Lee kissed Sam and kissed Sam all over. For some reason Sam did not stop Lee from kissing Sam on her neck, her chest, and her cheeks. Finally they both fell asleep together in bed.

The next morning. "Queen Nelia, I don't want Lee to go back, but I need him to go back. Can you send him home?" Says Sam. Few hours later. Lee was forced to get packed. Sam packed up all his bags and threw them out of the bedroom. "Why, are you pushing me away like this Sam. I want to be with you right now." Says Lee. "I know, but the thousandth time I told you. I need you to go home to see what is going on at your house." says Sam. "Can't you come with me, then?" Says Lee. "Lee, I don't think I belong in that world anymore. I belong here." Says Sam. "A couple days ago when I was in that cell, you wanted to leave and now you want me to leave. Do you not like me?" Says Lee. "No, I like you, Lee. I just think that you need to figure out what is going on at your house for now, please don't fight me." Says Sam. Lee looks at Sam. "You are lucky that I love you." Says Lee in a sad sigh. "Okay. Let's get you downstairs with all your stuff." Says Sam. Sam and Lee walk down the stairs getting ready for the portal for Lee to go back home for awhile. Lee still did not want to leave Sam alone here in this realm, but Lee did not have a choice. Queen Nelia summoned a portal to the otherworld for Lee to head home. Lee looks behind him seeing Sam looking at Lee as he walks toward the portal. Lee throws his bags into the portal and runs at Sam hugging her and kissing her on the forehead. "Sam, I you are lucky, that I love you. Otherwise, I would be mad at you." Says Lee. "I know that you love me. Lee I am doing this because I think that you need to go home anyway to just make sure that your family is okay. Get to know your family before they either abandon you or turn out to be a lie, but Lee, I just want you to know that you are not abandoning me or a lie. You are my love, and I love you. Just please don't come back to fast. Come back when it is a great time to come back." Says Sam. "I will." Says Lee. As Lee and Sam let go of each other. Lee looks back toward the portal, then looks back at Sam. Lee kisses Sam on the lips and walks toward the portal. Lee was gone out of Sam's sight. Sam teared up a little bit after when Lee left Sam's realm for good. The portal closes.

"Robert, what is that noise." Says Gretel. "I don't know." Says Robert. Suddenly a vortex comes through the living room ceiling. "AHHH." Says Lee. Everyone runs into the room to find that Lee was on the ground with bags, then the vortex disappears. "Lee, we have been looking for you everywhere. Where have you been this entire time?" Says Dad. "I have been in another dimension this entire time. I am sorry. I did not know there was going to be a search party for me." Says Lee. "Oh, these people there not for you. We are just grieving right now. We lost people two days ago." Says Dad. "Wait, Hazel is back." Says Lee. "Yeah, she is back." Says Dad. "Why, do you sound angry at me?!" Says Lee. "LEE, we have been looking for you for days. We thought you died. And now you are telling me that you have been in a realm this entire time." Says dad. "Well, it's true my friend Sam lives there." Says Lee. "Lee, I swear to God. I don't have time for jokes right now." says Dad. "I can tell, but I am telling the truth." says Lee. Dad walks out of the room mad, but happy that his son is alright. Hazel walked up to Lee hugging him. Lee felt pain and fear from Hazel. Hazel and Lee talk for a few moments about what has happened over the past few weeks. Once Hazel done talking. Lee could not believe it, but at the same time he can believe it.

CHAPTER 30

ASSASSIN!?

A guy was running toward a big man, the big man looked like he was not panicking, but the tiny guy that was running at the big guy. He looked scared to death. The tiny man walked up to the big guy. "Sir there is someone going around killing everyone right now." Says the tiny man. As there were alarms going off and screaming. "Well, the one thing I want you to do is protect me." Says the big guy. "I am not good at fighting sir." Says the tiny man. "You are a wimp." Says the big man. Both men run down the hall as they continue hearing alarms going all around. They stop in spot for a moment. They stopped, because of the pile of dead people. They were a bit more scared. Especially the big guy. There was blood all over the place. The floor was red, there was one person alive in that pile of people. He was alive, he put his hand up at the two men, saying help. Suddenly there was a knife in his throat. It came from the ceiling, above them. The person jumped down behind them. That was killing everyone, they threw themselves at the big guy. The tiny guy froze and did not move. The killer stabbed the big guy, in the head. He fell to the ground dead. The killer turned toward the last guy that was standing right there. The tiny guy looked at the killer. He noticed that the killer had a mask on, but the tiny man knew that the killer was a girl. The killer stud there looking at the man, but the killer just left him alone. The killer ran away going cloak. The man that was left in the ship he fell to the ground crying, saying thank God, I stayed alive. Before the killer leaves, the killer flies into the sky. Raising their hands at the ship. Suddenly the ship was up in the air. The killer was smashing the ship. Inside the boat the guy that thought he was going to be the only one that survived, but he ended up getting crushed by being inside the boat. His body exploded everywhere. Leaving the rest of that room covered in more blood. The killer then teleported away. Leaving the ship, as a squashed ball on the ocean.

TO BE CONTINUED

Printed in the USA
CPSIA information can be obtained
at www.ICGtesting.com
LVHW090459211123
764514LV00002B/109

9 798891 004085